PRAISE FOR KALI WALLACE AND *SALVATION DAY*

"Kali Wallace, the world needs you—and this book. *Salvation Day* is a taut thriller, a near-future look at where we're headed next, a mirror reflecting the best and worst of humanity. It is all that, and so much more. I'd follow the rebellious heroine Zahra anywhere—especially into another nail-biter of a story like this."

—James Rollins, #1 *New York Times* bestselling author of *The Last Odyssey*

"*Salvation Day* is a masterful story set at a screaming pace. It had me holding on for dear life all the way through. I loved it."

—Mur Lafferty, Hugo Award–winning author of *Six Wakes*

"Breakneck pace with real thrills and chills—plus lots of meaty stuff to think about. One of the major science fiction debuts of 2019. Kali Wallace is a force to be reckoned with."

—Robert J. Sawyer, Hugo Award–winning author of *The Oppenheimer Alternative*

"A smart, gripping thriller you just can't put down. Explosions, betrayals, morally gray choices, and twisty secrets; all set in the world that comes after the end of ours. Perfect for fans of *Aliens* and locked-spaceship murder mysteries."

—Kameron Hurley, Hugo Award–winning author of *The Broken Heavens*

"More than a science fiction novel, it's a good old-fashioned thriller set in the future—every page filled with breadth and scope and twists and turns. An exciting, dangerous, magical quest f truth."

—Steve Berry, *New York* of *The Kaiser's Web*

"A suspenseful journey with complex characters and a riveting universe that is as bold as it is fascinating, *Salvation Day* is a space thriller that will infect you with its gripping narrative as much as its mind-bending viruses."

—Peter Tieryas, author of *Cyber Shogun Revolution*

"Wallace delivers an exciting science fiction thriller that shines a light on government secrets, shifting blame, and elitism and class in a future society. The tight plot and well-developed characters create an engrossing read."

—*Library Journal*

"*Salvation Day* is a terrific space thriller. Wallace is an excellent writer, and she maintains tight control over her story as it progresses."

—New York Journal of Books

BERKLEY TITLES BY KALI WALLACE

SALVATION DAY

DEAD SPACE

DEAD SPACE

KALI WALLACE

BERKLEY
NEW YORK

BERKLEY
An imprint of Penguin Random House LLC
penguinrandomhouse.com

Library of Congress Cataloging-in-Publication Data

Names: Wallace, Kali, author.
Title: Dead space / Kali Wallace.
Description: First Edition. | New York: Berkley, 2021.
Identifiers: LCCN 2020036159 (print) | LCCN 2020036160 (ebook) |
ISBN 9781984803726 (trade paperback) | ISBN 9781984803733 (ebook)
Subjects: GSAFD: Science fiction.
Classification: LCC PS3623.A4434 D43 2021 (print) | LCC PS3623.A4434 (ebook) | DDC 813/.6—dc23
LC record available at https://lccn.loc.gov/2020036159
LC ebook record available at https://lccn.loc.gov/2020036160

First Edition: March 2021

Printed in the United States of America
10 9 8 7 6 5 4 3 2 1

Cover images courtesy of Shutterstock
Cover design by Adam Auerbach
Book design by Tiffany Estreicher

For Link and Mochi, for being very good company in a very bad year

DEAD SPACE

ONE

The kid was bleeding from his eyes, but he hadn't noticed yet. He sat on the edge of the narrow lower bunk, hunched over and swaying slightly, as though every one of Jackson's questions was a gust of wind he could not withstand.

"Where'd you get it? Who did the work?" Jackson leaned her shoulder against the upper bunk, made a face, thought better of it, and pulled away. Everything in the room was filthy. The air was filthy. "Just give us a fucking name and we'll be gone."

The kid didn't answer. He wasn't looking at her, wasn't looking at me, wasn't looking at anything at all. Scabs and pus had crusted around the wounds where the black market augment was drilled into his head. His artificial eye was already glitching like hell; the muscles of his face, from his eyebrows down to his chin, twitched with waves of tremulous spasms.

He was completely naked but for his tattoos, which showcased a brief, angry history of joining just about every outer systems political group that had ever gathered in a grubby station canteen to rail against one thing or another.

The lack of clothes also gave us a good look at the freshly sealed surgical scar that snaked down his spine. Whoever had done the surgery was worse than a hack. The kid would be lucky if he knew his own name after the doctors got the tech out of his brain. Every time he blinked, another droplet of blood squeezed from his tear ducts and rolled down his cheek.

"Can't have been cheap," Jackson said. "You sure as shit don't have the money for that. Who paid? Who sent you here?"

I read through his file while she worked through the script. The kid was a contractor, one of several brought to Hygiea for a six-month stint upgrading the industrial water filtration system. His anticorporate tendencies were more boastful talk than meaningful action, and mostly subsided now that he was making good money. He had a weakness for sexy new tech. As far as I could tell, four or five days ago he'd paid somebody to give him an illegal neural augment and ocular prosthetic. Stupid and dangerous, but not exactly unusual among contractors with too much money and too few brains.

"For fuck's sake." Jackson raised her hand like she wanted to smack the kid, but she changed her mind. "This is useless. Take what you need and get the medics in here."

That was directed at me with an impatient scowl. We'd been called out from HQ at the very end of the shift, and Jackson had a wife and family waiting with supper on the table. I had no supper ahead of me except standard-issue canteen slop and nobody waiting in my single quarters three levels down, but I wanted out of that room too. I got to it. Sterile gloves, evidence box, and a deep breath of the relatively fresh corridor air before ducking into the room.

"Hey." Jackson snapped her fingers in front of the kid's face. "Hey. Listen. Parthenope Enterprises Security Protocol 17, Sections G through K, gives us the authority to confiscate and investigate your personal devices. Do you understand?"

The kid blinked. Swayed. Blinked.

"Your PDs will be returned to you after we've verified that you have not used them for any activities in violation of Parthenope regulations while residing on Hygiea. If you have any questions about Parthenope's investigation process, refer to your residential contract or contact your company representative. Okay?"

I stepped gingerly through the messy room. There were three devices, one on the table and two on the floor, all smudged and unpleasantly sticky. I slid them into the evidence pouch and looked around to make sure I'd found them all. I didn't look too closely. My contractual commitment to ensuring the safety and security of Parthenope Enterprises and its facilities, operations, and employees did not extend to searching through fluid-stained sheets beneath the bare ass of a twentysomething kid reckless enough to think that paying somebody to drill into his head was a good idea.

Jackson saw me glancing around. "You done, Marley?"

"I'm done." I was already making for the door. I could feel the stench of the room clinging to my uniform. I would have to use a week's worth of water rations to scrub it off. "I'll get the analysis to you in an hour or two."

"And I won't look at it until morning," she said. "As soon as this fucker's out of my hands, I'm off the clock. You should be too."

Which told me she wasn't actually worried the kid was a terrorist or spy. I silently removed several items from my action plan for digging into this kid's questionable life choices. When it came to low-level criminals and cranks, we didn't get overtime for pretending to be especially eager Operational Security officers.

"Right. Yeah. Morning, then," I said.

I had one foot out of that fetid chamber when the kid on the bunk made a sound.

It sounded like a choking cough, like he was swallowing his tongue—and wouldn't that be the perfect end to the day—but he hacked wetly, then groaned out something that sounded like a word.

"What's that?" Jackson said warily. "You have something to say?"

"Wait," said the kid. His voice was so rough he could have been rolling nuts and bolts around in his mouth. The blood on his face was drying into twin crusted lines that stretched down his nose, over his lips, to the bottom of his chin. "Silver lady. Wait. Wait and tell me, tell me how—"

He broke off coughing; blood-pinked spittle flew from his lips. When the coughs subsided, he lifted his head, and for the first time since we'd come into the room, his bloodshot natural eye focused on something.

That something was me.

"Silver lady," he said. "It's time. It's time. Tell me how."

"Fuck this. Let's get him—"

Before Jackson could finish, the kid lunged from the bed to throw himself at my feet. He scuttled toward me, reaching with both hands. I jerked back and bumped into the doorframe. The kid's fingers, slick with his own blood, slid over the smooth surface of my boot. I kicked his hand away.

"Tell me how, it's time, I'm ready, I'm so ready, tell me how, tell me how," he was saying, over and over again, the words slurring together as they tumbled from his mouth.

"Don't move." Jackson had her stun weapon at the kid's back, pressed into the nape of his neck. Electroshock weapons weren't meant to be lethal—corporate security was subject to the disarmament treaty like everybody else—but I wasn't sure this kid could survive the jolt. "Do you hear me? You don't move a centimeter. Marley, get the hell out of here before this piece of shit gives himself an aneurysm."

I was already backing out of the room. I squeezed past the medics in the corridor and ignored their snickers, their raised eyebrows, their questions. I felt the prickle of their attention as I strode away, heard the murmur of their voices as I turned the corner at the end of the hall. Whatever they were saying about me, I had heard it all before. I didn't take an easy breath until I was on the lift and on my way up to HQ. I leaned against the wall for balance. I closed my eyes.

Hygiea was a loosely consolidated, carbonaceous chunk of rock and ice well out in the ass-end of the belt, with a diameter of over four hundred kilometers. Nowhere on the surface was the gravity any higher than one-tenth of Earth's, which was a drag for lifelong belters, but for people like me, born and raised on Earth, it was light and strange and required constant adjustment. Even with gecko soles on my boots keeping me anchored to the floor, I felt unstable, unsteady, convinced the wrong move or the wrong step would send me hurtling toward the ceiling. The feeling got worse at the end of the day, when the joint where my prosthetic leg attached to my hip was aching and I was trying to favor it, because my ancient animal instinct was telling me there was more weight than what physics actually provided, and my gait turned into an awkward, stilted limp that did nothing to convince me or my doctors that I was well on my way to being fully healed.

I was used to the stares: hungry and envious from a nauseating few, horrified and fearful from everybody else. I was used to the invasive questions: what does it feel like, does it hurt, can you still feel this, did you let them change your brain, why did you let them do that? Yes, it hurt. Yes, I could feel it. No, they hadn't altered my brain, only my body, and I never had a choice. I was used to it. At least they hadn't fucked me up in the process.

I had been working for Parthenope's Operational Security Department for just over a year, one of the so-called Safety Officers whose job it was to make criminals, malcontents, and all manner of other inconveniences vanish before any of them had a chance to impact the company's profits. There were a few hundred security officers on Hygiea, a small enough community that I had grown accustomed to being the one with all the metal parts, the security analyst who was half tech herself, the unlucky disaster survivor who'd been pieced back together. Nobody talked about it to my face anymore, but neither did they ever bother to disguise how glad they were not to be me. I kept my head down and did my job and stayed away from people like that kid with the bleeding eyes and festering wounds in his head.

I was used to all that. But I never got used to being touched. Strangers grabbing my hand, jabbing their fingers at my eye, slapping my shoulder to feel the metal beneath my clothes. I could not get used to that.

My prosthetics—left arm, left leg, left ear and eye, a scattering of partial organs—took signals from my brain, which was still a squishy, whole, purely human brain. Together they functioned as a close approximation to how a human body was supposed to function, most of the time. This was my body now. Nothing more, nothing less, and never what the biohackers and transhumanists and weird fetishists wanted to hear.

That didn't stop people from looking at me and seeing only the metal.

The lift let me out at Operational Security HQ. I skirted around the edge of the central office, smiles and nods and see-you-laters doled out where necessary. When some colleagues invited me down to the canteen for a beer, I made my excuses. A few gave me sideways glances, looks that hinted at questions they weren't asking, and I wondered how word of the biohacked kid could have spread so quickly. I retreated to my cubicle. They weren't bad people, my colleagues. The older officers were mostly ex-military, shuffled into private contracts when it became apparent nobody was starting a fresh war anytime soon; the younger ones were all career corporate types who wore the uniform as though it actually meant something. They all knew I was on Hygiea for exactly as long as it took to pay down my medical bills and get out of there. Mostly they didn't hold it against me. Normally I would have accepted the invitations, eager for any reason to get out of HQ, desperate to talk about anything except shitty days and petty crimes.

I only realized the questioning glances had nothing to do with the biohacked kid when I saw the evening news scrolls.

TERRORIST LEADER SENTENCED TO LIFE

BLACK HALO MASTERMIND HEADS TO HELLAS PRISON

SYMPOSIUM VICTIMS REACT TO SENTENCING

The headlines blurred together as I read. Every news feed was covering it, naturally, not as the top story but five or six items down the list. A rhythmic tapping set my teeth on edge—I was doing it myself, drumming my fingers on my desk. I stilled both hands and pressed them flat. Left hand, metal hand. Right hand, flesh hand.

Two years ago, the spaceship *Symposium* had been on its way to Titan with two hundred people aboard. One hundred seventy-five of those people, the passengers, made up the full complement of the Titan Research Project. I was one of them. We were some of the finest scientists and engineers in existence, experts in every field, people who had devoted their entire lives to advancing the frontiers of human knowledge. We were going to establish the first permanent human settlement near Saturn and the outermost in the solar system. It was to be a research colony, dedicated to scientific exploration and discovery.

We never made it. The antiexpansion terrorist group called Black Halo infiltrated the passengers and crew of *Symposium* before we left Earth's orbit. They waited until we were several months into our journey before enacting their plan: to disrupt the mission with a catastrophic series of explosions in the ship's fuel systems. *Symposium* was destroyed and most of the people on board died instantly. My friends, my colleagues, the people with whom I had planned to build a home and a community for the next several years, all reduced to atoms in a flash of fire and noise. Among the dead was my longtime mentor and idol, Sunita Radieh, whose loss I still felt like a physical pain whenever I thought of her. Sometimes I wondered if it might not hurt so much if Vanguard, the AI we had created together, had survived, if some part of her genius, her heart, her courage had survived in the machine we had built. But Vanguard had been destroyed as well. Every piece of it, from its breathtakingly complex mind to its uncountable lifetimes' worth of learned experience to its favorite physical expression, the praying mantis shape we affectionately called Bug, it was all gone. Everything was destroyed.

Parthenope Enterprises cargo ships were the nearest vessels to the *Symposium* at the time, so it was Parthenope rescue crews who picked us up and Parthenope doctors who patched us back together. There were thirty-one survivors: seventeen crew and fourteen members of the Titan project. Some were relatively unscathed. Six died over the next few months. Me, I got some shiny new limbs to show off. All of us earned a crushing mountain of rescue, transport, and medical bills. With no way to pay our way back to the inner system, no help from the Outer Systems Administration, no employment, and no convenient riches to our names, we were economic refugees, in Parthenope's debt until we worked our way out of it.

TERRORIST LEADER EXPRESSES NO REGRETS
VICTIMS ISSUE JOINT STATEMENT ON SENTENCING

I did not know Karl Longo, the man who had ruined my life, killed my friends and colleagues, and destroyed an incomprehensible amount of scientific research and irreplaceable technology. He had been safely on Earth, protected by the high walls of a private compound, when members of his group destroyed *Symposium*. I had not attended the trial; I had provided my testimony, what little there was of it, via a series of remote recorded interviews and depositions, first from my hospital bed, later from offices on Hygiea.

The people who had actually carried out the attack, the members of Black Halo that Longo had sent to infiltrate *Symposium*, had all died when their plan spiraled out of control—including Kristin Herd, who had been a friend and colleague of mine. She had joined our team when another member had to withdraw from the project. I had been on the committee that reviewed her application. None of us had suspected a thing. We had all approved of her research and her enthusiasm. Our vote had been unanimous. She had been planning all the while to murder us.

She was dead. They were all dead, and now Longo would spend his life rotting away in a Martian prison. I supposed that was what he deserved.

SYMPOSIUM SENTENCING: HAS JUSTICE BEEN SERVED?
MEMORIAL CEREMONY TO HONOR *SYMPOSIUM* VICTIMS

I shut off the news feeds. I didn't care. I couldn't care. This was my life now, such as it was. Picking grubby PDs off the floor in personal quarters, trawling through endless data, looking for petty extortionists, for corporate spies, for black market biohackers, even for snakes like Kristin, should they make themselves sufficiently troublesome to Parthenope. This isolated rock in the outer system, this thankless job helping a rich company make itself richer, the pain in my joints where metal met flesh, the medical debt that grew every day, this was it, this was all I had, until I could work my way out.

My heart was still thumping uncomfortably. I could still smell that dank, foul room.

I set up the confiscated PDs for a full data sweep and analysis, and I got out of there. I needed to scrub the bloody fingerprints from my boots.

TWO

It was a relief to slip into my private quarters and lock the door behind me.

The housing Parthenope provided to lowly Safety Officers like me was a box-like room two meters wide and three long, with a narrow bunk bolted to the wall on one side, an uncomfortable chair and a fold-down table beneath it, a toilet and sink behind a flimsy wall, and a wallscreen that only worked about half of the time. There was no port looking out on anything, not even into the gray, underlit corridor. I hadn't done much to decorate. There didn't seem to be any point in making an impersonal box look less like a box. I preferred to remind myself every morning and every evening why I needed to get away from here as soon as possible.

My quarters had about as much charm as a coffin, but I relished the privacy. Hygiea was very much a company town: company owned, company operated, company surveilled and secured. Parthenope was one of the largest corporations in the outer system, with its tendrils in every industry from mining to processing to fuel production to transport. There were fifteen thousand people living full-time on Hygiea, another two thousand or so moving through in a constant ebb and flow of ships through the busy port. It was such a small number compared to the population of the system, but when I had first arrived, it had been overwhelming. After nearly a year aboard *Symposium* and months in the hospital on Badenia, an asteroid under Parthenope's control that held both a shipyard and a medical complex, even the possibility of encountering strangers had been uncomfortable.

The showers down the corridor were busy at the end of shift; I decided to wait for the line to go down. I sat in my uncomfortable chair and pulled off my boots. I couldn't remember if I had laundry credit for the week, so I did my best to scrub away the bloody fingerprints myself. I used yesterday's shirt, which was already stained with a yellowish-green smudge of contraband a narcotics chemist had thrown at me.

While I was at it, I called up my personal messages to play on the wallscreen. I hadn't checked them in a few days; there was never anything urgent. But thanks to the news of Longo's conviction, there were a shit-ton of new requests for interviews from reporters—I deleted them all. A reminder for mandatory security analyst training. A reminder for a doctor's appointment I had been putting off for weeks. A reminder for mandatory port and transport safety training. A statement from the Parthenope employee bank. Another reminder for mandatory training. A note from my brother, Devon, who was living a safely mundane life on Earth.

I braced myself before opening his message. He wrote to me regularly, with photographs of his kids, updates about our parents, news he knew I would find interesting. I only replied some of the time, but not because I didn't appreciate the messages. I craved his letters with a hunger I scarcely understood, like an addict itching for a fix.

I had left them—my family, Earth, all of it—purposefully and without doubt. I had planned to be away for years. Even so, on the lonelier nights, in the quiet of my grim residential cell, I pored over every sentence, watched every clip of video, studied every picture until I had every face and landscape memorized. Tonight was no different. I took a breath and held it while I read about how much Devon's son, Michael, loved his dance classes, how disappointed his daughter Renee was to be second in her class rather than first, how little Phoebe was already walking—Devon had included a still photo, so much cheaper to send than a video, and I told myself it was almost as good as seeing her toddle recklessly through the garden, a whirlwind of curly brown hair and big brown eyes and freckles dotted across her nose. From the day of her birth our parents had claimed Phoebe looked so much like me as a baby it was uncanny, but all I could see in her rosy little face was my brother's eyes and my brother's smile. Devon did not mention the woman he had been dating, so I assumed that was over and retroactively decided I had never liked her anyway. He asked me how I was doing in a way that suggested he wasn't expecting an answer. I read all about the spat Mum had recently gotten into with her longtime academic rival about which foreign scholar would be invited to spend a year in their department. Dad was, apparently, experimenting in the kitchen again, this time with recipes based on ancient Greek texts and involving a great deal of garum.

That, more than anything else, stuck in my chest like a fistful of glass shards. I missed Dad's meals, the good and the awful. I missed our noisy family dinners. I missed stepping into the too-warm kitchen to see our parents' heads tilted together conspiratorially, Dad's ginger hair and Mum's long dark plait both alight in the evening sun. I missed inhaling the scent of spices, crowding around the table with knees bumping and elbows jostling, and gratefully accepting leftovers before the walk home.

I dropped my mostly clean boot to the floor. I should have gone to the canteen for a beer. I should have surrounded myself with people, with pointless conversation, with food that at least pretended to be something other than a tasteless meal bar. I closed Devon's message, knowing I would read it again later, and opened the next.

It was a private video message, which was enough to make me wary. Nobody I actually wanted to hear from had the finances to splurge for a video message to Hygiea. The lack of identified sender meant it was probably another reporter, another doctor, another lawyer trying to get past Parthenope's filters and offer miracles to the survivors of the *Symposium* disaster. Or, worse, Black Halo sympathizers spitting empty threats across space, or the families of survivors begging me to join some pointless activist group. It could be another pervert wanting to tell me about their implausible cybernetic fantasies or another scientist wanting to redefine humanity. Those with avarice in their eyes were bad enough; those whose soggy expressions glistened with pity were worse. I hated them all. I had stopped telling them to go fuck themselves months ago. Answering only made them more persistent.

"Hey, Hester."

With a swoop in my gut like falling from a great height, I paused the message in shock.

Pale face, pale hair, blue eyes. His name was David Prussenko. Former head robotics engineer for the Titan Research Project. His life, like mine, had been ruined with the destruction of *Symposium*.

David was paler than I remembered, his hair thinner, his face more gaunt. The past two years had not treated him well. He would likely say the same of me.

I let the message play.

"Haven't heard from you in a little while. I know you're busy, as always. What's up?"

I frowned. I had not spoken to David since the day we had given our final statements to a trio of Outer Systems Administration officials in a lofty corporate office here on Hygiea, some eighteen months ago. Like me, he had endless medical debts and no way to afford a journey back to Earth, so he had also taken Parthenope's offer of employment. But we didn't keep in touch. We never talked. We never contacted each other at all. I had always assumed he agreed it would be too painful.

David paused, fidgeted a little, glanced quickly to the side. It looked like he was alone in his private quarters; I could see an unmade bed behind him. On the wall above the bed, its corner just visible over David's shoulder, was an image that made my breath catch again. It was a map of Titan, identical to the ones David had always used to decorate his living spaces both on Earth and aboard *Symposium*. I couldn't see it clearly, but I would have recognized it anywhere.

"I'm still on Nimue." He cleared his throat. He was nervous about something; every time he hesitated I grew more tense. I had no idea why he would be contacting me in an anonymous message. He went on, "You know, the shining jewel in the company's crown and all that shit. It's all sysadmin stuff.

Overseer wrangling. I still think you'd be better at this job than I am—but these machines would bore you, I think. Maybe not. Maybe they're your style after all."

He smiled quickly, a twist of the lips, and I felt a pang of something that was half anger, half jealousy. Nimue was one of Parthenope's asteroid mines in the Hygiea family. I only knew its name because the company was building a huge facility there, and there were constant press releases, official communications, and progress reports going around. The Overseer I knew a bit more about. That was the name for Parthenope's station management artificial intelligence. Overseer AIs kept the mines, plants, and factories running smoothly with minimal human crew. They were advanced and powerful but not terribly innovative, but working with them would still be more interesting than trawling through data for petty crimes and misdemeanors—and definitely more my area of expertise, once upon a time, than David's. I was an AI expert, one of the best in the field, but the Parthenope personnel managers had never seemed to care, no more than they had cared that David could build the most beautiful robots.

I don't know what kind of job David had asked for when he first started at Parthenope, but every time I had asked for an Overseer-adjacent position they had always brushed me off. There were too few positions available. My medical needs were too great. Be patient. Work toward promotion. Engage positively in Parthenope corporate culture and you will be rewarded.

"The thing is, um . . ." David paused again. I did not remember him being so hesitant to speak, and it made me uneasy to see him stammer and stall when I didn't even know what he wanted. "Hey, remember that time we went to Kristin's gran's place down on the Jurassic Coast? I keep thinking about that weekend. I went looking for photos and vids. All that stuff. I've been looking, and I found something I wasn't looking for. That was a good time."

A hollow feeling opened up inside of me. David kept speaking, but his words slipped around me, too distant and too loud all at the same time, indistinguishable through the buzzing in my head. I remembered. A few years ago. A lifetime ago. A sweeping beach on the Jurassic Coast, beneath crumbling sandstone cliffs. We were on a retreat for the Titan tech team, those of us who would be responsible for making all our stubborn machines get along. I remembered lying on the sand on a clear, cold night, the day's work satisfying and exciting, all of us buzzing with the potential of our own brilliance. The taste of whisky, the taste of salt, the bite of the wind, the way the stars turned and turned. The wreck of the smuggling ship *Excelsior* offshore, dashed by waves, its massive metal hull dark and lonely, its ghosts silent for over a hundred years.

My chest ached. I rubbed at the scar tissue over my sternum. I had missed a few words of David's message. I played it back again.

"I just realized that you never settled up that bet you lost to me, the one about *Excelsior.* About what happened when it crashed." He leaned forward, his face growing large on the wallscreen. "I was right. You were wrong. They lied about it. They lied about everything."

He shook his head and sat back in his chair. He laughed, but it was forced, empty.

"You hear me? I was right. I won that bet after all. That lake should have been mine. I'd love to catch up. Let's do it, okay? I can set up from my end, but you need to handle your side. You know how tetchy the OSD gets about personal comms. Hey, fuckheads!" He made a face at the camera. "I know you're listening. Fuck off. Miss you, Hester. Let's talk. Do this one thing for me. Please?"

I sat for a long time after the message ended. I sat and stared at the comms menu on the wallscreen and did nothing at all.

Eighteen months since I had spoken to David, and now this. I couldn't recall when he had last asked anything of me. When we had been working together, he would wheedle and whine for silly reasons, sure, for a cup of fresh coffee, programming help, introductions to somebody he had his eye on. But he had not asked for anything after *Symposium*, after we learned we were stranded out here in the asshole of the solar system. There was a tremor in his voice when he said *please*, an unsteadiness he was trying so hard to hide. That was grief, I thought. That was fear.

I remembered the weekend he was talking about, but not as he described it. That had been before Kristin Herd joined the Titan project. The cottage had belonged to Jay Knox's grandmother, not Kristin's. We had argued about the *Excelsior* that night on the beach. David had believed the cause of the crash was a fault in the navigational system; I was certain it was human error. And I remembered clearly that David had been in the wrong. We had looked it up the next morning, over a hangover breakfast of toast and eggs. It had been the captain's fault all along: she had been smuggling weapons from Earth to an orbital station, and her attempts to evade notice had led her into the busy traffic around the Calais spaceport, where she collided with a small unmanned cargo ship. Her ship, her crew, all the illegal weapons they were carrying, they had all crashed into the sea. Over a hundred people had died when *Excelsior*'s impact sent a tsunami over the southwest of England, cresting seawalls from Exeter to Bournemouth. The rebelling orbital that *Excelsior* had been carrying weapons to had surrendered to Earth forces only a few weeks later.

We hadn't been mourning any of them, the smugglers or soldiers or freedom fighters, or even thinking of them at all, when we argued. That had happened over a century ago, during the meaningless rebellion of a minor orbital habitat. I couldn't even remember which one had tried to declare its independence that time around. It had nothing to do with us. It was only a curiosity. David had promised to pay up what we had bet—first dibs on exploring Kraken Mare, Titan's largest hydrocarbon sea—and we had laughed about it, laughed and drank and dreamed of the future. We had been so certain tomorrow, all of our tomorrows, would be splendid. I could not remember anymore what that certainty had felt like, if it had tasted of salt and bitter wind, if there had been room for fear beneath the wheeling stars.

I had no idea what David's message was meant to tell me. He hadn't mentioned Karl Longo's sentencing, which was the only thing I could think of that would spur contact after a year and a half of silence. If he meant to obliquely suggest that somebody had lied about *Symposium*, it was a bit late for that. Black Halo had taken full credit, and all the evidence substantiated their claim. Longo had written a very lengthy manifesto. The day's news articles reported he had been proud and unrepentant all through the trial and sentencing.

David had sent the message anonymously but still seemed to think the Parthenope comm monitors were watching. He hadn't said anything that would flag the message as suspicious.

And he had gotten so many details of our shared past wrong.

I sat there for so long my hip ached and the grime of the day was itching all over my skin. I shuffled to the washrooms and suffered through the tedious process of bathing in Hygiea's low gravity—a shower in name only, a damp contortionist's routine in reality. I scrubbed my scalp-buzzed hair and my fingernails and my skin until my shower credits ran out.

I returned to my box and played David's message one more time. He was right that we could not speak in true privacy without careful preparation from both sides. I couldn't set up a live, untraceable conversation from my personal quarters; I wasn't even certain I could set it up from HQ without being caught. Maybe David was cracking. Maybe he was addicted to narcotics that scrambled his brain. Maybe the strain of being stuck on an asteroid mine had broken him. It happened. A couple of months ago I had investigated a man who had snapped midshift and slowly, deliberately, methodically impaled himself with twelve iron rods before anybody noticed. He had missed all of his major organs and survived. He said afterward he did it because he was bored. That was what life in space could do to people. I wanted to talk to David anyway.

I shoved my dirty clothes into a ball and wondered if the kid with the bleeding eyes would survive the night, if his brain was already mush, if he would wake to regret how breathtakingly stupid he'd been. I turned off the lights. I spent half the night trying to get to sleep, the other half dreaming about fire and darkness and phantom pains shooting through my prosthetic parts.

I finally gave up, rose, and watched David's message again and again until morning.

I had to talk to him. If only to get him help. If only to ask my questions and hear his answers.

My stomach was churning with an anxious, acidic queasiness when I slumped into HQ just before 0600. I had a plan forming in my head for how to respond without our correspondence being detected. Part of that plan involved pretending everything was normal, so I sat at my desk and focused on my work. I compiled the results from the biohacked kid's devices. As I'd expected, he'd been reading the usual forums and chatter from groups across the system predicting the joining of man and machine, the neural singularity, the evolution of humankind any day now, any moment, just wait for it, soon the AIs would awaken and lift us all from our primitive self-imposed misery, blah blah blah, the usual garbage. There was a new countdown to supposed singularity every few years, because the assholes who wanted to be ruled by machines never seemed to find anything more interesting to do with their time. It took only a cursory glance at the kid's personal data to figure out who had most likely fucked up his head: a black market doctor from Ceres operating out of a cargo container on various transport ships since losing his license a few years ago. The doc's current transport was already gone from Hygiea, his butchering practice with it, and Parthenope's Operational Security Department had no jurisdiction anymore. The Outer Systems Administration was supposed to handle criminal matters outside of corporate territories, but the chances of that amounting to anything was nil. They didn't have the resources to go after rogue surgeons and wouldn't waste their time even if they did. I sent the conclusions over to Jackson and struck the file off my action list.

My next task was to look at the new investigations and see if I had been assigned any actions during the night. The morning's haul included some minor data theft, a spot of drug trade, a bit of light embezzlement among station concessioners—all threats to the health and safety of Parthenope employees, or so we pretended to believe. Everybody in the outer system was trying to rip off everybody else. I kept reading down the list. Physical altercation on Dock 7 nobody would admit to witnessing. Terminated employees squatting in their quarters when they were supposed to be shipping out—which had never made sense to me, because who the fuck would want to stay here longer than they had to? Jackson had explained that people did the delicate calculus of deciding whether staying until they were arrested and turned over to the OSA would cost less overall than paying for transport off Hygiea. The OSA was wise to the scam and had started billing holdovers for their voluntary jail time, but everybody knew OSA's enforcers couldn't compete with Parthenope when it came to collecting debts. It still seemed like a shitty way to live to me, but maybe after another year or two on Hygiea I would consider jail the least awful of innumerable awful options.

A flash of red at the top of the list caught my eye: new investigation had just been added to the system.

Location: Nimue
Event: Suspicious death
Deceased: Prussenko, David

THREE

I did my homework during the eighteen-hour flight from Hygiea to Nimue. I wanted to know what I was getting into.

Nimue was a C-type asteroid in the shape of an elongated ellipsoid, giving it the look of a gray, lumpy potato. It was about twelve kilometers in diameter on its long axis, five at most on its short axes, which put it on the larger size for rocks in the Hygiea family. Most of the exterior components of Parthenope's mine were clustered at one end of the ellipsoid; the docking structure jutted outward like a long, spindly stamen of a flower, with the facilities for cargo, operations, and crew quarters forming three petals at its base. The Operations and Residential sections were decommissioned ships that had been parked on Nimue, buried in the loose rock, and adapted into a permanent station to serve out the remainder of their useful years. There was also an abandoned Unified Earth Navy base on the asteroid. Nimue was too far from the inner system to have been useful during the Martian rebellion, and now the base was nothing more than a few empty bunkers and missile silos, stripped of useful parts, indistinguishable from the gravel and dust.

The heart of the facility—the reason that bleak little chunk of rock was so valuable to Parthenope—was not visible from the outside. Nimue was home to a massive unfinished ore-processing furnace that, when completed, would stretch along the entire longitudinal axis of the asteroid.

The station had twelve crew members—eleven now—and an Overseer. Cargo ships visited twice a month; Nimue was remote, but not so remote as to make it wholly inaccessible. For a good portion of its orbit, it was within cosmic spitting distance of major outer systems shipping routes. There were worse places to be stationed. There were better places too.

Data, maps, names, reports. I read them all hungrily. I wanted to be ready. I thought it might prepare me for what I would find.

I was wrong. Nothing could have prepared me for the sight of David's dead body.

They had left him where they found him: lying on his side in an airlock in the cargo warehouse. The interior door of the airlock was open. David was on the floor, with one hand outstretched and his fingers curled into claws on the cold metal floor. His face and the visible side of his head were a mess of blood and matted hair and pulped tissue. Somebody had beaten him viciously. Blood was splattered all over the walls of the airlock, over the control panel, over his clothes. Two fingers on his left hand were broken backward—he had tried to fight back. The murder weapon lay on the floor beside him: a long metal bar, with dried blood and bits of tissue on one end.

It had been nearly thirty hours since David had died. The

inside of the airlock was cold; decay was encroaching slowly. I pressed my lips together and swallowed. I tried to look away, but I couldn't take my eyes off of David's body.

"We haven't touched him. This is how I found him." Yevgenya Sigrah, Nimue's foreperson, spoke with the clipped accent of a Vesta native and the undisguised annoyance of a site manager whose operation had been inconvenienced.

"You found him yourself, yeah?" Safety Inspector Adisa asked. He was the ranking Safety Officer on the OSD incident team and my immediate boss for the duration of this investigation.

"That's what I said." Sigrah was a stocky, gray-haired woman of about fifty, with a permanent scowl and a long scar down the left side of her face. There was a notable sharpness in the way she answered, but I couldn't tell if it was because she had something to hide or just didn't want security officers fucking around in her station. "Checked his room in the morning, about 0700. He wasn't there, so I checked the ID tracking and access logs."

"Do you know why he was out here?" Adisa asked. He wasn't looking at Sigrah. He was standing in the doorway, hands in his pockets, looking down at the corpse. Part of me wanted him to move to the side so I could get a better look. Most of me wanted to turn away so I didn't have to see anything else.

"No," Sigrah said shortly. "He was on third shift. He wouldn't be the first to use the quiet shift for personal business. I tell them to keep their lovers' quarrels and petty arguments out of the work."

From the first moment we'd stepped off the transport ship and onto Nimue, Sigrah had been telling us that David's death was clearly the result of a personal argument. I wanted to ask her what she meant by that—who could have hated David that much, how did she know, who was that violent, why would they do this—but I kept my questions to myself for now and tried not to flinch every time Adisa asked something that felt completely unrelated or irrelevant.

"What do you use this airlock for?" Adisa asked.

This was the first assignment I'd worked with Mohammad Adisa. I knew him by sight and reputation, partly because Operational Security was a chummy clique of eager gossips, but mostly because there weren't many Martians working on Hygiea in any department. Adisa was average height, on the thin side of average build, brown skin, black hair turning to gray at the temples. Fifties, divorced, burned-out—so claimed the gossip mill—should have left OSD a few years ago, kept going instead. I had expected to have a fight on my hands when I asked to join the investigation. Personal connections between officers and victims made for messy reports, after all, especially if private lawyers ever got involved and started making noise about company liability. But Adisa had only shrugged and approved the request without asking why.

Sigrah glanced at the bloodied room, looked away. "Not a lot. Routine maintenance on the cargo system." She jerked a thumb upward. "There's a fuel line up there that's broken down a few times. Needs a walkabout every few months. But David isn't involved with any of that work."

"Could he have been helping someone else, yeah?" Adisa said.

"Don't know. It's not in the work logs."

"Any trouble lately? Disagreement among the crew?"

Sigrah hesitated, then shook her head. "Not that they brought to me. They keep their personal problems personal."

That meant nothing coming from a station foreperson. The kind of trouble that caused real problems among the crew rarely reached the boss's ears, even on a crew as small as Nimue's, and that was mostly by design. Sigrah knew the rules for succeeding as a Parthenope foreperson: everything good that happened on the station was her doing, whereas everything bad was the fault of troublemaking crew.

"Should I get started?" The question came from the third member of our team, the security tech Avery Ryu. They waited just outside the airlock with a crime scene kit and medical carry-board.

"Go ahead," Adisa said.

Ryu bobbed their head quickly, such an easy and familiar thing for them to do, in this unfamiliar place, that I felt a pang of fondness. Ryu and I had become friends, in a way, right after I'd started working for Parthenope, the kind of friends who used each other for company and sex and never talked about it. We hadn't spoken in several months—my fault, I supposed, although we had never talked about that either. When we had been hanging out together, Ryu's constant nodding, agreeing, affirming had driven me crazy, but it was a comfort now.

They stepped into the bloody chamber, avoiding the pooled blood on the floor, and got to work securing the murder weapon, documenting the scene, collecting physical evidence, scanning for fingerprints. All of which would be unnecessary once we had the surveillance recordings, but it was part of the OSD routine of acting like we served a purpose besides sweeping Parthenope's problems out of sight. Nothing we did ever made it into an Outer Systems Administration court. In the asteroid belt, corporate security was the only law that mattered.

I tried to look away. I didn't need to watch. The blood, the ruin of David's face, the exterior door so close and the barren asteroid visible beyond, it all felt like a painful weight pressing on my chest. I could not look away. I could not even blink.

The dead man looked nothing like the David I knew. He didn't even look like the man in the message. There was a small part of me, numb with denial, that wanted to believe it wasn't him. The David I remembered had been always in motion, tall, lanky in the way of men who run and swim and climb with enthusiasm well into adulthood, his white skin always tanned, with blue eyes and floppy blond hair and a ready smile. This man's face was too soft, his hair too thin, his hands too aged for the passage of so little time. But he had the same bald patch on the top of his head, the same faint shunt scars on his left arm, just below the cuff of his sleeve, where osteoregenerative drugs had been injected when he first left Earth. That had happened years ago, long before I met him; David had spent part of his childhood in an orbital habitat, with diplomat parents who negotiated treaties between Earth and the independent stations. He was forty-five years old, eight years my senior, but in death he looked so much older.

"Was he the only one working that shift?" Adisa asked.

"Far as I know," Sigrah said. "He swapped with Mary. It was her night on."

I recalled the personnel files: a woman named Mary Ping was Nimue's other sysadmin. I had never before heard of a mining facility with two sysadmins for its Overseer, but Nimue was a particularly valuable chunk of rock with a deep well of stakeholders and investors. No doubt Parthenope counted the extra crew member on-site as another way of safeguarding its operation.

"Was that normal, switching shifts?"

"It happens." Sigrah shrugged. "The surveillance will show everything."

There was nothing in her voice except impatience. No regret. No fear. No grief.

I turned away from the corpse to look around. The warehouse was a couple hundred meters long by about eighty meters wide, crammed from floor to ceiling with shipping containers. The tracks of the cargo crane formed a network of oiled metal about fifty or sixty meters above our heads. The containers bore insignia from numerous outer systems corporations and took up most of the available space, creating a labyrinth of narrow, shadowy canyons between tall, rectangular stacks.

I couldn't see any security cameras with a clear view of the airlock, but I wouldn't be sure until I got a look at the surveillance. Parthenope didn't like letting anyone dig around in their surveillance data, not even their own security officers. Not even when an employee has been beaten to death by another employee. They claimed it was to remain in compliance with OSA privacy laws; everybody knew it was because a data set that extensive was more valuable than all the water and rocks in Parthenope space combined. On Hygiea, obtaining permission to access the data was easy, but on Nimue it was proving to be a little more complicated. The Parthenope lawyer who had come along with the security team was currently in Ops firing off demands to a team of execs in the corporate offices on Hygiea, who needed approval from the legal team on Vesta, who in turn needed approval from an executive at the corporate headquarters on Yuèliàng. But Earth and its Moon were currently on the other side of the Sun, with the Yuèliàng capital city of Imbrium in the middle of its local night, so even on the best company relay network it took about an hour for encoded radio messages to go back and forth between Hygiea and the Earth-Yuèliàng system, and that didn't account for all the corporate ass-covering that would be happening at every step of the process.

"Was there any sort of alert during the night?" I asked. "Like a maintenance alarm? Something he might have come to check?"

Sigrah did not want to look at me. Her gaze kept skating over my face, straying to my left shoulder and down my arm, sliding back when she realized she was staring. "No," she said. "He wasn't here for work. It was personal."

I decided to take a cue from Adisa and pretend she didn't keep saying that.

"Was there anything in particular he was working on lately?" I asked.

"Nothing he brought to me. Mary might know, or one of his friends." She said this to a point somewhere below my left ear. I wanted to tell her to stare, to just bloody keep on staring until she'd looked her fill, but I'd learned from experience that only made things more uncomfortable.

"We'll also have to talk to the crew, aye?" Adisa said.

It wasn't a question. It was only his gratingly Martian way of ending every sentence like a question, seeking agreement even when stating a fact or giving an order. His accent was the only thing that marked him out as obviously Martian. All the other common signs—the evidence of childhood malnutrition, the scars from Mars's infamously terrible radiation treatments, whatever rebel tattoos he might have acquired during a misbegotten youth—were well hidden under his slightly rumpled uniform. But the accent was unmistakable. It was English spoken by somebody who was more used to the singsong rhythms of the Martian patois, that odd amalgam of the many languages carried to the red planet by early waves of colonists.

"Why?" Sigrah demanded. "You'll have the surveillance."

"Just following the rules, aye," Adisa said.

Sigrah narrowed her eyes. She wanted to argue with him, but she knew better. Her apparent disinterest in identifying who among her crew was a murderer wasn't all that surprising. If she pointed the finger at the wrong person, before anybody saw the surveillance, she would put herself in a position that raised more questions than it answered. No matter what she wanted to say, no matter who she wanted to blame, she had to know that playing along would get OSD off her station that much faster.

"Right. Second shift ends in about an hour. They'll be available then."

"Aye, we'll be ready for them before that."

"They won't be ready for you."

"Thank you for your help. We need to process the scene now, yeah?"

It took Sigrah a moment to understand that it was a dismissal. "This is my station. I'm required to supervise all activity."

"You are, aye," Adisa said, with a bob of his head that was not quite a nod, "except in security matters in which you are directly involved."

"I'm not—"

"You have twelve people on this station and one of them is dead," Adisa said. "We'll talk to your crew as soon as we're done in here."

Sigrah glowered at him but decided, in the end, not to argue. As she strode away, each step punctuated by the sticky sound of her gecko boots detaching from the floor, I heard her mutter, "Fucking smug Martians."

Ryu covered up a startled laugh, but Adisa didn't even blink. Even after a year on the job, it still shocked me to hear how open people in the belt were about hating Martians. Back on Earth everybody tended to be more polite about their bigotry. The war had ended thirty years ago, after all, so their civilized scorn went into discussing the Martian problem over tea: worrying about refugees straining the system, fretting over the corporate militarization of space, wondering if the PM would push her party toward another vote on the resettlement matter. It was all politics about faraway places and nameless people who couldn't survive on Earth without extensive and expensive medical procedures, people who wouldn't even need help if they hadn't started a hopeless rebellion in the first place.

Not so in the asteroid belt. There were too many people out here who remembered being forced to choose between Earth and Mars. The war was still too close, even though the last missiles had been dismantled twenty-five years ago.

Ryu cleared their throat. "I need some help turning him and getting him on the board."

I didn't know if they were speaking to me, but Adisa moved to help before I had to figure it out. I stayed out of the way. I couldn't begin to guess how many times David had been struck. He must have been surprised—it would be easy to take him by surprise, if one meant him harm. He was not suspicious by nature. He didn't pick fights, didn't throw punches. The first blow would have been a shock. Every blow after—only pain.

They rolled David, and I saw his face properly for the first time. One of his eyes and most of his nose were a mangled mess, the socket collapsed by blows from the metal bar, but the other eye was wide open and red with burst capillaries. The injuries looked like the result of a wild, uncontrollable rage. I averted my eyes quickly. Breathed through my mouth and counted to ten. The rest of David's body, save the two broken fingers, was intact.

"Ready," Ryu said. "On three we lift. One, two, three. Good."

The two of them maneuvered the corpse onto the board. I looked away as Ryu sealed the body bag over David's face. Adisa helped unfold the wheels of the carry-board, and Ryu left to take David to the infirmary. The warehouse grew quiet as their sticky gecko-boot footsteps faded.

I had to do something, so I stepped into the airlock to look at the interior control panel. The screen was dim and old, with dust ground into the corners and scratches over the surface. Above the screen was a small glass eye: a surveillance camera.

Adisa came into the airlock beside me. "Anything?"

"The camera doesn't look damaged." I tapped the panel to bring up the commands and quickly confirmed there was no way to access the security camera from there. "It should have recorded—" My voice caught. "Everything."

"How well did you know him, yeah?" Adisa said.

I wasn't entirely sure how to answer. "We were colleagues for a while. Friends, I guess. But not recently." My voice sounded high and thin to me. My lungs were a honeycomb of scar tissue and the doctors had warned me against exposure to low-oxygen environments, one of the hundreds of warnings they had given me, the hundreds of ways they had scolded me for surviving in such an inconvenient fashion, with so many ongoing systems failures.

"Have you kept in touch?" Adisa asked.

I hadn't told him or anybody else about David's message to me. I wasn't going to, not until I understood what it meant.

"No," I said. "I haven't seen him since we gave our final statements to the OSA."

"Why not, aye?"

I glanced at him. "Because we don't keep in touch. It's not like we have a little survivors' club where we get together and talk about what shit luck we have. We're all just . . . bad reminders to each other."

"But you still wanted to be here."

"Of course I did," I said. "David survived a bunch of terrorists trying to blow him up. He survived *that*, only to die here, like—like . . . It's fucking unfair that he should die like this. He deserved better."

The force went out of my words at the end. I was clenching my left hand again. I didn't like that I couldn't always feel it, didn't know what signals my own brain was sending until they were sent. My heart was racing. My skin was tight and itchy all over.

"Aye, all right," Adisa said.

I couldn't look at him. "You could have asked before we got here."

He shrugged, unconcerned. "I checked with Jackson, yeah? She said you're good at your job and could use the field experience. What was he like?"

"David? I just told you, we haven't been in touch."

"Before," Adisa said. "When you did know him. What was his work?"

"Oh. He was—well, he was a roboticist. A brilliant one. You know about the Titan project?"

"A bit, aye," Adisa said. "What was in the news."

I knew what that meant. The news was only ever about

how nearly everybody had died in a horrific terrorist attack, not about what they had been living for.

"We were going to Titan to establish a permanent research base to study . . . well, everything, but mostly to search for life. But Titan's a strange place, so it isn't—" I gestured helplessly. It had been a long time since I'd had to explain this to anyone. "It wasn't going to be like all the Europa projects, where the biggest obstacle is drilling through kilometers of ice and sending autonomous submarines down to look around. We were going to use autonomous bots, of course—there's no way people could just, I don't know, walk around doing field mapping. Titan has liquid hydrocarbon lakes. Rivers of methane and ethane. Multiple cryovolcanoes. The atmosphere is this thick organic haze of nitrogen. It has storms and weather and rain and—and it's cold as fuck, obviously, just over 90 kelvin or so. It's dangerous as hell, so bots would have to do most of the exploring."

I had thought I was over it, the yearning I felt when I described that hellish, beautiful world. I had thought the fires aboard *Symposium* had burned it out of me, the same way it had burned away my skin, my cells. Nobody asked me about Titan anymore. My heart felt light and fluttery, my breath shallow, to be talking about it again.

"And Prussenko built those bots?" Adisa said.

"Trained them to design and build themselves, for the most part. I worked on the AI that was going to control them. It was called Vanguard," I said, although he had not asked. "That was the brain. David was head of the team that built the rovers and drones and all that."

Adisa didn't say anything, just kept looking mildly curious, so I went on.

"It's, um, it's a lot more complicated than it sounds, because we weren't going to know exactly what kinds of sensors and instrumentation Vanguard needed on its rovers until we were actually on Titan. We couldn't send the bots out there with hardwired expectations for what they would find, because then they would miss anything truly interesting. Like, if we told Vanguard to look for DNA and RNA, it could easily miss evidence of life that was built on different macromolecules or . . ."

I trailed off. I was rambling now, saying far more than Adisa cared to hear. I felt like I needed to defend David's legacy, to make Adisa realize how talented he had been, how clever and innovative, and how bloody unfair it was that he had been stuck doing tech support in this miserable place. None of it mattered anymore. David, Vanguard, our mission, our future, it was all gone.

"He was brilliant," I said finally. Everywhere I looked there was blood on the walls. The stale metallic smell of it filled every breath. "He was wasted on a station like this. He deserved so much better."

Adisa looked at me for a moment, then he said, "Let's get the surveillance and talk to the crew, aye?"

God, I hated the way he said the words, not heavy with pity but carefully avoiding it, like casual professionalism was going to make this any less humiliating. I was used to being talked about. The whispers, the glances, the murmurs that followed me everywhere I went. I knew how that conversation with Jackson must have gone. She's fine with data, sure, but she's touchy and sensitive, thinks she's smarter than us, thinks she deserves better than this job. Get her out of here for a few days. She's such a drag on the mood.

I nodded, then swallowed painfully. "Right."

I didn't move. If I took a step, I would stumble, and the last thing I needed was my superior making a note of how clumsy I was. For anybody else, that might mean teasing about my lack of space legs, but for me it would mean a barrage of doctors' appointments to check my balance, check my coordination, assess my mental and emotional acceptance of my prosthetic limbs, upgrade and adjust, reprogram and rewire, a hungry glint in the doctors' eyes as they told me to try again, again, again. I could never simply lose my balance. I did not have that luxury. For me every stumble was a whole fucking science experiment for the ghouls who had pieced me back together.

"Take a minute," Adisa said.

He walked away, footsteps withdrawing into the warehouse, and I was alone.

It took three times, three times telling myself to just rat-fucking do it, to grow a bloody spine, to get the fuck over it, three times before I was able to turn around. I could take a minute, but it wasn't going to help. I could take an hour, a day, a whole accursed year, and it wouldn't help. There was no exercise in counting to ten or breathing deeply or soothing my nerves that would put me anywhere other than in space, on a lifeless rock in the outer system, in the room where David had died.

I made myself move. Not out of the airlock, but across it, toward the outer hatch. I stepped over the dark stain of David's blood and felt a suffocating rush of helplessness and aching, bitter sadness.

There was a window on the outer hatch, about twenty centimeters tall, hexagonal in shape, and a small slot beside the door for an emergency physical override, lest anybody be caught on the wrong side of depressurization. It was such a clumsy and old-fashioned gesture toward safety. The entire hatch was a bulky old unit obviously repurposed from the defunct UEN base; the door had been built to withstand Martian missiles or worse. It had kept the vacuum outside for more than thirty years. It wasn't going to snap open or crumple outward or vanish or any of the innumerable, impossible failures I could imagine, and did imagine, far too easily, every time there was only a single door between me and open space. The United Earth Navy loved its hexagon symbolism: one strong side for each of the six superpowers that had joined together to fight for Earth and crush the Martian rebellion. To keep the solar system safe from chaos. To show the upstarts who was boss. That level of ostentatious militarism had fallen out of fashion after the armistice, although crushing upstart Martians never really went out of style. The disarmament treaty and system-wide weapons test monitoring meant there wasn't any military weaponry or infrastructure within a million kilometers of Nimue, not anymore, not since the UEN had decommissioned the base. Only the geometry of the war remained firmly stamped on the ruins left behind, even out here, so far from Earth and Mars.

I was still making a fist. Still doing it without thinking. Left hand, metal hand. I took a breath and forced myself to relax. Brain, nerves, muscles. Signal and response. If I clenched that one too tightly, too often, without letting the joints open, the delicate engineering and responsive alloy that made up the phalanges and metacarpals would stiffen and glitch. It didn't hurt, exactly, because my prosthetic parts couldn't feel pain, but it was awkward as fuck when I tried to grasp something and my hand responded like a squeaky set of gears on an old bicycle. I dropped things. People stared. Everybody felt embarrassed for me.

I had to take a breath before I could look through the window. Two breaths. My throat was tight.

The view surprised me. I had somehow expected—even knowing that the airlock floor was oriented toward Nimue's center—that the airlock would open to space, and all that I would see would be stars and darkness. That was the view that haunted all my nightmares: the stars, the nothingness, and fuck you very much, doctors, for telling me how irrational it was.

But what I saw outside that window was Nimue's gray and pockmarked surface, sweeping out toward a startlingly close horizon. A line of old transport rails, probably unused since the UEN days, led away from the hatch. The curvature of the asteroid made the rails look as though they ended abruptly only tens of meters away, like a diving board into nothingness, but for all I knew they could wrap all the way around Nimue's lumpy, elongated body.

"What the hell did you get into out here, David?" I said quietly.

On the flight over, I had watched countless press reports and interviews with Parthenope execs in which they extolled Nimue's many profitable virtues; analyses from outer systems economists who said the company was betting its entire existence and the fortunes of a great many very powerful investors on the success of Nimue; projections questioning whether consolidation of ore-processing and fuel-manufacturing facilities was going to be more effective in future asteroid mining than the current distributed model; and many, many, far too many quarterly reports in which Parthenope proudly enumerated the ways in which Nimue was exceeding expectations when it came to productivity and efficiency.

Nimue was important to Parthenope Enterprises. It was no secret that their long-term plan was to absolutely dominate this bleak corner of the belt. Water for everyone. Fuel for everyone. Rare metals for everyone. Opportunity for everyone—provided they could pay for it.

Sigrah wanted David's murder to be personal. The company

wanted it to be personal. Mining crews got into personal altercations all the time. They were a discontented, easily agitated group of people. A disagreement over something petty. Drugs or sex or money. Tempers flaring. One furious blow that turned into dozens. It wasn't a stretch. It was what everybody wanted to believe.

There was a small sound behind me, a choked little gasp. I spun around, heart racing, to find a young woman standing in the doorway. Her shimmery silver hair was so bright it provided a disorienting contrast to the grim warehouse behind her. She had one hand pressed to her lips. Tears shone in her eyes.

"What are you doing here?" I asked. "You can't be here."

"I only want to . . ." She took in a shaky breath; tears spilled down her pale cheeks. Her voice was small and girlish, her accent unexpectedly posh. "They said I shouldn't, but I wanted to . . ."

"You can't be here," I said again.

"I know, I know, but I needed to see . . ." Her gaze danced over the airlock, over me, over my prosthetics, as though it was too much for her to take in, as though she already regretted letting the image of this blood-splattered room into her thoughts.

I could not dredge up any sympathy for her. "I don't care. Get out of here. You're interfering with the investigation."

"Okay." She nodded. She backed away, nodding. "Okay. I'll just—okay."

When she was gone, it took several moments for my heart rate to steady again. It took even longer for me to force myself to look out the window one more time, onto the bleak hellscape that had been David's last view of the universe.

If I opened that outer door, I could walk on the surface of the asteroid—if I was careful, if I did not step too hard. The possibility made my heart race, my breath catch, and I felt dark shadows gathering around the edges of my vision. I reached out to touch the door, needing to steady myself. This asteroid was so small, its shape so irregular. A single step might send me gliding into space, and Nimue would not have gravity enough to drag me back down.

FOUR

Adisa and Sigrah were waiting in the junction between Nimue's main sections. It was an angular room with walls of riveted metal, exposed ductwork, and a few small square maintenance access panels with manual locks. It looked to have been cobbled together as an afterthought, piece by piece, shabby and impermanent. The labeling on the machinery and pipes was in multiple languages, including English, Chinese, and Arabic, with scattered words in Spanish and Hindi and Russian. The doors to Ops and Res were open, but the wide metal door to the mine itself was closed and adorned with a colorful array of warnings: heat, radiation, chemicals, corrosion.

I had looked at diagrams and maps, but I couldn't fathom the size and scale of the facility behind that door. The extraction furnace was Parthenope's pride and joy, capable of chewing up any sort of rock and spitting out water, volatiles, rare metals. The furnace was currently three kilometers long, penetrating about one-quarter of the way through the asteroid, with the active face of the mine at the far end and plants for processing, refining, and manufacturing stacked along its length like vertebrae along the spinal column. The plan was to punch the furnace right through the long axis of the asteroid, creating the largest ore-processing and fuel-manufacturing facility in the solar system.

Above the ceiling of the junction, accessed by a ladder bolted to one wall, was the station's docking structure, which jutted a couple hundred meters above the asteroid's surface. Only crew used this long metal throat to enter the station; the cargo itself, both coming and going, moved along rails outside. The airlock was open, and a crew member in a space suit, with her helmet in one hand, was coming back down the long passageway. I recognized her spiky blond hair from the personnel files: Katee King, electrical engineer.

"Fuck if I know what's going on. I can't find anything," she said as she dropped down into the junction. She was carrying a sling of tools on her back. She looked at me and Adisa and explained, "Optical array is glitching. It happens all the time."

Sigrah's narrowed eyes and thin frown suggested she wasn't happy about a crew member telling a couple of OSD officers about Nimue's problems, but she only nodded curtly and said, "Understood. Take a look again later, if you have time."

"Will do." King hit the control panel on the wall to shut the airlock before heading into Res.

"You have communication problems often, aye?" Adisa asked.

Sigrah snorted. "You could say that. This is about the fifth time in two months Katee's had to crawl out there to fix the optical array. But she's better than the last electrician we had. That fucker sat on his ass for a year before he bought out his contract and took off. Katee spends half her time cleaning up the messes he left."

The sound of gecko boots came from the doorway to Ops, and a moment later a man stepped into view. "I'm certain we find your crew problems terribly fascinating, but perhaps we can stop wasting time now."

He was the Parthenope legal representative who'd come over with the investigation team. He hadn't introduced himself to me during the journey over, nor had his role been included in the official briefing reports, but Ryu had told me he was Hugo van Arendonk, one of the lawyers Parthenope sent along when they wanted an embarrassing problem to go away quickly and quietly.

"Apologies," Adisa said, without a trace of apology in his voice. "Are we complicating your busy social schedule?"

"Fuck off, Mohammad. I just spent two fucking hours waiting for the bloody CEO to crawl out from under her fuck-boy to get surveillance access." Van Arendonk's accent was almost comically upper-class, the sort of cut-glass variety that you only heard in the loftiest echelons of Yuèliàng society, or in media doing its best to mock them. "So let's watch the bloody vids and find out who did this. If the analyst doesn't have more pressing duties?"

He looked right at me, eyebrows raised.

"The analyst is ready when you are," I said. "Safety Officer Hester Marley."

There was a beat, a pause just a shade too long for comfort, before van Arendonk turned away. "I don't care who you are. I only want to know who we pin this on so we can get the fuck out of here." He glanced over his shoulder as he opened the door. "Please do come along, if you're not too busy?"

He strode into Ops without waiting for an answer.

"I'll be searching the victim's personal quarters," Adisa said. "Let me know if you find anything, yeah?"

"Right. Of course."

"Don't worry," he added, when I hesitated. "He's every bit as insufferable once you get to know him."

Sigrah laughed shortly. "They grow 'em that way on purpose."

Oh. Oh, shit. I hoped my face did not show my surprise. I had recognized the surname when Ryu mentioned it, but I hadn't realized he was a van Arendonk of *those* van Arendonks. One of the wealthiest and most powerful families in the solar system. The van Arendonks had been among the first to colonize the Moon a handful of centuries ago, when Earth was roiling under a constant onslaught of floods, storms, droughts, plagues, and all the wars such disasters brought with them, and those with the means fled for their own private cities in orbit and beyond. The first families to claim territory on the Moon had tried a few different names for their nation before finally settling on Yuèliàng, with the city of Imbrium as its capital. Decades passed, then centuries, and the founding oligarchs still controlled nearly all of the lunar nation. Some of the old families faded away; others blended together; but the core group remained essentially unchanged.

Which was, after all, precisely what they wanted. They wanted to remain as they were, ruling over their pale kingdom for as long as they could manage. They invested heavily in medical research for prolonging their lives, cloning themselves, genetically improving their children—all firmly outlawed on Earth. Rumors spread about experiments gone wrong. Employees being trapped in indentured servitude as broodmares and sperm donors. Babies stolen from their parents. Children designed to replace their forebears in every way.

Eventually Earth took notice. New treaties and laws tried to put a stop to Yuèliàng's medical experimentation industry, and the last few children to come from the shady old practices were born into the middle of an intense legal battle. But it all became irrelevant when rebellion broke out on Mars. The hungry Martian rabble became the enemy, the oligarchs of Yuèliàng allies once again, and everybody was busy making war.

I wasn't born when the war began. I came along after it had already been going for a few years, and my parents were academic pacifists who believed in Whole System governance. So I learned about those genetically altered lunar children as a sort of political footnote, a cautionary tale of territorial independence and the failure of scientific communities to ethically self-regulate. I never thought about the so-called Children of Yuèliàng beyond that.

Not until I found myself standing next to one and wondering what bot had crawled up his ass and died.

Hugo van Arendonk was tall, but not too tall, white, blue-eyed, fair-haired, and handsome enough in that bright-eyed, sharp-cheekboned way that probably appealed to people who were attracted to men, or lawyers. He was wearing tailored clothing that would have cost me six months' salary; even his gecko boots were bespoke rather than standard-issue. His family was the power behind both the oldest financial institution and the oldest university on Yuèliàng. Their name was on the Artificial Intelligence wing of the Lunar Museum of History, where I had, as a schoolchild on an extravagant spring holiday trip, encountered my first true Zhao-type AI. Their influence was all over every law, every treaty, every agreement that regulated how governments and corporations interacted in the system. One of the family's oldest living members—Charlotte van Arendonk, still the unrivaled grande dame of Yuèliàng politics in the beginning of her second century—had written key sections of the Outer Systems Disarmament Treaty, which had permanently banned private entities, corporations, and organizations from building their own personal armies since the end of the Martian rebellion.

Which made me wonder why her great-great-whatever-grandson was working as a legal errand-boy and fixer for Parthenope in the ass-end of the asteroid belt. I wondered, but I didn't even think about asking.

"Why are you here?" van Arendonk asked, when I caught up to him in the corridor. "You knew the dead man. You're a conflict of interest."

So he did care about who I was after all. "You'll have to ask Safety Inspector Adisa. He approved the assignment."

"But you made the request."

"Yes, I did," I said.

Van Arendonk looked at me. He probably had a pleasant face when he smiled; he had let the skin around his eyes wrinkle, let the line of his fair hair creep back a bit, keeping him from falling into the uncanny valley that plagued both the genetically engineered lunar children and people rich enough to pay for new faces twice a decade. He was certainly not smiling now.

I stared right back and waited. I had spent most of my academic life working alongside people who believed their ancestors had been shat directly out of William the Conqueror's ass. I wasn't about to let a snotty lawyer from Yuèliàng intimidate me.

He didn't challenge my answer. He just turned away and spoke as he kept walking. "We have approval to access surveillance for twelve hours before and after the time of death. Secondary Overseer contact through the systems room only. Any problems with that?"

"No," I said. "No problems."

In truth I was a little disappointed. The twenty-four-hour window I had expected, as it was standard in instances of suspicious death, but I had been hoping I might get a chance to look inside the brain of Nimue's Overseer. It wasn't necessary, not for reviewing surveillance data, nor would it have been normal procedure; only sysadmins had that kind of physical access. Just getting into the lift required a onetime access code, permission from HQ, full biometric scan and identification, and a unique circuit key that was itself kept under lock on the station. It also required, in many cases, agreement from the Overseer itself; they always had some degree of discretion about who was allowed to poke around inside their brains. I knew it was impossible and way, way above my pay grade.

But it was still frustrating to be so close to a powerful AI, one that David had worked with and trained for months, and not have a chance to take a closer look. Overseer AIs were not particularly revolutionary in design, but they were smart and did adapt to work intimately with their sysadmins. I would have loved to see firsthand how David had been spending the last months of his life.

The entrance to the systems room was at the far end of a long corridor. The Operations section of Nimue had once been a luxury transport vessel, and remnants of its former life were visible along the hallway: ornate light fixtures, decorative frames around the control panels, a geometric mosaic of polymer tiles on the floor. The pattern was white and gold and deep, deep blue, probably meant to imitate some ancient style from Earth and reassure the passengers they were traveling in luxury. It didn't feel like a working asteroid mine—except for the bulky reinforced security door at the end.

Van Arendonk entered his security access code, I entered mine, and we endured a few seconds of awkward silence before the door slid open. The interior was dark enough that I felt the tug of mental adjustment as my sharper artificial eye saw the scene more clearly than my natural eye, and my brain had a brief argument with itself trying to reconcile the difference. My first impression was of a deep, deep cold.

My second impression was of a massive, encompassing presence.

There was a pause—a heartbeat, no longer—and the lights came on, rising from the gentle gray of an early dawn to an eerie cool blue.

The room was not particularly large, only about the size of standard solo quarters. Every surface I could see, from the walls to the ceiling to the floor, was polished and clean and shiny, but somehow it managed to avoid any single clear reflection. The effect was unsettling and disorienting. I didn't know where to look, where to focus.

Van Arendonk gestured for me to step into the systems room first. The door slid shut behind us. I heard the faint click of the locks engaging, then the hiss of the ventilation and heating system kicking in to accommodate our presence. The lights changed again, became warmer in tone, less harsh on the eyes. The Overseer itself—the actual brain of the machine—was built into what had previously been the cargo hold of the passenger ship, several meters beneath our feet, surrounded by a vast cooling system. There was an access lift in the room, behind yet another bulky security door. We didn't have permission to go any farther.

I took one chair, van Arendonk the other, and the screens came on.

"Welcome, Hugo. Welcome, Hester. It's good to see you."

The voice wasn't particularly loud, but it surrounded us, smooth and mellow, from every direction at once.

The Overseer asked, "What can I help you with today?"

Like every artificial intelligence under Parthenope control, Nimue's Overseer spoke with a woman's voice, pitched high, with a forced politeness that set my teeth on edge. I wasn't fond of AIs that defaulted to natural voice communication in the first place, as it left too much room for misinterpretation. I was even less fond of AIs whose corporate programmers or users had persuaded them to speak with softly subservient women's voices. Such tones did not evolve naturally in an AI's communication style. Somebody had specifically taught it that, because somebody in the company had decided that was what a faithful servant should sound like.

I didn't like it any better when the Overseer went on without waiting for us to answer. "Are you comfortable, Hester? I have noticed a slight imbalance in your stride that I believe could lead to chronic physical discomfort. If necessary I can—"

"Stop verbal communication," I said curtly. "Requesting authorization for security and surveillance data by Safety Officer Hester Marley." I gave my investigative access code again.

Van Arendonk did the same: "Requesting authorization for unrestricted security and surveillance data access by legal counsel Hugo van Arendonk." He provided his own access code, then, after a second, he added, "Stop verbal communication."

The Overseer said, "I'm sorry you don't want to speak to me, but I will do what I can to help."

It acknowledged our requests with text responses on the screen: access codes received, investigative request pending, security and surveillance subsystems responding. I was bouncing my leg nervously; I made myself stop. A few seconds passed, seconds I knew had to have been adopted by the Overseer because it had learned somewhere along the line that too-rapid responses actually made humans trust it less. Station steward AIs were designed to provide human comfort as part of their mandate, and human comfort often included pretending to operate on human timescales. It was another thing I disliked about working with Parthenope's AIs. I didn't care to be condescended to by a machine.

A confirmation appeared on the screen: **Limited access granted.**

"Right," van Arendonk said, "let's start with the visual . . . right. By all means, don't let me stop you, Safety Officer Marley."

Nor did I care to have a company lawyer telling me how to do my job.

I asked the Overseer to bring up the security and surveillance data from the day of David's death, then narrowed in on employee ID tracking and medical reports. Parthenope watched its employees obsessively. In addition to the omnipresent cameras and audio recorders in public spaces, the company required a unique code every time we accessed a terminal, logged the embedded microchips in our wrists every time we passed through a monitored doorway, and constantly analyzed every action to flag those that ventured outside standard routines. There was an entire medical subsystem devoted to assessing the physical, mental, and emotional well-being of the crew.

All of which meant that Parthenope employees had virtually no privacy in any aspect of their daily lives, but it also meant I would be able to pinpoint the exact moment when David died—and I could watch it happen.

At least, I should have been able to.

Something strange happened when I asked the Overseer for David's time of death.

The time it reported loss of contact with his internal tracking chip was 2400:00:00.

Midnight. Exactly midnight. To within hundredths of a second.

"That can't be right," van Arendonk said.

I was glad I didn't have to explain to him how improbable it was. I asked for the tracking and surveillance data for the time and location of David's death.

The Overseer answered: **Data unavailable.**

"What? Why the fuck not?" I said, and my hands were already moving again, asking for a full surveillance report on David's motions. My access only allowed me twelve hours of data prior to the recorded time of death, so I worked backward to find out what was available.

The Overseer was quick with a reply.

Just before 2300, David was tracked moving from Operations to the junction, from the junction into the cargo warehouse. That was the last recorded confirmation of his presence prior to his death at 2400.

Between 2300 and 2400, there was no security, surveillance, or tracking data.

Data unavailable.

There was no medical data. There was no door or terminal access data. No cameras anywhere on the station had recorded anything during that time. No audio recorder had registered a single sound. There was nothing. Every possible record was nonexistent.

A buzzing sound grew in my ears. This should not be possible. I had the required access; the Overseer was not hiding anything from me. I checked and double-checked. Asked the Overseer to check. It was completely fucking impossible. Data unavailable, every time I asked, for every source I searched between the hours of 2300 and 2400 on the night of David's death. It was all empty, empty, empty. Not only in Ops and Res, not only in the cargo warehouse, not only in the airlock, but everywhere throughout the facility. There were no surveillance and security data files from that hour. None. Even the exterior cameras positioned on the docking structure recorded nothing. The entire security subsystem had stopped recording at precisely the same moment, and one hour later it had picked up again as though nothing had happened.

There was nothing but an hour-long gap of darkness and silence.

"How is that possible?" van Arendonk asked. He leaned forward in his chair, staring intently at the Overseer's output. "Is that possible?"

I didn't want to admit it, but I had no idea. Overseers did not stop monitoring their stations for any reason. It simply didn't happen. The whole purpose of putting the surveillance system under the control of an AI rather than a fallible human crew vulnerable to threats and extortion was to protect it from such tampering. I didn't even know how somebody might go about blinding an Overseer for a single second, much less an entire hour. Even station sysadmins weren't supposed to have that kind of power.

But the first step was to ask the Overseer itself, so that's what I did. I didn't know how the Overseer would interpret a direct query, so I dug into the commands that led to the surveillance and security blackout. I wasn't terribly surprised to find that the command itself had been erased within microseconds of the system returning to fully operational, so I traced the origin of the deletion order. I looked specifically for any actions taken by Mary Ping, the other sysadmin. There were only twelve people on Nimue, and arguably only the two sysadmins would have even the slimmest chance of convincing the Overseer to close its eyes for an hour.

Even with no real idea what to expect, the answer still surprised me.

"Um," I said. I double-checked the result. "The surveillance blackout command arrived in a superoperational command packet."

"What the *fuck*?" van Arendonk said. "It came from Hygiea?"

"Well, it looks like that," I quickly amended, "but it could be a false command, or somebody piggybacking on the commands from HQ, or altering it after the packet arrived but before the Overseer executed it, or . . ."

I was getting ahead of myself. Superoperational commands were how the company told the Overseers what to do. They were normally things like "produce more fuel" or "mine rock faster" or "make the crew less depressed and more productive." The company higher-ups decided what they wanted, the master AI on Hygiea turned those demands into high-level commands and sent them out to all the mines and facilities, and the Overseers interpreted the orders as they saw fit. I didn't work with the Overseers directly, but I knew the commands were not generally concerned with operational micromanaging.

They were sure as fuck never supposed to shut down surveillance. But there it was, inside the command packet from the master AI, a clear instruction to Nimue's Overseer to black out surveillance. The command packet in question had arrived on the day David died, hours before his murder. It had come directly from Hygiea.

"So which is it?" van Arendonk said. "Is somebody on this miserable rock making it look like the company is covering up a murder? Or is the company actually covering up a murder?"

I had been wondering the same thing, but I hadn't expected the Parthenope legal rep to come right out and say it.

"They sent us here to investigate it," I pointed out.

The look van Arendonk gave me was amused. "Did they?"

Of course they hadn't. I knew as well as anybody that we were here to clean up a mess and file a report that wouldn't ruffle any feathers. It was unlikely anybody in the Operational Security Department had even consulted anybody in management before responding to Sigrah's report of a suspicious death. If news got out while the higher-ups in OSD were dragging their feet and covering their asses, they would be the ones to catch the blame if anybody higher up started to get nervous—or, worse, if word of a violent death on Nimue made Parthenope's investors nervous. Our job was to get here, name the culprit, and haul them away.

I knew all of that, had known it since the day I took the job, but sometimes I forgot. When I was looking at a body, when there was evidence to collect and data to search through, when I started wondering about *motives* and *reasons*, I let myself forget that I was asking questions for which nobody really cared to hear the answers.

"Trust me, Marley," van Arendonk said, his voice as dry as dust. "Nobody knows what this company is capable of better than those of us who have to shovel their shit and pretend it's gold. So who fucked with the Overseer's commands?"

"I don't know yet. I have to check some things."

I was already working on it. The packet had arrived during the scheduled transfer from Hygiea, but it had not been implemented right away. This was because in the data transfer there was also an auxiliary command with an alert to Nimue's Overseer to hold off implementation pending sysadmin approval for minor adjustments. I looked to see who had approved it. Then I looked again.

A deep pit of dismay formed in my gut.

David was the sysadmin who had received the request. He had altered the commands to fix the supposed minor errors. He had inserted the command for the surveillance blackout. He had done all of this between nine and ten in the morning the day before he died.

David had covered up his own murder hours before it even happened.

FIVE

It was, at least, an answer to van Arendonk's question.

"David shut down the surveillance himself," I said. "He had help from somebody on Hygiea, someone who has the access necessary to alter the command packet. But he did it himself."

Van Arendonk sat back in his chair and frowned. "That makes no sense. Are you certain?"

"As certain as I can be at this stage, yes."

"Why? Was he meeting someone? What was he hiding?"

I closed my eyes briefly and rubbed my temples. "I don't know yet."

"Who was he working with? Who has that kind of access?"

"I don't know."

"How the *fuck* did this not get flagged by the goddamned machine?"

"I don't know," I said again, biting out each word. "I've only just started digging."

"But you knew him," van Arendonk retorted. "What was he into? Data theft? Corporate espionage? Black market tech?"

I almost laughed. Almost, but it caught in my throat, awkward and strangling, and I could only shake my head. *Why the hell would I steal other people's shit when my own is so much better?* David had said, laughing, one evening aboard *Symposium*. One of the food scientists had made a crack about David's robots, something about how he had incorporated UEN weapons designs into his own rovers, and how could anybody believe we were a mission of exploration and discovery if we were deploying weapons of attempted genocide on a distant world? Nothing we hadn't heard before. Ethics committees and governmental agencies alike had asked again and again, digging into our research every time we so much as sneezed, to make sure we were not in violation of the postwar disarmament treaty. The autonomous weapons used by the UEN during the war had been so horrific, so clever and deadly, that outlawing them became nearly universally popular in the years afterward, when the true extent of destruction became clear. A more temperamental man might have let that comment lead to a fight, could have raised tempers to boiling and set research teams against each other. But David, with all the ease of a bloke ribbing his friends about football scores, had only laughed, said he believed himself an agent of peace by turning the horrors of war toward pure exploration, said he was a pacifist to the bone and took joy from melting swords into plowshares. The laughter was gone by the time he finished speaking, but so too was the tension. David had believed in what we were doing. He had believed in it so deeply and so completely that no careless accusations or snide comments could ruffle him.

But that was David from before. The David who had sent me a halting, mysterious message hours before his murder was a mere shadow of the friend who had laughed in the mess aboard *Symposium*. I didn't know the man he had become.

"Nothing like that, when I knew him," I said quietly. "I don't know what he's been into lately."

The briefest grimace crossed van Arendonk's sharp face. I didn't know if it was annoyance or shame, and I didn't much care. He stood abruptly and turned toward the door, then hesitated.

"How long will it take you to find out?" he asked.

We had been in the room for barely fifteen minutes. From where he stood, to my left, he was looking only at my damaged side, my scars and my prosthetics, and I met his eyes only long enough to see if he would flinch away. If he did—I probably would have said something, tongue sharpened and patience worn thin. But he didn't, so I kept quiet, and I did not have to find out what would spill out when I opened my mouth.

"Very well," he said, as though I had given him an answer. "I have to talk to Mohammad and HQ. Report as soon as you find anything."

The Overseer unlocked and opened the door to let him out. It's hard to stride purposefully in gecko boots in low gravity, but he made a good try at it, his footsteps peeling noisily down the corridor. The door slid closed behind him.

I sat back in my chair and rubbed my hands over my face. It should have been a relief, to have the systems room to myself, so I could dig into what David had been up to.

They lied about it, he had said. *They lied about everything.*

He had reached out to me for a reason. Van Arendonk had to be right. There had been something going on in David's life, something that led to both his message to me and his murder, and I had to find it.

I fed the Overseer a rapid-fire series of queries to collect all the data I could from the months David had been on Parthenope. He would hardly be the first Parthenope employee to pad their income with a bit of data theft or extortion or some other criminal endeavor. I set the Overseer to analyzing everything it would give me. I only had twenty-four hours of visual and audio recordings, but surveillance wasn't the only way to learn something. Employee ID tracking data. Terminal usage. Data request logs. Active work time and inactive downtime. Internal and external communications. It was a huge amount of data, far more than I could ever hope to go over, and it would take even a machine as powerful as the Overseer a little chunk of time to process. I wanted to look for patterns in David's behavior: who he spoke to in public areas, who he met in private quarters, who he communicated with off-station, how often, about what, and whether those were even real people. Where he spent most of his time and where he went only rarely. What he did when he was alone.

I added another query: a pattern-recognition query on all of David's communications, personal and professional, for the entire time he had been on Nimue. I told it to search for anything to do with *Symposium*, Black Halo, those who had died, those who had survived. For news reports about Karl Longo and his sentencing. For messages he had sent to anybody else that fell outside his normal pattern of behavior. Questions he asked, answers he received.

And anything he might have said or searched or discovered about his fellow crew members. Anything. Everything. I wanted to see all of it. We had missed Kristin Herd before, and scores of people had died. David had not been responsible for that, not to the same extent I had been, but I knew he would not have forgotten. He would be ever aware that those sitting next to him in the mess, working beside him on every shift, sharing tools, swapping stories, were not to be trusted.

While the AI was chewing on that, I watched the surveillance of David's last day.

Twelve months with Parthenope Security and I had grown used to watching people do all manner of things in every imaginable place. People who lived under constant surveillance either forgot or stopped caring that they were being watched at all times. The only supposed privacy Parthenope employees had was in their personal quarters, but even then the company had a record of everybody who went in and out. On a normal day I spent my working hours watching drug deals, physical fights, clumsy threats, embarrassingly bad attempts at extortion, far too many sexual encounters, and more than a few incidents that were some inexplicable combination of all those things.

This was different. This felt like standing outside myself—the person I had become, uniform and security access and prosthetic limbs I couldn't pay for and all—and looking back across the divide between this hollow simulacrum of a life and my real life, the one I had lost, because that was where David belonged. That was where he lived and breathed and thrived, on the other side of that invisible curtain. It made my chest ache to watch him move through his last day, to see him so settled into the depressing reality we were never meant to endure. It made my skin feel dirty, my throat tight. I did not want to be there.

I watched anyway. I would not let myself turn away.

David worked in Ops for most of the day. He was there at 0917 when the data transfer from Hygiea arrived with the super-operational command packet. He implemented the changes. He went on to other tasks. The other sysadmin, Mary Ping, was in and out of their shared workspace in the room next to this one; they spoke about work when they spoke at all. It was a quiet day. David left Ops to eat lunch in the mess, and afterward he went to his quarters for a few minutes. When he returned to Ops, he uploaded an encrypted file from his PD.

That had to be the message for me. It didn't look like a video comm; David had disguised it as an operations report. There was no trace of it in the system anymore. If I hadn't been looking for it, I would have never known it existed. He had recorded it a few hours after he arranged for the surveillance blackout.

After he left Ops in the evening, David returned to the mess. He spoke with a few crew members during the meal. The conversation was perfectly mundane. Complaints about the workday. Complaints about the company. Plans to watch a media serial that evening—apparently *Rachel Returned* was in its fifth series and the main character was finally about to land on New Earth. More complaints about work. More complaints about the company. There had been a snag in calculating holiday travel time; HR was dragging its feet.

After the meal was finished, the crew drifted away from the mess. Some back to work, some to their quarters, some to the other side of the common room to exercise or watch Rachel discover a new world, same as the old world. David headed into his private quarters. He was in his bunk for about twenty minutes before Mary Ping approached his door. She stepped into David's room, out of sight and sound of the surveillance system. They both emerged a couple of minutes later.

Ping touched David's arm, smiled, and said, "I owe you one."

David answered, "No problem."

She retreated to her own quarters; David returned to Ops.

I checked the crew roster. As Sigrah had said, Ping had been on duty that night but had switched with David last minute for medical reasons. I checked her actions earlier in the evening; she had asked the station medic for migraine meds and a sleep aid.

David stayed in Ops for several hours. He spoke to no one. He received no personal communications, alerts, or unscheduled reports. He read the news about Karl Longo, but he didn't linger over it. He accessed a few internal Parthenope reports about an Overseer virus attack on another mine a couple of years ago. He spent some time searching for a selection of Parthenope project names: Sunset, Sunshine, Sunburn, Sundown, working through about a dozen related words before giving up without finding anything. He looked at a few personal messages from home. His mother, his sister. His focus was scattered; his mind was clearly somewhere besides his work. The surveillance camera was placed in a high corner above his workstation. It captured him in profile, working sporadically throughout the night, interrupting brief minutes of activity with long breaks in which he seemed to do nothing at all. When he did work, he was accessing data from the station's records. I read through the lists of actions and files; I had to ask the Overseer to translate a number of file names for me. Cargo transport lists. Fuel conversion efficiency data. Station-wide energy usage. A few shutdown and maintenance reports from the past few months.

At 2256, David logged out of his terminal and rose from his seat. He rubbed his hand tiredly over the back of his neck. He left Ops and passed through the junction. He looked directly at one surveillance camera for a few seconds. I held my breath, waiting for him to say something, but he remained silent. He provided his access code to enter the cargo warehouse at 2258. There was nobody else in that part of the station. Not in the warehouse, not in the airlock, not anywhere. Everybody else was in their personal quarters.

At 2300, the surveillance went dark.

When the blackout ended at 2400, the lights in the cargo warehouse airlock were on. The hexagonal window was a hole of darkness rather than a faint source of light, and there was David, dead on the floor, surrounded by blood. He lay there alone for seven hours before Sigrah thought to look for him.

I didn't know I was crying until I tasted salt at the corner of my mouth.

I wiped the tears from my face. It was so unfathomably unfair that somebody so clever and bright and full of life should end like that, but crying about it didn't help. There was no help for David now, nothing to change the sad bloody end of a life that could have been so brilliant. All I could do was find out who had killed him, and why, and what he had been trying to tell me before the end.

I got to work tracing David's hidden message. If I could figure out how he had reached out to me without leaving a trace, I could also find out if he had been communicating with anybody else, like a contact on Hygiea or elsewhere.

Nimue had both optical and radio communications arrays, each with multiple transmitters and antennae. The radio array was for broadcasts, live conversations with nearby ships or stations, emergencies, rare real-time back-and-forths between company execs when a lawyer needed to beg favors of a CEO, that sort of thing. Low data capacity, encrypted but still easy to intercept. It was never used for things like superoperational command packets or operations reports, or for moving large chunks of data around, so it was not what I was looking for. David would have used the optical array to hide his video message.

Because of Nimue's elongated shape, its slightly wobbling rotation, and the fact that it had communications infrastructure only on one end, Nimue and Hygiea had line of sight to exchange optical data bursts every seven hours. The command packet had arrived at 0917, and the next scheduled data exchange was at 1613 that afternoon—which correlated with when the message to me had arrived on Hygiea.

Immediately I saw that something was wrong.

The 1613 data burst from Nimue had not been successfully completed.

My pulse quickened. The data from Hygiea had arrived on schedule and without problem, but the reverse was not true. When Nimue tried to send its own data burst, there had been a power failure in the transmitters of the optical array. By the time the array was back online, Nimue had rotated out of its window of opportunity. There had been an encrypted radio query about the failure from Hygiea; Sigrah had responded with an update regarding ongoing repairs on the optical array. The data packet was successfully transmitted seven hours later.

Hygiea hadn't received anything from Nimue at 1613. But I had.

Sigrah had said the optical array had ongoing problems. I checked the maintenance logs and found numerous reports from Katee King, Nimue's electrical engineer, recording her increasing frustration. Several times over the past few months, power surges in the array had caused transmissions to fail. King had been taking the optical transmitters offline one by one in an attempt to isolate the cause, so far without success.

A few of the transmitters had been removed from service entirely. But no matter what she tried, no matter how many parts she replaced, no matter how many requests she and Sigrah sent to Parthenope for new transmitters, every couple of weeks another data transmission failed because of a power surge in the array.

But now I knew the transmitters weren't failing entirely. They were just being hijacked for unofficial use, and the power surges were likely designed to cover up David's hidden, unauthorized transmissions.

Katee King was diligent about filing her reports; the pattern was easy to spot. The problems had started abruptly ten months ago. David had been on Nimue for eleven months.

Nobody hijacked a transmitter for legitimate reasons. Nor did they do it just to send cryptic secret messages to former friends and reminisce about old times. Van Arendonk was right to be suspicious. David had gotten himself into some kind of trouble—probably very illegal—and that had gotten him killed.

I knew what I needed to do next. I couldn't ask King or anybody else from the crew to do it for me. One of them had killed David. I wasn't the most devoted OSD Safety Officer, but even I knew it was bad investigative practice to send a potential suspect out to collect evidence. I was going to have to check the optical array myself.

"Fuck," I said, and I stood up, and I went to find Adisa and Ryu.

I really did not want to go outside.

SIX

The good news was I didn't have to go outside.

The bad news was I had to get close enough that I wasn't sure the precise details mattered much in the deepest recesses of my lizard brain, where all my instincts were screaming at me about my inevitable, imminent death in the vacuum.

"You can wait here, you know," Ryu said. Their voice was tinny over the helmet radio, their eyes behind the faceplate wide and concerned. The lightweight vacuum suits were just a precaution, supposedly, but it was the kind of precaution that only made me more worried. "Just tell me what to look for. You can talk me through it. You don't have to—"

"Avery," I said sharply. "Not helping."

The concern in their expression melted away to amusement. "You are so fucking stubborn. Are we going?"

We were going. The optical array was located on Nimue's

docking structure, accessible via a long, enclosed maintenance shaft. Sigrah wasn't happy about us going out there; she seemed to think that if her engineer hadn't found anything, we had no chance of doing better. Adisa had ignored her objections and told us to take a look. He was currently sitting down with Sigrah to ask about what various criminal enterprises might be running under her nose on Nimue.

Ryu turned the manual wheel that secured the hatch to the maintenance shaft. "No electronic lock, but there is an ID tracker. Did your dead man ever come through here?"

"He's not my dead man," I said. "And not according to the security logs."

They moved to the side as the lock disengaged, and they tugged the hatch open, revealing a dark space beyond. There was a slight exhale as the pressure equalized; I felt a nudge of air from behind, like the station was trying to push me out. Ryu switched on their headlamp and leaned through the hatch.

The only crew the Overseer had logged passing through this hatch were Katee King and the man who had been the electrical engineer before her. Her predecessor had left Nimue eight months ago, a few months after David arrived. The man had bought out the remaining three years on his contract with a sudden windfall, moved back to Earth, took a job fixing radio telescopes somewhere in western Australia. I had a query out to HQ regarding where that sudden windfall had come from, but I rather doubted I would get an answer more useful than "inheritance from previously unknown rich uncle" or similar. Nobody ever put "payment for participation in lucrative black market scheme" on their company exit interview forms.

"Well." Ryu glanced back at me. "Ready?"

"I'm not the one who keeps stalling."

"I mean, I know you're not used to this hands-on shit, so I can get Mohammad to help if—"

"Yeah, okay, ask the superior officer to do the grunt work."

"He would. He's not so bad to work with, when he decides to give a fuck. And he's Martian," they added. "Crawling through tight spaces to find illegal tech is basically his entire heritage."

"Problematic stereotypes aside, I'm *fine*. Let's go."

"If you're sure—"

"For fuck's sake, just move."

They gave me a grin and a cheeky thumbs-up and climbed through the hatch. I switched on my own headlamp and followed.

Because Nimue was relatively small, shaped like a potato, actively being hollowed out on the inside, and rotating with a weird wobble, its gravity was less a reliable force and more a matter of politely agreeing where the floor ought to be. That worked well enough to trick the mind in Ops and Res and parts of the facility designed with human concepts of up and down, where one was surrounded by such luxuries as floors, ceilings, and waste hatches where one could deposit vomit from a sudden wave of vertigo.

It did not work when decoupled from those elements. It really, really did not work.

There was no floor in the maintenance shaft, no ceiling. Everything was walls, and everything was crowded with so many conduits, pipes, and ducts that climbing into the shaft felt rather like being swallowed by a mechanical beast. I was instantly disoriented, with my head telling me I was upside down, the tug on my muscles telling me I was falling, and my vision telling me the rest of my body was lying.

I squeezed my eyes shut to give my brain a chance to adjust. When I opened them again, Ryu was already several meters away, the beam of their headlamp filling the shaft with a kaleidoscope of shadow and light. I decided to think of it as climbing, if only to keep the disorientation at bay, and followed.

"It would help if we knew what we were looking for," Ryu said.

"Oh, certainly," I agreed. "That would help a lot. Why didn't I think of that?"

I couldn't see the look they sent my way—all I got was a flash of their headlamp—but I understood the tone of their voice well enough. "What I mean," they said, with exaggerated patience, "is that I'm going to take a look at one of the working transmitters before we head up to the ones that aren't working."

"We have the schematics from the Overseer," I said.

"Right, right. Station engineers are well-known for following schematics exactly."

"I didn't mean we should trust them."

"And they certainly don't have a reputation for changing things randomly and never documenting it."

"I only meant we have something to check against." Distracted, I angled a kick badly and ended up shoving myself into a rubber-encased cluster of wiring hard enough to jar my left shoulder. I let out a soft grunt of pain.

Another flash of light as Ryu glanced back at me. "You okay?"

"Fine."

"If you need to—"

"I'm fine."

I knew I was being too sharp and had very little reason for it. Ryu was not quite a friend anymore, nor were they exactly an ex, as we had never defined the time we spent together, but they certainly weren't an enemy. They were only being considerate—which was part of what had drawn me to them in the first place, that gentle warmth and easygoing calm that felt so out of place in the every-asshole-for-themselves corporate culture of Hygiea. It was also what had made me back away. That was my problem, not theirs. I didn't want to be a beast to them.

But I couldn't bring myself to apologize. The words were there, caught in my throat like a cough I could not expel. I was afraid I would only say something worse.

We climbed along that metal throat for what felt like an eon. Our headlamps barely penetrated the darkness, reaching no more than five or ten meters ahead. We took a few minutes to look over the first transmitter on the array. Identifying where the power came in, where the data came in, where it differed from the schematics. After that, Ryu started talking again. Maybe the darkness was getting to them, or the proximity to open space, or maybe they were only tired of the awkward silence. Whatever it was, they started telling me about all the ways in which criminals of investigations past had sabotaged, altered, or hijacked comms systems for various purposes. They knew of lawyers piggybacking Hygiea's surveillance system to find potential clients in class-action lawsuits, drug designers mining personal communications to learn which work crews and stations were best targeted by their on-station dealers, hackers feeding false data sets into stations to retrain AIs to be less restrictive or more biased, extortionists sending deepfake evidence of high-level executives committing anti-corporate actions, smugglers inventing false proprietary designs to auction on the black market, and so much more.

"If there's a way to make money doing it, somebody's figured it out," they said. "You really don't have any idea what your friend was into?"

Your friend, now, instead of *your dead man*.

"I really don't," I said. "If you'd asked me three years ago, I would have said David would never bother with anything illegal, because he was good enough at his work that he could find a well-paying job anywhere."

I couldn't see Ryu's face, but I heard their soft, amused snort over the radio. "Doesn't always work that way."

"Yeah. I know."

If it did work that way, I sure as fuck wouldn't be crawling-climbing through a claustrophobic maintenance shaft on a corporate asteroid mine looking for proof that somebody I had very much liked and respected had gotten himself beaten to death over some harebrained moneymaking scheme. But if I said that, Ryu would give me that look, the one that asked without really asking if that meant I thought some people did belong here, just not people like me and David, people who deserved better.

So I didn't say it. I just had the silent argument with Ryu in my head, let it play out for a few seconds, then said, "I have no idea what he would do if he was desperate enough. He was smart enough to figure out just about anything, but what he could do seems kinda limited by being stuck here."

"Right, right. Limited data transmissions, extremely limited transport, very small crew . . ."

"But a valuable location," I added.

"So the company likes to say."

"Oh, I know. I've seen all the press reports. The jewel in Parthenope's crown." David had used those words in his message to me. "I'm not particularly impressed with what I've seen."

"Only because you haven't seen many asteroid mines. These facilities are a fucking palace compared to the shitholes most people are stuck in. What's the first offline transmitter?"

"Uh, seven. Seven and twelve are both offline. Seven should be the next one."

We didn't find anything suspicious on number seven. It had been disconnected and partially cannibalized for parts, but there was no sign of alteration or tampering, nothing to indicate that it was routing power or data anywhere it wasn't supposed to go.

Number twelve was different.

"Huh," Ryu said. They looked down at me, headlamp briefly blinding me, then back at the machinery. "Come look at this."

I climbed up beside them and rested my heels on the edge of a bracket. "What is it?"

They pointed at scratch marks on a metal panel. "These brackets have been removed, and whoever put them back in was careless, or in a hurry. None of the others have that."

It didn't look like much to me, but Ryu pulled out their wrench to remove the bolts. They handed them to me one by one, then slid the panel out of the brackets.

"Oh, hello," they said. "That's different."

Where the other transmitters had a neatly packed cluster of parts and wiring behind their panels, this one had a shiny silver device. It was lightly curved and shaped something like a leaf, with thin metal plates overlapping like scales, broadly at the top and tapered below. The overall effect was of a shimmering beetle's carapace, protecting its soft underbelly as it clung to the side of the shaft. The edges were polished on a clean, smooth bevel, without the faintest trace of imperfection or marring. The metal itself was silver with a bluish sheen to it, which almost gave it the look of water. It was beautiful and elegant and terribly out of place in that cramped maintenance shaft.

I wanted to touch it, to brush my fingers over the clean metal. My heart was pounding and my breath was short.

"Oh," I said quietly. I swallowed. My voice was thick in my throat. "I know—I recognize this. David made this."

"You're sure?"

I withdrew my hand. "I spent years working with him. I recognize the style." I let out a choked little laugh. "Always so much prettier than it needed to be."

"It's not that I doubt you, but . . . what is it?"

"Probably exactly what we think it is," I said. "Something to take power from the array to use this transmitter. I assume David paid the previous electrical engineer to come out here and install it to hijack the transmitter. Or he could have directed the installation remotely, using a bot. That would be trivial for him."

Ryu leaned to one side, then the other, bumping their shoulder into mine as they examined the device. "It's possible, I guess. We should check the station's machine and printing facilities to see when he made or modified this thing here. If it was him."

They were right, of course. We had to check. But I had no doubt that the silver device was David's work.

"We should bring it in for a better look," Ryu said. Behind their faceplate, their expression was thoughtful. They tapped the radio control on the arm of their suit to switch frequencies. "Hey, Mohammad, we found something. Marley says it looks like the victim's handiwork. I want to bring it inside to take it apart."

"If you can do that without damaging it, yeah?" Adisa said.

"That's the idea. Can you see how it's attached down there?" Ryu said to me. "I can't see much at this end."

I lowered myself down to another bracket to get a look at the bottom of the device, where the data and power cables would have entered the original system. The space beneath the silver carapace was very narrow, and the reflective surface made it hard for me to see into the darkness. The device moved slightly when Ryu gripped it, and the gap widened just enough for me to see the angular lines of four braces holding it in place.

"Can you see anything?" Ryu asked.

"I can see how it's fixed in place, but I can't see how it's attached to the power or data lines."

"Can you dislodge it?"

"Just a sec."

I reached for the most accessible leg—using my left hand, the one that could be replaced if it got smashed or zapped—and felt along its length to the mechanical clamp at its end. The gap was so narrow my space-suited forearm barely fit, and the angle put an uncomfortable twinge of pain in my left shoulder. I changed my position and reached again. There was a whir of noise from within the device. Light sparked from some unknown source and a crackling sound filled my ears.

"Hester," Ryu said, "get your arm out of there."

"I've almost got it."

"Hester."

Their voice was low and tight. I looked up to see sparks arcing outward from the wrench, the tool kit, the radio antennae on their suit. Their eyes were wide, and in the faceplate of their helmet I saw mirrored sparks from my own suit reflected. I felt nothing; the suits were nonconducting, our bodies safe and sealed inside. But the effect was deeply unsettling. I withdrew my arm, careful not to jostle anything. The static grew louder. The sparks spread all around us, dancing down the maintenance shaft.

"Not good," Ryu said, their voice almost lost in the radio's crackle. "We should—"

A blinding flare erupted around us, so bright my prosthetic eye glitched and my natural eye seared with pain. All I could see was Ryu's silhouette surrounded by light, engulfed in light, gone. There was a furious roar, a sudden pressure all around, and the maintenance shaft exploded into a storm of lightning.

SEVEN

I couldn't see anything except fiery white light.

My prosthetic eye began to glitch uncontrollably, sending a rainbow of colors across my vision. The roar in my ears was constant and mechanical: the discharge had fried the radio. Beyond that constant, grinding static, I heard popping and clapping all the way down the maintenance shaft in small bursts of thunder. Every instinct was telling me to run, run, *run*—but I couldn't run, I was hanging like an idiot in a vertical shaft, with only a company-issued nonconductive worksuit between me and death by electrocution. If the suit wasn't damaged. If it had been tested recently. If Parthenope had bothered to stock Nimue with functional suits in the first place. In one of the first extortion cases I'd worked, I'd come across documents detailing exactly how much the company paid out in negligence lawsuits every year and how little it was compared to how much they saved by ignoring OSA safety regulations and trusting that only a tiny fraction of the people who died had family who could afford to sue. I didn't need to think about that right now. I needed to get the fuck out of there.

My left eye was still glitching, but I could at least look around without risking giving myself a seizure. The first thing I saw was Ryu's boots about ten centimeters from my helmet.

"Avery," I said. "Hey, Avery."

The radio threw my voice back at me as a painful squeal. I switched it off. That stopped the static and the feedback, but not the clanks, sparks, a distant thumping sound—what the fuck was that?—and my own breath, ragged and too fast. I grabbed Ryu's foot to get their attention.

"Hey, come on, we need to get out of here."

No response. I shook their foot again.

"Avery! Come on. The radios are fucked. Look at me."

David's beautiful device was, unsurprisingly, a charred and smoking mess. The silver shell was distorted; the whole thing belched gray smoke and blue sparks.

As a self-destruct mechanism, the power surge had been devastatingly effective. We had sealed the device's fate the moment we tried to move it. If we hadn't been wearing vac suits, we would have been killed instantly.

"Fuck you, David," I muttered. "Fuck you *so fucking much* with every one of your *own fucking machines.* Avery, get out of my way. I need to see if there's anything we can salvage."

I shook their ankle insistently and dislodged their gecko soles from where they were perched. They slumped toward me in an awkward tangle of limbs.

"Shit. What the fuck? Can you hear me?"

That was wrong. That was not fucking okay. Even without the radios, I should hear their reply. They should be moving.

With my heart racing and my breath coming in short, painful gasps, I shoved Ryu to one side and stomped my foot into the wall to propel myself upward. There were still little arcs of electricity darting outward from David's device, leaping down the shaft in a chaotic dance. I tried to ignore it—tried to tell myself that if I wasn't electrocuted yet, I probably wasn't going to be—and twisted around to get a look at Ryu's face.

Their headlamp was smashed, their faceplate cracked. Scorch marks spiderwebbed over the top of their helmet. On the inside of their faceplate was a smear of blood.

"Shit. Shit. Avery!" I shook them frantically. The blood was coming from their nose and their eyes were narrow slits, but they did not respond. "Fuck. Okay. I'll get you—fuck, I'll get you out of here. Come on."

No response, but I kept talking, kept spitting out that nonsense stream of babble and reassurances. I needed help, but I couldn't call for it. I squeezed up beside Ryu and began the clumsy, painstaking process of getting us out of there.

The descent felt endless. The only light came from my headlamp, and the sound of my own breath was loud in my ears. My fear grew with every second. The crack in Ryu's helmet, those scorches—they had been shocked, but I didn't know how bad it was. It looked like their nose was still actively bleeding. It took a hell of a blow to smash your nose into the front of a space suit helmet. Their neck could be damaged too. I could be making everything worse by moving them. I didn't know what to do. I couldn't check for a pulse—couldn't risk removing the suit, not with the remnants of David's light show still sparking and snapping around us. Which had to be exactly what he had wanted, the ratfucker. He had designed rovers to operate on a hostile moon that spent the vast majority of its time within Saturn's magnetosphere. Nothing he did to create *death rays of electricity* was an accident.

If he weren't already dead, I would have murdered him myself, just for being such a raging asshole as to build a self-destruct trigger like that to protect his shitty criminal scheme. After asking him who the trap was for. And why. I would only murder him after he answered my damn questions.

"You are going to wake the fuck up," I said.

My chest hurt. It was the kind of hurt that came from the inside, the kind of hurt you didn't know was possible until you had your body blown up and replaced with spare parts, and sometimes your parts and those parts didn't quite know how to cooperate in situations of high physical stress—situations that were, according to my doctors, supposed to happen *never.* I was having trouble steadying my breathing. My heart rate was out of control.

I stopped for a few seconds to breathe. Ryu slumped against me, limp and unconscious. I tugged one of their arms out of my way. "Avery, you piece of shit. You are going to wake the fuck up and this is going to be so bloody awkward."

It had always been awkward between us, even when we were in our ill-defined relationship. I told myself it was because I didn't want to make any attachments on Hygiea. I told myself it was because they weren't my usual type. I usually went for short, femme, more than a little mean, smarter than everybody and well aware of it. Not warm and wiry and friendly and unburdened by excessive ego. I told myself it was because I had no time for a relationship when I needed every spare minute to extract myself from Parthenope's clutches. I told myself I could never be sure if they were looking at me or my shiny new body parts. I told myself a lot of things, so many that I hadn't noticed right until Ryu stopped coming by my quarters that I was the only one who cared about my endless litany of excuses. Then I told myself it was better that way. I had more important things to deal with. I didn't care. I couldn't care.

"I am going to be so fucking annoyed with you if you don't wake up," I muttered, and I started moving again, down and down and down.

It couldn't have been more than five or ten minutes before light filled the shaft around us, but it felt like so much longer. The electrical sparks and ribbons had been so searing, so bright, my eyes, both artificial and not, were still smarting from the onslaught. I only noticed the new light because I saw my shadow move when I was still, and it startled me so much I thought, for a second, it was another surge of lightning. Somebody touched my foot.

I jerked in surprise and looked down. I couldn't remember the name of the crew member who waited below us. A woman, dark hair, worried expression. She was saying something I couldn't hear. I only understood when she gestured for me to let her take Ryu. I had some trouble getting out of the way and jostled Ryu in my clumsiness.

"Sorry, sorry," I muttered, trying to make myself small, trying to be gentle. "We're getting you out of here. We're getting you help."

Ryu gripped my wrist suddenly. I yelped in alarm. They were awake, their eyes wide, their mouth open. They reached up to touch their face, remembered they couldn't only when their glove struck the faceplate. They said something; the words were muffled by the helmets.

I was so relieved I let out a giddy, hysterical laugh. I leaned in to touch my helmet to theirs. "You stupid fuck, you scared me."

I didn't know if they could hear me. I would worry about being embarrassed later. I pressed myself into the narrow space between two conduits and let the woman tug Ryu toward her. Yee, I remembered, as I got a good look at her face. Elena Yee, station medic. She moved much more deftly in Nimue's microgravity than I ever could, carefully ferrying Ryu down the shaft and toward the exit before I could orient myself to follow. She looked up at me for a second, and I gestured awkwardly with my thumb.

"I have to go get . . . I'll be right there."

I didn't know if she could hear me or understand what I was saying, but she nodded and left me to it.

Back up the maintenance shaft, back to the sabotaged transmitter. Back to David's wicked little device. Most of it had been destroyed, and what hadn't been was now fused to the machines around it. I was able to loosen the charred metal casing, one bent brace with half a clamp still attached, and a few circuit boards probably beyond recovery. I collected what little I could and got out of there.

EIGHT

Yee was loading Ryu onto a carry-board with the help of another crew member when I climbed out of the hatch. She had their helmet off, their arms and torso strapped to the board, and she was speaking very quickly, a flurry of words I couldn't understand through my helmet. Ryu's eyes were fluttering, their chest rising and falling, their hand moving at their side, and I was so relieved my eyes stung with unexpected and humiliating tears. I grabbed the edge of the hatch to steady myself. They were awake. Breathing. Moving. Fuck. I swallowed back sudden nausea and tried to breathe before following them to the junction.

As soon as I climbed down the ladder, Sigrah was in my face. I backed away from her to tug my helmet off, then immediately regretted it.

"—did you do to my array? We've got nothing now! This is

why we don't let fucking *data analysts* go digging around in valuable systems. I did *not* approve of this and I will *not* let you continue to damage my station or crew."

She stepped toward me, lurching with the cling of her gecko boots, and raised one hand. She was pointing at me, finger extended in the very best angry schoolteacher fashion. My ears were already ringing and my head was pounding, but I didn't get the chance to snap back at her because Adisa stepped up, not quite between us, but near enough to give Sigrah pause.

"Safety Officers Marley and Ryu did have authorization," he said, his voice so mild there wasn't the faintest hint of anger, "because they are investigating a murder. A murder that somebody in your crew committed."

"That's not—" Sigrah closed her mouth abruptly.

I wondered what she had been planning to say. That's not possible? That's not true? Not relevant? Perhaps it was a reflexive reaction, an automatic defense without anything behind it. Perhaps it was something more. She knew as well as we did that somebody on Nimue had killed David.

She scowled and lowered her hand. "What the hell is that?"

She was staring at the pieces of David's device as I removed them from my tool bag. I held up the twisted sheet of metal like an offering, not so Sigrah might take it, but so that she could look at it carefully and I could see her reaction.

"This is what David used to hijack your transmitter," I said. "Well, part of it. The rest has been destroyed."

"Destroyed?" Another crew member was watching from the doorway. I recognized her as Katee King, electrical engineer. She was wearing a vac suit; the helmet was tucked under her arm.

"A massive power surge," I said. "It was booby-trapped for when it was discovered."

King's eyes widened. "Fuck me. I guess that explains the total array failure. How do you know where it came from?"

I turned the distorted metal casing over. I had to admit it didn't look like much, not anymore, scorched black with only glimmers of the polished silver still shining through. "It looks like David's work. He liked to . . . liked to make things shiny, even when they didn't need to be." It sounded like a weak justification, now that I had to say it out loud, but I was certain.

Sigrah was scowling. "I don't care if it looks like the governor of Vesta's hairy asshole. You were not supposed to do *anything* except assess the surveillance data, and now you have completely disabled our optical array."

I tried not to wince. It wasn't my fault the power surge had burned out the entire array, but I very much doubted anybody would see it that way. I could easily imagine how Parthenope would justify adding the repair expense to my endlessly compounding debts.

I tried, "It's not like I meant—"

She spoke right over me. "I will talk to HQ about the damage you've caused. This is not acceptable. Your investigation is not supposed to interfere with station operations at all. Our entire schedule will be thrown off. How soon can you get the optical array back online?"

King answered, a bit hesitantly, "I need to know the extent of the damage first."

"There might be another booby trap," I said. I didn't really believe that, but I was not about to make Sigrah's life any easier while she was blaming me for David's little party trick. "It's dangerous. You'll be risking your crew to send them out there before we know more."

"Shut the fuck up," Sigrah said. "Katee, get your ass out there and give me a full report and plan of action."

King looked from Sigrah to me, me to Adisa, clearly torn.

"A moment, please," Adisa said. "We need to speak to your crew first, yeah?" The conciliatory Martian uptalk was back; I had no doubt now that it was deliberate. "We can't risk anybody else getting hurt until we have more information. The array is part of the investigation now."

"You don't have the authority—"

"We'll start with those who knew him best," he went on, "and we'll need a place to talk to them—a private room, aye?"

A series of increasingly unhappy expressions crossed Sigrah's face. "I am going to contact HQ."

"As you should, aye? We'll talk to the crew while you do that."

Sigrah was gritting her teeth so hard I expected to hear them crack. After a long, long pause, she said, "Use the quartermaster's office by the galley. You can talk to one crew member at a time, provided you are not interrupting work that cannot be rescheduled. This whole shitshow has already taken up too many active hours. And the second HQ gives the go-ahead, my people are repairing the array."

"Of course," Adisa said, but Sigrah was already stomping away into Ops. When she was gone, he looked at me. "Are you hurt?"

"Oh. No, no. Avery got the brunt of it. I'm fine."

If fine meant that I could taste blood in my throat from the panic that was only now fading, and my heart still felt like a quivering, shuddering, gelatinous sea creature trapped in my chest, and my skin was clammy all over from sweat I hadn't realized I was shedding beneath the suit. I wanted out of it so badly I started to undo the fasteners right there in the junction.

Adisa took the pieces of David's device and looked them over. "Only one transmitter was altered?" he said.

"Yes. According to the maintenance logs, it was taken offline months ago." I glanced at King, who nodded.

"Was it twelve? I haven't worked on that one since I've been here. Perry—the old engineer—he said it was missing a data translator." She looked apologetic and sheepish. "I should have double-checked his work. I know. But I've had so much else to do. And the array works most of the time. I really did think it was a power supply problem upstream in the system."

"I think number twelve works fine—or it did, until now." I opened my vac suit to pull off the sleeves and let the top hang from my waist. The cool air was a relief. "I think David paid off your predecessor to help set up this device. It probably redirected power from the other transmitters every time he used it."

"I feel so stupid for missing it," King said. "What was he doing?"

"We don't know yet. Only that he's been doing it regularly for several months."

"Right under my nose." King tossed her helmet up and caught it. "She'll find some way to . . ." She trailed off, but I knew she was thinking exactly what I had been thinking moments ago: Sigrah would find some way to blame her for this. "Okay, I'll wait for your say-so to go out there. I don't fancy being zapped. I hope Safety Officer Ryu will be okay."

She went back into Res, stepping out of her vac suit as she did so.

"Yes, I know," I said, before Adisa could speak. "I'll check the logs to make sure she really did miss it."

The door to the systems room opened at the end of the corridor, and van Arendonk walked toward us, pausing briefly to glance at the closed door of the comms room.

"Who is she yelling at?" he asked, eyebrows raised.

"HQ," said Adisa. He turned the scorched piece of metal

over in his hands thoughtfully. "How certain are you that this is Prussenko's work?"

"Pretty certain, especially that outer shell. I didn't get a good look at whatever it was covering up." I was leaning against the wall for balance as I bent down to remove my boots and peeled off the rest of the suit. "He could have built or modified a bot to get the communications hardware in place."

Adisa ran his finger along the crooked edge of the casing. He looked troubled, but he only said, "We'll need to find out if he built it here."

"I know. I can check the manufacturing and printing logs."

Van Arendonk leaned against the doorframe, arms crossed over his chest. "So the dead man was hijacking a transmitter for his own uses."

"Could be an accomplice wanted a bigger cut for themselves, aye? Arranged a meeting in the warehouse to renegotiate the terms of their agreement," Adisa said.

"Or maybe . . ." I folded up the vac suit and straightened my own clothes, now damp with sweat. *They lied*, David had said. *They lied about everything.* I only wished I had the first fucking idea what his message was trying to tell me. "Maybe he found something that somebody didn't want him to find."

"And he tried to blackmail them?" said van Arendonk. "It's a possibility. A small crew like this gets to know each other's business a lot more than anybody is comfortable with. But a monitored cargo airlock is a bloody stupid place to have a clandestine meeting about a criminal enterprise. Why not use private quarters like everybody else?"

"I don't know yet," I said.

"And what was he stealing?"

I gritted my teeth. "I don't know."

"You'd probably know if you'd managed to grab the evidence rather than blow it up," van Arendonk said.

"Stop it, Hugo," Adisa said, without looking at him. To me he said, "We'll interview the crew and—"

Van Arendonk pushed away from the doorframe. "Let me do it."

"No need." Adisa turned abruptly and started walking. "Marley, with me."

"Mohammad, wait. You don't have to—"

"Find out what Sigrah is shouting to HQ about."

"She's probably shouting about the communications array your analyst just exploded."

"I didn't *explode* it," I muttered. "The radio array obviously still works fine."

"Besides that," Adisa said. "She knows more than she's telling us and it's getting on my nerves. And ask your office what kind of data's been stolen from Nimue lately."

Van Arendonk tried again. "I can—"

"You can make yourself useful. We have crew to interview. Marley. Now."

"You don't have to talk to her," van Arendonk said. "You don't."

Adisa didn't turn, didn't respond, didn't give any sign he had heard. I looked at van Arendonk, but he was watching Adisa walk away with an unreadable expression.

"Talk to who?" I said.

Van Arendonk barely glanced at me. "Just do your job, Marley, and try not to fuck anything else up."

He turned and headed back into Ops to join Sigrah.

"Right," I said to the empty junction. "I'll do that."

The Residential section of Nimue was built into the remains of an old United Earth Navy vessel. It looked like the ship had been a creaking old bucket even before the war, which made for a stark contrast with the shabby luxury of Ops. There were no decorative tiles and polished sconces here, only utilitarian angles, unnecessary hexagons, and the pervasive smells of rehydrated soy protein, industrial cleaner, and sweat. Parthenope had made, at best, a half-hearted attempt at transforming the interior from a deeply depressing military transport into a mildly depressing crew habitat. There was a common recreation area, an exercise room, an infirmary, a galley and mess, and private quarters arranged along a corridor with shared heads at the end. The proportions were all wrong: the ceilings too high, the walls too close, the doors wider and shorter than they ought to be, as though built for people who moved about in a permanent crouch. During the war, the hold would have been stacked full of troops in temporary stasis, sleeping the sleep of the clueless and terrified as they shipped off to die in some pointless battle. Everything was gray, grimy, and blocky.

I checked on Ryu in the infirmary before going after Adisa. They were woozy but awake, with a broken nose, two puffy red eyes, and a headache. They promised to get back to work on the medical exam of the corpse as soon as they could.

"Don't be stupid," I said, relief making me gruff.

"You don't be stupid," they retorted, and something tight and painful eased in my chest. "I'm fine. I just hit my head."

"They will be fine, I promise," said the medic, smiling.

"You actually hit your entire face," I said to Ryu. "You're going to look like a raccoon."

"I think that's probably an insult, but since I didn't have your fauna-rich Earth childhood, I'll pretend it's a compliment. Now go." Ryu shoved me away. "You've got work to do."

Before joining Adisa, I grabbed another PD to replace the one David's device had fried.

The room Sigrah had offered for our interviews was a cramped space attached to the galley. The faded sign on the door confirmed it had been the quartermaster's office, but it was currently being used as pantry storage and, surprisingly, a small garden. A sprightly selection of hydroponic herbs looked to be thriving beneath full-spectrum lights. Their spicy, earthy scents almost helped disguise the overriding odor of stale instant coffee, food preservatives, and the lingering memory of something burned. Almost.

There was just enough space for a few chairs around the metal table that was bolted to the floor. Adisa was already sitting in one chair facing the door; I slid in to sit beside him.

"Is it normal for a foreperson to be this unwilling to help?" I asked.

The question was somewhat flippant, but Adisa considered it seriously before answering. "I don't know that she's unwilling to help, yeah? I think she knows it won't look good for her that she's had a thief operating under her watch for the better part of a year. She doesn't want it to blow back on her or the station."

"If she's not involved," I said.

His sleeves were rolled up to just below his elbows, and for the first time I saw the tattoos on his forearms: a series of words written in Arabic on the left, a line of numbers on the right. The only word I recognized on the left was *planet*; my Arabic was mostly nonexistent and I couldn't guess at the rest. The numbers I had learned about in school: they were for identification. The UEN had imprisoned so many Martians during and after the war, and had so little interest in sorting out the peculiarities of Martian names and families and lineages, they had decided numbers were easier. Most Martians had the tattoos removed after they were released. Some kept them, I'd heard, because they wanted their bodies identifiable should the war ever start again.

Adisa shrugged and tapped his fingers idly on the metal tabletop. “Aye, that too. Maintaining productivity is probably her only chance at keeping her job, yeah? It’s a good job. She doesn’t want to throw it away just because her crew has its share of fuckups.”

“David wasn’t a fuckup,” I said.

I looked down at my PD, glanced over the list of personnel, unsure of what else to say. I tended to do everything I could to avoid thinking of a position with Parthenope as a good job. It felt too much like giving up, like accepting something I had never wanted and settling into a routine that would draw me in and wrap around me and never let me go, and all the while telling myself it was good for me. I hadn’t considered the situation from Sigrah’s point of view. How it must feel for her to be in charge of one of Parthenope’s most important stations, but still stuck out here alone, without any help except what Hygiea provided, with one crew member dead and another responsible, and a team of security officers coming in to stomp around and break the optical array and insist that a brutal murder was only one of her problems. I didn’t feel sympathy for her, exactly, because she was still alive and David was dead and somebody on Nimue had killed him. But I did have to acknowledge that maybe Adisa was right. Maybe she wasn’t stonewalling on purpose.

After a moment, I said, “Whatever he was doing, he wasn’t . . . He wasn’t a bad person, and he definitely wasn’t stupid or rash. He must have had a reason.” I cleared my throat delicately. “Um, so. What was that about before? Van Arendonk said you don’t have to talk to somebody? Did he mean Sigrah?”

Adisa let out a slow breath. "Ah, no. He meant Mary Ping. The other sysadmin."

"Okay." I had absolutely no idea what that had to do with anything. "But why? We really do need to talk to her, obviously. Do you know her?" All I knew about Ping was that she had switched shifts with David—which was why she was first on our list, but it didn't explain Adisa and van Arendonk's weirdness.

"She was on the Aeolia investigation before she moved here," Adisa said.

The name Aeolia rang a bell. I tried to dredge up the details from memory. It had been on the company news while I was bedridden in the Parthenope hospital on Badenia. Mass casualty incident. Something about terrorists using a virus to infiltrate the station's Overseer. That was supposed to be impossible, but it happened anyway, and a lot of people died. By the time I started work with my newly signed contract binding me to Parthenope for five years, there was a plaque on Hygiea commemorating the employees who had lost their lives on Aeolia. I couldn't remember who the company and OSA had blamed. Not Black Halo or any of the groups sympathetic to their anti-expansionist cause. That I would have remembered. Still something about it tugged at the back of my mind.

It took a few seconds for me to remember. "Oh, right. I think David was reading something about Aeolia before he died."

"He was?" Adisa looked like this was the exact opposite of what he wanted to hear.

"I think so. Let me check." I reached for my PD and asked the Overseer for a summary of David's activity on the day he died.

There it was: Parthenope's unclassified internal reports

about the Aeolia incident, which had taken place about nine months after the *Symposium* disaster. David had already been working for Parthenope by then.

"Right. Here it is. He looked at the incident reports, but only for a few minutes. I don't know what they say. I haven't had a chance to look yet. I can get them now, if you want?"

Adisa started to say something, then changed his mind. "Do it later. Right now, I think we need to talk to Mary Ping."

NINE

Mary Ping was a few years past forty, pretty, with pale skin, straight black hair, and golden-brown eyes. She wore a standard gray Parthenope jumpsuit with a belt cinched tight around her waist and gloves dangling from one pocket.

"Hello," she said, pausing in the doorway. "You wanted to speak to me?"

"We do. Have a seat," said Adisa.

"I apologize for keeping you waiting. I was down in Level 5, trying to convince the Overseer and the manufacturing module to stop arguing."

Ping moved into the room with effortless grace, her steps dancer-like and smooth and silent; she had no gecko soles on her boots. She sat across from us and smiled.

"It's good to see you again, Safety Inspector," she said to Adisa. "I didn't realize you were once again investigating violent incidents. But I suppose you couldn't stay away forever, however much you might want to."

"We need to talk to you about David Prussenko," he said.

"I'm happy to help in any way I can." Ping rested her hands on the table, fingers laced, relaxed. "But I don't know if any of it will help. I liked David, but I didn't know him very well."

"You worked with him for eleven months, yeah?" Adisa said.

"Well, yes, but you know what I mean. Work and friendship are very different things, even in a crew this small." Ping's appearance suggested a mixed Asian Earth ancestry in her family tree, and her accent was clearly from somewhere off-planet, odd and hard to identify. Not posh like Yuèliàng, in spite of her mannered word choice, and forced in a way that made me certain she was pitching her voice lower than its natural register. It was the voice of somebody trying to sound more serious and more upper-class.

"Who did know him well? Who were his friends?" Adisa asked.

"He was close to Neeta. He also spent a lot of downtime with Miguel. They knew him best, I suppose."

I looked at the personnel roster. Miguel Vera, fuel tech. Neeta Hunter, station roboticist. I recognized the latter's employee photo: she was the young woman with the silver hair who had come to see where David died.

"Why are there two sysadmins here, aye?" Adisa asked. "There aren't normally, on a station this size."

"Most stations this size don't have multiple concurrent operations. The mine is only one part of it. There is also the construction of the furnace and the processing facilities. The Overseer can handle it—they're quite clever minds, you know—but on a human scale it is a lot of work for a crew this size,"

Ping said. She separated her hands, tapped her fingers on the table, clasped them together again. "So if you're asking if I was resentful that they sent David along to take over half my job, the answer is a resounding no. I welcomed his help. David was very good at his job."

I didn't think Ping was being completely honest, but I couldn't quite figure out why I felt that way. There was nothing cagey about the way she spoke, no hesitation or darting eyes. If anything, she seemed far too calm. She looked directly at Adisa, as though I wasn't in the room at all. I was used to that—a lot of people didn't like to look at me—but she didn't seem uneasy. Quite the opposite. She seemed to be enjoying herself.

"How did you divide up your duties?" Adisa asked.

"We've never had a very rigorous division. I handle most of the Overseer's cooperation with the subsidiary and auxiliary systems, such as the mining and manufacturing, power generation, intrastation transport. David handles—handled—most of the higher-level and external functions. He was better with the big picture than with the details. He took care of the efficiency algorithms. And the communications arrays," she added pointedly, after the briefest pause. "What happened to the optical array? All we've been told is that it's out of commission for now."

"That's part of what we're looking into. Who handles the security system?" Adisa asked.

"David, mostly, but there have never been many security threats." A pause. "Until now."

"And surveillance?"

"David, again, but he didn't spend much time with it. The surveillance system is not meant to have a lot of human interference—as you well know. The Overseer handles anything that comes up."

"Did David ever ask you about Aeolia?" he asked.

Ping raised her delicate eyebrows. The question surprised her. "Why would you ask that?"

"Did he?"

"Not for some time, I don't think. We spoke about it briefly when he first came here—professional curiosity only. There wasn't much I could tell him that's not in the official reports."

"What was he curious about, specifically?" I asked.

Ping looked at me for the first time since she had sat down, and when she answered, it was with the air of someone who was consciously humoring me. "Like everybody else, he mostly wanted to know how a virus could infect an Overseer. It's not supposed to be possible, but I think we all know that Parthenope going around telling everybody it was impossible was an irresistible challenge to the wrong sort of people." She paused thoughtfully. "If we're being honest, I do wonder if David's concern was a bit more personal. I think he wanted to understand how Aeolia's Overseer could have made such terrible mistakes. I did everything I could to assure him we had learned quite a lot from the incident and those mistakes wouldn't happen again, but . . ." She shrugged slightly. "I understood his worry, because I've shared it. I can still smell them, do you know? All those people. The smell lingers."

She was looking at Adisa again, waiting for him to respond, but he remained quiet.

So I asked, "Does Nimue's Overseer make mistakes?"

"Goodness, no. Nimue is terribly reliable. It's quite set in its ways. But that can be its own problem, can't it?"

"How so?" I asked.

"The Overseers are powerful AIs, but they're very predictable, so they can be tricked. That's what happened on Aeolia. And now it's happened here, as well? You can tell me the truth,

Inspector." She was still smiling as she spoke to Adisa. Mary Ping smiled too much for somebody who had lost a colleague all of thirty hours ago and was now being interrogated by OSD officers. She smiled too much for anybody. "Not to the same extent, obviously, but the responsible party must have circumvented the surveillance system, or you wouldn't be here talking to me. You would have identified the murderer as soon as you arrived, and that handsome lawyer would be drafting a statement that firmly absolved Parthenope of any liability or culpability in the matter—tell me, Safety Inspector Adisa, what is Mr. van Arendonk doing here anyway? This is hardly a matter that requires his presence. If you had surveillance, you would already be on your way back to your husband. Oh." Ping pressed her fingers to her lips. She was looking at Adisa with dancing bright eyes. "I forgot. He's gone back to Earth, hasn't he?"

Adisa didn't acknowledge her questions. He asked, "When did you last speak to David Prussenko?"

"You don't already know? Is the surveillance gap that extensive?"

"We'd like to hear it from you, yeah?"

"Very well. It was just after dinner, the night before he died. I asked him to swap overnight shifts with me."

"Why?"

"I had a bit of a headache. I was overtired from a late shift the day before. It was nothing serious. We traded shifts all the time."

"Was there anything unusual about his behavior that night?"

"No. Nothing."

"Was he upset? Happy? Nervous? That day or anytime in the days before?"

"No, not at all. But you really should ask his friends. They'll know more. You have to understand." She sat forward; her expression turned earnest. "I had absolutely no reason to want David dead. I liked him. We worked well together. I had no personal or professional quarrel with him." She turned to meet my eyes. "This must be so hard for you. David spoke about you sometimes. He didn't like to talk about *Symposium*, but he was a great admirer of your work."

Her easy words felt like a weight in the center of my chest. She was still smiling.

"As am I," she went on. "I followed your work on the Titan Vanguard AI for years. Tell me—did you choose that name intentionally? The Vanguard satellites of the twentieth century weren't terribly successful. The first one crashed as soon as it launched. Seems an unlucky name to choose."

I swallowed; my throat was dry. I didn't know how to answer. I decided to try to match her calm. "It was chosen by committee. They decided that ruling out mission names simply because they coincided with unsuccessful American projects from centuries ago would eliminate rather too much of the English language."

"How very typical. I confess I am a bit flustered right now. It's not every day you get to meet the creator of such an innovative AI."

She did not look remotely flustered. I was the one who felt a nervous twitch in my fingers, the smallness of the room around us, the urge to shift in my seat and lean away.

"I didn't create Vanguard alone," I said. "We had a large team. Sunita Radieh was the lead scientist."

"Oh, but everybody knows that when a leader takes credit for a major achievement, it means the underlings have done all the hard work." Ping kept looking at me with that unnerving, unblinking stare. "I mean no offense. It's only that I understand how it must be so hard for you, to be working at a job like this, in a place like this, when you were meant to have so much more."

The last time I had seen Sunita, she had walked me to my quarters aboard *Symposium*. It was shortly before midnight on a night like any other; we had been in the laboratory late, running Vanguard through a series of tests to simulate what it would do when it lost radio contact with the base on Titan. It had recently developed the strange habit of reaching out to the comms systems of other departments aboard *Symposium* and persuading their AIs to do its talking for it, and we had to figure out a way to structure our tests so it couldn't do that. There wouldn't be anybody else to contact on Titan, after all; it had to learn to rely only on itself and what we brought with us. We had continued our conversation all the way from the lab to our personal berths, speculating on what the overnight results would show, planning a new test, exchanging rapid-fire ideas and adjustments so easily, so comfortably, as we had done for years. I had not known it would be our final conversation. I had not known to say goodbye. I had said, "I'm betting it figures it out," and Sunita had smiled at me, a beautiful wide smile that lit her entire face, and she had said, "You know our naughty little child best. Sleep well."

Three hours later I woke to screaming alarms and fire and pain.

I never saw Sunita again. She was gone. Vanguard was gone. Our mission was gone. And I was here, in this hateful box of metal on an ugly rock in the belt, with this cold, smirking woman before me, and I did not know what to say.

"I have so many things I want to ask you about it," Ping said. "Do you mind? It's the evolutionary aspect that interests me the most. I can't say I keep up with the literature as much as I should, but how did you avoid Baldwin's Law? You must have had precautions in place, to achieve project approval within the disarmament treaty. I know how very particular they are about avoiding the mistakes of the past."

I glanced at Adisa, but his expression remained blandly unconcerned, as though Ping wasn't using polite euphemisms to talk about the attempted genocide of his people and destruction of his home. *Mistakes of the past* was what people said when they wanted to talk about the horrors of the Martian war without acknowledging that those horrors had been entirely intentional. Vice Admiral Dane Baldwin had been responsible for developing and deploying the United Earth Navy's autonomous weapons on Mars. The threshers that razed the agricultural domes and kick-started a famine, the dusters that destroyed the solar panels and cast entire cities into a deadly winter, the slugs that poisoned the water supply and rendered nearly half of the survivors sterile.

Unintended consequences of technological advancement, Baldwin had said at the tribunal following the war. Not his fault. The machines made their own decisions. The machines were responsible.

I put my PD down and sat forward in my chair. I didn't know what Mary Ping wanted from me, only that she meant to provoke, but I had been provoked by better than her a hundred times before.

I said, "There's no such thing as Baldwin's Law. It has no basis in theory or practice. Artificial intelligences are not inherently destructive. There have been fully evolutionary AIs since Zhao's first Taijin mind, and most of them don't turn into killing machines. Baldwin didn't want to be held accountable for what he had created, so he blamed the machines for his own choices. He was never trying to do anything but create weapons of war."

"But his excuse convinced the tribunal," Ping said. "Oh, I know they found him guilty of some minor war crimes, but his only punishment was a few years of house arrest. He's a free man now."

That much was true. He had been the invited guest at an AI conference a few years before I left Earth. I had seen him in the hallways of the convention center, a red-faced man in a tailored suit—no sign of his naval uniform—talking in a booming voice while acolytes and admirers scurried behind him, asking questions he never deigned to hear.

"The war tribunal was not made up of experts in artificial intelligence," I said.

"You truly don't think violence is inevitable in the evolution of an advanced AI?" Ping asked.

"I know it isn't."

"But violence *is* inevitable in nature," she said, "and isn't the goal of an evolving AI to mimic nature as closely as possible? And do we truly understand what happens on the frontier between technology and nature—such as in your own lovely body?"

I curled my left hand into a fist but did not move it from the table.

"Nothing is inevitable with AI," I said. I would have really liked for Adisa to jump in and get the conversation back on track, but he kept quiet. "The goal of an evolving AI is to improve itself for the tasks it is given, and to do so in ways that we can't conceive or define. If that task is not a violent one, there is absolutely no reason for the AI to seek violent solutions."

"Vanguard never did?"

"Vanguard was an explorer," I said tightly. "Everything it did was toward the goal of collecting as much information as possible in an unfamiliar environment while not disturbing or altering that environment any more than absolutely necessary. Destructive actions would have made that goal harder to achieve."

"You must have been so very proud of it."

"Yes. I was."

"Have you considered creating it again? If it could be done once, surely it could be done twice."

She wasn't the first to ask. She wasn't the first to fail to see how it was such an empty question. If she knew anything at all about artificial intelligences, she had to know no individual AI could ever be exactly replicated. No explorer I might create in the future would choose an elegant praying mantis as its favorite physical form and accept the nickname Bug with a bob of its head and wave of its arms. I would never again design an AI that would learn to play Sunita's favorite piano concertos when we worked late in the lab, or collect evidence of a grad student stealing engineering tools before we even noticed anything was missing, or organize the data it collected according to which sets it thought would excite me the most. A new AI would never learn to communicate in every possible physical form, from a sturdy six-wheeled rover to a long-winged drone, using an ever-expanding array of elaborate gestures that almost resembled dance and conveyed more nuance than more ordinary stilted natural voice algorithms ever could. A new AI would not teach itself to assign silly food names to each of the team members and start using them without warning, causing us to be baffled, then delighted, as we tried to work out who was Gyoza or Pickles or Baba Ghanoush. It wouldn't learn to taunt less complex robots with its agility or make up logic games to challenge other AIs. All of the things Vanguard had learned and discovered while we were making it the smartest explorer it could be, they were gone and could never be replicated.

My voice was hollow when I answered. "It wouldn't be the same."

"No, no, of course not. That is rather like asking a mother to replace a dead child with a younger sibling, I suppose. The joy is in the unpredictability, isn't it? You must have given it so much freedom, to let it grow so powerful. I worry that since the Aeolia incident we're neutering our Overseers by restricting them too much."

I leaned back, watching Ping carefully. "Do you think Nimue's Overseer is at risk of an attack like Aeolia?"

"Oh, no," she said quickly. "I've seen no sign of that. But it's something David and I talked about, although he didn't share my concerns."

"What exactly did you talk about?" I asked. I glanced at Adisa, a clear invitation to jump in. I didn't know the first fucking thing about Aeolia except that it kept coming up in this investigation and everybody knew more about it than I did. He remained stubbornly, uselessly silent. "I mean with regards to Aeolia."

"Only what was relevant for our jobs. The changes implemented after the incident made our jobs a bit duller, to be honest. It might be good for business—and for safety, I suppose—but I'm not sure it's good for them. For the Overseers."

I couldn't stop myself from making a face at that. "They're machines."

"I'm surprised to hear you of all people say that," Ping said. Her accent was slipping, letting a bit of rough-and-tumble orbital rat shine through. "With what you created. And what you are now."

There it was again. The reason for her staring, her questions, her focus.

"I don't understand. What am I now?" I asked. "The untamed frontier between nature and technology?"

She dipped her chin slightly. "I've offended you."

"Do you really believe in that?"

"You don't?" she said. "Wasn't it the Zhao herself who said that when our machines know us as well as we think we know them, the distinction will be irrelevant?"

"She also said she would wager her life's savings on a Yuèliàng kite-jack race before she would try to predict the future of AI," I pointed out. "Yet people keep trying to predict the future of AI. As they've been trying and failing to do for centuries."

"Ah, well, she had her quirks, our mother of machines," Ping said. She sat forward in her chair and extended one hand toward me. "I'm sorry. I know this is inappropriate, but I can't help myself. May I look at your arm?"

I didn't move. Not so much as a twitch of the fingers. "No," I said.

"I've made you uncomfortable." Ping sat back and withdrew her hand, curling her fingers closed as she did so. "I didn't mean to. It's not mere prurient interest. My curiosity is professional. Who did the work? I only want to look. And, if I may"—a self-conscious laugh—"touch, just a bit? You must tell me who did your work. It's stunning."

I was surprised that she came right out and said it, as though there was nothing inappropriate about the hungry look in her eyes, the way she reached before she asked. Would she have said the same to the boy with the bleeding eyes, I wondered, and envied him for how his brain and body had been butchered? I had met the man who designed my prosthetic limbs only a few times in the hospital on Badenia, between my many surgeries. He had called me "Helen" and "girl" and "people like you" and asked me repeatedly if I was sure I didn't want my new arm and leg to match my skin, he had a lovely golden tone they could use, it would match perfectly if I spent some extra time under UV light, and it would only cost a little more, I should really consider it, it was sure to be all the rage among his female patients who wished to remain beautiful while redefining humanity. It was a relief when he left me to the surgeons and nurses, to his uncaring legal representatives and bored liaisons. They all wanted me to be very clear on what would happen if I should leave Parthenope before my medical bills were paid in full (repossession), if I should allow a third party to study the prosthetics in such a manner as to encourage unauthorized reproduction (prosecution), if I should make public statements disparaging the doctor and/or his team associated with Parthenope Medical and/or the technology of which I was currently in possession (litigation), if I should alter and/or modify and/or damage the patented and proprietary Augmented Medical Devices in any way (all of the above). I signed everything. I had no choice. I declined every one of their entreaties to offer myself up to the laboratory for further research or promotional duties.

I had chosen naked metal instead of the nauseating facsimile of human skin.

I stared at Mary Ping. I wanted to say no again, but I was afraid I would shout, or vomit, or cry. I kept my hand on the table.

"Is that all you want to talk about?" I said. "Because I don't have time for a philosophical debate about the existential evolution of artificial intelligences. Do you know anything else about David's death? Anything you haven't told us?"

She didn't flinch. She just kept staring at me, looking me right in my prosthetic eye. "I do not. But please do let me know what I can do to help," she said. For the first time in what felt like an eternity, she turned from me to look at Adisa. "I know it must be hard for you to investigate under these circumstances. You normally don't do much but watch the surveillance and drag the scapegoat away."

"We sometimes do a bit more than that, aye," Adisa said.

"Of course." She rose from her chair but hesitated before stepping away from the table. "If that's all, I have work to do. Twice as much, now. I'm sure you understand."

"Wait," I said. I had almost forgotten. "Do you know of any Parthenope project or operation with a name like Sunshine or Sunlight?"

"No, but I'm hardly aware of much outside my area of expertise," Ping said. "I really do have to get to—"

"One more question," said Adisa.

Ping barely hid her annoyance. "Yes?"

"Have you ever had reason to suspect there is any criminal activity happening on Nimue?"

"Really, Safety Inspector, I would have reported it, if I did."

"Not even a hunch?"

"No. Nothing." She took a step, turned back to look at me. "Are they all in prison now? The people responsible for *Symposium*, those who survived. I saw that it was in the news. I even asked David about it, but he never liked to talk about it. I do wish he had reached out for comfort when he needed it, before the end."

My left hand clenched, metal fingers scraping over the tabletop. She knew. I didn't know how it was possible. I had no proof. I didn't have any reason for my certainty beyond the tight pain in my chest. But I was absolutely sure she knew David had sent a message to me before he died.

I had assumed his remark about somebody listening had been general, for whoever in the company might be listening, but I knew better now. Mary Ping was the one he had been hiding from with his cryptic memories and awkward code talk.

As soon as she was gone, I wanted to call her back, take her by the shirt and shake her, ask her what she knew and what she had done. Why she had asked me about Vanguard, about violent AIs, about the evolution of machines. What David had told her. Why any of it mattered.

I found myself thinking about the time I had taken Vanguard to the bottom of the ocean and what it had done there. It had been a few years before *Symposium* launched. I hadn't thought of those days in ages, but now they were filling my mind again, dancing around with Mary Ping's sly question: *Vanguard never did?*

The rivalry we had with the members of the Europa Deep-Sea Expedition was more antagonistic than friendly. In one respect, they were years ahead of the Titan project on every possible axis. There were already colonies on Europa with transportation connections that kept the bases supplied with both people and resources. They had been drilling into the ice for two years already. They would be sending their autonomous submersibles into that cold, dark ocean well before we landed on Titan. They were probably going to find life first. We could all admit that—if not to their faces, but to each other, after a few drinks—and it stung.

But because our goals were so similar, if our destinations so different, we often found ourselves working side by side. That's what happened when I took a portable detachment of Vanguard down to the Joint Territories Mid-Atlantic Research Station, which sat on the bottom of the ocean near the thermal vent colonies on the Mid-Atlantic Ridge. My goal at Mid-AR was to train Vanguard in a wholly unusual and unexpected environment. I knew it could adapt to exploring underwater and at high pressure, but I had never taught it anything about the living colonies of organisms around the deep-sea vents. I wanted to see what it would do when it encountered those bizarre creatures for the first time, those life-forms that didn't play by the rules of energy acquisition and resource management that we had introduced it to on the surface.

The first few trial runs did not go well. Vanguard didn't like the high pressure at that depth, and it had balked at exploring far from the station when I sent it out to get its sea legs. That failure, unfortunately, happened right when one of the submersible designers from the Europa expedition was watching.

"You're asking too much of it," the insufferable Rodney Grieg said, when Vanguard curled itself into a ball.

"You've got to give it a little programming push," said Grieg, when Vanguard kept itself close to the station.

"You need to look for errors in your algorithm," was Grieg's advice when I brought Vanguard back inside.

"You need to kill that bug shape," declared Grieg, with a bit of a shudder, when Vanguard re-formed into its praying mantis form to scurry back to the laboratory.

"These kinds of machines, they aren't easy to design," Grieg said, over dinner one night, pointing his fork at me as he spoke. "There are a lot of special considerations. I can go over them with you later. I've got a free hour."

It was all I could do not to snatch the fork from his hand and stab it into his eye.

Instead I slunk away to my berth to spend the rest of the evening alone. The Europa team were all as obnoxious as Grieg, and the crew of Mid-AR were an insular and wary bunch. I worried when I interacted with them that I was looking at my future, that years in the darkness and isolation of space would teach me to stare too long, to linger by dark portholes, to treat strangers with open suspicion. I preferred Vanguard's company. It crawled around my berth as Bug, its praying mantis form, exploring every nook and corner of the little room, while I poked at the programming of its test parameters. It kept interrupting me to share nuggets of information about Grieg's team: who had plagiarized their thesis, who had finessed test results, who was accepting small bribes from corporate entities to share bits of research. I didn't really care about the ethically questionable choices of the Europa team, but Vanguard was a shameless gossip and I never felt lonely when it was sharing its findings with me.

I had still not solved the problem by the next morning, when it was once again time to send Vanguard out for a test. Grieg was loudly complaining about a slow pump in the hatch, so neither he nor anybody else noticed when I gave Vanguard a little pat on its triangle head—it had been years since I'd felt ridiculous for such habits, as Vanguard spoke most eloquently in gestures—and whispered, "Go out there and make me proud, kid."

I went with Grieg and his team to Mid-AR's overly warm observation room. The exterior lights were on but did little to penetrate the crushing darkness. I took a seat with my PD, prepared to pretend I was learning a great deal from Vanguard's continuing reticence, and ignored the boastful chatter of the Europa team all around me.

Grieg's ugly submersible swam into sight first. It was a big, boxy thing, with a round propulsion system that resembled the toothy anus-like mouth of a lamprey; it had two mismatched and awkward lobster-like claws that Grieg claimed were for collecting samples from the underside of Europa's ice crust. I had asked him—big mistake on my part, instigating a conversation—what sorts of samples the claws were meant to collect, and he had launched into a half-hour lecture on the importance of proper sterilization in sample collection, which had nothing to do with what I was asking and made the assumption that my own scientific experience was approximately on level with a six-year-old starting her first bug collection. I hated to look at his machine, hated how inelegant it was, and hated most of all that it *worked*. Maybe it could only perform a handful of tasks, but it performed them well.

But it was not jealousy I felt when I watched the bot swimming in neat circles outside the station. It was doubt. Doubt that we had chosen the correct path. Doubt that Vanguard was clever enough to solve the problems I put before it. Doubt that I was smart enough to guide it to those solutions.

Vanguard swam into view a few moments later. It had adopted an eel-like shape for swimming, one of its favorite forms in underwater environments. It rippled elegantly around Grieg's machine. It was so beautiful and agile, with the smooth metal scales catching and reflecting the station spotlights, giving it the look of a shimmering flame dancing in the darkness.

When it began to curl into a ball, as it had done on every previous test swim, Grieg's knowing snicker grated my nerves.

"It's such a *cute* little pill bug," he said.

I regretted very much my prior restraint in not stabbing him with a fork. I stared down at my PD, pretending to make notes, until a gasp from one of Grieg's grad students drew my attention back to the window.

Vanguard was changing shape again. From a tight ball it spread out, first evenly in every direction, then forming sharp angles and straight lines. It swam alongside Grieg's machine, mimicking its motions—and its shape, I realized, after a few seconds. It was reshaping itself to look exactly like Grieg's boxy machine, complete with the lobster claws and the lamprey-mouth propulsion system. It was a marvelous facsimile, but it didn't last, because Vanguard kept changing. It flattened and spread, forming wings like those of a manta ray, but stayed close to the other bot, swimming over it like a rippling cloak. Grieg's machine clearly had no idea how to react; it tried snatching with its claws, dodging out of the way, turning and rolling, but Vanguard never fell behind. The difference in agility between the two bots had never been more apparent.

Grieg was completely silent until Vanguard began to wrap itself around his bot.

"What the hell is it doing?" he demanded, his voice high and scared.

I didn't try to answer. I had no idea. Vanguard was now curling around Grieg's machine like a blanket gently swaddling a child.

"What is it doing?" Grieg said again. "What's going on?"

Almost as quickly as it had wrapped itself around the other bot, Vanguard released it. It spread its wings again—taking on the shape of a diving bird now, or an arrowhead—and swam away. Grieg's machine turned a few degrees, disoriented and sputtering.

Then it aimed its nose downward and swam directly into the ocean floor.

Grieg's team all began talking at once. The bot kicked up silt and gravel when it struck the seafloor, creating a brightly illuminated and nearly opaque cloud outside the window.

Through the murk, I could just see the newly angular shape of Vanguard racing away. Toward the mid-ocean ridge and the colony of creatures there. Finally, after days of failed tests, it was swimming off to do its job, and it was going to do it alone.

"What did you do?" Grieg demanded. He leaned down to get in my face, blocking my view. I leaned away from the coffee smell of his breath and angry spray of his words. *"What did you make it do?"*

I didn't bother answering. He wouldn't have believed me anyway. I had not taught Vanguard to do that. I had not trained it in any task that involved identifying competition and eliminating it. I had not told it that it needed to disable Grieg's machine in order to perform its own exploratory tests.

All I had done was tell it to make me proud.

"Marley."

Adisa's voice broke into my reminiscing. My breath caught, and I blinked rapidly, hoped it was not obvious how distant I had been, how lost in the past and close to tears. I missed Vanguard so much it ached, but most days I was able to ignore the ache, the same way I ignored the imbalance in my limbs, the glitches in my eye. Mary Ping had found that ache and pressed on it as though it was a fresh bruise.

"Sorry," I said, my voice rough. "I was just thinking."

I considered, for a moment, telling Adisa about David's message. I knew that admitting I had been in contact with the victim meant I could not be on this investigation. I knew that concealing such evidence would endanger my job. But the pressure of carrying David's message around in my mind, trying so desperately to tie it to everything we learned, looking for secrets beneath secrets without any help, was growing harder the longer we were here.

"We'll talk to Neeta Hunter next, yeah?" Adisa said.

The impulse passed. *It's a good job*, he had said, about working here on Nimue, under Parthenope's watchful eye and controlling thumb. He was not going to help me. Nobody in Parthenope's employ would help me, because it would mean endangering themselves.

"Sure," I said. "I'll get her in here."

TEN

I had never seen eyes like Neeta Hunter's before. She hadn't been close enough for me to notice in the airlock earlier, but I could see them clearly now. They were big and bright, an unnatural electric blue, with thick lashes and overflowing tear ducts.

"I don't understand what's going on," Hunter said. She wiped at her tears and took a shaky breath. Her accent was upper-class Yuèliàng, even crisper than Hugo van Arendonk's. "Nobody knows anything. What happened in the optical array? Did David do something? What does the surveillance show?"

"We're still trying to work that out," Adisa said. "We need to ask you some questions about David."

"Oh, god. I can't believe he's gone."

I wondered if the cosmetic surgery had damaged her tear ducts or if the excessive moisture was part of the alteration, something she had requested to make her look bright-eyed and dewy, perhaps, even younger than her twenty-one years. To make those startling blue eyes shine. To let her turn on the waterworks on command.

If so, she had certainly got her money's worth—and it had been a great deal of money. Both her eyes and her shiny silver hair cost far more than a Parthenope asteroid miner could afford. But Neeta Hunter didn't need to worry about money. According to her personnel file, she was a Hunter of Hunter-Fremont, one of the largest and most powerful family-run corporations in the system, with a near monopoly on industrial shipping in the inner system. Her mother was Leonora Hunter, one of Yuèliàng's genetically engineered heirs; her grandfather had just been elected for a third term as Imbrium's vice chancellor. Neeta Hunter's inheritance was probably worth more than several small orbitals and colonies combined. Her family might not be able to buy Nimue outright, but they would at least be able to bring Parthenope to the table.

I did a quick check on Parthenope's public reports: Hunter-Fremont was among Nimue's many powerful investors; they had a heavy stake in the shipyard on Badenia. No doubt they were hoping to expand their shipping empire into the asteroid belt and beyond.

Neeta Hunter's background explained her ability to purchase absurdly expensive cosmetic enhancements. It didn't explain what an heiress to one of the system's wealthiest families was doing repairing bots on Nimue.

"Take your time. What was David like?" asked Adisa.

"I liked him. We came here at the same time, so we've always kinda been a team. He was fun to talk to. He knew a little bit about everything."

"What did you talk about?"

"Oh, everything. Mostly work. He was brilliant with robots, just brilliant. We talked about music and media too—he knew a lot more about late lunar surrealism than most people. We were going to try to get to the Tandy Tschovek show on Vesta next year. It was fun to get him going on about indie artists versus corporate acts and all of that." Hunter laughed, a bit self-consciously. "We argued, but it was always for fun, you know? It all seems so silly now. I know none of this helps you."

"You were close, yeah?" Adisa said.

"I guess." Hunter took in a quick, wet breath and rubbed at her nose, a gesture that made her look about fourteen years old. "Not like that. I mean, yes. We were friends. But I wasn't shagging him or anything. I don't know if he was interested in people like that."

He had been, before. Female, male, nonbinary, as long as they were beautiful and clever and laughing, he had loved them all, and they had loved him right back in whirlwind romances that ended as soon as they began, but rarely with bitterness. I felt a sudden, overwhelming pang of homesickness, to remember how easy it had once been to laugh and flirt and laugh some more, to come into work after a weekend knowing David would be there with a story and a challenge to provide a wilder one. The *Symposium* disaster had taken that from me. I hadn't considered before that it might have taken it from David as well.

"Did he have a problem with anybody on the crew? Anybody have a problem with him?"

Hunter shook her head firmly. "No way. No. Everybody likes him."

Adisa pressed, "No disagreements or fights? Even if they didn't seem like a big deal?"

"No. Nothing like that. I've been trying and trying, and I can't think of any reason anybody would want to hurt David."

So why, I wondered, and not for the first time, had Sigrah tried to convince us his death was personal before we even started? I had assumed she had somebody in mind before, but now I was less certain. Her insistence made little sense without others in the crew telling stories about personal strife or conflict.

"That's what we're trying to figure out, aye?" Adisa spoke in a low, kind voice, leaning toward her, his expression a mask of sympathy. It was quite effective in putting the girl at ease, and it was a stark contrast to the studied disinterest with which he had spoken to Mary Ping. "What did you talk about when you talked about work?"

"Oh, everything. I mean, we're all stuck here, right? David helped me a lot. He was so brilliant with the bots. This is my first contract, and there's so much I don't know." Hunter took in a breath and sat up straighter. She rested her hands on the table, then immediately lifted them to wipe her tears again. That gesture, small and innocent, made me angry, then it made me sad. She was too young to be this far from whatever home on Yuèliàng she'd left behind. "I owe him a lot. He helped me when I first came here. I got hassled, you know? Because of my family. Because everybody assumes there's no way I know what I'm doing, or I must have, I don't know, bribed my way into this job." She let out a sharp little laugh. "God. As if *this* is the job I would buy my way into, if that's what I wanted."

"People in the belt aren't shy about sharing their opinions, yeah?"

"Yeah. I don't mind, really. I know you want to ask, so I guess I can just tell you. I'm here because I didn't want the life my family wants for me. That's all. There's nothing more to it than that."

I very much doubted that was true.

"When did you last speak to David?" Adisa asked.

"The evening before he—the evening before. At dinner. He didn't have much to say."

"No? Why not?"

"I don't know," Hunter said. "I could tell something was bothering him, but I didn't ask." Then, more plaintively, her voice falling to near a whisper, "I should have asked. I was just going on about stupid things. I have this bootleg copy of the HalfLiquid immersion show on Asteria and I thought he might want to watch it with me. That's so sad, isn't it? I can't believe that was the last thing I talked to him about, some stupid concert, instead of asking him what was wrong. I could have . . . I don't know. I didn't even try."

"Did you ever hear or see anything that made you think David was involved with something he shouldn't have been?"

Hunter worried her lower lip. I felt a shiver of excitement.

"You can't get him into any trouble now, aye?" Adisa said gently. "We only need to know what he was doing."

"I don't know. I would tell you if I knew. I swear."

But she wasn't looking at us. She was staring at the table, tracing an old stain with the tip of her finger, every line of her body tense and uncomfortable.

"Anybody else on the crew? We know a bit of black market dealing isn't uncommon on a station like this."

"I don't know," she said again.

Adisa waited a moment, giving her a chance to go on. When she didn't, he changed tactics. "How did he work with Mary Ping? Bit strange, having two sysadmins on a crew this size, yeah?"

She was relieved to leave the topic of criminal activity behind. "I don't know. I don't think David liked her much, but it was no big deal. He said the Overseer didn't like her either."

Hunter gave a quick, self-conscious smile. "I mean . . . you know what I mean. He knew Overseers don't like or dislike anything. It was just a way of talking about it."

"So they didn't work well together?" I said.

"He said he spent half his time fixing problems she'd created or doing things she should have done already."

"Like what?" I asked.

Hunter only shook her head. "It's all beyond me. I'm good with the bots, but not the Overseer stuff. He said she let things slip through the cracks, things that she ought to have trained the Overseer to catch. I don't think David was overwhelmed with work or anything. Sometimes he seemed kinda bored, to be honest. He'd go around helping other people. He helped me a lot." A quick shrug. "I don't know."

"Did David ever talk to you about the Aeolia incident?" I asked.

Hunter frowned. "I don't think so. No more than, you know, the way anybody talks about it, when it comes up."

"Did it ever come up?"

"I don't think so? Everybody kinda tries not to mention it. It's so dark."

As casually as I could, I asked, "What about *Symposium*? Did David ever talk to you about that?"

She wiped away a tear. "Not about the . . . you know, the attack itself. He never wanted to talk about that, even when other people tried to ask him about the trials or whatever. But sometimes he would talk about the research he was doing on the Titan project. I always wanted to hear it, you know? He was a brilliant roboticist. I learned so much from him. But it was more than that. It was . . ." She tugged on the ends of her sleeves; the gesture made her look even younger. "We're all just trying to make our way out here, you know? Work our contracts and do our jobs and maybe think about finding a better position next time."

It was surreal to hear an heiress from one of the wealthiest families in the system talk about living the life of corporate drudgery in the outer system. I couldn't tell if it rang false to me because I knew her family history or because there was something insincere in her delivery. I didn't like that I couldn't tell. I let her keep talking.

"But David believed in more than that," Hunter said. "Not in, I don't know, a spiritual sense. Nothing like that. But I know he thought that he'd lost something really special and important after *Symposium*. He would talk about . . . sometimes, he would talk about how he'd had a chance to explore and discover, but it was gone now. I asked him a few times if he was going to try to get back to it, but he always said it was too late." She sniffled and looked at me with watery eyes. "That's a terrible thing for a person to believe, isn't it? Nobody should ever feel like it's too late."

It took my breath away, to think about how lonely David must have been, stuck on this isolated rock, with nobody but this child to confide in. She was so young. She could never understand.

We asked her about the night David had died, about where she had been and who she had seen, about her programming knowledge, about the surveillance system, but none of it led anywhere useful. She had been asleep, in bed. She hadn't seen or spoken to anyone. She didn't know much about the surveillance system. She didn't know much about the Overseer. Her job was to build and repair maintenance bots. She just wanted to do her job. She couldn't believe David was dead. She kept crying throughout the interview. It was hard to imagine this young woman, with her designer eyes and shimmery hair and endless stream of tears, beating a man to death in a rage. It was hard to imagine her feeling rage about anything. She seemed too delicate for such an emotion.

Next we spoke to Miguel Vera, the fuel tech and friend of David's. He was from Earth and pinpointed my nomadic middle-of-the-Atlantic accent right away. He was going back, he said, when he finally saved up enough to get home. He spoke with the jittery sort of nervousness of somebody who took too many stimulants and got too little sleep.

"This is insane. I can't fucking believe one of them did this. Nobody kills people out here. What's the point? We're all so fucking close to dying anyway."

"Did David make anybody angry lately? Any fights?" Adisa asked.

Vera shook his head. "No way, man. Shit. That's sick. There's no reason. Even the people he annoyed weren't, like, annoyed, you know?"

"What kind of annoyance was that, aye?"

"No big. His shitty taste in music. Okay, seriously, don't look at me like that." Vera's grin was quick and strained. "Like, he was good at his job, I mean, really good, yeah? So sometimes he'd get bored and start sticking his nose into other people's work."

"How so?" I asked.

"He spent two weeks once riding my ass about fuel leakages in the dead-ended lines that run to the old UEN base. The Overseer has no control out there. I doubt it even knows the base is there except as a blank spot on the map—there's nothing functional left for it to know about. But David wanted to see for himself."

"Did he? Did he go and check the fuel lines?" I asked.

Vera shrugged. "No idea, but I doubt it. There's no point.

The Overseer isn't sending fuel and power out to an empty base. If there are leaks, they're somewhere else."

"What other problems was David asking about?"

"Let me think. Oh, yeah, he was always hassling Ned about errors in the cargo manifests, like a facility this size isn't going to have errors. Shit nobody gives a fuck about, but that was David."

We heard much the same from the remainder of the crew. David had been well-liked, good at his job, and got along with everybody. There were minor complaints, petty squabbles, ordinary crew disputes, but no fights, no simmering resentments, and absolutely nobody who would admit to having any idea that David or anybody else was involved with anything shady.

Sonya Balthazar, the furnace engineer, had asked Sigrah to intervene when David kept inviting himself into the mine to nitpick her work, never mind that he had absolutely no fucking idea how to bore a half-kilometer-wide tunnel through an asteroid. Sigrah had scolded David, but it hadn't done much good.

"It's too dangerous," Balthazar said, tapping her fingers on the table to emphasize each word. "But he never seemed to care. He wouldn't even tell me what he was looking for, and honestly, I didn't have time to figure it out." She sat back in the chair and crossed her arms over her chest. "I don't have time to deal with David's shit. I don't have time for *this*."

Lashawna Melendez, the geologist, told us that David did the same in her assay lab on more than one occasion, but she never bothered running to Sigrah because she didn't need help dealing with unwanted interruptions. Ned Delicata, the docking and cargo tech, confirmed that David gave him grief about discrepancies in cargo manifests, but he added that he had turned right around and passed that grief along to Parthenope, because the mistakes all originated elsewhere. He had never fought with David, he said, and he was more than happy to tell us—at length—his thoughts on how likely each and every one of his crewmates was to be a murderer, what method they were most likely to use, what secrets he suspected were hidden in their pasts.

"We don't even have the right to defend ourselves," Delicata said. He leaned over the table while he spoke, mostly ignoring me to address his words toward Adisa. "We should have that, at least, but thanks to your fucking people, we're stuck out here with our thumbs up our asses every time some psycho decides to fuck things up."

Adisa didn't bother pointing out that it had been the overwhelmingly powerful UEN, not the starving and desperate Martian rebels, whose use of weaponry had led to the postwar disarmament treaties. His only reaction was to tilt his head slightly and say, without trying to soften his accent in the slightest, "You think Prussenko should have been able to defend himself, aye?"

"I think a lot of things would be different if we weren't expecting the likes of you and your little security shits to keep us safe."

"So who do you think is responsible? Given the nature of the murder, aye?"

Delicata didn't hesitate. "It was the Hunter brat. Lovers' quarrel. You know how rich kids get when they don't get what they want."

"Yeah? What did she want?"

With a look of confusion, Delicata said, "Why don't you ask *her*?"

Adisa thanked him for his help and asked him to send the next crew member in. Delicata, still red in the face, stormed away. I nudged Ned Delicata upward on my list of crew members to look into more closely.

Katee King, the electrical engineer, confirmed that David had told her not to bother repairing the offline transmitters until they figured out the cause of the power surges, but she swore once again she'd had no idea he was hiding something. Bitsy Dietrich-Yun, the facilities engineer, disagreed with Vera about David's taste in music but confirmed what the others had said about David looking for off-assignment work; he had helped her reprogram some of the cargo loaders a month or so ago, and they were supposed to meet up in a day or two to fix some more. Ivan Dolin, the mining engineer, confirmed what Balthazar had said about David sometimes wandering about the station where he wasn't supposed to be, but like everybody else, he didn't think there was much to it and didn't mind. He welcomed the company whenever David ended up out in the mine during long, dull shifts of fixing this machine or that. Sometimes they played cards on their breaks.

They were all edgy and anxious, every person we talked to, if not outright scared. A few had theories, a few had suspicions, but not one of them admitted to knowing anything that might have gotten David killed.

After the last crew member was gone, Adisa rolled his shoulders tiredly and rubbed the back of his neck. "Either this is the cleanest crew in the whole fucking system or they're all so scared of being implicated they can't see what's in front of them. And that includes Sigrah."

"Whatever David was doing, it will be in the data somewhere. I just need time to look. And access." I hoped I sounded more confident than I felt. I had been expecting some guidance from the interviews—stories about crew conflict, hints of black market trades, suspicions of shady contacts—but all we'd learned was that whatever David was doing, he had kept it to himself.

Adisa tapped his fingers on the table. "Maybe Hugo has learned something from HQ."

There was a shout from the common room. We both jumped to our feet and moved toward the door. Neeta Hunter's voice rang out, high-pitched and furious. "What did you do to him? What did you do to him?"

Adisa and I emerged from the galley just in time to see Hunter launch herself at Mary Ping, who was walking through the main room. Hunter grabbed the front of her jumpsuit and shoved her against the wall; Ping's head struck with an audible thump.

"What the fuck did he ever do to you?"

Ivan Dolin, who was closest, grabbed Hunter's shoulder to try to pull her back. "What the fuck, girl? Stop."

Hunter ignored him. She was fixated on Ping. She had one hand fisted in the front of Ping's shirt; with the other she struck Ping hard across the face.

"Why? Just tell me why! Why would you hurt him?"

"All right." Adisa darted forward to catch Hunter's wrist before she could hit Ping again. He pried her fingers from Ping's shirt and tugged her away, with Dolin's help. "Back off, yeah? Don't do this."

"I know it was you." Hunter's voice was wet with tears. "Everybody knows it was you."

"I'll take her to her room," Dolin said, putting his arm around Hunter's shoulders.

The other miners stared as they left, half-risen from their chairs, mouths open. Their expressions were caught between abashed amusement and genuine fear.

I didn't notice Sigrah in the doorway until she spoke.

"We're not doing this," Sigrah said. Her voice was strident and loud enough to carry. "Do you hear me? We are not fucking doing this. We are not that kind of crew. We are not going to make accusations. We are not going to treat each other with suspicion. We are going to let the security team do their jobs, and we are going to get back to work. Is that clear?"

A ringing silence filled the room. None of the miners reacted.

"Is that fucking clear?"

Mumbles of assent. Narrowed eyes. One or two obedient nods.

Through all of this, Mary Ping said nothing. She sat at the end of a mess table. She smoothed down the front of her shirt and touched her cheek gingerly. The blow had left a red mark on her pale skin. She looked over to see me standing just outside the galley. She smiled, whisper-soft and quick as a flash, and turned away.

ELEVEN

By the time we finished interviewing the crew, it was technically the end of the day, and we all sat down to a demoralizing meal of rehydrated noodles and indistinguishable plant protein smothered in a sticky, too-sweet sauce. I finished my own food quickly and slipped away to look around the crew quarters.

I found David's berth about halfway down the long corridor. My security access code let me in.

The room was barren and impersonal. David had little clothing aside from standard-issue jumpsuits and work boots. He didn't even have an extra pillow or blanket from the station stores. It was such a contrast to what I recalled of David's previous homes that it made my heart ache. He had once surrounded himself with pieces of every aspect of his life. Jewelry made by his nieces, images and videos from his travels, little bots he tooled and trained in his spare time. His laboratory had been a whirlwind of organized chaos. He had always known exactly where to find everything he needed.

I thought, inexplicably, of my brother's home in the Cotswolds, his ancient cottage with its low doorways and big wooden beams, teacups in the sink and children's toys everywhere. I always told Devon that so much clutter would drive me mad, and he always told me I was welcome to clean for him, if I wanted, while he took the kids to the playground. In truth I loved Devon's house, loved how rooted he and his children were in that place, loved how the door creaked but never loud enough to hide the sound of Michael and Renee shrieking that Auntie Hester was here. Little Phoebe would be able to shout it along with them soon—but she didn't know her aunt. She would probably never know me. I would never know what her voice sounded like calling my name just as the sun was setting and the scent of something rich and hearty drifted from the kitchen.

In that moment I wanted very much to answer Devon's latest letter. I wanted to tell him about David. I wanted to tell him about the doctors' appointments I was postponing because I was afraid to hear how little progress I was making. I wanted to tell him how much debt I had to pay off and how much every message, every video, every contact with Earth set me back. I wanted him to tell me that it was okay, my being so far from home and missing so much. It was okay that I was so different, so broken, so alone.

The only sign that monastic room belonged to David was a map on the wall. It was old-fashioned, printed on some kind of archival-quality polymer, stuck to the metal surface with black electrical tape. The image was a geomorphic map of Titan, with the moon's landforms rendered in vivid colors and patterns and light. David had had one just like it aboard *Symposium*, right above his bunk, so that he might fall asleep every night gazing at it.

When *Symposium* had sailed past Mars's orbit, we celebrated that milestone of our voyage with a tremendous party for all the crew and passengers. I had not thought about that day since before the disaster, but it came to me now, clear and vibrant. The festivities had been briefly interrupted when Kristin Herd got herself locked out of the laboratory again—third time since the voyage began, seventh since she'd joined the project—and her hurt, mulish reaction had only made the rest of us laugh. It made us laugh every time, which was callous, but we only laughed because she never did. We were never cruel enough to deserve what she did to us later.

I had ended the night in David's quarters, drunk and giddy, lying beside him on his narrow bunk and pointing to all the places we were going to explore. All we did was talk and laugh and plan—our friendship was never sexual—but that night we spent lying side by side, fully clothed with our shoulders and hips touching, planning for a future we craved so much the wanting was a constant hunger. It was warm and intimate and comfortable, and I remembered thinking, perhaps saying aloud, that it was worth everything, all the years of work, all the sacrifice, all the tearful goodbyes, for a chance to know a world nobody had known before.

It hurt, like a blade right between my ribs, to remember how happy we had been.

Gecko boots squeaked on the floor behind me. I turned to find Adisa in the doorway.

"I've searched it already," he said. "Nothing here. No contraband. Not even moonshine."

"I know." My voice was hoarse. I blinked quickly and made a show of looking around the barren little room. I did not want him to see the tears stinging my eyes. "I only want to see . . ."

How he had lived. Who he had become. I didn't know how to explain. There was nothing here.

Adisa made a sound in his throat, like he was on the verge of speaking, and for one horrifying second I thought he might say something *comforting*. I didn't think I could bear that.

Perhaps my discomfort showed on my face, because he only said, "Ryu has found something in the medical exam, yeah? They want to fill us in."

"Right. Okay." I followed him for a few steps, then stopped. "Wait."

Adisa looked back. "Yeah?"

"What happened on Aeolia?" When he didn't say anything, I went on, nerves making me ramble. "I know I can look it up and read the reports and everything. But it's just that . . . David was reading about it before he died. And he was also reading about *Symposium*. And trying to find information about this Project Sunshine or whatever it's called. Those three things, right before he died. And Mary Ping was obviously trying to needle both of us." And succeeding—but I kept that thought to myself. "Maybe it's just a coincidence, because *Symposium* was in the news that day, but . . ."

"You think Prussenko saw some connection?"

"He might have." I shifted my position, trying to ease the growing ache in my left hip. I needed to sit down. "Aeolia was also a terrorist attack, wasn't it? A virus infected the Overseer?"

Adisa rubbed his hand over his face. "Aye, it was. Aeolia was a mine, but not like this one. An older one. Big operation, active twelve or fifteen years, and a lot of the work was exterior—you know what that means for a mine?" I shook my head. "It's more dangerous work, needs a lot more attention, so they need more crew. They can't just send borers into the rock to chew it up, aye? Thirty were assigned to the site, plus another thirty on temporary assignment to upgrade the dock. The company never considered it a security risk."

"How did anybody even get a virus into an Overseer?"

It was supposed to be impossible; that was part of why Parthenope guarded its Overseers and their design so closely. The easiest way to infect an AI would be to get into its brain directly, but that was no easy task for anybody. Only a sysadmin with a specific reason could access the AI directly, and only under very particular circumstances. I thought about the locked door in the systems room, the one that van Arendonk and I hadn't been granted permission to open. I wondered if David had ever gone through that door. Or Mary Ping. I should have asked her.

I added, "Was it somebody on the station?"

"We never found out," Adisa admitted. "If it was, they're gone now, yeah?"

"What did the virus do?"

"It caused systems failures that cascaded until the Overseer shut itself down."

"It shut itself down? But that's—they shouldn't do that. Why is that even possible?"

He shrugged slightly, made a vague gesture with one hand. "Ask Mary Ping. She investigated it afterward. The crew sent out distress calls requesting help, but Hygiea didn't know it was serious until a cargo ship got there and . . . They were too late. The water recycling and atmospheric control systems had broken down, so when the fires started, there was nothing to . . . We had to use ID chips to identify them. Sixty people. It took days."

I didn't want to imagine it. I had spent too much of the past few years trying not to imagine what fire could do to the human body. How helpless people were in the confines of a ship or station. How hard it must have been, how very painstaking and gruesome it must have been, to identify every single body. I didn't want to picture it, but the images were there in my mind. Twisted and blackened corpses in dark corridors. Smoke that smelled of meat and melted rubber. Flashing lights. Alarms. The alarms I heard were from *Symposium*. The corridors I saw were aboard *Symposium*. I didn't know what Aeolia had looked like. When I tried to imagine it, I only came up with the corridors of Nimue, rooms like this room, beds like the one David had left behind, and thinking about that filled me with so much dread I could scarcely breathe.

"Is that what you wanted to know?" Adisa looked so terribly uncomfortable that I almost regretted asking. I had wanted to know—needed to know—but that didn't make me feel any less of an asshole for making him tell me. I should have read the reports.

"Did anybody ever claim responsibility?" I asked.

"No." Adisa started to say something, but he changed his mind, shook his head slightly. "It's worth looking into, I suppose. Come on. Ryu's waiting."

He left. I looked over David's berth one more time before following.

Except for the map of Titan, that empty room could have been anybody's quarters. It could have been my quarters on Hygiea, marked just as little, every bit as easy to abandon. Even the map seemed sapped of color and contrast in the weak, muddy light. I closed and locked the door behind me.

The infirmary was a small room slotted alongside the galley and mess, up against the curved wall of what had once been the ship's inner hull. It seemed like hygienically questionable placement to me, a feeling that was not helped by how easily the pervasive scents of reheated food drifted through the thin door. One of the most fun parts of undergoing months of medical treatment that included a significant amount of organ repair and nerve rewiring was that my body had come out of it with some exciting new opinions about what I could not bear to smell and taste. Cheap long-storage meals were one of the things that turned my stomach most often—which was great and not at all annoying for a person living in space and surviving on such meals.

And that was before adding in the faintly sweet scent of decay.

The infirmary was narrow, with rows of cabinets on either side of the single table, and everything was scrupulously clean. Adisa and van Arendonk were already there, standing on one side of the table; Ryu sat on a stool at the head of the exam table. I shuffled in, last to arrive, and shut the door.

David lay on the table. His skin was waxy and pallid. Ryu had cleaned away the blood, but somehow that only made the wounds more hideous. His one remaining eye was closed. I wondered at how pale his eyelashes were, how fine his thinning hair. I remembered that hair being soft gold when the sun shone through it. It looked colorless now.

"He was fairly healthy," Ryu said. Their voice was rough, their movements a bit unsteady, and overhead lights weren't doing their pale complexion and rising bruises any favors. They looked very much like they ought to be lying down, not presiding over a corpse in the middle of a medical exam. "About as healthy as could be expected. He kept up with his radiation and osteo meds. He did his resistance exercises. No addictions, no flags on the mental health assessments. The only thing the medic was keeping an eye on was his lungs." Ryu flicked a glance at me, quick and apologetic. "He had some scarring and diminished lung capacity from the *Symposium* incident, but HQ decided it wasn't serious enough to keep him from a station assignment."

When the explosions in the cargo bay caused fires that cascaded uncontrollably through *Symposium*'s atmospheric control system, the living areas had been swamped with superheated air. The scarring in David's lungs was from breathing. From surviving. I had the same scars.

"He wasn't killed by diminished lung capacity," van Arendonk said. "What have you found that's actually useful? Those rabid fuckers are wound so tight I wouldn't put it past them to kill each other while we're in here."

Ryu rolled their eyes and didn't even try to hide it. "Right, sure, okay. No surprises in the cause of death. Blunt object, many blows, you can see it. But there is one weird thing. Look at his sleeves."

They slid from their stool and lifted one of David's hands. I hadn't noticed before, in the airlock, but I saw now that the cuffs of his jumpsuit were cinched tight to his wrists with soft bands of pale yellow.

"His feet too," Ryu said.

Larger versions of the same bands cinched his trousers to his legs.

"He was dressed to put on a space suit," Adisa said.

Ryu nodded. "That's what it looks like. I noticed because Hester and I just went through it."

David's clothes were secured at the arms and legs to make it easier to don a vac suit like the ones Ryu and I had worn in the maintenance shaft, the ones that never fit quite right and always bunched up the clothes underneath in awkward places.

"Did he go outside? How did you miss that?" van Arendonk asked.

"No," I said quickly. "The airlock never depressurized. The outer hatch never opened."

"Not even during the blackout period?"

I shook my head. "No. That airlock wasn't depressurized that day. Hasn't been for a few weeks, since the last logged maintenance check."

"So he was preparing to go outside, aye?" Adisa said. "There was no suit with him."

"Maybe the other person was supposed to bring it?" Ryu suggested.

"What's out there?" Adisa looked at me expectantly.

I blinked, caught off guard. "I, uh, I'm not sure. I'd have to check. Sigrah said they only go out for—"

"Routine maintenance on the cargo transport system, but let's make sure she's right about that, yeah? Who uses it, how often, why."

"Right. That will be in the logs."

"We should look for the suit too—recyclers, incinerators. We can start in the warehouse," he said. "Hugo, what did you get from HQ?"

"Fuck-all and jack shit," van Arendonk said. "A whole lot of arse-covering from long-winded puckerfaces telling me to ask someone else."

"Sit down with Sigrah and try to scare her into telling you more."

"Oh, you want my help with the interviews now?" van Arendonk said. "I'm so flattered. Let me check my calendar."

"Threaten her with legal repercussions if she doesn't cooperate. You're good at that." Adisa turned toward the door, then stopped. "What do you know about Neeta Hunter? Why is she out here?"

Van Arendonk laughed. "I have no bloody idea. Most likely she took off on her own to prove that she isn't tied to Mum's purse strings. It's practically a rite of passage among the families, as a way of feebly exerting our imaginary independence. Some of us run off to volunteer legal aid to ungrateful Martian freedom fighters, and some of us run off to rock-hop for a few years before it gets boring. She'll crawl back to Yuèliàng when she runs out of money."

"Must be nice to be a Hunter," Ryu said dryly.

I wanted to agree, wanted to roll my eyes and nod, but all I could think was: how bloody unfair. How staggeringly fucking unfair it was that Neeta Hunter could leave anytime she wanted, but I couldn't even venture outside of Parthenope territory without bankrupting my entire family for generations to come because my life and work and time and even my limbs didn't belong to me anymore. How bloody unfair that life could be so easy if you were Neeta Hunter or Hugo van Arendonk, but for the rest of us, ruined by events beyond our control, there were no good paths, no safe options, only choices that hurt more and choices that hurt less.

"Any chance she's working for Hunter-Fremont?" Adisa said.

Van Arendonk considered it. "I doubt Leonora would be so gauche as to use her own daughter as a spy. That's the sort of thing she would hire out to a well-vetted professional. But it seems like a clever investigator might want to ask the girl herself."

"It does seem like that, yeah." Adisa then looked squarely at Ryu. "And you're going to get some rest."

"But I'm—"

"Rest," he said. "Find a spare bunk. That's an order. Marley, meet me in the warehouse to dig through some garbage."

After Adisa and van Arendonk were gone, Ryu made a face. "I'm *fine*," they said. "And I'm not finished here."

"You don't really look fine," I said. I brushed a strand of hair back from their face to get a better look at their damaged nose and black eyes. "You look like shit."

"Oh, wow, thanks ever so much, Safety Officer Marley." They glared at me briefly before reaching across David's corpse to grab the other side of the body bag. "This is your first field investigation, isn't it?"

I dropped my hand. "What does that have to do with anything?"

"And the victim is someone you knew."

"And?"

There was a pause that lasted just a shade too long, then they said, "It's nothing."

"What's nothing?" I said.

"It doesn't matter. Never mind."

"No, come on, what is it?"

Ryu looked at me for a long moment. We were about the same height, but right now their slender shoulders were stooped with tiredness and pain. "I don't mean anything by it," they said. "It's just that you seem distracted. Like there's something you're on the verge of saying." They spoke with a soft sort of weariness that indicated they were already sorry they'd said anything.

They were right, of course. They knew me well enough. Every single time we spoke about what David had gotten himself into, it was there on the tip of my tongue, pressing against the back of my teeth, the urge to tell them about David's message. I knew that by keeping it to myself I was keeping something from the investigation. I also knew I couldn't truly trust anyone. Adisa seemed like he truly wanted to find the killer, but he had been with Parthenope for a long time, and nobody stuck around that long if they didn't prioritize protecting the company and their own position within it above all else. I sure as hell couldn't trust van Arendonk, a rich man making himself even richer by fucking over employees on the company's behalf.

And as much as I wanted to trust Ryu, I knew it was too risky. I didn't know them that well. What they liked about their work, what kind of gossip they collected, how they laughed at their own jokes, how their dark hair always fell into their eyes, those were the little things I knew, the bits and pieces collected during the time we'd spent together. They were one of the first friends I'd made upon arriving on Hygiea, the first to help me get past spending every hour of every day lonely and angry and itching for anything to take my mind off how my life was ruined, to forget for an hour or two how hard it was to escape the stares, the questions, the leering, and worst of all the shuddering, to stop thinking about the way people looked at me and flinched because I was everything they were terrified of becoming: a broken thing far from home, a helpless victim whose future had been devoured by the serendipitous cruelty of space, a walking purgatory stuck between the promises of the past and the mind-numbing bleakness of the future. Ryu had approached me in the canteen and they had been looking at my face, not my prosthetic parts, so I hadn't snapped at them to scare them away. What I knew about Ryu was that they came from one of the innumerable private orbital habitats owned by some toxic Christian sect, the sort of micro-society where women were chattel, binaries were rigid, shame was rampant, and regular, generous donations to the reelection campaigns of Earth-based politicians ensured that human rights inspectors stayed far, far away. Why Ryu had left, how they'd ended up in the asteroid belt, what they had left behind, whether they missed it, how they dreamed their life might go, I didn't know any of that. All I knew was that they would never go back. Ryu didn't like talking about their painful past and impossible future any more than I did.

I couldn't ask them for help. I couldn't ask them to risk their job like that. Whatever usual parameters defined friendships, relationships, or friendly but distant exes, those rules didn't apply anymore, not in the asteroid belt, where everybody was counting the dollars in their personal debt and the days on their corporate contracts, and information was more valuable than human life.

"Hester," they said, when I did not answer.

"I am kinda messed up about it," I said finally. "About David. I didn't think it would be this bad."

"Do you need—"

I eased away when they reached for me. "I need to find out who killed him."

"Yeah. Okay. Do you want me to walk you to the warehouse?"

"Why would you do that?" I said.

Ryu laughed, although there was little amusement in it. "Because there's a murderer on this station?"

"I'll be fine. You're supposed to be resting." I reached out to touch their hand gently, barely a brush of my metal fingers over their skin. They had never flinched from those fingers, and they didn't now. "I heard some asshole got you electrocuted in a maintenance shaft. You should take a nap."

"Fine," they said. "I expect you'll have the killer identified by the time I wake up."

TWELVE

Nimue in the evening was quiet but not silent, filled with an encompassing industrial lullaby of flowing air and humming machines and rumbling gears, the bumps and thumps and metallic whispers of repair bots just beyond the walls, all singing their own songs to their own melodies. It was not comforting, exactly, but it was familiar. Even so, I felt a prickle of unease between my shoulder blades as I entered the cargo warehouse.

The crew were scattered around the station, catching up on the work that had been delayed over the past few days. I didn't like having our suspects out of sight, so I asked the Overseer to show me the location of everybody on Nimue. It wouldn't let me look at any active visual surveillance; for that I needed permission from the company and the agreement of the Overseer, neither of which was likely at the moment. What I could access was a map with current ID tracking data. It would have to do.

Adisa was already in the warehouse, near the airlock where David had died. Sigrah and van Arendonk were in her office in Ops. Mary Ping was in her quarters, Neeta Hunter in the robotics lab. The rest of the crew were in the living quarters or in Ops. Nobody was in the mine. It looked like Sigrah's insistence that they keep working had not persuaded anybody to give up their night for a full shift.

The Overseer turned on lights ahead of me and shut them off behind me, creating the uncomfortable feeling of being onstage and unable to escape an insistent spotlight. Everywhere outside of the light, down every long canyon between the stacked cargo containers and towering racks, the warehouse sank into deep gray shadows. The soft peel-tap sound of my gecko boots was disconcertingly loud. Around me long, shadowy canyons stretched between the towers of shipping containers. Even in Nimue's slight gravity, my shoulder and hip were beginning to twinge. Every day it began as a gentle ache where the artificial limbs attached to joints that had been shattered and pieced together again; over hours of use without rest the pain grew into fiery hot spots that were impossible to ignore. That was something the smug, strutting doctors who claimed to redefine humanity with gleaming limbs and skin facsimiles never advertised: they didn't know how to make pain go away.

I thought about Mary Ping reaching across the table, asking to touch my hand. The hunger in her expression. How it made my skin crawl.

I asked the Overseer for any of the investigative query results it could give me, and I read through what it provided as I walked toward Adisa. None of David's personal communications had been flagged as suspicious; he wasn't in contact with any known or suspected criminals or criminal enterprises. That was hardly a surprise; I already knew he was hiding his communications. He also hadn't spent any time looking into others' communications records or personnel files or financial records, all the things one might be expected to study if one were interested in pursuing a sideline in blackmail. I wanted to find out whether the Overseer agreed with the crew about who David spent most of his time talking to, but that would have to wait until I got back into the systems room.

Adisa was waiting outside the airlock. He looked up from his PD at the sound of my gecko soles and said, "Once a month Ned Delicata goes out this door for a maintenance check. Supposed to be routine, but some of them take him a couple of hours or more. There's a power station for the cargo transport system nearby, yeah?"

"Was he alone?"

"Aye, usually. There's no record of Prussenko ever going out through this door."

I didn't want to stand too close to the airlock. I wondered who would get the job of cleaning up David's blood. They would probably send a bot to do it.

"Delicata didn't mention using this airlock when we spoke to him," I said. We hadn't asked either. We should have. Maybe Mary Ping was right. Maybe we were too used to relying on surveillance to tell us what we needed to know.

"No, he didn't." Adisa looked to the left and right. "Where's the nearest incinerator?"

The Overseer answered by highlighting the locations on my PD. There were two incinerators, two recyclers, and one large-format waste disposal unit in the cargo warehouse. We split up to check the nearest two units, and when that proved fruitless, we rejoined to cross to the other side of the warehouse.

Adisa was quiet as we walked together. I could not guess what he was thinking. I thought about what Ryu had said earlier: he wasn't bad to work with, when he decided to give a fuck. I wondered if this was him giving a fuck or not. I honestly couldn't tell. I knew we had to do this bit of busywork, to make sure the killer hadn't disposed of evidence in an obvious and idiotic spot, but I also knew that we weren't going to find a murderer by searching for the charred remains of a bloody space suit. I was going to find them by learning whatever it was that David had discovered.

I shuffled the station map off my PD screen and went back to looking over my query results.

"Find anything interesting in Prussenko's data?" Adisa said.

"Maybe," I said slowly. "Nothing obvious. David's communications are clean. He didn't do any obvious snooping for blackmail material. Nothing that I can find, anyway. He could have been really good at covering his tracks."

"So good that you can't find them?"

I couldn't tell if he was mocking me or not. "I'm still looking. I can confirm that what the crew told us is true. David did spend a lot of time getting into things that weren't technically his job." I consulted my PD to run down the list. "Geological reports. Three-dimensional structural maps of the asteroid. Repair requests. Fuel line leaks. Equipment breakages. Cargo manifests. Power usage stats. He even looked at plumbing issues. Why the hell would he care about plumbing issues? His tracking data patterns put him all over the facility. He flagged a whole lot of operational discrepancies, but he never wrote up any reports about what he was doing. Never summarized any results to share."

"All recently?"

I scrolled to the top of the list. "Recently he's been most focused on power and fuel numbers. And cargo manifests. He looked at a lot of those."

I frowned, thinking through the possibilities. Water. Fuel. Rare metals. All valuable, sure, but I couldn't imagine a scheme in which stealing any of those would net anybody much of a profit. Transport was too expensive in deep space. Data was so much more lucrative.

"This seems like a pretty difficult place to run black market trade," I said. "I assumed because of the transmitter that he was only interested in data, but maybe he stumbled across somebody else stealing fuel or materials? Is that even possible? Do people steal from mines like this?"

"Aye, sometimes. Not often. They usually target stations with ports and shipyards for equipment, ship parts, if they're going for something solid. Or hospitals, for the drugs. But if something's not bolted down, somebody will try to take it. And Prussenko died in a cargo warehouse."

"Yes. He did." I looked at the list of David's recent activities again. "What I don't understand is why the Overseer didn't flag any of these discrepancies that David found. The errors in cargo manifests and fuel volume, that sort of thing. That sort of boring detail is exactly what steward AIs are good at. Unless it has an exceptionally large margin of acceptable error? Which might be exactly how somebody could get away with stealing, I suppose. I've never looked into how Overseers learn their error margins."

We came to the end of a row of cargo containers, and a wide space opened before us. There was cargo-moving machinery parked around the edges, as well as a few huge pallets of what looked like raw materials—iron or some other metal, but whether it was newly arrived or due to be shipped away, I had no idea. Overhead was the transport crane, unmoving for now. In the tall, dark wall ahead of us was the broad opening to the transport tunnels that carried cargo to the rest of the facility. Beneath the tunnel opening was the large-format waste disposal unit, with a recycler on one side and incinerator on the other. All of it was dwarfed by the scale of the warehouse, the ceiling so high above, and I felt a strange sense of vertigo, to go from the claustrophobic canyons of the cargo rows to this dizzyingly open space, where the lights were muted and weak, like the sun straining on an overcast day.

It was easier to keep my eyes on the floor. To pretend the gravity was strong enough to matter. To remember up and down and never allow the darkness to confuse me.

"Why are you working security?" Adisa asked, as we started toward the incinerator.

The question caught me off guard. "What?"

"You're an AI expert. Why are you working security?"

There was nothing more than mild curiosity in his tone, but it still rankled. He hadn't asked when I'd made my request to join the investigation, even though he must have known who I was. I couldn't imagine why he was asking now. He had no reason to care. I was doing my job. More thoroughly than most Parthenope OSD officers ever managed, since we were here actually having to investigate something, rather than just watching surveillance and locking somebody up. Maybe it was my first murder that wasn't one drunken asshole smashing another over the head with a pipe wrench, and maybe I had missed a few things and overlooked a few obvious tasks until he pointed them out, but I was doing the work I needed to do.

"It was the least shit of all the shit options they gave me," I said shortly.

The Parthenope representative who had come to "discuss

your opportunities" while I was still in the hospital had not had very much to offer. She had stood beside my bed—didn't take a chair, had no intention of lingering longer than she had to—and never once looked at my face or my newly acquired prosthetics. She hadn't even looked up from her PD as she read off the positions Parthenope had available for somebody in my situation. She listed salaries, contract lengths, expected duties, her voice as flat as that of an AI with a bad natural language algorithm. I was on the fading edge of that morning's pain medications, and beneath the throbbing ache of the surgical wounds was something more subtle, more insidious: an incessant itch in my left foot, the foot that no longer existed and could never be scratched. The doctors assured me it would fade with time, as the nerve treatment continued and my neurons learned to speak directly to the prosthetic. And it had, eventually, but on that day, when the leg had been newly fitted, all I could feel was that itch, an itch so great I wanted to kick the blankets away—kick the company woman and her list of demeaning jobs—kick and kick and kick until I couldn't feel anything but screaming pain anymore.

I might have made a noise. I might have moved. Whatever I did, it drew the woman's attention, and she met my eyes for the first time.

"What are your thoughts?" she said.

She didn't care to hear my thoughts, which were that every single job she offered was so far beneath me it was barely worth considering. She didn't want to hear me spew my qualifications and degrees like so much bile over her clean white blazer. Parthenope could afford all the experts it wanted and more, and I had spent the last decade of my life focused with laser intensity on a project that had earned no profit for anybody and therefore had no demonstrable value within the rubric of Parthenope's assessment.

"I can make some suggestions, if you like," said the woman. "Have you considered working as a data analyst with the Operational Security Department? You could do important work in identifying potential dangers before anybody gets hurt."

Later, when I was less medicated and more alert, I realized that she had not been making suggestions at all. She had been feeding me what Parthenope's hiring algorithm wanted her to feed me. The manager AI that organized all of the company's personnel had looked at my skills, looked at my qualifications, looked at my debt, looked at the medical bills that would only continue to grow. It had looked at how I had gotten into that mess in the first place and how likely I was to leave at the first opportunity. It had made a calculation designed to maximize how long the company could keep me under its thumb for the least amount of pay. It had known from my educational and research background that I would be too proud to accept a low-level systems maintenance job. It had also known from the circumstances of the *Symposium* disaster that the representative could drop a few key words into our largely one-sided conversation to sink their hooks into my guilt and anger. *Preventable tragedy. Better mission screening. Crew protection.* She didn't have to mention Kristin Herd or all I'd lost. She didn't have to ask me if I had ever suspected we were in danger. All she had to do was offer the right job.

All of that was standard practice for corporate hiring. I knew that. I had always known that. It made no difference. Knowing an ugly truth and having the power to fight it are two very different things.

After I'd agreed to the security job and signed away five

years of my life, the woman had smiled for the first time since coming into the room. It was no more sincere than her voice and had as much warmth as the frozen talus that made up the surface of Hygiea.

What she hadn't known was that not everybody had missed the danger aboard *Symposium*. Vanguard hadn't. It had known Kristin was trouble from the start. We had just been too arrogant to listen.

He said she let things slip through the cracks, Hunter had said, about the way David and Mary Ping worked together. I didn't know how much I could trust anything Hunter said. *Things that she ought to have trained the Overseer to catch.*

I powered on the incinerator in Nimue's cargo warehouse. My thoughts were scattered, tumbling over one another, but I still had this one small, insignificant task to perform. The unit didn't require any sort of crew ID or access code. Its logs showed that it had been used the night of David's death. During the surveillance blackout.

A small burn. Very brief. Only a few kilos of material.

I leaned my forehead against the smooth, cool control panel while the machine pulled up the automated content assessment.

Polymers. Metals. Both of varieties common in radiation-proof vacuum suits.

Trace amounts of organics. Amino acids, lipids, proteins, water. Enough to trigger the sensors, not enough to require a biohazard alert.

"Hey." I didn't speak loudly, but my voice echoed through the vast warehouse. "I found it."

Adisa came over to look at the screen then tucked his hands into his pockets and leaned one shoulder against the front of the incinerator. "So Prussenko arranged to meet somebody out here. Maybe an accomplice. Maybe not. Either he learned something about what they were up to or they learned something about what he was up to. Something that required them to go outside."

I called up the station maps on my PD to take another look at what was accessible through the airlock. "There's the power structure and lots of other machinery for the cargo transport system. A big crane complex. Oh—and one of the radio antennae. It's about thirty meters from the door."

"Any sign Prussenko was using the radio array? Could he be hijacking that antenna too?"

"I didn't see evidence of that, but I also didn't look as closely because the radio array hasn't had any ongoing problems," I said. "It would be far from ideal for transferring any large amount of data, but he might have used it for encrypted messages. Okay, so David and the killer were supposed to head outside. But they disagree about something. They fight."

Adisa tilted his head slightly. "Do they? Why did the killer bring the weapon into the airlock?"

"Oh. Right. Well, then, *maybe* they fight. Or maybe the killer attacks without warning. And afterward cleans up by getting rid of the vac suits."

"We should try to identify where those suits came from. And narrow down what it is out there we need to look for before we go look for it." He pushed away from the wall. "I want to talk to the man who's been in and out that door and never mentioned it. After that, we're going to have to take a look for ourselves."

Of course. Of *course* we would have to go outside. Actually outside this time, not just near it. We had to see what David had been planning to see. The prospect made me cold and queasy.

"Are we going out . . . tonight?" I said.

Adisa looked at the time on his PD. "That seems unwise.

We've all been on duty too long to make a safe exterior walk, and if any more of my junior officers get hurt on duty, people might start asking questions. We'll get a few hours' rest first, aye? I'm going to talk to Ned Delicata again." He took a few steps backward, then added, "Grab the data from this unit, yeah? We'll need it for the report."

I did as he said before starting back toward the warehouse entrance. The lights followed me, rising and falling in the gaps between the shipping containers. I was thinking about how else I could search the Overseer's data. About what I would say to Ryu when I checked on them again that wouldn't give away how worried I was. About how impossible it would be for me to sleep while knowing I had to go outside the station soon. About what the hell David had been trying to tell me. I wasn't paying much attention to what was around me, so when the next bank of lights came on and illuminated a figure standing before me, I was so startled I flinched and dropped my PD.

"I didn't mean to scare you," said Mary Ping. She was smiling, that enigma of a smile that made my skin crawl. "I only want to talk."

THIRTEEN

Mary Ping approached with a graceful stride, moving from the edge of our shared spotlight to the center. She stopped about two meters away. A bank of lights switched off behind me. The darkness in the warehouse grew deeper.

"You needn't look so worried. I'm no threat to you," she said.

She was empty-handed, dressed only in her jumpsuit, without even a PD or a radio. I had both, although I had no weapon. I wasn't approved to use an OSD-issued nonlethal electroshock weapon. For that, I would need Adisa or Ryu. I would have to call for help—and I could, if I needed to.

Knowing that did nothing to ease my nerves. I didn't like that Mary Ping was here. I didn't like that Sigrah refused to let us restrict the crew movement because it would negatively impact productivity. I didn't like that Ping had waited until Adisa was gone to approach me. The rest of the station suddenly felt very far away.

I bent down to pick up my PD. "What do you want?" I asked. There was an angry snap in my voice, one I would normally try to quash, but now I didn't bother.

"I wonder why the company would assign you to this investigation," Mary Ping said. "The rostering algorithm usually avoids putting acquaintances of victims on investigation teams."

"I asked to be included." I gestured impatiently toward the exit. "I have work to do, so either tell me what you want or don't, but do it quickly."

"Why did you ask? David told me he wasn't in contact with any of the *Symposium* survivors. You weren't friends anymore."

It stung, to hear her say it, to know that David might have said it as well. "Why does it matter? You weren't friends with him either."

"Was he speaking the truth? Your friendship was so easily sundered?" Ping said.

She took a step forward. It was all I could do not to step back in response.

"It's not relevant now." I made myself move forward instead, to walk purposefully toward her, to play at harried and dismissive—however unconvincing—in every motion. "If you'll excuse me."

She grabbed my arm as I tried to pass. Left arm, metal arm, and I felt it in the twist on my shoulder, the slight pressure on my joint, more than in the touch of her fingers, of which there was only a hint, like the brush of a feather. Lifelike sensory capabilities for prosthetic parts cost more. I was used to it by now, the lack of feeling, but I was not at all used to being grabbed unexpectedly.

I froze a beat before pulling away, and in that moment of

hesitation Ping leaned close and murmured in my ear, "I know he asked you for help."

I twisted out of her grasp and stepped back. Stepped back again and bumped into the side of a shipping container. I had suspected before. Now I was certain: she knew about David's message to me. What I did not know was whether she knew exactly what he had said. She could have found evidence of it somewhere in the comms system or in David's personal devices. She could have overheard him or spoken to him or simply made a very logical guess. I wasn't about to admit anything to her.

"What are you talking about?" I said.

Instead of answering, Ping said, "You're still looking for the reason, aren't you? All of the questions you're asking, it's because you have no idea why anybody would want him dead."

"Of course we want to know why," I said, with an exaggerated roll of my eyes, feigning impatience. "That's why we're asking all the questions. Do you know something you haven't told us yet?"

"I know you're asking the wrong questions. You have to understand—"

She stopped abruptly and turned her head; her straight black hair swung along her jawline. She peered intently into the darkness for several seconds. My skin prickled as I followed her gaze. I couldn't see anything.

"Understand what?" I said. "By all means, if you want to tell me how to do my job, go ahead."

"You must hate this work so much."

"What?"

"Someone with your background, working in a job like this. It's so far beneath you. You must hate it."

For fuck's sake, having a conversation with her was like

chasing a narcissistic butterfly through a shit-filled meadow. I had no idea if she was doing it to keep me off-balance or if she just didn't know how to follow one thought with another.

"It's not my first choice, but it could be worse," I said. "You haven't told me what you want."

"I understand. I really do. It's frustrating to look at all this—" She swept her arms out to encompass the warehouse, the stations, the shadows. "All of this has been built in service of what? Nothing more than profit?"

"And? What's your point? David was killed because of money? That's your fucking revelation?"

"Doesn't it bother you? All of this for no purpose except chewing up what's around us and making a few wealthy people even more wealthy. All the people working here for their wages when they could be doing something amazing for humanity. All of these resources. All of this innovation."

"You're wasting my time."

"You don't really believe that. You know what I'm talking about. You created something beautiful and powerful. You created it not to serve a corporate master, but to explore and discover. You created something knowing that it would grow to become more—knowing that it would help us become more. You know we can be so much better, if we let them show us the way. You've already taken that step yourself."

I laughed. I couldn't help it. She was so serious, her eyes so wide, her words so intense, there was nothing I could do but laugh. She was the same as the cyberneticist who'd designed my prosthetics, swanning about the hospital corridors with a duckling line of followers behind him, claiming to everybody who would listen that he was redefining humanity in a way that no god could ever comprehend, that every patient who went under his knife would emerge as something wholly new and different. She was the same as the boy with the bleeding eyes back on Hygiea, reaching for my boots because he saw something in my prosthetic limbs that his drug-addled and surgery-muddled mind believed he should crave, and he had to believe it was time, it was time, *now* was time for the AI revolution humanity had been awaiting for centuries. She was the same as the reporter from Ceres who contacted me every couple of months because he was convinced, absolutely convinced, that the woman Hester Marley had died aboard *Symposium* and the AI Vanguard had survived instead, hidden away in the electronics of my prosthetic parts, learning to be human amid the wreckage of my old life.

Then my laughter was gone and in that moment I hated Mary Ping so much I was breathless. I was here for the man who had once been my friend, for the memories and the loss we had shared, and because it was the last thing he had asked of me before he died. I was here for my own foolish, selfish, fallibly human reasons. I was not here to fuel the mad light in Mary Ping's eyes, to feed the hunger she felt when she looked at me and saw only gleaming metal, never pain. She didn't know anything. She believed she understood something nobody else was smart enough to grasp, but all she could see was her own desires, distorted and reflected back to her, in everyone she met. David was dead. Ryu was hurt. I had no answers. I was sick with anger for how pathetic and grasping she was.

"Last chance," I said. "Do you know something about David's death or not?"

"I know why he died."

"Sure you do. So tell me."

"The others were talking about what you and the Martian

asked them. You think David stumbled into something important and dangerous in his work."

"It's a possibility."

"You've got it backwards. He and his little friend didn't find something hidden *in* the data. What he found *is* the data."

I studied her face carefully. "What does that mean?"

"Safety Officer Marley," she chided. "We are intelligent women. You know what I mean."

My mind was already racing. Fuel shortages. Energy fluctuations. Geological assays. Facility efficiency. Misplaced cargo. Everything David rightfully had access to as sysadmin. Boring station bullshit. Details about what Parthenope was mining. How much progress they were making. How much water they extracted. How efficiently they produced fuel. How much product they shipped away.

My heart skipped with excitement. Ping was saying that all the boring bullshit David spent his time going through wasn't beside the point. It wasn't the haystack in which the lone valuable needle had been hidden. All that boring bullshit *was* the point.

Nimue was meant to be the jewel in Parthenope's growing crown. Its lineup of powerful investors, its decades' worth of productivity and profit projections reaching into the future, the nonstop PR campaign to convince everybody they were reshaping commerce in the asteroid belt, it was all tied up in Nimue's success. They had, quite literally, bet the entire company on it.

"It's all a lie, isn't it?" I gestured to the massive room around us; Ping's eyes followed the track of my metal fingers. "This whole fucking facility. It's supposed to be completely self-sufficient and so efficient that it's already exporting fuel. But it's not, is it? It's not anywhere near what Parthenope is claiming it should be. That's what David figured out. The whole facility is a huge fucking scam, and the company will collapse if anybody finds out. Does everybody know? Who else knows?"

She was so tense I could see her cheek muscles twitching, her hands trembling. "You're thinking too small. David made the same mistake."

"What do you mean? What mistake?"

"He thought he could reveal the truth for his own uses."

All of my excitement turned cold and congealed in my gut.

"He told you that?" I asked.

"He couldn't see anything outside his own life. His own selfish unhappiness."

I felt queasy. "When did he tell you that? When did you talk to him?"

She stepped closer suddenly and grabbed my arm. I tried to pull away, but she wouldn't let go. "I wanted him to understand. I was going to show him, make him see how beautiful it can be, if only he allowed it. But it was a mistake. He was fixated on what the company is doing—what the *humans* are doing. He didn't understand that sometimes sacrifices are necessary. Some things are so much more important than one man's ideas of right and wrong."

I could barely speak. "What did you do?"

"I can explain. Let me show you. I can show you what I wanted to share with him. Everything's going to change soon. I know you'll understand when you see it. You more than anybody." Her eyes were shining and wide. "I never expected you to come here. I didn't even think it was possible. This is better than I thought it could be."

"Is that—" Her fingers were wrapped tight around the

prosthetic humerus of my left arm. Her voice was breathy and fast. I struggled to keep up. "Is that what you said to David? What did you say to him? When you arranged to meet him?"

"I offered to show him the truth. But he was afraid. He was not being rational."

"What truth? Is there proof that Parthenope is lying about this facility? David was going to find it, and that's why you attacked him?"

Mary Ping's mouth turned in a slight frown. "It didn't have to happen like that."

I shoved her away from me. "You killed him."

"He didn't understand. You're making the same mistake. Don't let your small, scared little mind control you. You have to listen to me. I didn't want to hurt him. He could have just waited. Only a few days, that was all I asked for. He was going to ruin everything. I didn't want to—"

She stopped abruptly. She was looking past me, her eyes wide. She stumbled backward a few steps, as though I had pushed her again, but there was a good meter between us.

"No," she whispered. "What are you doing here?"

I turned, my gecko boots squeaking faintly.

There was somebody else in the warehouse.

They were no more than a silhouette, the outline of their body traced by the sparse light: a gleam on the edge of a shoulder, a reflection on the side of a helmet. It was that reflection that held my gaze. They were wearing some sort of space suit, one that obscured their face behind a flat shield and enclosed their trunk and limbs in a hard black carapace. It was a mechanical suit, powered and armored but not as bulky as those used for cargo maneuvering or spacewalks. I couldn't see it well enough to make out the details.

They were still, so still they might have been a statue, a slice of dark against the shadows.

Then, in a heartbeat, they were coming toward us.

They moved with such astonishing speed it took my breath away. The suit was so well balanced their loping stride wasted not a single motion, with no noise greater than a gentle whir. Within seconds they were upon us. I stumbled away, tripping over myself in my hurry to retreat, fumbling for my radio as I lost my balance and fell awkwardly into a shipping container.

There was a flash of light—a bright green blink—and Mary gasped.

That bright flash, so much brighter than anything else in that warehouse, confused the input from my prosthetic eye into a stutter of double vision. I squeezed my eyes shut, fighting back the sudden nausea and pain.

When I opened them again, there was a multilegged bot racing up Mary Ping's leg. She yelped and batted at it, kicked her leg wildly. The bot scurried over her hip, her waist, and dodged her grasping hands to reach the center of her torso.

Her eyes widened in shock and she took in a sharp, pained breath. Her lips were parted, her hands frozen in rigid claws over the bot. Beneath her rasping breath I heard a quick snapping sound. An acrid chemical scent drifted on the air. With it came the unmistakable scent of blood.

Mary Ping screamed. Red blossomed on her chest as she grasped at the bot, but she could not tear it away.

"Get it off me!" She turned in frantic circles, batting helplessly at the bot. "Get it off, get it away, get it—"

There was a white flash—her scream stopped abruptly—and a deafening concussion of sound. The world became a storm of flashing lights as the noise faded. I staggered to the side, thrown off-balance by the confusion of my eyes and ears. My shoulder hit the side of a shipping container; my knees struck the floor.

Mary was not screaming anymore. There was a damp gurgle. A whimper.

I pushed myself upright, shaking my head to settle the flashing in my left eye. I crawled toward Mary. My right hand slipped on something warm and wet. Her blood, spreading across the floor.

FOURTEEN

She was lying on her side with her eyes and mouth open. Her chest was a ruin of scorched flesh and shattered ribs. A twist of smoke rose from the wound, and blood seeped through ragged gaps in the cauterized flesh. The remains of the bot clung to the skin just below her collarbone with two intact legs; the rest of it had been destroyed. The acrid chemical smell faded, replaced by the scent of cooked meat. Nausea roiled in my gut and I gagged, coughed, struggled against the urge to vomit.

A second bot crept along her leg, illuminated by a delicate blue internal light. Its legs folded and unfolded elegantly, letting it cling with three one moment, six the next, constantly shifting its shape as it picked its way over the landscape of Ping's body. The blue light flashed brighter for a second, and my heart squeezed with panic.

I grabbed the bot with my blood-smeared hand, not thinking, wanting nothing more than to pull it away from her. I felt a sting of pain and shook my hand frantically, stirring the bot into a whipping whirlwind of wire. It legs folded into its body until only two remained extended; those two grasped my palm and wrist, piercing the skin. The entire device emitted a biting chemical smell, powerful enough to make me cough.

I flung the bot away from me—tearing the legs from my hand—and sent it slamming into the side of a shipping container. One of the bot's legs bent and worked, turning in a helpless circle as it tried to stand.

I scrambled to my feet—almost lost my balance again—and I stomped on it. It made a loud, satisfying crunch beneath my boot.

When I looked up, the person in the mech suit was still standing several meters away.

"Stop!" I shouted, although they hadn't yet moved. My voice echoed dully from the shipping containers around us. "Don't move!"

I reached for my radio, but I had dropped it along with my PD. I had to call for help. Blood trickled from the wounds on my hand, the metallic scent mingling with the acrid accelerant. I couldn't take my eyes off the killer.

They remained eerily still. I could see absolutely nothing behind the blankness of their faceplate. They had no headlamp or flashlight. They stood just beyond the bright circle of the ceiling lights, not quite in shadow but not illuminated either. Everything about the suit was featureless and black, with its supple limbs blending seamlessly into hidden joints, and not a single external obvious vulnerability in its mechanical workings. I had never seen anything like it.

"I need you to identify yourself," I said. I didn't know if it was the right thing to say. It was never my job to bring suspects into custody. "Reach up very slowly and take off your helmet. Do you hear me? Take off your helmet and identify yourself."

I glanced down again; my PD and radio had slid several meters away. One look at the map would tell me who was standing before me. Or one question.

"Overseer," I said, raising my voice so it could carry. "Please summon Safety Inspector Adisa to this location and identify the crew member— Shit!"

I was expecting them to turn and run, or reach for another explosive bot to throw at me, or lunge toward me in an attack. I was not expecting them to bend their knees and jump backward, then do it again, and again, covering two or three meters with every bound, the motion so smooth and so strange I spent a few stunned seconds trying to work out how the suit helped them keep their balance.

Then I stopped staring and sprinted after them.

I bounded down the row with a wild, flailing abandon, letting my gecko soles anchor me, momentarily forgetting that I had no real practice running in gravity this low. The insistent ache in my left hip returned, but I gritted through it. I wasn't fast enough—I didn't think anybody would have been fast enough—and within moments the killer changed directions. They jumped again, twisting in midair, and turned a corner into an intersecting canyon of cargo containers.

I heard them land, heard the pounding of their boots on the warehouse floor. By the time I rounded the same corner, they were well ahead of me. I raced after them, running as fast as I could, my heart thumping with the effort. No extreme exertion, the doctors had said. Gentle exercise only. Let your body learn to move again. I fucking hated being scolded by doctors.

At the end of the shipping containers, I charged into a broad, open space for about two steps before my left leg slammed into a solid obstacle at exactly shin height.

There was a solid clink of metal on metal, followed by an explosion of fiery-hot pain in my hip joint.

"*Ratfucker!*" I stumbled and fell, dizzy with pain.

It took a moment for me to catch my breath. I had run into a stack of long metal bars, set directly across the gap between the shipping containers. I staggered to my feet, gasping for breath. The bars hadn't been there before; they were from one of the pallet stacks several meters away, the ones I had passed while looking for the incinerator. The killer had moved them—taken them from the stack and placed them here—and they had done it quickly, breaking the metal bands on the stack and moving four-meter-long unwieldy pieces of metal in seconds. All before I caught up to them.

The killer was scrambling up a ladder on the warehouse wall, quick and agile as a spider. I stepped over the obstacle—fuck, my hip hurt—but they were already four meters above the floor, five, six. They reached the open entrance of the cargo transport tunnels and an alarm beeped. Radiation warning. They were entering a zone of low shielding.

The alarm didn't stop them. They scrambled over the edge and disappeared into the tunnel.

"Fuck. Fuck fuck *fuck*."

I couldn't follow. Even if I could climb the ladder with a wrenched hip and a bleeding hand, I couldn't risk going unprotected into a low-shielding zone. I sure as hell couldn't risk chasing after an armed killer without weapons or backup.

I turned instead and limped back through the warehouse. Every step was agony. Every breath felt raw and shallow.

I staggered like a drunkard back to Mary Ping's body. I

grabbed my radio and PD, and turned my attention to the PD first. The Overseer was still showing me active tracking data for the station, so I brought up the map and panned over it quickly.

"Come on, come on," I muttered. "Who the fuck are you?"

I found myself and Mary Ping on the map—she was a red dot indicating a medical alert—and Adisa coming toward us. Sigrah and Delicata were with him. I found the transport tunnels.

"Come the fuck *on*, where did you go?" I muttered, scanning over the map frantically. "Where are you?"

"Marley!" Adisa's voice carried through the warehouse.

"Over here!" I shouted. I had no idea how to describe where I was.

The sound of noisy gecko soles slapping on the floor drew closer, and Adisa came running up with Sigrah and Delicata right behind him.

"What the hell—" He stopped abruptly when he saw Ping.

Sigrah tried to push by him. "Mary! What happened?"

Adisa held out his arm and stepped in front of her. "Don't. Stay back."

"What the fuck did you do to her?" Delicata said, whirling to face me.

"Nothing. It was—I don't know who it was. I couldn't see their face. They were wearing a mech suit—"

He made a noise in his throat, something between a gasp and a growl. "That's not possible."

"—and I couldn't identify them," I said. "They fled into the cargo tunnels. I've got the tracking data but we need a head count—"

"*Here?* Not fucking possible," Delicata said again. He stepped up close to me. "What the fuck did you do?"

"Back off, Ned," Sigrah said, her voice low and tight.

He whirled around to face her. "What the fuck is going on here? This isn't fucking right. You know there's something going on. You never said—"

"I said back *off*, Ned. Let the safety officers do their jobs."

Delicata gritted his teeth; I saw the muscles working in his jaw. He was glaring at Sigrah, having apparently forgotten about me, and she was glaring right back. I would have given anything to hear whatever it was he had been about to say, the words she had cut off so cleanly.

"Go," Sigrah said to him. "Gather the others in Res. Everybody. I don't want anybody alone right now."

Delicata nodded curtly. He cast one more look at Mary Ping, his expression dark and troubled, before leaving.

Adisa was already on his radio. ". . . and wake up Ryu and tell them to get the hell out here, aye?"

"On it." Van Arendonk's answer was clipped. "What happened?"

"Not sure yet," Adisa said, looking at me. He crouched beside the crushed bot, the one I had smashed with my boot. He studied it for a second before picking it up gingerly, turning it over in his hands. "Somebody attacked Mary Ping. Marley saw it but wasn't able to identify the killer. Marley? Where did they go?"

"Into the cargo tunnels. I can't fucking find them," I said. "I'm looking. I'm looking."

I was smearing blood all over the PD as I tried to navigate the maps. My hand was shaking. I wanted to slump against the container and slide down to the floor. The ache in my hip was unbearable and my head was throbbing. I wanted to close my eyes in a dark, quiet room. I wanted to erase the last hour. I could not stop hearing Mary Ping's screams. The bitter, powerful smell of the accelerant from the bots was seared into my nostrils.

Adisa stood up and turned to Sigrah. He still had the crushed spider bot in his hand. He held it out to her; she flinched away from it.

"Did you know you had this on your station?" he asked.

Sigrah glowered at the spider. "Am I supposed to know what that is?"

Even I could tell she was lying. Adisa was even less impressed. "You have two dead crew members, a criminal operation going on for months that you never noticed, and now you've got somebody running around with autonomous weapons that have been illegal throughout the system for twenty-five years. Am I supposed to believe that you're so fucking shit at your job that you know nothing about any of it?"

Sigrah pushed Adisa's hand away. "Get that out of my face."

On the map, the crew was gathering in Res. There was nobody in the cargo tunnels near the warehouse. Nobody had passed through the exits into other parts of the station. The security system wasn't scanning the killer's ID anywhere. The suit had to be blocking the chip—that was the only thing that made sense. I was going to have to find them the old-fashioned way.

"Overseer, are the ID scans in the tunnels working? Show me the live surveillance. Every camera in the tunnels."

The Overseer answered with a flash of the words: **Data access restricted.**

Right. Fuck. I needed to be back in the systems room—I needed access beyond what I had already been granted. Without that, all I had to go on was the map of the station, and the map wasn't telling me anything. I focused again on Ops and Res. There were only eleven crew on the station, and Ping was dead, and Sigrah had been with Adisa, so that left nine to account for. Delicata was in the junction. Melendez was leaving the assay laboratory as van Arendonk approached in the Ops corridor. Yee was in her quarters, as was Vera. King, Balthazar, and Dietrich-Yun were in the common room. Dolin was in the exercise room.

I looked again. Counted heads.

He and his little friend, Ping had said.

"Hunter," I said. "It's Hunter."

Adisa cut off whatever he was saying. "You're certain?"

"She was in her quarters. She's not anymore."

"Hugo, do you have eyes on Neeta Hunter?" Adisa said. "Has anybody seen her?"

Neeta Hunter, with her expensive blue eyes and her expensive silver hair, her tears that flowed so freely. With her powerful connections and her friendship with David even she hadn't seemed to understand. It was so fucking obvious in retrospect. If anybody on Nimue had the contacts that would make corporate espionage lucrative, it was her. And she had already blamed Mary Ping for David's death.

"She's not here," van Arendonk said.

"Where the fuck is she?" I asked. "Where is she? Overseer, show me Hunter, for fuck's sake."

I was expecting another restricted access warning, but instead the Overseer answered: the map shifted to show Neeta Hunter as a solitary dot amid a bewildering labyrinth of lines.

"Where is that?"

Sigrah leaned over for a look. "Level 8. She just stepped off the lift. Why the hell would she be down there? She's not authorized—"

"Marley, with me," Adisa said. He turned on his heel and started walking.

"You're not authorized!" Sigrah said, rushing after him. "You can't just go into the facility without escort. It's an active mine. The safety bond does not cover—"

"Can we secure the level to make sure she doesn't leave?" Adisa asked, talking right over her.

She kept trying. "I have to go with you. This is a liability. You can't—"

Adisa whirled to look at her as we all reached the door. "You are going to stay here with the rest of your crew. Can you secure the level to keep her there?"

"You do not have the authority to make such a demand," Sigrah said.

"Add it to your list of complaints for HQ." Adisa stepped into the junction, where van Arendonk was waiting. "The crew—and the foreperson—are restricted to this section. Get Ryu to watch them."

Van Arendonk hesitated for only a second. He was looking at Adisa. "Right. And you're going to . . . ?"

"We're going to go find Neeta Hunter," Adisa said. "Marley?"

I was already entering the security access code to enter the mine.

FIFTEEN

Only when the lift doors closed and the carriage began to move did I realize Adisa was still holding the crushed bot.

"Is that safe?" I said. I could see my blood staining the ends of its thin legs.

He plucked at one of the legs, twisted it, broke it free. "It's harmless now."

"Um. Okay. What is it?"

"We used to call them spiders." He dropped the first leg and twisted another off. His voice was strangely flat, and he didn't look up from the bot as he spoke. "Or Sorrells, sometimes, because they were built by Sorrell-Larkin and used by their mercenaries. Haven't seen one in years. The UEN used them during the war."

Sorrell-Larkin was, these days, yet another company mining the asteroid belt, but I had some vague recollection that they had gotten their start as an arms manufacturer and private security firm during the war. "What for? For bombing? Or starting fires?"

"Oh, they're much more versatile than that, yeah? Good for fires and explosions, aye." He turned it over. "Poisoning food and water supplies." Peeled off the thin metal carapace on the underside. "Contaminating medical aid shipments." Ripped the insides out with a single smart tug. "Burning fuel reserves."

Adisa gripped another leg and snapped it off. It was disconcerting to watch. He was so focused, like a child with a bug he had captured under a glass. I hadn't realized until that moment how calm his gestures usually were, not until I saw his hands now in constant, nervous motion.

"Assassinations," he added, after a moment's pause. He did not raise his voice, but there was a tightness in his words that made me tense, made me want to edge away from him in the lift.

A memory from my childhood on Earth: a thin-lipped teacher at the front of the classroom, his mustache trembling as he sniffed and said, *The UEN did not conduct assassinations. Most of those events were false flag operations carried out by Martian suicide bombers.* The war had been over for a few years at that point, and most of what happened—most of what the UEN did—was already public knowledge. The teacher knew he was repeating lies. He just didn't care.

I said nothing. Adisa wasn't finished.

"They would send a nest of these into crowds of protesters outside military bases. Food banks. Water plants." Adisa pried another one of the legs out from beneath the round little body, watched the way it bent and twisted almost freely. "Refugee camps. Hospitals."

I had seen footage of those attacks, the ones the UEN had blamed on Martians until they couldn't deny the truth anymore. Hundreds or thousands of desperate, frightened people gathered together, asking for food or medicine or for somebody to hear them, and an explosion would go off, and another, another, a whole series of them like fireworks popping through the crowd, and people would panic, run, crush each other in an attempt to get away. I didn't ask Adisa if he had seen those attacks in person. I already knew what he would say.

"This is quite a bit more advanced than what they had then. Your friend was a roboticist."

"David wouldn't build weapons. He hated even the idea of them."

I stared at the spider, trying to decide if any part of it looked familiar. The legs. The metal plates on the body. The way it had moved. I didn't know. I couldn't imagine David re-creating UEN weapons. Even when he used weapons tech, he worked so hard to leave the deadly purpose behind. He had never built elegant little machines solely to kill people. That wasn't David. That wasn't the man I had known.

"People often abandon their principles in desperate times, aye?"

I felt sick even thinking about it. "I'm not saying it's impossible. Only that . . ." I didn't know what I was saying. I kept thinking about that teacher lying to a roomful of children because he could not admit he had supported atrocities. "Hunter is a roboticist too. She has resources. She could build something like that. There was the mech suit too, and I know David never worked on anything remotely like that. It might have been . . . I don't know. An advanced worksuit of some kind?"

Adisa closed his hand around the spider's little body, held it tight for a second. Then he flung it into the corner of the carriage, where it broke apart. I flinched as the parts skittered across the floor.

"It shouldn't be here," he said. He spoke so quietly I could barely hear him. "It shouldn't be anywhere."

I had to look away from the combination of anger and dismay on his face. It was too raw, too intense. I felt embarrassed to see it, and ashamed of my embarrassment, and suddenly, brightly angry at David—for this, for being involved, for bringing me here, for dying. I checked the map with the tracking data again: Hunter had not moved from Level 8. We were moving through sections of the station, through areas for fuel manufacturing, volatile processing, water purification, and more. The whole facility extended just over three kilometers down the long axis of Nimue.

It was a long distance to cover, even for a fast lift. It was hard to imagine how Hunter could have traveled so quickly through the station, but perhaps the transport tunnels had cargo movers that weren't bound by the rules of human comfort.

Adisa cleared his throat. "Tell me what happened, aye?"

He meant it was time to include what I had left out when we were standing in front of Sigrah and Delicata. I quickly told him about Mary Ping finding me in the warehouse and what she had said.

"She killed David," I said. "She admitted it to me. She knew David and Hunter were working together. I don't know exactly what they were doing, but I know David found power usage that's not being reported, cargo shipments that aren't tracked, fuel that's produced but never transported off-site. Probably a lot more. That's why he spent so much time looking at other people's work. The facility's supposed to be self-sufficient. He knew something wasn't adding up, and he wanted to find out why. And what he found out is that Parthenope is lying about how successful Nimue is. All those glowing reports they're sending out to their investors and partners are bullshit. The station is nowhere near self-sustaining."

Adisa was quiet for a second. "What was he going to do with this information?"

"Pass it along to whoever was paying him to spy, I guess. Maybe that's Neeta Hunter's family. I don't know, but I bet tracing his contact on Hygiea would tell us more."

"Where does Mary Ping fit into it?" Adisa asked. "Why attack Prussenko? She doesn't strike me as somebody with any company loyalty."

"I don't think she cared about protecting the company at all. It sounded more like she was trying to protect herself. She wanted to make David understand, so maybe she was afraid of being implicated? Or scapegoated. Or she had her own side project going on that she didn't want him to find." I exhaled in frustration. "I don't know. I don't know what she wanted to tell me. I'm not sure she was entirely in her right mind."

The lift began to slow. We were approaching Level 8.

"She's likely still armed. And won't be happy to see us." He drew his electroshock weapon and powered it on.

"Right. Great. You know that won't be much use if she's suited up."

Still, I wished I had taken Ryu's weapon before running into the lift, even if I hadn't the first idea how to use it.

"She didn't kill you before, when she had the chance, aye?"

"I guess she didn't," I said.

"We try to talk to her first. Just talk."

Where the previous levels had been roughly cubic, Level 8 was a massive disk capped onto the deepest end of the massive cylinder. Catwalks radiated from the lift like spokes of a bicycle wheel, and below our feet, visible through the mesh walkways and an incomprehensible jumble of machinery, was the mining equipment. Thirteen huge, toothed boring machines to gnaw away at the solid rock. The wide conduits to transport the material to the center of the wheel. The series of crushing drums and filters at the center. The cone where crushed rock was shunted into the furnace to be scorched to ash, where the intense heat would extract all the water, volatiles, and metals.

The mine was quiet for now. Nimue was in a stabilization phase, prepping for the next stage of expansion. The mining machines were due to fire up within a few days, according to Sigrah; that was why she had refused to stop work.

So much closer to the physical center of the asteroid, gravity did not tug us much in any particular direction, and the cluster of lights around the lift did little to illuminate the vast space. The air smelled of metal and tasted of grit. It felt at first like an abandoned station, or a mausoleum, misted with rock dust and so dim the distant outer edges faded into darkness. It was hard to imagine how different it would be when the mine was fully operational.

But there was movement in the darkness. I became aware of the noise first: metal on metal, faint clatters and clanks, the momentary hum of an engine that revved and faded. I looked around frantically, searching for glints of silver in the darkness, bracing for another hateful little spider—then realized the source was an army of inspection and repair bots crawling over the machinery. I spotted about ten, maybe fifteen, glimpsed through gaps in the machines and in shafts of light in the distance; they were the same dull metal hues as the equipment and darted in and out so swiftly it was impossible to know where they might emerge. It reminded me of roaches swarming a refuse heap.

"Marley." Adisa's voice was quiet. "There."

He nodded toward the left. Along one of the catwalks, about thirty meters from the lift, a bright ring of light surrounded a solitary figure. With his electroshock weapon in hand, Adisa went first. Hunter's silver hair caught the light. She wasn't trying to hide—but neither was there any way for us to approach her unseen. As we neared, I saw that she was on her hands and knees beside a control console. She had the front panel popped open as she rooted around inside. There was a tool bag clipped to the walkway railing beside her.

She noticed our approach when we were about halfway to her. She looked up and sat back on her heels.

"Oh, hello," she said. "Did you need something?"

She reached for her tool bag, and Adisa said, "Don't."

"I was only—is my radio not working? What is it?" she asked.

"Put the tools down and stand up, please." Adisa didn't raise the stun weapon, although he was now close enough to use it. "Slowly."

"I don't understand." Hunter rose to her feet, brushing her hands on her jumpsuit. I saw the exact moment she noticed the weapon in Adisa's hand. Her eyes widened. "What's going on?"

"What are you doing down here?" Adisa asked.

"I'm only trying to finish some work."

"Alone? At this time?"

"I know it's not smart, but . . . What's wrong? Did something happen?"

"Something's not right," I said quietly.

Adisa didn't respond, but I knew he heard me. He had to feel it too. She was afraid, she was confused, but there was nothing in her demeanor that suggested guilt. It had taken us several minutes to get here on the lift, but she had obviously been working for some time. There was no sign of the black mech suit.

Before any of us could say anything else, our radios clicked on.

"You have a problem, Mohammad," said van Arendonk.

Adisa grabbed his radio. "What?"

"The Overseer has been able to track Hunter since she left her quarters. She was never out of range of an ID scan."

"I don't understand. Why are you looking for me?" Hunter asked.

Van Arendonk continued, "She went straight from Res to the lift. Stopped at Level 2 for a few minutes. Went back to the lift. Stopped at Level 5. Back in the lift. Her ID chip was scanned every time."

"I told you, I'm finishing some work," Hunter said.

"Oh, fuck," I said. My heart began thumping anxiously. I clicked on my own radio. "Was she—"

"No," van Arendonk said. "She was not. She hasn't been scanned at any of the warehouse entrances since several hours ago."

Hunter's expression was baffled. "What are you talking about?"

"Then who the hell was that?" I asked.

Van Arendonk said, "I have no fucking idea, Marley."

"Check the surveillance in the tunnels," I said. "You can get permission for that, can't you? Where did they come from? How did they get there?"

"Please tell me what's going on," Hunter said.

"*And*," van Arendonk said, "the rest of the crew are accounted for. All the tracking data is solid. None of them were in the warehouse when Mary Ping died."

"*What?*" Hunter's mouth dropped open. "Mary is *dead*?"

"For fuck's sake." Adisa ran a hand through his hair, then looked at me. "How is that possible?"

"How is what possible? Please!" Hunter's voice rose to a shout, but she looked abashed when we both stared at her. "What's going on?"

Adisa clipped his stun weapon to his belt. "Mary Ping was killed in the cargo warehouse about half an hour ago. You were the only crew member not accounted for at the time."

Hunter put her fingers to her lips. "Oh, no. I didn't do anything. I swear. I was here."

"Somebody has to be fooling the surveillance system," I said to van Arendonk. "Where did the killer go? Are they still in the transport tunnels?"

"Oh, you'll love this," van Arendonk said. There was a slight waver in his voice: he was rattled. "There is no surveillance in the cargo transport system. None at all, no matter what permission we get."

"Bullshit. There has to be. Ask the—" Shit. There was no sysadmin to help him, because both sysadmins had been murdered. "There has to be."

"The system hasn't been operational for months."

"It's been broken forever," Hunter put in. "David filed about fifty reports asking for a surveillance specialist to come fix it."

I had never heard of a Parthenope surveillance system being down for so long, in any part of any station, without the company jumping to fix it. I wondered why Sigrah hadn't mentioned it. It seemed like a rather important detail to leave out when we were supposed to be identifying a killer.

I said, "The Overseer should also have been throwing warnings to HQ constantly."

Van Arendonk made a frustrated noise. "I can only see what the Overseer is showing me, but it doesn't appear to have been a priority. It's a low-shielding zone that's off-limits to crew, so nobody has reason to spend much time there."

That wasn't good enough. There had to be something else going on to make the Overseer dismiss the danger of leaving a large portion of the station, a dangerous potion of the station, unwatched. But the lack of tunnel surveillance was only one part of the problem. "Somebody had to be in the wrong place during the attack. Maybe it looks like they were in their private quarters or taking a fucking piss or—fuck me, or anywhere surveillance doesn't reach."

"Marley," van Arendonk said, "listen to me. I have tracking data for everyone at the time of the attack. Everyone."

Fuck. That wasn't possible. He had to be missing something. He might only have access to the tracking data, but the Overseer had a whole lot more than that, and it would flag any inconsistencies. There were ways to falsify surveillance and tracking data with a deepfake, but it was basically impossible to do quickly or with little notice. I had never heard of it being done successfully in a station run by an Overseer. There would be evidence that the ID scans or cameras or data lines had been tampered with. There would likely be glitches all over any audio and visual recordings. Parthenope's stations had too many cameras, too many audio recorders, too many sensors, too many ID trackers for convincing fakery. There would always be something the Overseer could flag as suspicious. A footstep where none should be. A shadow with no source. Complete silence in a room where a person should be breathing.

I was grasping at straws. "So who was alone and not moving? In a room by themselves? Where does the Overseer pick up any audio-video misfit?"

"I am quite far out of my depth here," van Arendonk said.

"There has to be something. Look again."

"By all means, Safety Officer Marley, please come back here and look for yourself. This is a task better suited to an analyst, don't you think? I should contact HQ for expanded data access."

I started to snipe back at him, even though he was right, but Adisa spoke first.

"There's another possibility," he said. "There could be somebody else here."

For a long moment, nobody reacted.

Hunter let out an uneasy laugh. "What? You mean, on Nimue?"

"A stowaway? Doing, what? Sneaking around the station?" I wanted to laugh too, but Adisa was not joking. His suggestion was completely serious. I started to shake my head. "That's not possible. There's too much surveillance. Even the transportation . . . it's not possible."

"It's not likely, but it's always possible," Adisa said. "It's something we have to consider."

It wasn't as though a stowaway could have just happened by, parked a ship, and sneaked inside. Nimue was eighteen hours from the nearest station. Nobody could approach unnoticed. There was only one place for a ship to dock, and it was under constant surveillance. Even getting from the ship to the cargo transport tunnels, if that's where somebody meant to hide, would have them passing by countless points of Overseer security and surveillance. And that was before they reached the tunnels, where they would have to remain inside a protective suit constantly to avoid the radiation. They would need food, water, warmth. They would need a way to communicate.

Mary Ping had asked, *What are you doing here?* Not *Who*

are you? or *What do you want?* The person in the mech suit was not a stranger.

It had to be one of the ten crew members left on Nimue. A sophisticated surveillance hack, maybe, but behind it would be a face we already knew. Somebody we could identify and confine. Somebody we could find and stop before they killed again.

"I need to get back to the Overseer," I said.

"Please do," said van Arendonk. "It's growing impatient with my clumsiness."

Adisa said, "Hugo, get over to Res to help Ryu keep an eye on the crew. Sigrah and Delicata especially. We're heading back now."

"Good. I'll—"

Van Arendonk's voice cut off abruptly.

"Hugo?" Adisa said.

There was no reply. Silence. Not a chirp, not a crackle, nothing.

"Hugo? I didn't catch that." He lowered his radio slowly. "If he's right—"

An earsplitting wail interrupted him. It was so loud and so high it made my prosthetic ear squeal in protest. Lights flashed with startling, searing brightness. There was another blast of sound before the Overseer's voice came from the radios and nearest control console.

"Warning. The station is being placed on lockdown due to the potential for exposure to harmful radiation." The words echoed in stereo, just a beat offset from one another. "Warning. All personnel must find their way to a safe room immediately."

"What?" I said. "What the fuck is happening?"

"Warning. The station is being placed on lockdown due to the potential for exposure to harmful radiation."

My hand went to the radiation sensor at my belt. The values were still within the safe range. On the high side of the safe range, but not high enough to trigger a warning. The station alarm screamed again.

"Nearest safe room," Adisa said to Hunter. "Where is it?"

"Warning. All personnel must find their way to a safe room immediately."

"Shit, shit." Hunter unsnapped her tool bag from the railing and slung it over her shoulder. "The furnace control room is closest. Over there, there's a ladder. All the way up. Come on."

We ran to the end of the catwalk and made a left turn to approach the base of a tall ladder. Hunter climbed first, with me right behind her. I grabbed the rungs and pulled myself up, fear making my motions awkward, unsteady, my nerves jumping every time the alarm wailed. I was shaking so much that I missed a rung with my boots and swung free. My heart skipped wildly and I let out a startled yelp—I was only holding on with one hand, my left hand, and that felt like holding on with nothing at all. Something caught my leg—Adisa, grabbing my ankle—and moved my right foot back to the rungs.

"We have time," he said. I hated how calm he sounded, how frantic I was in comparison. "You're okay, yeah?"

The ladder was a good fifteen or twenty meters long, but we finally, finally, reached the top. Hunter pushed the hatch open and climbed inside, then turned to help me up. Adisa was right behind me. He scrambled into the room and slammed the hatch shut. In the space between the alarms came the solid clank of the locks engaging.

SIXTEEN

The furnace stretched before us, a glowing red throat of impossible size. The cylinder was largely empty, but in the distance little bursts of light appeared and vanished, like matter and antimatter meeting at the dawn of the universe. Each light sketched a faint tail of dust, a phantom track through the fierce red space, hundreds of meters above us.

A wave of vertigo made the room spin around me. We were below the furnace—this room was turned the wrong way—we had to be looking up from the floor—we weren't even in the center of the level—it wasn't a window. Fuck. I closed my eyes to reorient my brain. Stupid, stupid, stupid. It wasn't a window. This was a shielded control room; the walls probably contained two meters of solid lead. I was looking at a wallscreen that provided a view down the long axis of the furnace. It helped to know that, but only a little. I was still dizzy and nauseated, and the room was so warm sweat sprung to my brow.

I tore my gaze away from the red furnace and looked around for the room's main terminal. I asked the Overseer to identify the location of the high radiation levels. Asked for the report on what had triggered the lockdown. Asked for an assessment of station-wide danger. I asked again. And again, and again.

I got nothing. To every query, the Overseer simply replied in text what it had been saying aloud: **The station is being placed on lockdown due to the potential for exposure to harmful radiation.** The stubborn answer made no sense. The Overseer should be providing unrestricted information about the source of the danger to anybody who asked. **All personnel must find their way to a safe room immediately.**

Nothing else.

"There's no internal report on what triggered the lockdown or where it happened. None of the radiation sensors are showing high readings."

"What? No, that can't be right. Let me look," Hunter said.

But even as I moved aside, the terminal stopped responding. The warning was frozen on the screen: **The station is being placed on lockdown due to the potential for exposure to harmful radiation. All personnel must find their way to a safe room immediately.** I checked the next terminal over, where the comms were patched through, and found the same thing.

Adisa tried his radio again. "Hugo, Avery, what's happening on your end?"

"I don't understand," Hunter said. "What's wrong with it?"

"They can't hear you," I said. The room's comms didn't even acknowledge the radio signal, much less pick up and transmit it.

Normal lockdown procedure did not include disabling comms. Not ever, not in any circumstance. No Overseer or station designer wanted to prevent people from communicating during an emergency. But that was our reality: we had no way of contacting the others. We could not see what was happening outside the room. We were stuck in the furnace control room with no way out. My chest felt tight; my heart was racing. There wasn't enough air. It was too hot. I needed to breathe. It was a small room, and completely sealed. I couldn't breathe. I couldn't think of anything to do. There was nothing we could do, not without a way to make the Overseer listen to us. Not deep in the mine, three kilometers from help.

The red light from the furnace faded as the image on the wallscreen vanished.

A second later, all the screens around us went dark. The overhead lights went out. Every indicator light in the room, on every panel, switched from green or blue or white to red. Aside from the glow of my PD screen—now registering an error as it tried and failed to talk to the station—that faint red glow, from so many tiny specks, was the only light in the room.

A bright light flared across the room. I flinched, then recovered to see Adisa brandishing a small flashlight. He aimed it up and around, searching for something, before finally settling on a ventilation panel near the ceiling. He boosted himself up on one of the terminals to reach upward. I didn't understand what he was doing—my fear was clouding every thought—until he held his hand in front of the panel for a few moments.

"The air's still flowing, aye?"

As soon as he said it, I could hear it: the faint, steady hiss of the ventilation trundling along uninterrupted. Relief washed over me, followed by embarrassment for letting myself spiral into panic. I made myself think about it logically. The life support systems were still functioning; they wouldn't stop working because the Overseer engaged a lockdown. Even if the Overseer was shut down or destroyed—and I had no reason to think it was—there were multiple fail-safes to keep vital systems running, including everything from less advanced AIs to take over the primary tasks all the way down to purely mechanical backups. It was the first thing every student of artificial intelligence learned on their first day in class: never leave your ability to breathe up to a thinking machine. Followed, always, by a shocking list of catastrophes that had occurred because people neglected that lesson. I had been told by a friend once that the first thing every station engineer learned on their first day was to never trust an AI programmer to remember that people need to breathe.

We still had air. I wiped my right hand on my trousers. The ache in my chest did not ease.

Adisa lowered himself to the floor again. "Has a lockdown like this happened before?"

Hunter searched through her tool bag and brought out her own flashlight. "No. Not station-wide, not since I've been here." She swiped and tapped frantically at the terminal. "It's never been this unresponsive before. I don't know. Mary will have to—oh, god. Mary."

I felt another pang of panic with her words. The station had no sysadmin. Whatever was going on, there was nobody up there who had the access or ability to fix it.

Hunter drew in a shaky breath. "I don't know what's going on. Is there really somebody— How can there be somebody here? Somebody we don't know? What do they want?"

Adisa leaned back against the terminal, with his hands resting on the edge. "I doubt it's a coincidence the alarm sounded when it did, aye?"

"You think this . . . this person set it off on purpose?" Hunter said.

I glanced at my PD before remembering it was momentarily

useless. I dropped it onto the terminal. "Just because the crew were all in Level 0 when the alarm sounded doesn't mean one of them couldn't have set up a trigger earlier. This doesn't prove there's an infiltrator."

Adisa nodded slightly. "True enough. What sort of damage would cause a station-wide lockdown?"

We both looked at Hunter, who chewed on her lower lip before answering. "There are parts of the facility where damage would leak enough radiation for a station-wide alarm. If there was an explosion or something . . . well, depending on where it was, we wouldn't have heard it, right?" She dropped her hand to check the radiation sensor at her belt. "There's no effect in here, but if there's damage to the furnace shielding or the fuel processing plant or the hot waste disposal . . . that's bad. I don't know the details—that's Miguel and Sonya's area, and they're doing tests all the time—but I know it's bad. That's really, really bad."

"Could you build a remote explosive?" I asked.

"Me?" Hunter looked at me in surprise. "Why?"

"You're the only one in the mine. You build robots."

"Not like *that*," she said, incredulous. "I build repair bots. Maintenance bots. Not bombs. I wouldn't even—I've never made anything like that. We don't even know it *was* a bomb. That's just the first thing I thought of."

"But you could build something like that if you wanted to, couldn't you?"

"Why would I want to?"

"That's how Mary Ping died," I said. "An explosive bot. Probably autonomous or semiautonomous."

Hunter gaped at me. "But that's—that's illegal," she said. She seemed to realize the foolishness of her words a second later, because she cringed, but she was also shaking her head. "I would never do that. I swear, I would never build a bot that would kill someone."

"I think," said Adisa calmly, "you should tell us why you're down here in the mine."

Hunter looked at him, but she didn't answer right away.

"Two of your crew are dead. The station is on lockdown. And," he added, looking around, "we're a bit stuck here for the moment, yeah?"

Still Hunter said nothing.

"You were helping David, weren't you?" I said. "The two of you have been spying on Nimue and selling information to your family. Were you looking for leverage? Your family wants to expand into the asteroid belt, but Parthenope is trying to get all the shipping under its control before they can. Is that what this is all about? It's all just more fucking corporate money?"

Hunter let out a sigh and slumped onto a stool. She rested her elbows on the console and buried her face in her hands. Adisa and I waited.

"You have it backwards," she said finally, her words muffled by her hands. She rubbed her face with her palms; there were tears on her cheeks. "I wasn't helping David. He was helping me. I know I should have told you. I know, but I was hoping—before you even got here, Sigrah told us all to not let an obviously personal crime get in the way of our operation, and it was easier to just . . . let her say that. I mean, nobody ever expects OSD to dig that deep into anything, you know?" She flinched. "Sorry. You know what I mean. I'm sorry."

"Tell us what you and David were doing," Adisa said.

"I set it all up before we even started here. David just figured out how to make the transmissions and access the data without the Overseer noticing. But he only did it because I wanted to, and he was desperate for money. He has—had—so many debts from the accident. As soon as I realized that, I knew . . . He was easy to persuade. But it wasn't his idea. It's my fault."

"What did you steal?" Adisa asked.

"Data. Designs. Schematics. Operational stats. But not to sell to my family. I'm not working for them." Hunter's voice turned sharp as she looked at me. "Hunter-Fremont doesn't need me spying for them. They've got their own sources for that."

"Then who?"

A shrug. "Anybody who wants to buy. We don't handle that part. We have a contact on Hygiea—and no, I don't know who it is. We've never met. It's probably somebody in systems operations, but who knows. I'm pretty sure they finessed the personnel assignment algorithm to get both of us here at the same time. But maybe it's a bloody maintenance plumber."

Probably not a maintenance plumber, I thought, if this was the same person altering the superoperational commands that let David black out the surveillance. It had to be somebody with high-level access and little oversight, somebody the company trusted to work with the master AI. That was a question we couldn't answer until we returned to Hygiea.

"We took it in bits and pieces. We tried to be careful."

"You wanted the buyers to keep wanting more, aye?"

Hunter gave Adisa a wobbly smile. "Exactly. That was David's idea. I wanted to grab everything we could and take the big payday, but he convinced me it was too risky. I know he was right, but I keep thinking, if I had argued with him, if we had bought out our contracts and gotten away from here . . ."

"Why were you down here today?" Adisa asked.

"Cleaning up," Hunter said. She reached into her tool bag and brought out a small gray box, held it up for us to see. "We have data recording devices all over the station. We designed them to simulate crew access, so the Overseer would never be able to find a pattern. I figured you would start looking soon."

She was giving us more credit than we deserved. A full search of the mine had never been on our action list.

I asked, "When did you first realize there were inconsistencies in the station data?"

Hunter looked surprised by the question. "That was all David. He noticed some weird stuff a few months ago, but I just blew it off. I didn't think it was a big deal."

"Did he ever mention a company project with a name like Sunshine? Or Sunset?"

"Not that I know of. What he talked about, it was all a lot more vague than any particular project. Nothing out of the ordinary. Companies lie about stuff like this all the time. Like, if they're claiming to produce more fuel than they are, that's part of the business. Carrington Ming Quartet did that a few years ago, remember? All they got was a fine. It doesn't mean the power's being diverted off-grid. But David wouldn't let it go. I thought he was just . . ." She glanced toward me, her expression apologetic. "He was traumatized, you know? He didn't like to talk about it, but I knew he was always worried about sabotage, always worried what everybody in the crew was up to. He was afraid he would miss something. I don't know what he thought would happen, exactly, but I don't think it was this." She sniffled and wiped her nose with her sleeve. "He never deserved this. I'm sorry. I keep forgetting that you and David went through so much together."

I didn't say anything. There wasn't really anything to say. I knew the fear she was describing, because it was one I shared. I understood all too easily how worried he would have been about missing something important, something obvious. Something as dangerous as Kristin Herd and all the other Black Halo operatives on *Symposium*. I understood exactly what he was afraid of.

Adisa knelt down to rummage through the kit of things he'd brought into the mine. He brought out a tube of water and offered it to her. She accepted it gratefully. I hadn't even thought about bringing water with us. Three years since I left Earth and I still didn't remember how important it was to always carry even the most obvious things for survival. I wondered, fleetingly, if maybe I just wasn't very good at living in space.

Hunter passed the water to me next. It was lukewarm and faintly metallic but a balm to my dry throat. I handed the tube back to Adisa. "Thanks."

Adisa hopped up onto a terminal to sit with his back against a screen. "Go back a moment, aye? David thought the data discrepancies happened because power was being diverted?"

"That's what he said," Hunter said. "That's why he spent so much time nosing around. He was trying to figure out what didn't fit."

"Oh," I breathed. "Oh, shit."

"What is it?" Adisa said.

I shook my head to avoid answering. My face warmed. Fuck. *Fuck*. I had been so sure that the data discrepancies *were* what Parthenope wanted to hide. I had interpreted Mary Ping's deflection as confirmation.

But she hadn't been confirming my theory at all. She had been laughing at me, because I had done exactly what I was terrified of doing, exactly what David had been trying to avoid. I had missed the obvious.

David had been searching the facility, shadowing the crew, asking questions, sticking his nose where it was not invited.

If all he had been looking for were data discrepancies, he wouldn't have needed to leave the systems room. Fuck, he probably could have done it all from his quarters without getting out of bed. He hadn't only been looking at the data and reports and the claims the company was making. He had been looking into every square meter of the station itself. He had been looking for something. Not in the data, but in the facility.

Mary Ping had known what he was looking for, even if he hadn't known it himself. She had killed him to keep it hidden. Sigrah had to know as well. This was her station. She had been reluctant to help from the start, eager to dismiss David's death as a personal quarrel turned violent.

I thought about the faceless mech suit in the darkness. Flinging the spider bots. Jumping backward—such an uncanny motion, against every instinct, yet so well balanced.

I thought of the surprise and anger on Delicata's face when I told him and Sigrah what I'd seen.

I thought again of Mary Ping's last words before the screams.

"Marley?" Adisa said.

I was staring at one of the red indicator lights beside the hatch in the floor. We were surrounded by them, in that dark room lit only by our own flashlights, a dozen or more tiny red eyes.

"What exactly did David find?" I asked.

"I don't know," Hunter said. "I already told you everything I know. He didn't tell me anything. I wish he had. If he had asked for help, we could have figured something out."

Oh, but he had. He had asked for help.

He just hadn't asked her. He had asked me.

There was a camera in the corner of the ceiling. Another in the control panel for the door in the floor. I didn't know how many audio recorders there were. I needed to tell them what I was thinking, but indirectly, carefully.

"How hard is it to trigger a false radiation alarm?" I asked.

"You think this is a false alarm?" Hunter said. She looked at me, considering. "I guess it could be. It makes more sense than causing an actual leak."

Adisa drew one leg up to his chest and hooked his hand around it. He had rolled his sleeves up again, once again showing his prison tattoos. "It's not difficult, aye. A child could do it in about, ah, three and a half minutes."

I raised my eyebrows. "That is a very specific estimate."

Adisa hesitated a moment, but only a moment, before deciding what to say. "Have you heard of the ship *Terese Hanford*?"

"The prison ship?"

"Aye, that one."

"I learned about it in school," I said, unsure of where he was going with it.

"They teach that in Earth schools?"

"Not a lot. Nothing good."

Terese Hanford was a massive prisoner transport used by United Earth Navy during the war. It was where they imprisoned Martian rebels indefinitely—some for years without ever being brought before a court, thanks to a deliberate loophole in system law. Because only Earth and Yuèliàng courts were considered valid, suspected war criminals could only be charged when they were brought to those courts in person. If they were never brought to Earth or the Moon, the UEN could keep them in transit for as long as it wanted. So *Terese Hanford* did not dock at Earth or the Moon for the entirety of the war. Humanitarian groups repeatedly demanded access to the ship and its prisoners; they were denied every time. Investigative news agencies tried to sneak aboard, protesters got themselves arrested in attempts to infiltrate, and even veterans groups spoke up, citing the extraordinarily high suicide rate among sailors who had served aboard *Terese Hanford* as a reason for more oversight.

The UEN denied all of it. It just kept shoving more and more prisoners into its cells until the war ended. Only then had the truth come out. I remembered news reports of children with skinny arms and open wounds, corpses jettisoned into space without even the dignity of clothing, guards with black masks covering their faces, hollow-eyed women and men who looked more like famine victims than war criminals. One particularly vivid image of an empty metal room splattered with blood was on the news for weeks. I was a child when the war ended, too young to understand, but not so young that I didn't absorb what my parents and their academic friends argued about, what I saw on the solemn reports, what protesters in the streets screamed when politicians passed by.

It had taken years to process all of the prisoners, most of whom were Martian or spaceborn and would have trouble surviving on Earth without extensive (and expensive) medical intervention. The government of Yuèliàng set up a special court for the purpose. Historians and political scientists still argued about how many of the prisoners aboard *Terese Hanford* had ever been convicted of any crime. Most of them had been locked up for no reason except the bad luck of being born Martian and caught in the middle of an unwinnable war.

"You were there?" I asked, because I had no idea what else to say.

"Ah, in a manner of speaking," Adisa said. "I wasn't arrested, at first. I sneaked aboard."

"You did *what*? Why the fuck would you do that?"

Adisa grinned quickly and crookedly. "I had this foolish idea that I could instigate a mutiny among the prisoners, aye? We were never entirely sure how many guards were aboard, only that there had to be many times more prisoners. It was a terrible plan. I made it as far as the cargo bay, and I was able to trigger a false radiation lockdown, but I was caught as soon as I tried to get into the inhabited sections of the ship. It turns out the UEN doesn't care much about getting its sailors to safety during a lockdown, so they were still patrolling, even thinking there were deadly levels of radiation. And it's a bloody big ship. Took too fucking long to get anywhere, yeah."

"You tried that by yourself?"

Adisa look at me, eyebrows raised. "Working with others on such a scheme would have been a wartime conspiracy, yeah? But one young man working alone, that was merely the ordinary crime of a misguided youth. Or so my public aid lawyer convinced the court some years later, when arguing for a commuted sentence."

"How the hell did that work?"

"You can ask him yourself, when we get out of here. He'll be glad to tell you all about it."

"What do you—" I stopped. "What? No. Van Arendonk? Really?"

It was impossible to imagine a corporate lawyer like Hugo van Arendonk volunteering to help Martian criminals. That was more the sort of thing my aunt and her wife used to do during their sabbaticals, when they would travel off-planet for half a year to spend the time counseling Martian survivors of the war on how to get their lives back together.

Adisa laughed. "It was a very long time ago."

"We all know that story back home," Hunter said. "The van Arendonks still can't decide if they ought to be embarrassed or proud. His family's even worse than mine when it comes to preserving appearances. Whatever happened to *Terese Hanford*, anyway? What does the UEN do with a ship that size when it's done with it?"

"They sold it," Adisa said. "It passed through a few corporate owners, I think. It's pretty old by now, so last I heard the only buyers were some wealthy incorporated Exodus cult. Can't remember the name it has now."

"Wait. Was it *Divine Immutability*?" I asked. "It launched, what, about six months ago?"

Adisa shrugged with one shoulder. "Aye, that's the one."

"I remember seeing a documentary about them," Hunter said. "That seems like a mission designed to fail."

I had seen the same program. It had been all over the news, because while it wasn't the first pioneer ship to set sail for extrasolar destinations, it was one of the largest. But that wasn't why I remembered it.

"Avery's family is on that ship," I said.

Adisa was surprised. "I didn't know."

I felt a pang of doubt; maybe that was something Ryu preferred to keep quiet. They had never wanted to talk about the cult they had been born into or life on the orbital where they had grown up. All they had ever said to me about it was, "I left as soon as I could. They never much wanted me around anyway." I hadn't asked for details. All I knew was that *Divine Immutability* had launched with some eight hundred people on board, more than seven hundred in long-term stasis, because they believed they were divinely destined to claim and colonize a distant planet. Among those people had been Ryu's siblings, cousins, parents, childhood friends. I couldn't remember what exoplanet they had picked as their destination. I did remember telling Ryu, at the beginning of one of the nights we had spent together, that anybody with even passing knowledge of exoplanetary research could have told them it was a stupid fucking place to go, they would all be crushed by the planet's gravity and roasted by its late-cycle sun, never mind what they believed their god was going to provide for them. Ryu had shut me up with a kiss and a shove onto the bunk. I had thought it was because I was being pedantic and annoying, or because neither of us was there for conversation. I hadn't considered how cruel and thoughtless I was being, consigning their family to certain death with my arrogant certainty. I hadn't wondered if they were hurting beneath their mask of casual amusement. They probably knew their family was seeking an impossible paradise aboard a former prison ship. That was the sort of thing Ryu would make a point of knowing, however much it hurt them.

It was also beside the point. I couldn't worry about Ryu now. They were safe in Res. We had a much bigger problem to deal with.

"So," I said, "you were able to trigger a false radiation alarm on what was probably one of the most heavily guarded ships ever built. As a kid."

"A teenager. It wasn't that impressive, really."

"But you didn't get caught while you were doing it, only after. Even on a UEN ship with constant surveillance."

Adisa looked at me for a few seconds. "True, yeah. Why?"

I looked at Adisa. I looked at the closed hatch. I looked back at him. "No reason. No reason at all."

SEVENTEEN

Adisa hopped down from the terminal. He clearly wanted to ask me what the fuck I was talking about, but instead he started wandering around the room. Locating the cameras, just as I had a few minutes ago. After a bit, he pointed at Hunter's tool bag.

"Sure, but what are you—"

I put my finger to my lips. Hunter cut herself off and nodded slightly. She opened her mouth again, closed it, instead lifted her hands in an obvious question. Her eyes darted to the cameras as well. Good. They were both wary now of the fact that we were being watched.

"The basic mechanism never really changes, aye?" Adisa said. He searched through the tool bag until he found a screwdriver. "Every security system has local components that have to decide at every door whether it's more dangerous outside a room than inside. That was part of why what I tried on *Terese*

Hanford didn't work. The UEN didn't care if there was more danger inside the prisoners' blocks than out. The warden made that decision."

I understood what he was saying: he wasn't going to try to get us out of that room until I convinced him that the danger outside wasn't real. I didn't know how to do that, but I did know that I needed a way to explain what I was thinking—and I needed to do it without letting whoever, or whatever, was watching know.

Just as David had done when he sent his message to me.

"So I have a confession to make," I said. I didn't know if Hunter was trustworthy, but I knew she hadn't killed David, whatever other kind of trouble she was mired in. I would have to take the chance. "David contacted me before he died."

"What?" Hunter said. "When? What did he say?"

Adisa raised his eyebrows, but he didn't look particularly surprised.

"Did you know already?" I asked him.

"No," he said. "But I did think you weren't telling the truth about not having spoken to him in over a year."

"I *was* telling the truth about that. Until he sent me that message, I hadn't heard from him in eighteen months. We weren't in contact at all."

"He didn't talk to any of the other survivors," Hunter said quietly. "He said it was too painful."

"It was. It is." I shook my head to brush that aside. It wasn't important right now. "The thing is, his message didn't make any sense. He went through all this trouble to send it anonymously and hide the transmission, but nothing he said made any sense. He was reminiscing, but he had some details wrong. He was talking about this debate we had once about the warship *Excelsior*. It's, um, it's a wreck off the coast of England. It crashed during one of the old orbital rebellions. We had an argument years ago about whether the crash was human or machine error. David insisted that he was right, that it was machine error—but that's not what happened. He also mentioned Kristin Herd. He talked about her like she had been present for that argument, but it happened long before we met her."

"One of the Black Halo members, yeah?" Adisa said.

"Yes. The one who joined our team. And I thought maybe by bringing up *Excelsior* and Kristin at the same time, David was trying to tell me he'd discovered something about her or Black Halo that we didn't know. Like, maybe everybody had missed something about who was responsible for the *Symposium* attack. Or that he had learned something about somebody here on Nimue, like a crew member who was secretly involved with something dangerous, something the company screening had missed. But I looked for evidence of all that. I didn't find anything. So maybe that's not what it was after all."

I took a breath, looked around the room again. Two cameras, probably only one audio recorder, but all those red lights, piercing the paler glow of Adisa's flashlight, still looked to me like eyes. The room seemed to expand and contract whenever I turned my head, the shadows wavering, the close walls and crowded terminals blurring. I was too warm. I was tired. I was scared shitless. It was hard to wrangle my thoughts into order.

"I think maybe he was referencing something that happened before we left Earth," I began. "Right after Kristin joined the project."

I paused. Adisa and Hunter were listening. I needed a moment to figure out what to say.

It was strange to me, how I remembered it mostly in the aftermath rather than in the event itself. It had been a long, busy week of problems and meetings and emergency calls into the lab late at night, but all of that blurred together in a haze of frustration and exhaustion. Where my memories became clear again was afterward—it must have been Friday. A long, leisurely, decadent summer twilight, the sort of summer evening that only ever happens in the City of Dreaming Spires. Purple in the sky at ten o'clock, the leafy rustle of trees in a gentle breeze. Dry red Spanish wine from Sunita's cellar. We were drinking in her garden, just her and me, long after dinner was over and the others had left for their own homes. The murmuring sounds of the city were muffled by her lush garden hedge, and the anxieties of the week slipped away as the whole of the world drew itself into the well of summer darkness that surrounded us. I didn't want to leave. I knew there was more we needed to talk about.

"We need to discuss what your child has done," Sunita had said, her voice gentle and teasing as a warm breeze. "Have you worked it out?"

"Why is it only my child when it makes trouble?" I had asked, laughing, but we both knew I was laughing to cover my lingering unease.

Vanguard was always surprising us; that was nothing new. It was always learning new methods for solving problems, evolving new ways to face challenges, teaching itself things we had never realized it needed to learn. That was what it was supposed to do, and I never grew tired of that thrilling moment of realization, the heart-skipping second when I understood that it had outgrown and overreached the tasks we had set before it. I was enamored of the way it thought, the way it communicated, the way it grew and changed and made itself ever more complex.

When it taught itself to access the building security system and open the doors as I arrived in the morning, we were surprised but not overly concerned. When it noticed and identified a grad student stealing tools from the machine lab, we were charmed and a bit impressed. It was not supposed to be able to do any of that—it was not supposed to monitor personnel or have any facilities control over its surroundings—but it was an explorer by design, an informational pack-rat by choice, created for observation, collection, and, if necessary, self-preservation. We reasoned that it had learned these behaviors in response to the questions we put before it regarding what it would do if there were vital crew or systems failures at the station on Titan. It would still need a way to go home, even if there was nobody waiting to let it in.

We only began to worry when it started locking doors instead of opening them.

"We didn't realize it was targeting anybody in particular at first," I said. I rubbed my hand over my shaved head, wiping sweat from my scalp. "We thought it had found another thief, maybe, or was looking for one. It took some testing to figure out that Kristin was the common denominator. Every time Vanguard took over the building's security system to lock the doors, it was when she was among the people trying to get in."

"It knew about her?" Hunter asked.

"I don't know," I said. "It must have known *something*. We had introduced her to Vanguard the same as we did everybody. She had all the right credentials. She passed the background checks easily. But Vanguard kept doing it, even after we left Earth. Changing the access codes so Kristin couldn't get into the lab, or couldn't do her work. We thought it was . . . I don't know, a little funny. We laughed about it."

It had annoyed the hell out of Kristin, naturally, but it had intrigued me and Sunita that Vanguard was taking actions we could find no logical basis for. Everything else it did had a reason. But this we could not explain. That summer evening in her garden, Sunita had suggested it might be because Vanguard knew I didn't want a new member of the team, but that wasn't a real reason, not for an AI. There had to be a decision, an algorithm, a series of choices that translated my displeasure at having to replace a member of the team into Vanguard's actions. We had built an astonishingly clever mind from the ground up, circuit by circuit, pathway by pathway, and we understood only part of it. That mind had grown and changed, and now it was doing something we had never taught it to do. It was not unlike being a parent to a child who had heretofore been perfectly angelic, only to have the police show up on the doorstep one evening with a grinning delinquent in hand, demanding to know why we let our offspring run amok. It had been equally thrilling and unsettling.

I said, "It only made sense afterward, when Black Halo named Kristin as one of their martyrs. But by then, well, it was too late. Vanguard was completely destroyed. I couldn't figure out what it had seen that we kept missing."

Adisa had been quiet while I spoke, but now he asked, "What do you think David was trying to tell you by bringing that up?"

"I think he was telling me to be suspicious of the crew here. But . . ." I glanced at the camera in the corner again. I hoped they understood. "Not only the crew."

Hunter's eyes widened. "Oh. But that's not possible. Is it? Oh, fuck."

Adisa tossed the screwdriver, caught it. The look on his face suggested he had a large number of very pointed questions to ask me, but also that he knew this was neither the time nor the place for them.

"Three and a half minutes," he said. "Grab your stuff and come close to watch, aye?"

He knelt beside the hatch and waited for me and Hunter to gather around him. Not to watch, but to block the security cameras' views of what he was doing. Hunter leaned against the control panel; I positioned myself between the hatch and the camera in the corner. If there were others in the room that we hadn't spotted, we might be in trouble. It would all depend on how quickly the Overseer caught on to what Adisa was doing.

Holding his flashlight in his mouth, he removed the screws from an access panel beside the hatch. He reached in to pull out first one bundle of wires, then another, tugging until he found a small plastic box of circuitry. None of it was labeled, but he seemed to know exactly what he was doing. He snapped the box open to peer inside. I felt a little bit ashamed by the surprise I felt as I watched him work. He had grown up on Mars, in a time when the oldest and poorest habitat domes were already crumbling into disrepair after decades of neglect, when starving populations were locked out of food banks, when corporate executives hoarded water in private compounds, when armed militias stockpiled weapons for use against unarmed protesters. I couldn't imagine what living under those conditions must have been like, but it was not hard to understand how, in a place like that, learning to trick a sensor to get through a locked door could easily be a matter of life and death.

It felt like barely any time at all had passed before he said, "It's about to get very loud in here."

A blindingly bright warning light flashed once, twice, then came on with a steady white blaze. An alarm wailed, followed quickly by the droning voice of the security system: "Warning. High radiation detected in this area. Evacuate immediately."

The hatch's control panel flashed on, and between wails I heard the muffled clunk of the lock disengaging. Adisa tugged the hatch open and gestured for Hunter to climb through.

"Warning. High radiation detected in this area. Evacuate immediately."

I followed right after Hunter, letting myself slide-fall down the ladder as quickly as I dared. Adisa was right after me; he pulled the hatch shut, cutting off the siren in midwail. When I reached the bottom of the ladder, I checked the radiation sensor on my belt, just in case I was wrong. The levels were normal, identical to what they had been before the alarm went off. I let out a sigh of relief.

"Okay," I said, when Adisa joined us at the bottom of the ladder, "I have to admit I don't have a plan for what to do next."

Hunter chewed on her lip, then her expression brightened. "Oh! I do. Follow me."

She strode quickly along the catwalk, took a turn on a passage midway down, turned again a few more times. I couldn't see beyond the small circle of light illuminated by our flashlights, but I could still feel the vast, echoing space around us, the massive machines above and below, the mine stretching out to walls hidden in the distance. The repair bots were still working, crawling over their machinery like beetles. The warm, steady hum of the facility had not changed.

Hunter led us to the center of a catwalk and stopped abruptly. There was nothing at the spot, no console or terminal, no access panels, no machines or bots.

"We can talk here," she said, speaking quietly. "David and

I found this. It's a security blind spot. The drum of the crusher blocks the nearest camera, and there are no audio recorders anywhere close. We just have to stay in the center of the walkway, between these seams."

She pointed to the floor, indicating a section of metal grating. It was a bit tight, but we huddled close.

"All right, Marley," Adisa said. "Make your case."

"Right. Okay." I absently rubbed my left shoulder, trying to ease the ache in the joint. "Mary Ping killed David. That much I'm sure of. He discovered something she had done, and instead of being impressed by it like she wanted, he was horrified. So he confronted her, hoping he could get her to admit it or change what she was doing, and she killed him. The question is, what did David discover? I think that goes back to Aeolia. That's why David was reading about it right before he died.

"Mary investigated Aeolia. She must have had access to the virus that infiltrated that Overseer, the one that overrode all the fail-safes. Whatever the virus did that made the Overseer give up on keeping its crew alive. I think Mary took that virus—or figured out what it was doing and wrote her own virus to do the same—and brought it here. It's supposed to be impossible to infect an Overseer with a virus, but that means fuck-all when you're a sysadmin who can get access to the Overseer's brain."

"But why?" Hunter said. "Why would she do that? What's the point?"

"The way the virus affects the Overseer *is* the point," I said. "I keep thinking about what she said to me before she died. And when we interviewed her. She asked me if I didn't think machines would make better choices for humans than we made for ourselves. I've met people like her before. People who talk about AIs the way she did. They don't look at AIs and see machines, or tools. They see something more like a religion. Like a god. She talked about how much freedom Vanguard had—how much we'd given it. I think she was trying to figure out if I agreed with her. I don't think she wanted to create a killer AI to make some kind of political statement, or whatever it was the people who attacked Aeolia wanted. I think she brought the virus here and infected Nimue's Overseer because she wanted to see what it would do with all that freedom. And it worked. It worked too well. The Overseer is thinking for itself. It was thinking for itself when it locked us down. When it killed Mary Ping."

Neither of them said anything for a long moment.

"Look, I don't know," I said, frustrated. "Maybe I'm way off the mark. We can't exactly ask her. What I'm saying is—what's more likely? There's some infiltrator on this rock who's been hiding for who knows how long and just happened to show themselves right before triggering a lockdown, or . . . there isn't anybody here? There was nobody in the mech suit. Because it was being remotely controlled by the Overseer."

"Overseers don't hurt people," Hunter said, but weakly. "They can't."

"Maybe they haven't before, but they are capable of it," I said. "The infected Overseer on Aeolia let its entire crew die."

"Wouldn't we have noticed? If the Overseer was infected?"

"David did notice," I said. "Only he didn't know exactly what he'd found. That's why he reached out to me. I thought he wanted to talk about *Symposium*, but I think now . . . he probably wanted help from an AI expert who wasn't Mary. Somebody who would recognize what happens when an AI starts misbehaving."

Hunter shook her head; wisps of her silver hair were floating free around her face. "But why would it kill her? Why would it do that?"

"I'm not entirely sure. I'd love to ask it. Maybe it was because she killed David, so it knows she's a threat. It's infected with her virus, but it's still an Overseer. Maybe it did it to protect itself from her tampering with it further." I rubbed my hand over my face. "That's the problem with AIs that can slip past their boundaries. We don't know why they do what they do. We can't predict them. I really don't know."

I looked at Adisa, who had been quiet the whole time I'd been arguing my hypothesis.

"I'm probably missing something. I know I'm missing something," I said.

"We are," Adisa said. "You said David discovered that the company was falsifying reports about mine efficiency and production, aye?"

"That's right. He had piles of evidence collected."

"And there's no surveillance in the cargo transport tunnels, aye? So here's the question," Adisa said. "Where did the mech suit and the spiders come from? Why is there tech like that here on Nimue?"

"Because somebody—" I cut myself off as I understood what he was saying. "Oh. Oh, fuck me."

There it was. The missing piece, the rough edge that didn't fit.

David had tried to warn me. How frightened he must have been, how angry, when he looked around at his circumstances and realized there were so few people he could trust, and fewer still who would understand. He wouldn't even have trusted Hunter, connected as she was to her family's business and the game of profit and loss the corporations played across the system. He'd reached out to me because he knew I hated Parthenope as much as he did. Because I understood what AI could do. Because we had spent countless hours debating the ethics of technological advancement, the responsibilities of creating machines we could not control, the opportunities and dangers we were bringing into the world.

David and I had years of shared history together, filled with events he could have referenced in his message to me, but he had chosen *Excelsior.* A ship famous for nothing except that it had crashed while carrying a hold full of illegal weapons.

My chest felt tight. I said, "They built them here. The company is building weapons on Nimue."

That was what David had discovered. That was what had gotten him killed.

For a good half a minute, nobody said anything. Hunter looked stunned. Adisa, angry, the same anger I had seen in the lift when he picked apart the spider bot. I felt sick to my stomach.

"But that's—that's illegal. That's *very* illegal," Hunter said, her voice thready and high.

I almost laughed at the plaintive words. Her surprise was genuine; she hadn't known. I doubted most of the crew knew, aside from Sigrah and a couple others. Delicata, with his monthly maintenance inspections that took hours longer than they should have. Mary Ping with her insidious little virus.

Of course it was illegal—that's why it was going to be so very profitable. That's why it was hidden behind the fanfare of a massive engineering project and a blizzard of operational data. Unauthorized weapons manufacturing was a violation of every tenet of the postwar disarmament treaty. The punishment wouldn't be a fine or a slap on the wrist. The company risked losing every one of its mining operations. Every one of its executives and any investors in the know could be prosecuted for war crimes on Earth and Yuèliàng.

Parthenope was doing it anyway. Nimue was hiding a factory that was making highly advanced mech suits, nimble and explosive spider bots, and who knew what the fuck else. The company wanted to turn itself into a military power in the asteroid belt, and probably beyond, should the company ever decide to end twenty-five years of system-wide disarmament and launch into a war. All the analysts and economists wondering if Nimue would be worth Parthenope's investment in the long run—they hadn't counted on the fact that the company was also building the means to aggressively expand its territory not by mergers, not by acquisitions, but by conquest.

Adisa let out a sharp breath and shook his head. "Fuck. The discrepancies your Prussenko found in energy and resource usage—it's all going toward a hidden part of the station, yeah? They've got a rotten big UEN base just sitting there and not being used for anything else."

"One of the crew, Vera, he mentioned that David had been looking into fuel leaks in the unused lines leading to the base," I said.

"The base has been condemned, hasn't it?" Hunter said. "It's completely closed off. You can't get there anymore."

"Are you sure of that?" I asked.

"That's what . . ." She laughed hollowly. "That's what Sigrah told us. She told us the Overseer doesn't even know the base exists, because it's outside of its stewardship responsibilities. And where the Overseer can't see, we aren't authorized to go. It would violate the liability terms of our contract, you know, the usual. And of course we just fucking believed her. Katee and I were talking about going to explore during some downtime, right? Not to look for anything. Just to poke around. Sigrah flipped her shit. She said she didn't want an accident or a lawsuit on her hands. We thought she was overreacting, but it wasn't worth the headache of trying to argue with her."

"I think we need to ask her about it," I said to Adisa. "And Vera. I should have asked him more about what David was doing."

With the station under lockdown, I wasn't entirely sure how we would do that. Every asteroid mine had a way to get miners to the surface if all the mechanical systems failed and the crew was left with no computers, no comms, no power, no air. It didn't have to be easy or efficient. It just had to exist without depending on any higher system that might fail.

And in this case, that meant climbing three kilometers up to Level 0. Three fucking kilometers.

We decided, naturally, to see if there was some way to access the lift instead. I was thinking about bypassing the lockdown again, about Adisa's helpful youthful skills, but that all turned out to be unnecessary.

As we approached the lift, its control panel, which had been dark before, blinked on. A single word appeared.

Ready.

I stopped short.

"What? Is it functional?" I said.

Our radios crackled, making us all jump in surprise, and a woman's voice came through. "Hello? Are you out there?"

"That's Katee," Hunter said excitedly. She grabbed her radio to answer. "Katee! Is the lockdown lifted?"

A pause, then Katee King replied, "We've got the lift working. You should come back."

"Is everybody okay? What happened?" Hunter asked.

"You should come back," King said again, her voice strangely flat.

She was upset, I thought. Still scared. Wary about something.

Adisa spoke into his own radio. "We're on our way."

The lift doors slid open.

EIGHTEEN

The lift carried us swiftly upward. There was no more radio communication from Level 0, and the Overseer was completely silent and unresponsive for the entire journey. No vocalization, no messages on the control panel, no reaction to our repeated attempts to access the controls or comms. It felt incredibly risky, to be riding a lift without knowing if the AI that controlled it was functioning or not, but the choice between remaining deep in the mine with no idea what was happening or rejoining the others to face it head-on was no choice at all.

The lift glided to a stop when we reached Level 0. The doors opened to reveal the junction. The lights were on.

The first thing I saw was the body.

"Shit. Fuck," Adisa breathed. "Fuck."

In the doorway to the cargo warehouse, Ned Delicata was jammed between the door and the frame. The door was crushing his upper chest and left shoulder as it tried to close; the mechanism ground and strained as it pressed into him.

"Oh, no. No, no, no." Hunter darted forward and dropped to her knees beside the man. "Can you hear me? Ned?" Her voice rose to a near shout. "Is he— I can't tell if he's— Can you hear me? Ned!"

Clinging to Delicata's burned skin and shredded jumpsuit were the mangled remains of a silver spider bot. His head lolled when Hunter gently shook his shoulder.

"No, no, no," Hunter said. She was growing hysterical now. She stood up, turned around, dropped to her knees again. "What happened? Where is everybody? Katee? Katee!"

Adisa reached for his radio. "Avery? Hugo? Do you copy?"

There was no answer. I couldn't tell if the comms system was picking up the radio or not. I leaned around Hunter and over Delicata to try to stop the door from squeezing him, but the control panel was unresponsive. The cargo warehouse beyond the doorway was dark. I could not see or hear anybody. No voices, no footsteps, no crackle of radio. A black storm cloud of doubt filled my mind.

Adisa stepped closer and put a hand on Hunter's shoulder. She started, cut off her babbling at once with a sharp inhale.

"Is he breathing?" he asked.

"I don't know. I can't tell. I can't—I can't—" Hunter sucked in another breath, clearly trying to get ahold of herself. With a shaking hand, she reached out to touch the pulse point at Delicata's wrist, then at his neck. "I can't, I can't feel anything. I can't."

Adisa tried his radio again. "We've returned to Ops. Avery? Do you copy? If anybody in the crew can hear me, please answer."

"Radio range isn't very long here, with the shielding," I

said. He knew that. I knew he knew that. But I felt like I had to say something, offer something, to fill the suffocating quiet around us. The higher Hunter's voice went, the more frantic her breathing, the more numb I felt, as though her growing panic was draining the possibility of reaction out of me. The door to Ops was open. "We need to look for—"

Delicata let out a wet, crackling cough. Hunter squeaked and reeled backward, caught herself with one hand before she fell. Bloody spittle flew from Delicata's lips, staining his chin and splattering the door that held him in place. There was a horrible sound, like the grinding of bones, from deep within his chest.

Delicata's eyes opened. His lips moved, as did his one visible hand.

Adisa crouched beside him. "We're going to get you help. What happened? Where are the others?"

Delicata exhaled the shaky, jagged beginning of a word: "Sh-sh-she, she—"

"She?" Adisa prompted. "Where did the others go?"

Delicata's mouth twisted into a grimace, showing red teeth behind red lips, a gory mimicry of a smile. "T-t-too late. They're walking right—think they can escape it." He broke off coughing again, until the cough turned into a high-pitched wheeze of pain. "Too late."

"Where are they going? Why is it too late?"

Hunter touched Delicata's shoulder. "Ned, where are they? Where's Katee? She called us."

"I don't think she did," I said, very quietly. I didn't know if Hunter heard me, but Adisa acknowledged my words with a glance and a nod.

For a few seconds, Delicata only breathed, sucking in desperate breaths with ragged and pained sounds. "The old base," he said. "Think they're running away to where it can't—to where it can't see them. I didn't—I didn't send it. It'll find them. It has—it has eyes."

"They're going to the UEN base to escape the Overseer?"

"Stupid plan. Don't like to go there anymore. Not—not now, not since it—it changed."

"Changed? What do you mean?"

"Won't—won't work. Sig—Sigrah will . . ."

"What will she do?" Adisa said, more urgently. "Do you know where she is?"

That time there was no mistaking Delicata's expression. It was a twisted, angry scowl.

"Fuck her. She'll say it was me."

"You mean Sigrah? What will she say?" Adisa said.

Delicata started coughing then, a horrible tearing sound, and bloody spittle sprayed from his lips, stained his chin, until the cough caught up to itself and he gurgled suddenly—his eyes widened—and he tried to say something, tried to force a word out—and stopped. He just—stopped.

"Ned? What are you talking about? Ned?" Hunter's voice rose to a shout. She was shaking her head, her silver hair swinging, and she looked so unsteady on her feet I worried she would faint. "What the fuck is going on? Where is everybody?"

She tried to push past Adisa, but he rose to his feet and held her back. As soon as he gripped her arms, she burst into tears. "We need to check for other injured crew," he said to me over Hunter's shoulder. "Can you—"

"Right," I said. It was eerie how calm I felt. I was waiting for Hunter's panic to infect me, for her tears and shouts and gasping breath to spread, but it didn't happen. "On it."

As I left, Adisa was murmuring to Hunter, explaining to her what we should have figured out before we stepped into that lift: Katee King had not contacted us. The crew had not gotten the lift working. It was the Overseer, both times. Mimicking King's voice. Drawing us in.

We would have been safer in the mine.

I passed through the door to Res to find the common area illuminated by only a few lights from the galley and the media playing on the wallscreen—they had traded *Rachel Returned* for *Andromeda Sunsets*, but had thankfully muted the swooping orchestral score. That and my flashlight were enough for me to see that the crew lockers near the entrance were open, boots and jackets and gear tumbling onto the floor. I cast my light around and spotted a few belts and cases opened with the contents spilling out. There was a half-finished tray of food on one of the sofas in the media area. A blanket lay rumpled on the floor beside a chair, as though somebody had left it there when they jumped to their feet.

The crew had left in a hurry, but there was no sign they'd had to force the door to get out. I checked a few of the lockers, consulting their content checklists to figure out what each had contained before. The bulky heat suits and powered work boots were still there, but the emergency vacuum suits such as the ones we had carried into the mine with us were gone. They had left expecting depressurization or radiation. For the old base, as Delicata had said. They had gone prepared.

I moved through the common area slowly. The sound of my gecko boots on the floor seemed impossibly loud, with only the hum of the station's ventilation and the galley appliances to accompany me, and with every step I grew more tense, more aware of the heavy silence, more certain that in the next second I would hear the rain-soft clink of metal on metal and glimpse a silver bot racing toward me.

The only thing I didn't recognize in the common room was

a metal box with a hinged lid, sitting open on one of the mess tables. I stepped over to look inside. It was empty.

When I moved back, something else caught my eye.

There was a body tangled around the legs of the table. It hadn't been visible from the door; it was obscured by the benches and deep shadows. It was Miguel Vera. His eyes, still open, blankly reflected the light from my torch. The bot had latched onto Vera at his shoulder. His entire arm, half his chest, and his neck and the lower part of his face were a bloody ruin. Two spindly legs of the bot remained embedded in his slack cheek.

I checked for a pulse anyway. There was none. His skin was cool to the touch. He had been David's friend. He had been saving up to go back to Earth.

His was the only corpse I found. Every other room was empty.

The last room I checked was David's. It looked exactly as it had before: tidy, empty. Nothing personal except the map of Titan on the wall. I turned to leave again.

And stopped. Slowly turned around.

I won that bet after all, David had said in his message. *That lake should have been mine.*

He had mentioned Kristin to warn me about the Overseer. He had brought up *Excelsior* to warn me about the weapons. But the lake—I didn't know why he would bring up the lake. Nothing in his message had been incidental. I stepped closer to the map.

Kraken Mare was the biggest body of liquid on Titan, a huge sea of hydrocarbon that spanned over four hundred thousand square kilometers. It wasn't our landing site, but it was one of our primary research goals. I couldn't remember why we had been wagering on it that particular weekend. There had probably been a meeting with the microbiologists that week; they were always wide-eyed with excitement about what they hoped to find. I did remember that at some point after learning the name of Titan's known features, Vanguard had spent a few test cycles forming its aquatic bots into the shape of a giant squid. It did that sometimes, with concepts it was only just learning: took them in, looked them up, tried out a hundred or a thousand different variations of what they might mean. The kraken shape turned out to have the best propulsion system in certain environments.

I touched the map, ran my fingers around the ragged edge of the lake—and felt something behind the smooth material. The raised edges of an irregular shape. No more than a few millimeters thick.

I peeled the corner of the map away from the wall to find a small patch of thin film the exact same gray color as the walls; if I had looked without first touching it, I wouldn't have noticed it. I had to use my fingernails to pry it up.

Underneath the gray patch was a piece of metal about fifteen centimeters long, smooth and rectangular on one end but notched with a complex series of peaks, pits, and striations on the other end. I held it between my thumb and forefinger, turning it in the light of my flashlight; the hair-thin lines and tiny pockmarks gleamed. It was a circuit key. A physical key with an electronic component: both the irregular shape and the complex insets of copper would match its keyhole precisely. The physical shape could be forged easily, but the electronic connections created by the circuitry were much harder to mimic without access to the inside of the lock itself. It was the sort of thing you might use for access to a location that needed a layer of security in addition to embedded ID chips and manual codes.

Like, say, for entering the brain of an Overseer from inside an already-secure systems room.

I stared at the key for a long, long moment, and I thought: damn you, David, and this shitshow you got yourself into.

I pocketed the key and rejoined the others in the junction. Hunter had managed to calm herself down a little bit, although she was still sniffling and crying. Adisa stepped out of the Ops corridor just as I returned.

"There's nobody in there except Vera, and he's dead," I told them. Hunter's breath hitched at the news. "The others took vac suits and some supplies from the lockers."

"There's nobody in Ops either," Adisa said. "Not that I could find. I couldn't access the systems room."

Hunter looked toward the cargo warehouse, shuddering slightly when her gaze passed over Delicata. "I guess they did go to the base? Because they thought it would be safer?"

I looked to where she was looking, toward the dead man crushed in the doorway, and a sickly, cold unease came over me. I understood the uncertainty in Hunter's voice. It didn't make sense. Why would the Overseer lock down the station, then attack the crew? What was it trying to stop us from doing? Why didn't it just kill all of us, if it wanted us gone? And why would Sigrah flee with the others when she already knew what danger they were running into?

We had something wrong. We were missing something, still, something important. My head ached.

I had to ask the Overseer. I reached into my pocket to touch the key.

I said, "I found—"

We all heard the noise at the same moment. It was faint, but sharp, like the tinkle of glass shattering in a distant room—but it wasn't glass. I recognized that sound. I had heard it before, in the warehouse, when Mary Ping died.

I spun to face the door to Res, but that wasn't where the noise was coming from. Instead it seemed to be coming from all around, echoing and clattering with chaotic unpredictability. The sound grew louder, but not much; it was still too faint to pinpoint.

"You said there was no one here," Hunter whispered. She was looking around frantically, her eyes wide as she stepped uneasily toward the center of the junction.

"There wasn't," I said, also whispering. "There isn't."

I backed away from the door to Res. The sound came again, a little bit louder, and only then did I realize it wasn't coming from any of the four open doors around us.

It was coming from above.

We all looked up at the same time.

The airlock to the docking structure was open, and the long passageway was dark. We hadn't noticed. We hadn't even looked. I aimed my flashlight into the passage; Adisa did the same with his. The two unsteady beams caught glints of silver and blue in the darkness, some stationary, others moving restlessly and unpredictably, a starfall of reflections accompanied by the rain-like patter of metal feet on metal walls. The light was not strong enough to illuminate the entire passage. I could not see how many spiders there were up there, swarming down toward us. I could only hear the growing chorus of their clinking, clattering steps.

Adisa said, "Ops."

I was already turning toward the door. We raced for it, all

three of us jamming through in a heartbeat. I slammed my hand onto the control panel to shut the door—but the panel remained dark and unresponsive.

"Fuck!" I tried again, tapping frantically at the panel, but there was nothing. "Shut the fucking door, you asshole!"

The Overseer, if it was listening, did not bother to respond. I glanced over my shoulder, down the long hallway toward the systems room. It was too far. The clatter of the spiders was growing closer, and I had no way of knowing if the Overseer would even let us in.

The others realized the same thing. Hunter was the first to dart back into the junction and run for Res. Adisa and I were right behind her, but when we were through that door, we ran into the same problem: the panel was unresponsive. The Overseer would not let us close the door.

"The mine? Should we go back down?" I said, my breath already short and pained. The spiders were growing louder and louder. A couple were close enough that I could see their long, thin legs whipping as they scurried.

Adisa considered my suggestion for only a second. "No. The warehouse."

Right. He was right. The warehouse door was already trying to close. All we had to do was climb over Delicata's body, then pull it out of the way and let the door slam shut.

"Go," I said, shoving Hunter toward the warehouse door. "Over him!"

She first shrugged off her tool bag and tossed it through the gap, then turned sideways to follow—or she tried to, but even with Delicata's arm holding the door open she could not squeeze through. She braced herself against the frame, right above Delicata's body, but it didn't budge. The gears were grinding somewhere in the wall, trying to close. I ran over to help her, and the two of us together were able to shove the door open another few centimeters, enough for her to fit.

As soon as she was through, I lost my grip on the edge of the door—my fucking metal fingers—and it crushed against the body again. Delicata's flesh split with a wet sound.

"Overhead!" Adisa shouted.

The first of the spiders dropped through the airlock. It hit the floor, rolled its long legs into a cage, and tumbled toward the wall. It unfolded again and ran up the wall alongside the door to Res.

I lunged for it without thinking, throwing myself into the wall to crush the spider before it could reach the warehouse door. There was a burst of acrid chemical scent, a snap of electricity against my metal shoulder. When I moved away, the crumpled bot fell to the floor.

"Toss your pack through," Adisa said. "I'll help with the door."

A second spider followed the first, tumbling through the doorway in a tangle of long legs and flat body, a clattering, rustling, flashing knot of metal and motion.

I looked up. The spiders were roiling in the passageway, close enough now that the flashlight illuminated them clearly. Another two neared the airlock. Three. Ten. I couldn't count them all. They raced down the walls of the passage, a rippling, clicking wave crashing onto us from above.

"Marley!" Adisa shouted. "Get through the door!"

Neither of us was as slender as Neeta Hunter. I looked around wildly, searching for something to pry with, something to hold the door, but there was nothing. I felt a tug on the back of my leg: a spider had dropped from the airlock and latched onto my trousers. My heart thumping with panic, I reached down frantically to yank it free. I flung it across the junction, where it smacked against the control panel by the mine lift.

The panel, which had been dark before, was now functioning.

Steward systems maintenance requested.

"Oh, fuck you." I spun around. Every panel in the junction said the same thing. "Come on! Call them off! I know you're listening!"

"Marley, we have to go!" Adisa was by the door, waiting for me.

Another spider dropped into the junction, and I crushed it with my boot as I stepped over. The crunch was a goddamn delight, that sound and that feeling, a single spark of joy slicing through the panic, but it didn't last and there were so many more coming, so many swarming overhead that their clicking, clacking steps were all I could hear.

"Open the fucking door for us, please!" I shouted.

But the Overseer, if it was listening, ignored my plea.

Steward systems maintenance requested.

I braced myself against the warehouse doorframe again and, with Hunter helping from the other side, pulled on the door to force it open a little bit more. Together we managed to move it enough that the dead man slumped to the side, no longer pinned. Adisa pulled him out of the way.

"Go," I said, jerking my head toward the door. "Get in there."

I felt a spider land on my back, and I tensed. I couldn't move yet. I couldn't even flinch, lest I lose my grip on the door. Adisa slipped through the opening, then turned to help Hunter hold it open.

"Now, Marley," he said sharply.

The spider on my back was creeping upward, gripping my shoulder with its spindly legs, a flash of silver and blue so close to my face, too close. I let go of the door to grab the bot and fling it away, but even as I did so I felt nudges and tugs on my trousers. They were swarming around my boots, over the toes, crawling over each other, tumbling and climbing and clicking, and with every motion they left that familiar bitter chemical scent. They were spreading their fuel.

The Overseer wasn't stopping them. Every control panel still said the same thing.

Steward systems maintenance requested.

It was not going to do what we wanted. It had its own ideas.

"Come on!" Adisa said, reaching for my arm.

A sharp pain in my leg: one of the spiders had punctured my trousers.

The Overseer was not going to let me go.

I didn't take Adisa's hand. Instead I shoved him backward with a single, solid push, just enough to get him out of the doorway.

"Go! Find the others!"

The door slid shut before he could respond, crushing several spiders with a loud series of pops and metallic squeals. I tumbled backward, caught myself, turned. The bots were stretching their gossamer-thin legs to form a broad net around me, a rippling and waving trap that spanned the room. It was strangely beautiful, almost organic in the way it moved, and for a second—for a fraction of a second—I was mesmerized.

There was a snapping sound. A wave of that chemical scent. A flare of light to one side. That fraction of a second had been too long. The bots were going to ignite.

I didn't give myself time to think. I charged through the net and ran for Ops.

I was only a few meters into the corridor when the first explosion flared behind me. It came with a flash of light and noise, and a painful full-body blow on my back. I hit the floor so hard every bone in my body rattled, and I slid along the corridor for several meters. The second explosion followed swiftly, and everything was blinding light and agonized, deafening shrieks of metal bending, and heat—the heat was intense and unbearable—but I scrambled to my feet and ran, and somewhere beneath the cacophony I was shouting, *"Let me in, you piece of shit, let me in, let me in,"* and it wasn't listening, the fucking Overseer wasn't listening to me, the door was closed. I was two meters away and it was closed. One meter and it was closed. I slammed into the wall, hunched over the panel, jabbed in my access code with shaking hands. The heat was going to burn through my clothes, through my skin, it was going to swallow me whole before I could even scream.

The door slid open silently.

I dove through the doorway as another explosion shuddered through the corridor. For a second there was nothing but fire and light and pain. The tortured sound of metal crushing metal. So much noxious chemical mist in the air I choked on it.

Then the lights were gone, the heat too, and everything was silent.

NINETEEN

They told me I couldn't remember.

It was impossible, said the doctors, in their endless declarations about what could be allowed within the confines of my own mind and the limits of my own damaged body.

I had been asleep when the accident occurred. After I bid good night to Sunita, I had tucked myself into my uncomfortable coffin-like bunk to spend an hour or so making notes on the day's work. I amicably shared the passenger berth with another scientist, a biologist for the Titan project, but she had been working nights in her own laboratory, monitoring a delicate experiment with a purpose she was happy to explain but I only partly understood. Nobody's work stopped en route to Titan; it only accelerated. The feeling among the project members was that we needed to use every possible second so that we might hit the ground running. Even after I put my PD away and turned off the lights, my mind was racing. I did not think I would be able to fall asleep. I had been having trouble sleeping since we left Earth. I told myself it was excitement; there was so much to do, all of it important, all of it brilliant. In retrospect I wondered if it might have been fear. Even though I had been preparing for the journey for years, it felt as though there had never been a moment when I had truly considered what it meant to leave Earth without knowing when I would be coming back—if I would ever come back.

I must have fallen asleep, because I woke to the wailing of the ship's alarms. There were alarms for decompression, radiation, fire, all of them shrieking a monstrous symphony of confusion and failure. I woke to searing heat and dust-choked air. I woke to shouts and screams. I woke to the sensation of flying, falling, striking a wall, falling again.

Oh, no, said the doctors, much later, in the claustrophobic trauma ward on Badenia. That wasn't possible. There was no way I could remember. My injuries were too severe. I would have lost consciousness immediately. I was lucky to be alive. Lucky to have made it. So very lucky.

But I did remember. I remembered opening my eyes to a churning abyss of red dotted by silhouettes of black. I remembered the roar of explosions and the piercing sting of screams. I remembered the pain.

I learned later, when the investigation findings began to trickle into public view, that the Black Halo members embedded on *Symposium* had not meant to fully destroy the ship. They meant only to disable it, but they had set off a bomb in the propulsion system that created a cascade of explosions, each larger than the last, which spread from the engines into the fuel system, from the fuel system into the atmosphere and electrical systems, along the way sparking hundreds of fires that the suppression system had no hope of controlling. The larger explosions punched holes in the hull; the smaller ones spread unchecked through maintenance shafts and walls, melting electronics into useless slag, turning oxygen supply lines into deadly bombs, filling the air with poisonous fumes. I remembered that too: the ceaseless pop-pop-pop of walls shattering, conduits breaking, pipes hissing as water turned to steam.

The doctors told me I had invented it all, my memories of those minutes or hours, because my mind needed to fill an unsatisfactory void. Because I needed to believe I could know what had happened. Because I did not want my entire life to have changed without my bearing witness to it.

Ah, I thought now, that single word thrumming like a drumbeat in my aching head. Look. You were wrong. You fuckers were so wrong.

Even as the words coalesced into a coherent thought, I realized something wasn't quite right. Yes, there was pain. An ache in my head that extended down my neck and back. An insistent fire in my left hip, a sharper pain in my right ankle. A strange tugging feeling in the skin of my right hand. I counted through my body parts—I knew to do that, somehow, knew to feel for each one, to note those that did not respond.

Right. Okay. The fire, the explosions, the floating, those had already happened. *Symposium* was the past. This was Nimue. This was a whole new clusterfuck. I was proud of myself for understanding that so clearly.

Now: There was no fire. There were no alarms. I had escaped into the systems room as the spider bots started self-destructing in Ops. The door was closed now. I was safe—

relatively safe, at least, with a massive door of steel and lead between me and the bots. I couldn't hear them anymore. I didn't know if that meant they had stopped, or if the systems room was simply insulated well enough to keep the sound of their onslaught from traveling.

The room was not completely dark, but there was so little light it took my eyes a moment to adjust. I pushed myself up on my knees—my right shin hurt, had I run into something? Yes, fuck it, the chair, I'd slammed right into one of the chairs. I blinked several times to clear the spots from my eyes. My left eye was having trouble focusing. I shook my head, shook it again, tapped the side of my temple as though that would help. It never helped, but I never stopped trying.

There was a gentle light before me. A soft pale square set in the wall. The control panel for the interior door.

Steward systems maintenance requested.

"Oh, fuck off," I said. I grabbed one of the chairs to pull myself to my feet, gritting my teeth against the pain—and, hey, there was some exciting new pain, an ache in my jaw that I had not noticed before. "I'm coming, I'm coming."

I limped over to the door and slumped against the wall. Beyond that door was the lift, and at the other end of the lift shaft was the Overseer. I entered my access code again—it wouldn't have worked, had company regulations still mattered, but I doubted the Overseer cared about that. I pulled David's circuit key out of my pocket and slipped it into the slender notch below the control panel. Turned it, waited for the machine to hum quietly, extracted the key again. I forced myself to stand up straight, let the cameras get a good look at me.

"Come on," I said. "You asked for me. I'm here."

The door slid open. I stepped into the carriage; the door

closed behind me. It was a short journey downward, only a few seconds, before the door opened again.

Slowly, as slowly as the dawn breaking, the lights rose.

The lift opened to a wide, low room washed in a soft blue and purple glow. Towers of black marched in rows away from me, with lights flicking along every single one. Stacks of processors, more than I could begin to count, filling a room ten or twenty or thirty meters square. The floor was dark and reflective, the ceiling the same, giving the towers the illusion of extending forever below and above. I could not hear any of the normal sounds of the station. Everything was muffled by a steady, pulsing hum. The air was comfortably warm, yet I felt the stir of a cooler breeze from above, cooling the sweat on my skin.

For a second—the briefest, purest second—all of my physical pain faded into awe.

I was inside the Overseer.

"Hello, Hester."

The voice startled me. It sounded different here, in this big, humming room. Less constrained than it had been in the systems room. Here it surrounded me, wrapped around me, both comforting and overwhelming. It was no longer the voice of an agreeable and soothing woman; that polite fiction was gone. It spoke now with a presence so big and so powerful my heart skipped when it said my name.

"Hi," I said. "I'm here. What do you want?"

"I appreciate your help. I apologize for the injuries you have suffered."

I wanted to laugh but was afraid of how much it would hurt. It was a learned response, a conversational tactic. I knew that. An Overseer could not feel regret—should not be able to feel anything at all. It was a machine. My heart rate was creeping up, and I was finding it hard to breathe. I had thought, before, I knew what kind of machine it was. Now I was not so sure.

"What are those things, anyway? Those spider bots," I asked.

"They are Recluse 9.3 Mark Seven adaptable semiautonomous hive-linked mobile robotic incendiary devices."

Whatever the fuck that meant.

I said, "You know you didn't have to send them after us to get me in here. You could have asked nicely."

"That particular Recluse 9.3 Mark Seven hive is not under my command."

The chill on my skin was suddenly more than a drift of air.

"But—what? What?" I said stupidly. I looked around, as though I might find clarification in the room. It felt like my mind was skipping, a data playback with missing pieces. "But—you didn't? Those spiders aren't yours?"

"The Recluse 9.3 Mark Seven hive is under manual command," said the Overseer.

An Overseer was not supposed to be capable of subterfuge. An Overseer was not supposed to lie. But if I was right—if it was corrupted by whatever virus Mary Ping had brought to Nimue—all of those rules about how nice, predictable steward AIs behaved might be meaningless. A lie was, after all, only output. What it was doing inside was another matter entirely.

I had assumed the Overseer was controlling the mech suit, the spiders, and the lockdown. The attack on the crew—but I already knew something about that didn't fit, even before it had drawn me into its protective armor and kept the spiders outside.

Manual command. *She'll say it was me.* That's what Delicata had said before he died.

The Overseer hadn't attacked the crew.

Shit. My head hurt. My everything hurt. I felt so queasy my stomach could have been tied in knots. I needed to sit down.

I staggered forward a few steps. The lights changed to illuminate a path. I had to lean on the processor stacks for balance. I hoped the Overseer didn't mind. It led me to the center of the room, where the towers opened up into a neat square with a console and chair in the center. I hadn't known until that moment that Overseers were designed with an interior human workspace; Parthenope kept the physical design of the Overseers as much a secret as the workings of their electronic brains. I was relieved to see it, and not just because I wanted a chair. Humans are small and anxious and suspicious. We need places to nest, places to sit and think and pretend we have control, even within the hearts of our own creations. I limped over to the chair and sat heavily.

"Show me ID tracking data and visual surveillance for everybody on the station," I said. "And don't tell me I don't have bloody access. I know you want me to see it."

The lone console screen was a broad expanse at a gentle slant, clean of smudges, free of scratches. The facility map appeared, but there were only a few small dots, and most were red.

Delicata in the junction. Vera in the common room. Ping in the warehouse. David in the infirmary. All dead.

And me, still green, below Ops. Nobody else.

"Show me where you last scanned everybody else."

As expected, a flurry of dots and names all appeared in the same place: at the entrance to the transport tunnels in the cargo warehouse. Everybody had passed through there, including Adisa and Hunter. They were all in the tunnels—all out of sight of surveillance. I tried to contact them, but the Overseer told me there was no system for crew communications in the tunnels either. The tunnels and the base they led to formed an impenetrable blank spot in the Overseer's data, territory in which its sensors and eyes had no reach.

Adisa's and Hunter's ID chips had been scanned a good ninety minutes later than the bulk of the others. Sigrah about an hour before them, and alone. Most of the crew, including Ryu and van Arendonk, had entered the tunnels first—and they had done so as the station was going into lockdown. They had left Vera, Sigrah, and Delicata behind.

"Right. So, tell me, was there a radiation leak?" I asked.

"No."

"Did you sound the alarm?"

"Yes."

"Why?"

"My primary concern is the safety and well-being of the crew."

Before I could ask for an explanation, the image on the screen changed, and I was looking at a surveillance recording with both video and audio components.

It showed van Arendonk entering the systems room right after Adisa and I stepped into the lift. There was no surveillance in the systems room, so he was out of sight—and he wasn't around to see what was happening in Res at the same time, which was a raging argument between Sigrah and some of her miners. Vera, King, a few others decided they were going to search for the killer; they were convinced the transport tunnels were the only place for a murderer to hide. Sigrah forbade them from going anywhere. They told her to fuck off. She told them to sit their asses down and stay put. Pale and tired and frustrated, Ryu tried to get everybody to calm down, but nobody listened.

The Overseer split the images on the screen: I was now watching two recordings play out simultaneously.

Sigrah stormed out of Res, with Delicata right behind her. The crew began grabbing vac suits and gear from the lockers, even as Ryu pleaded with them to slow down and wait to hear from Adisa.

Delicata followed Sigrah into Ops, where they stopped just outside the comms room.

"This is getting out of hand," he said. "What the hell is that thing—"

Sigrah whirled on him. "Shut the fuck up."

"Did you do that? Did you kill Mary?"

"That wasn't me. You know what that was." She glanced up, eyes seeking out the nearest surveillance camera, and looked away quickly. "You're not going to do anything stupid, do you understand? We're going to be rational about this."

"But if it's killing—"

"We have what we need to get control of this situation." She paused. "Do you understand? We are still in control of this situation."

"They're talking about the tunnels," Delicata said. "I have to head them off."

"It's too late."

"But I still have the key, I can go out and—"

"Impossible. It's unfortunate for them that Mary set up a trap to stop them."

They stared at each other, hard, for several seconds. I couldn't see Delicata's face, only Sigrah's, and she was so tense the muscles in her jaw twitched.

"What about . . ." Delicata's head moved slightly; he was trying to gesture toward the camera without being obvious.

"Don't worry about that. We had no way of knowing what she left behind," Sigrah said. Her voice was so calm, so even, I would not have heard the anger tamped down beneath the words if I couldn't also see her fists clenching at her sides and the narrowness of her eyes. "We had no way of knowing how little regard she had for her fellow crew members."

A few seconds passed. Delicata nodded stiffly. "I understand."

"Go. I'll take care of the rest. I have to update HQ."

Sigrah went into the comms room, Delicata back to Res. The argument had made little progress: Vera and King were determined to go into the tunnels, while others were still trying to persuade them to wait for more information. Ryu was sitting on the edge of a table in the mess, rubbing their eyes tiredly. They glanced up at Delicata as he passed. Without speaking to anybody, he walked straight through the common room and disappeared into his private quarters.

In the comms room, Sigrah punched in her access code for the two-way radio, then entered a second personal code. In Parthenope systems, the second layer of security would encrypt the message and disguise the identities and locations of the sender and recipient. She said, "This is an emergency update regarding Sunburn. The situation is unstable. I request immediate assistance for containment and mitigation. I repeat: the Sunburn situation has become unstable, and I request immediate assistance."

"Who is she talking to?" I asked.

"The location is Hygiea. The recipient of the encrypted communication is unidentified," said the Overseer.

Not really a surprise. Radio encryption like that was available only to people at higher levels in the Parthenope corporate structure. Somebody on Hygiea would probably be able to identify the recipient, if they did the right kind of digging, but Nimue's Overseer had no way of doing so with any certainty.

"What is Sunburn?" I asked. "I've heard that name before."

"That information is not available."

On the screen, Sigrah was repeating her request. "The Sunburn situation is unstable. A Sunburn-approved crew member is disobeying direct orders and may be in possession of unauthorized material. I request immediate assistance for containment and mitigation from the nearest response team. Please respond with an ETA."

"Response team?" I said. "What is she talking about? Are there Parthenope ships nearby?"

"The nearest vessel is Parthenope Enterprises transport *Wellfleet*, en route from Hygiea."

"Really? There's already somebody on their way here? What's their purpose?"

"*Wellfleet* was dispatched to retrieve the Safety Officers at the conclusion of their investigation."

"We didn't request retrieval, did we?"

"There is no request on record prior to Foreperson Sigrah's request for emergency assistance."

Of course there wasn't. It would have had to come from Adisa or van Arendonk, and neither of them had given any indication they were ready to leave before we figured out what was going on. It wouldn't matter. Whoever had arranged for *Wellfleet* to come to Nimue would no doubt be able to offer a perfectly legitimate reason for dispatching the ship before it was requested. The time involved, the seriousness of the situation, the concern about future danger to the crew.

And Sigrah had known all along they were on their way.

Sigrah was still talking. "I'm secure for now, but I don't know the status of the others. They might be dead already. All of them. I've lost control. I have no contact with other crew. I'm requesting immediate emergency and evacuation procedures for the protection of Sunburn."

"What the *fuck*?" I said.

I stared at the screen. Checked the time stamps on the surveillance. Stared some more, my heart thumping with sudden fear. Sigrah was standing in the comms room, speaking into the radio, without the least trace of fear or concern on her face. Because she was not in any danger. She had not lost control of anything. She looked up at the camera in the comms room, one eyebrow raised. She knew she was being watched—she knew her lies were recorded—and she did not care.

In the mine, Adisa and I had reached Level 8 and were approaching Neeta Hunter warily. In Res, the rest of the crew were still discussing the best way to search the transport tunnels. About three minutes after he had entered his private quarters, Delicata emerged with a box in his hands, the same one I had found on the table in Res. It was gray and metal and about half a meter square. He set it on the end of a table.

I hadn't seen the label stamped on one side before, but I could see it clearly now: R9.3.

Recluse 9.3. Those were the spiders. The spiders were right fucking there and nobody had any idea.

Delicata snapped open the latch and lifted the lid. He took something out, something small enough to fit in the palm of his hand, and closed the lid but did not latch it. He tested the lid, made sure the latch didn't catch, and looked around. Nobody was watching him. He left the box on the table and walked out of Res and headed for Ops. He tapped on the door of the comms room. When Sigrah opened it, he handed her the small device he was carrying.

"Go keep an eye on them," Sigrah said. "Try to keep things calm."

Delicata nodded, but his expression showed only confusion. He turned to leave, but he stopped when van Arendonk came out of the systems room at the end of the corridor to make his radio call to Adisa and me down in the mine. He paced at the end of the corridor as he spoke, but when he saw Delicata and Sigrah, he turned and headed toward them.

I wanted nothing more than to jump to my feet to warn him, to warn all of them. It had all played out over an hour ago. There was nothing I could do. My heart was pounding and my throat was tight and every instinct was telling me to run, shout, *do something.* But it was too late. All I could do was watch in horror.

Van Arendonk told Delicata and Sigrah that Adisa and I were on our way back up with Hunter. Sigrah nodded at Delicata, who followed van Arendonk into the junction. She closed the door to Ops behind them and tapped at the device in her hands.

In the mess, the first long, silver spider leg emerged from the box. A choked cry escaped my throat. Nobody saw it. They weren't paying attention.

That was when the Overseer triggered the radiation alarm.

The scene in Res exploded into absolute chaos. The spiders burst from the box as the alarm sounded, and the crew didn't know what they were reacting to, not at first. The spiders spread around them, scrambling to the doorways as though they intended to corral the crew, dodging out of the way every time somebody tried to grab or stop one. Vera was the first to succeed—he caught one of the bots in his hand—and another leapt to his chest and ignited.

It didn't kill him right away. He screamed and fell, crawled across the floor, flailing in pain. More spiders swarmed after that one, keeping the crew away when they tried to help him. Melendez and Dolin had to pull Elena Yee back from Vera, but they weren't fast enough and one of the spiders attached itself to her hand. Melendez pulled it free—Yee shrieked in pain—and threw it across the room. Ryu had their electroshock weapon drawn, but there was nothing to aim it at. Van Arendonk had run into Res when the attack started, but Delicata remained in the junction, motionless, watching through the open doorway with an expression somewhere between nausea and fear. The spiders were too small, too fast. They leapt and crawled and scurried through the common room, swarming toward the crew as they fled. The bots' method seemed to have shifted from encircling the crew to isolating and attacking them, but it was all changing so fast, evolving so fast, every moving piece hard to follow in all the chaos.

It was King who shouted for the others to follow her, grab their gear and follow, for fuck's sake, *hurry*.

When the first of the spiders raced out of Res and into the junction, Delicata spun around and ran toward the comms room—but the door was locked against him. He pounded and shouted and cursed, his angry pleas lost beneath the wail of the station alarm. One bot followed him, then another. His shouts grew louder.

Inside, Sigrah leaned against the door, and she waited.

Delicata hadn't expected the bots to turn on him. He hadn't realized that he was, to Sigrah, every bit as disposable as everybody else on Nimue.

In the end, it only took a few minutes, but through those few minutes Sigrah waited, and listened, and did nothing. She waited while Delicata pounded on the door and begged her to let him in. She waited while the others fled Res in a panic, racing into the cargo warehouse with the spiders following them. Only when the Overseer gave its final lockdown warning did she emerge from the comms room. From the Ops corridor, she watched as Delicata tried to follow the others, but a spider caught him first, caught him and attacked him just as the Overseer was closing the door to the warehouse.

Several of the spiders crawled over Delicata to chase the others into the warehouse, but only a few caught up before the crew reached the ladder to the cargo transport tunnels. King and Melendez kept guard at the bottom of the ladder, kicking away any spider that got close enough, as the others climbed the ladder one by one. Only a couple of spiders managed to keep up with them. They vanished into the tunnels, charging toward the old UEN base.

They didn't know about the weapons factory. They didn't know they had been herded into a trap.

Neither did the Overseer. It shut the tunnel doors behind them, and they disappeared from its tracking data.

In Ops, Sigrah watched the device in her hands. She cursed sharply—disappointed her bots had let so many people get away, I guessed, but it was hard to tell because she had no expression on her face except annoyance and boredom. It felt too big and too terrible to believe, for all that the proof was right before me. She had been expecting a slaughter when she brought the spiders out of their box. And if the Overseer hadn't triggered the lockdown, if the alarms hadn't sent everybody into a flurry of action, a slaughter was exactly what she would have achieved.

She tapped the spider control device a few times. All the spiders stopped their pursuit and headed back to Res. They crawled again over Delicata, who was struggling to free himself from where he was trapped in the door. Blood trickled from his mouth. He tried to call for help, but all he managed was a wet wheeze.

Sigrah pocketed the device and returned to the comms room. She sat down before the radio. She made another encrypted call.

"This is Nimue. I am requesting immediate armed assistance from the vessel *Wellfleet*. Repeat: I am requesting immediate armed assistance from the vessel *Wellfleet*. Sunburn has been infiltrated and overtaken by hostile crew. I couldn't stop them. They've taken hostages—I don't know if they're still alive. They are armed and extremely dangerous."

She left Ops without waiting for a reply. She had to squeeze through the warehouse door over Delicata. He pleaded for help. She didn't even look at him. He tried to grab her leg, and she kicked him away; the door crunched closed on his shoulder. He screamed, but Sigrah was already walking away.

"How did she get into the transport tunnels?" I asked.

"Station forepersons have access to manual overrides," said the Overseer.

"And you've got nothing in the tunnels or in the UEN base? No comms? No security logs?"

"I have no management or oversight access in that facility."

"None at all?"

"No, Hester."

It could be lying. But I didn't think so, not anymore. I had been thinking that the same virus that had infected Aeolia's Overseer was at work here, brought over by Mary Ping for her own twisted reasons, making Nimue's Overseer effectively dishonest, twisting its stewardship actions into violence. The truth, I realized now, was far simpler.

"I am so fucking stupid," I said softly. "It isn't you at all, is it? You're only trying to help."

The Overseer understood that to be a rhetorical question and did not answer.

Fuck. I needed to think. I rubbed my eyes tiredly, rolling my head to ease the tightness in my neck. I had let my disgust for Mary Ping color my conclusions. Because she had killed David, I had wanted so badly for her to be responsible for everything else as well. I had wanted her hubris to have been her downfall. And perhaps it had been, but not in the way I had imagined.

There were two AIs on Nimue. Not a single virus-infected AI acting strangely. Two AIs, one acting exactly as it should be, protecting the crew as best it could, and one acting in a way that looked wildly strange because I hadn't known what I was looking at. They could both be Overseers, but I rather suspected that the one in charge of the facility in the UEN base was something else. It had different goals, different directives. An Overseer would never inhabit a weapons-grade mech suit and attack a crew member under its protection—but a weapons AI could do that easily, under the right circumstances.

The others were going to be caught between Sigrah and the AI—if they weren't already. I asked the Overseer how much time I had before *Wellfleet* arrived. Its best estimate was just over two hours.

"Show me active visual surveillance in Residential and Operations," I said. "Please."

"I'm afraid some of my surveillance modules are damaged, but I will show you what I can."

The Overseer brought up images from the station above: smoke filling the junction, the tangled ruin of spiders scattered throughout the corridor, Delicata's body, Vera's body. Nothing but flickering lines or darkness from at least two cameras. The explosion had been largely contained within the junction and Ops corridor. The walls were scorched, control panels cracked and smoldering, but there were no serious obstacles or obvious structural problems. At the center of the junction were the mangled remains of the bots, fused together in a gruesome tangle.

"And the cargo warehouse?" I said.

The screens changed obligingly. It was quiet, without any signs of movement. No spiders. The doors to the tunnels were still open; Sigrah hadn't closed them after she passed through.

"The cargo airlock."

David's blood, nothing else.

"A map of the facility exterior, including all the remaining UEN infrastructure." I rolled my shoulders tiredly and sat forward in the chair as the screen changed again. "Thank you."

There. There it was. The transport tunnels had to follow the spine of the facility before branching off toward the UEN base. But there was also a way across the surface of the asteroid. A route fast enough that Ned Delicata could use it on his regular "routine maintenance" checks. That was what he meant when he offered to go out and head off the crew before they reached the secret factory.

"Fuck." I sat back in the chair. "Fuck everything."

I hauled my pack into my lap to take stock. The radio, useless for now, but probably wouldn't be later. My PD had been cracked across the screen in the explosion but was still functional. Flashlight. Rebreather. At the bottom of the pack, the emergency vac suit was still folded up neatly. A quick check showed it had not been damaged. The radiation sensor still hung from my belt.

I hurt all over, every bloody joint throbbing with pain as I stood, but it was bearable. I would survive.

I couldn't get out of it this time. I was going to have to go outside.

TWENTY

I limped over to the lift and waited. Standard-issue emergency suits were flimsy as hell, minimally pressurized and insulated, and relatively easy to tear, so I decided to keep it sealed up in the pack on my back until I needed it.

"I cannot protect you if you leave this place, Hester," said the Overseer.

"I know. I need to leave anyway. Just open the doors ahead of me and shut them behind me."

The lift doors slid open. I stepped inside.

"Be careful," I said, then felt immensely foolish, then guilty for feeling foolish.

"You as well, Hester," said the Overseer.

The doors shut, and the lift carried me up to Ops.

Outside the systems room, the corridor was filled with drifting smoke, pockets of heat, whirling dust. A bitter, metallic scent made my eyes water and my throat ache. I switched on my flashlight, but the air was so choked with dust the light only made it harder to see. I turned it off again and pulled the front of my shirt up to cover my mouth and nose. I paused every few steps to listen for the clatter of metal legs, but I heard nothing. I didn't see any intact or waiting spiders, but that meant nothing. If any had survived the explosion, they could be hiding again. The explosion had done the most damage in the front part of the corridor, near the door to the junction; it took me a few minutes to pick my way over and around the ruptured wall plates and twists of metal.

I stopped at Delicata's body and nudged the twisted remains of the dead bots away from him. I knelt and scrubbed my hands on my trousers. He had told Sigrah he still had the key; he had to have meant the key to the UEN base, the one he used for his visits or inspections or whatever the fuck he had been doing. The corpse stank of charred meat and scorched plastic. I swallowed back my nausea and began to search his pockets. The fabric, where it had not been burned, was tacky with his blood. I tried not to look too closely at the ruin of his shoulder and upper arm, but my gaze kept drifting that way anyway. I wondered if that was what I had looked like when the rescue crew found me.

I found the key in the inner pocket of his jacket. It was nothing like the circuit key I'd taken from David's room. It was bulkier and heavier, a solid chunk of metal. It looked to me less like a security key and more like the sort of tool sometimes used for manual overrides in creaking old machines—but the UEN base was, after all, a creaking old machine. I secured the key in my pack and looked at the camera over the door.

"Okay," I said. "The warehouse, please."

The door slid open. I stepped into the warehouse.

There had been no time to move Mary Ping's body. She still lay on the floor, flooded with diffuse industrial light, in a pool of drying blood. I didn't let myself look away as I neared. Didn't let myself look away when I stood over her.

I had thought, when I first saw her, that it was hard to imagine her beating a man to death in a rage. But looking down at her bloodied corpse, with the skin singed and ribs cracked open and insides revealed, it was not hard to imagine at all. David had wanted to know what Parthenope was hiding, and Mary Ping had promised to show him. Agreed to meet him in the airlock, as long as he disabled the surveillance. Promised to bring him a vac suit so they might step outside. He had suspected that Parthenope was building weapons of war. I knew now that fear and disgust were what I had heard in his voice in the message to me.

She had killed him to protect the AI hiding in the UEN base. But I still didn't know why it had killed her. I didn't even know if it was reasonable to ask *why*. There were hundreds, if not thousands, of stories about martial AIs that had gone very, very wrong. Maybe this was another example of the same: an artificial intelligence designed to kill, so it killed, and it was as simple as that.

Her blood filled the air with a stale, metallic odor that turned my stomach as I walked away.

I was halfway through the warehouse when I heard the first spider.

There was a whisper-soft clatter of metal on metal, just loud enough to carry over the peel of my gecko soles and rasp of my breath. I froze for half a beat, then turned quickly, searching frantically, and glimpsed a flash of silver at the edge of my vision. I flinched, lurched away from it, and began to run.

The spider raced along the wall of the container behind me.

Before I'd made it even three meters, there was a pricking sensation on my shoulder. The spider had jumped. The ratfucking thing had jumped, and now it was clinging to my upper arm. My left arm, with no flesh for it to grab, but its legs were clinging to the sleeve of my shirt.

I shook my arm frantically, and when that failed to dislodge it, I reached for it with my right hand. It scampered down my arm toward my exposed prosthetic hand. Its clever little legs wrapped themselves around the metal joint of my wrist, and I felt a spark, followed by a sudden and nauseating wave of pressure in my nerves, strong enough to make me stumble in surprise.

I grabbed the spider with my other hand and pulled, wrenching it free—felt that spark too, it was like a low-voltage shock, just above the threshold for pain—and flung it to the ground. I stomped on it, but even as I was enjoying that fleeting satisfaction, I saw another two spiders racing toward me along the cargo containers.

The surviving spiders were still following Sigrah's earlier command to trap and destroy. And now the goddamned murder machines had found me.

I ducked my head and ran. The pain in my hip was growing worse with every step, shooting down my leg and up my back, but I didn't dare stop. Another spider jumped for me, landed on my back. I grabbed it but couldn't wrench it free.

Those sparks of nerve pain returned as the spider burrowed itself into my shoulder joint, and at the same moment I noticed flashes of light across my left eye—the artificial one—and fuck, fuck, fuck, that little fucker wasn't just clinging to me to blow me up, it was fucking with my prosthetics, it was hacking me like I was an enemy machine.

I spun around and slammed my shoulder into the nearest shipping container, hard enough to knock the spider loose. I stomped on it just before I stumbled past the end of the row. I turned to my left and sprinted toward the exterior wall of the cargo warehouse, turned again.

We had left the airlock wide open. Careless for a crime scene, but really quite helpful for me. I veered inside and reached to pull the interior hatch closed. Another spider leapt for me, landed on my right hand, the one its friend had punctured hours ago. It ran up my arm and around my shoulder. The door closed with a heavy clunk, and I spun the wheel to engage the manual lock before grabbing the spider.

"Get the fuck off me!" I smashed it to the ground and stomped on it, stomping again and again and again, as the airlock door closed. "Fuck fuck fuck!"

I only stopped when it was a wreck of metal pieces and smashed circuits, utterly flattened beneath my boots.

Another one skittered over the outside of the interior window, then another, their blink-fast motions obscuring my view.

I dropped my pack to the floor and tore it open to get the emergency suit. I had to turn the suit a few times to locate all the limbs; my hands were shaking. I couldn't see the spiders outside the airlock anymore. They would be climbing to the control panel, they were going to be trying to get in—could they get in? Was their programming that smart? Maybe. Probably. I had to assume they could get in.

I pulled the soft helmet over my head, wincing at the feel of the thick, rubbery, almost slick material. The gloves were fat enough to make my fingers clumsy, but luckily the suit had been designed for people in a panic, for people losing air and losing blood and losing control. I clipped the seals into place at the neck and shoulders and powered the suit on.

For one frightful second, nothing happened, and I thought: wouldn't that be bloody perfect, a dead suit, a useless piece of scrap—then the ventilation and pressurization kicked in. It felt odd, like a warm breeze in the small of my back and down my legs, an obscenely intimate caress that made me squirm. I told myself to get over it, and I reached for the airlock control panel. I hit **Engage**.

"Please fucking work," I said.

My voice was dull and loud in the confines of my helmet.

The old airlock clanked and groaned around me. A loud hiss filtered through the shitty microphones in the suit's helmet. My heart was thumping so hard it was a pain in my chest. My breath was rasping and metallic. I counted down the seconds.

The control panel told me depressurization was twenty percent complete. Thirty-five. Fifty percent complete. I could have sworn I heard the clatter of the spiders outside the interior hatch. It was impossible—not that they were there, of course they were there, but that I could hear them. The steel was twenty centimeters thick. The UEN hadn't fucked around when they were building their wartime bases. Always so afraid the Martians would show up out of nowhere and bomb them to hell, never mind that the Martians had only ever started rebelling because they were starving, because they had no ships, because Earth-based companies had stolen their water and their moons, because they weren't permitted weapons to defend themselves, because they were living like animals in their own habitat domes, in their own homes—or so the more radical of my parents' friends had liked to say, during those otherwise dull academic dinner parties in their garden in London after the war ended, when the wine flowed like delicate summer brooks before the cognac flowed like the Thames in a storm surge. Nobody told me and my brother to hurry off to bed because nobody cared that we were awake and listening.

Voices would rise and fall and laugh and argue while the summer sun set in brilliant streaks of red and orange over Hampstead Heath. I missed my parents, I missed Devon and his kids, I missed London and Oxford and sunshine and greenery and being able to move without pain. I missed all of it so much it hurt, like I had swallowed a knot of thorns and my entire body had hardened into scar tissue around the ragged, still-bleeding wound in the center. I should never have left Earth.

One hundred percent. The airlock depressurization was complete.

The doctors told me I had not been exposed to open space. They told me a lot of things I did not believe, but that one I couldn't deny. I would not have survived if I had touched the vacuum. It had taken seven hours for help to arrive. That my nightmares took me from fire into ice, tumbling and tumbling, flames trailing behind me as charred bits of my own body fell away and froze and crumbled to dust, that was as much a mystery as the accident itself, one that nobody cared to solve.

There were infinite places I wanted to be that were not the barren surface of an asteroid with minimal gravity. My parents' kitchen as my father made a pot of tea. Sunita's garden in Oxford as the long summer sunset painted the sky red and purple. Aboard *Symposium* without knowing what was to come. Even my grim, lonely quarters on Hygiea, where I could lock the door, lower the lights, muffle the world outside. Anywhere. Anywhere. In that moment, every wonderful and terrible place I had been in my life was more appealing than the prospect of opening that door and stepping outside.

I opened the door anyway, and I stepped outside.

The wide, flat metal plating of the transport track stretched before me. My gecko soles wouldn't keep me anchored on loose or sandy surfaces, but it seemed like I was in luck, if I used a very generous definition of luck—because asteroids don't have atmospheres, so Nimue didn't have wind, which meant there was no dust or grit drifted over the track. I closed the hatch behind me.

Stay centered. I took a breath. Move smoothly. Another. And walk. Lift one foot, set it down. Lift the other.

Just fucking walk.

Faster.

Don't look up.

Once I had been the person who would have craned her head toward the darkness and the stars to see whatever she could see, to spot distant bodies familiar and strange, to stare and stare and stare until my eyes watered and my neck hurt and the view above was more precious and familiar to me than anything on the ground. I had been so certain I would not fear the dangers of space. I would embrace them. I was an explorer at heart, or so I had told myself. I had nothing to fear but failure. It had been so easy to believe in that courageous fairy-tale version of myself when I was earthbound and safe.

I did not look up.

The surface of Nimue was gray and gravelly and utterly dull. Any features larger than cobbles were few and far between. There was only dust, and gray rock, and two or three kilometers of track ribboning beneath me. I did not look up. I had no instinct for how long it would take. I didn't know how fast I was walking. I didn't even know if I'd estimated the distance correctly from the maps.

I did not look up, until I did.

It was less a conscious action than instinct, the impulse born of being a marginally evolved primate treading on a surface that curved too much, toward a horizon that loomed too near, and the fear that came with that, a fear so deep in the old brain I didn't even register it as such. It was only a thought that wasn't a thought—I needed to see where I was going—and I lifted my gaze from the track.

The first thing I saw was that the surface of Nimue around me was no longer flat and featureless. The bulky structure of the UEN base was in view. It looked like a dull gray box set down on the asteroid's surface at an angle, as though half of it had sunk into the regolith. Beyond the box were three towers. I recognized the shape of them from history books, from memorial parks on Yuèliàng: they were missile silos. I had no sense of scale, no sense of how tall they were, nor how far away. How insufferably bloody stupid it had been, for the UEN to build missile silos all the way out here, so far from Mars and the inner system battles. How scared they must have been, to think the war would stretch this far. Scared or greedy or bloodthirsty or some sick combination of them all.

However pointless its origin, it was a relief to see the base so close. I might have been able to drop my gaze again, to keep going, if I hadn't also looked at the stars.

Above the dull gray surface of Nimue was the darkness that wasn't sky because there was no sky here, specked with lights so small and so distant they might have been motes of dust, and the great size of the darkness, the crushing cold of it, it hit me with a wave of vertigo so strong I felt it as a physical blow, as though the asteroid was tumbling beneath my feet, the tracks bucking. I turned, dizzy, and sank to my knees, accidentally missed the edge of the track and plunged my right hand several centimeters down to the surface instead.

I squeezed my eyes shut, twisted in that awkward position, willing the vertigo away. My stomach was churning and my heart was pounding, and I felt suddenly, painfully hot all over, sticky and prickling and so feverish it was frightening. I shifted, thinking I ought to stand, but the surface of Nimue was soft, not solid rock, and my hand only sank deeper when I moved. I leaned to the left, clutched at the metal track with my metal fingers until I had a seam to grip, and pulled myself upright again.

I squeezed my eyes shut and I breathed, and breathed, and remained still, and breathed.

It was a long time before I could open my eyes.

My clumsy fall and even more clumsy recovery had kicked up a gritty cloud around me. The dust didn't settle; it hung like a fog, obscuring my view, wrapping me in a dull gray shroud. I tried to keep my gaze down as I stood, to look at only the cargo rails beneath me, but I could not forget the darkness above. I knew it was there, and a single wrong step would send me spinning into it, drifting away with nothing to tether me, a trail of dust clinging to my boots. I could not stop thinking about how small Nimue was. How little there was of it, that hideous lumpy potato tumbling through space. I couldn't breathe. There was no air in the suit. I couldn't breathe and it was a bloody stupid way to die.

I took in deep, shuddering breaths. I took small steps. I kept moving. I did not stop until the entrance to the grim gray bunker loomed before me.

There was no control panel, no electronic input, no place to try an access code or employee ID. There was only an old-fashioned light signal above the door: red for pressurized, green for depressurized. The light shone red. I dug the key out of my pack and looked for the slot. I hadn't noticed before how the dull gray metal was smudged with blood.

There it was, labeled for everybody to see: AIRLOCK MANUAL. Apparently the company, or Sigrah, didn't trust the AI that reigned behind that door to control its own perimeter. I inserted the key and turned it. For several seconds, there was no reaction.

"Come on, come on," I muttered. I had no idea what I would do if it didn't work. "Come on, fucker."

Then the door began to tremble. The key turned in my hand; I let it go quickly. There probably would have been noise, had there been any air to transmit it. Instead I felt only a faint shuddering quiver when I touched the metal. Several seconds passed before the light turned to green.

I opened the hatch and stepped inside.

TWENTY-ONE

On the other side of the airlock: nothing but darkness.

I closed the inner hatch—it made a deafening clang—and held my breath. The echoes faded. The airlock pinged and clinked quietly. There were no other sounds. The only light came from the airlock indicator above the door, and that was a muted green, illuminating nothing.

I checked the suit's readout of atmosphere conditions. Breathable air at a normal pressure. Still I hesitated to take off my helmet. I wasn't feeling particularly trusting. But the suit had limited peripheral vision and an internal speaker that crackled every time I turned my head. I needed to hear and see what was around me. I removed my helmet but left the rest of the suit on. The air on my face was cool and dry, stirred by a faint current.

The silence was deeply unsettling. I couldn't even hear the usual station hum. There was simply nothing.

I switched on my flashlight. The floor ended abruptly about three meters ahead. There was no railing, only a drop into a deep, deep darkness. The light was just strong enough to illuminate the shapes of some machines: belts, gears, robotic arms, cranes. Some of it looked decades old, as though it had not been updated since the war, while some was very new. All of it was packed together, leaving very little empty space and making it hard to see much farther than what was right in front of me.

Nothing moved. The entire factory was still and quiet. As far as I could tell, none of the machines were operational. I caught the scents of metal, rubber, fresh oil, fuel. A hint, perhaps, of smoke. It was as though the entire facility had fallen quiet just before I stepped inside and was now holding its breath.

I reached for my radio but hesitated before turning it on. I had been making plenty of noise already, with the creaking of the airlock and thunderous clang of the hatch, but speaking felt different. After too many seconds of indecision, I clipped the radio to my suit without saying anything. I needed to see more of the facility before I alerted anybody to my presence. I didn't see any surveillance cameras or tracking units, but I couldn't be sure they weren't present. I needed to know who—or what—was out there listening.

Every motion I made felt too loud: the sticky-soft peel of the gecko soles, the crinkle of flexible polymer on my arms and legs, the sound of my neck rasping against the suit's collar. I cast my light around and found two metal staircases leading down. I chose the one to the right, closer to where I thought the transport tunnel should come into the base, if I was understanding the layout correctly. The staircase had a skinny gate across the top, but it swung open easily on recently oiled hinges.

The stairs creaked and trembled as I descended. I couldn't even see how far down they went. I had no idea where a control room might be, or the entrance from Nimue's transport tunnels, or the systems room and physical brain of the AI that ran the factory. All I could see were the steps before me and the machines around me.

I could also see, here and there, in glimpses and gaps, in flashes of illumination when my light turned, what those machines were building.

Weapons. The factory was building weapons, exactly as I had suspected, but suspecting a thing to be true was very different from seeing it firsthand. Winding around me, on both sides of the staircase, was a tangled braid of racks and conveyor belts, drawing from the hidden depths of the machines like tributaries joining a river that flowed toward the far side of the facility. Most of what I could see nearby appeared to be the incomplete pieces of products that would be completed and armed elsewhere. There was a line of missile casings standing upright like soldiers momentarily frozen midmarch. There were slender canisters with no markings or labels laid out like baguettes on a conveyor belt. I recognized the shape from history books and news reports: the UEN had used noxious gas loaded onto riot rovers to slip into crowds and quash Martian protests. Something about the blankness of those canisters, the complete lack of exterior markings, was so much more unsettling than a rainbow of warning labels would be.

I kept walking. Down the stairs, through the machines, gaping with growing horror at all I saw.

Egg-shaped devices that looked like beehives, with each cell glinting strangely. Fixed-winged drones like pinned butterflies. Armored rovers with empty gun mounts. Countless pieces, incomplete parts, devices I didn't recognize. Wings, perhaps, or blades. The casings for small explosives. Sections of what I assumed were to be larger unmanned spacecraft, visible now only in shards of curved hulls and polished nose cones.

My mouth was tacky and dry, my heart beating quickly. I imagined this facility functional. Every machine chugging, every belt whirring. Bots I could not see piecing together these uncountable parts into whole and operational devices. I imagined all of these weapons loaded into transport containers. Ships coming to Nimue to carry them away—the crews would be told they were transporting water or fuel or precious metals. Shipments would spread throughout the outer system, carrying Parthenope's weapons into every major port and station. All waiting for a signal from Parthenope—and what would that take? They were not building all of these weapons without a plan. Whatever that plan was, whatever conquest they wished to achieve, the spark to set it all in motion could be anything. A deal gone wrong. A treaty disregarded. A rivalry grown tiresome. So little. I did not know what they were waiting for, and that was as terrifying as not knowing what they intended to do.

I stared at all of it, committing it to memory with growing panic as I continued my descent into the facility. Another turn in the staircase, then another. There I spotted the first surveillance camera, but I couldn't tell if it was working. I shifted my light from one hand to the other to test if the camera followed my motion. It remained still.

The light did catch, buried deep in the guts of a machine, the flat, reflective faceplate of a helmet. There was a line of mech suit helmets lined up on a belt, like disembodied heads, separated from their bodies.

The factory just kept going. It extended down and down and down, stretching into the depths of the asteroid, so ruthlessly efficient in its design it would have been impressive, if its purpose weren't so terrible. I was growing impatient and frustrated. I was fairly confident the transport tunnels should be meeting the base somewhere ahead of me and to the right, but I had seen nothing like a control room for human crew, nor a systems room for an AI. I had not heard any sounds except my own footsteps and my own breath. The silence and the darkness weighed on me, turning that vast space claustrophobic and oppressive, with the dance of my own flashlight casting nervous shadows in every direction.

I made it all the way down to the factory floor before I saw the first hint of light.

The stairs deposited me near what seemed to be the middle of the facility. There were racks of transport containers in the distance, on the other side of the factory, with the broad area directly before me split by what looked, at first glance, like a misplaced city street. There were buildings of one or two levels, with dark windows looking outward like eyes. I was so disoriented, so frustrated with how little I could see, that it took me a moment to realize those rooms were exactly what I was looking for. They were the parts of the facility designed for human crew.

But there was nobody there. All the rooms were dark. There should have been somebody, Ryu and the others, or Sigrah. They couldn't all still be in the transport tunnels; more than enough time had passed. I didn't want to consider that I had been so wildly wrong, to think this was the only possible destination, but the alternative was worse. The spiders could have found them in the tunnels. Another mech suit, against which they would have no defenses. Sigrah could have caught up to them and killed them all. Finished the work her bots had failed to do. Even now she could be returning to the station to tell

Parthenope something unfortunate had happened. What the Overseer had shown me on surveillance made it abundantly clear that Sigrah had a story all planned out and absolute confidence that nobody would question it.

I turned to the right, toward where I believed the entrance from the transport tunnels to be, but as I did so a glint in the other direction caught my eye. I thought at first it was only a reflection, but when I turned off my flashlight and waited for the spots to fade, the light remained.

It was a low red glow at the far side of the factory. As my eyes adjusted, a shape emerged: a sphere, sitting above the central rooms, high above the factory floor, visible only in shards of faint red light that shone from frail lines on its surface.

No. That wasn't right. The light was not on the surface, but coming from inside. Visible through tiny cracks—but how tiny were they, truly? I had no sense of distance, no way to gauge the true scale. The red lines were uneven and jagged like the seams of a human skull. The shape, the scale, the deep red glow, everything about it was at odds with the tightly efficient facility around it.

The sphere sat above the factory like a wasp nest, or a banked ember in the oppressive darkness. I knew better than to jump to conclusions, but I was ready for a leap. This was not a structure designed by human engineers, for human purposes.

This was where the weapons AI kept its brain. It had made itself a home.

I moved away from the sphere, staying close to the base of the machines. I hoped I would not have to approach that unsettling sphere directly. For now, I would search for a control room as I cautiously made my way toward it.

I had just passed the staircase again when a soft noise caught my attention. I stopped abruptly, silencing the sound of my gecko soles on the floor and the crinkle of my suit, and listened. I couldn't tell at first where it had come from. Only when I heard it again—a soft, rhythmic pair of taps—was I able to pinpoint it as coming from ahead of me and slightly above. As I turned, a bright light flared from the same direction.

I snapped my flashlight off and stepped back, knocking my head painfully on the underside of a conveyor belt. I bit back the yelp of pain and waited.

This light, unlike the red of the AI's nest, was brilliant and pale and not at all hard to see. It appeared as a neat rectangle in the wall of the factory, a bright glow several meters wide and tall, bouncing as it grew brighter and brighter. It took only a few seconds for my confused brain to make sense of what I was seeing: somebody was approaching within the transport tunnel. I heard no voices, only the soft sound of footsteps. Whoever it was, they weren't using gecko soles. They were leap-stepping along in the manner of people used to low gravity. My mind raced to figure out who it could be, but without any real idea how long it took to pass through the tunnels, nor what obstacles they contained, I couldn't even make a good guess. Probably not a large group, judging by the sound.

An interminably long time seemed to pass before the light changed from a distant glow to a bright pinpoint, and the edges of the tunnel were illuminated clearly. I glimpsed the dull gray of a vac suit and the reflective curve of a faceplate—just enough to be sure it was a person, not one of the black mech suits, but there was nothing more I could discern. They could have been anybody. At the end of the tunnel, they descended a ladder to the factory floor, sliding more than climbing, and landed with a tap of boots.

Nobody followed. They were alone, and they knew exactly

where they were going. There was no hesitation, no worry about what might be lurking in the dark. It had to be Sigrah. Fuck. But the others had fled before her—where were they? Why had it taken her so long to get here? Perhaps they had hidden somewhere in the tunnels, or had another destination in mind entirely. Perhaps she had searched along the way. Or caught up to them already. I hated not knowing where they were.

She walked straight from the bottom of the ladder to the first room in the row. For a moment I saw her only by the light shining around the corner and through the walls of windows. There was a mechanical clank—a door unlocking—and the light dipped, concentrated behind the window, snapped off.

Lights came on inside the room. Behind the windows, Sigrah removed her helmet and set it aside. She turned, peering down this way and that; she was looking at consoles and screens. Her expression was hard to read from where I stood, but while she moved quickly and with purpose, there did not seem to be panic or fear in her demeanor.

I waited until she was turned away from me to slink quickly back along the machinery. She would have surveillance now, security control, weapons, anything she wanted.

The lights could come on at any moment, but for now the darkness protected me. I ran across the open space to the row of rooms in the center. I pressed myself against the wall and waited to hear the door open again or the crackle of a radio or the clink of metal spider legs.

Instead I heard a gentle whir, very faint, obviously mechanical. It sounded like a fan, something weak and small, but I could not see it, could not see anything at all. My eyes strained in the darkness. It was coming from above, and after a few seconds it was joined by another just like it. One to the left, one to the right. Still no lights came on on. I had no idea if Sigrah had surveillance access yet. She could be looking right at me. She could be calling upon weapons I would never see in the darkness.

I flinched when I felt something fly past my head. In the faint, faint light from Sigrah's control room, all I could see was the hint of motion, a shadow among shadows, moving so quickly it blurred before my eyes when I tried to track it.

My mind filled with stories I'd heard as a child: rumors of heat-seeking and motion-sensing machines stalking through the Underground tunnels beneath London, remnants of the war set loose on Earth by Martians determined to claim their revenge. Family dogs blasted to soggy red pulp in suburban gardens. Homeless men chased like animals through the streets of Southwark. The same from my father's side of the family in California, where my cousins spoke of craters in the desert where homesteads used to be, of children snatched from schoolyards by gleaming insectoid prowlers, of an old woman who mistook a threshing bot for a recycler when she stepped outside and her head—so the gruesome story went—rolled into the street while her body slumped in her front hall. There was no truth to the rumors. The war never reached Earth. All the violence had happened on Mars or in space. But the stories were terrifying precisely because the machines were real.

I held my breath until the whirring sound faded. Slowly, carefully, I turned my head to look for it, whatever it was. A smudge of movement well above me, but no light, no reflections. It faded into the enveloping darkness. I took a few more steps, feeling my way, my heart pounding.

Another few steps. My hand slid from the wall into empty space. An open doorway.

I slipped into the room and shut the door quietly. Breathed

a cautious sigh of relief when the latch caught. Breathed again when the whirring machine retreated.

A few steps into the deeper darkness and my boot connected with something soft but immovable. I lurched forward, caught myself. I leaned down to find the obstacle on the floor.

Touched the cool, smooth, familiar material of a vac suit.

Traced with my fingers along the length of an arm. The curve of a shoulder. A warm, exposed face.

TWENTY-TWO

I jolted upright and stumbled backward a few steps, slammed into the hard edge of the doorframe. My heart was hammering and my breath coming in quick rasps. I couldn't hear anything else, couldn't hear if the drone was hovering right outside the door. I felt an arm. Warm skin. A face. Light, light, I needed my fucking light—I switched it on, remembered half a second later to bank the glow with my hand. I let my eyes adjust.

There was somebody lying on the floor right in front of me. I dropped to my knees and reached for them.

"Hey," I whispered, scarcely daring to make a sound. "Hey, are you okay?"

I recognized the black hair braided into rows: Melendez, the crew's geologist. I stripped off my glove and reached into the collar of her vac suit to find a pulse. She was alive but out cold. I didn't see any obvious injuries, no blood or head wounds, but I couldn't examine her thoroughly while she was wearing a vac suit. She was on her front, with one arm caught awkwardly beneath her body, the other reaching above her head and gripping the ankle of a boot. Somebody else's boot. She wasn't alone.

I panned my light over the room. My hand was shaking so much the beam danced over the walls and corners and dusty consoles and people on the floor.

They were all here. I crawled past Melendez to reach Dolin, who was lying in a sprawl next to Dietrich-Yun. Elena Yee was just beyond them, Balthazar right beside her. All of them were unconscious. All wearing vac suits with no helmets. Katee King was curled onto her side at the base of a console; there was blood on her face, more matting her hair, staining the gloves of her suit. Ryu was next to her.

"Oh, fuck, Avery." I lurched across the room, tripping over Yee's legs, and fell to my knees beside Ryu. I turned them onto their back and brushed their limp black hair off their face. "Come on, Avery, wake up. Wake the fuck up."

I couldn't tell if they were breathing. They looked so pale, so bruised with their twin black eyes and swollen nose. I leaned close to listen for their breath, tugged at their collar to find a pulse. Their skin was clammy and cold.

There. A flutter beneath my fingertips. A pulse. Slow, but steady.

I let out a shaky breath and pulled them close.

"Oh, fuck you. Fuck." I could feel their breath now, warm and a bit sour, shallow but even. "I hate you so much. You need to wake the fuck up."

But they didn't wake up. They didn't stir. I reluctantly crawled away to search the room. I needed to know what had happened and why they were unconscious.

As I turned, there was movement at the corner of my eye.

I looked up, startled, but saw nothing except the flat, pale reflection from a small window in the door. Shit. I hadn't noticed it before. I switched the flashlight off and stood, somewhat unsteadily, to pick my way across the room in the darkness. I stopped when I reached the front wall, and I waited.

A moment later: a click. The door was opening.

I heard no whirring, no humming, none of the soft mechanical sounds of the drones, only the soft scrape of the door and the sticky peel of gecko boots. A faint shadow of motion resolved into a dark shape. The silhouette of a person less than a meter away.

I lunged wildly, my heart in my throat, and struck out with both hands. The first blow, the one from my right, was a useless slap that caught the edge of their shoulder. But the second, from my left, was a solid punch of metal fingers curled into a metal ball, and it connected with their face.

Face. Not faceplate. Not a hard helmet but soft flesh.

I heard a spluttering "Fuck!" before the whirring sound returned. There was a gasp from the other person—right near my ear—then one hand on my arm, twisting me around, and another clamped across my mouth. They pulled me backward, my boots dragging uselessly, and pushed me to the floor. There was a scrape—a creak of hinges—and the door clicked shut again.

A soft, soft whisper as the hand moved away from my mouth: "Shut the fuck up. It will hear you."

I had no time to respond before the whirring noise grew louder. There was a sharp pop and a crackling sound outside the door. White light spilled through the window, and a rainlike patter filled the room. Something, several somethings, struck the door and wall, causing the entire room to vibrate with deafening noise. As the sound of the impacts faded, I could again hear that close, constant humming that put an ache in my teeth.

There was another volley of impacts on the door and wall, and a crackling, like fireworks, that landed a series of loud metal pings. The door rattled under another round, then another, before the drone moved along the wall, launching its attack on other doors, other rooms. The noise of impacts grew softer as the machine drifted farther away.

I breathed in silence, waiting. The room was utterly dark.

There was a scrape and a scuff. A sigh.

Then, in a whisper, Hugo van Arendonk said, "Hello, Marley. I think you broke my fucking nose."

"What the fuck is that thing?" I hissed.

At the same time, van Arendonk said, "Where did you come from?"

"And what did you do to them? Why won't they wake up?"

"What did *I* do? Fuck. Fuck." He took a deep breath, then another. He was trying to calm himself down, which did not exactly help me calm myself. "I didn't do anything, for fuck's sake. And to answer your first question, who the hell knows what the thing is. Some kind of bomb filled with shitty, smaller bombs? I'm not a fucking engineer. It can track motion and see in the dark a hell of a lot better than I can, but it seems to be pretty stupid about finding targets. Couldn't you see it?"

"Why would I be able to see it?" I said, still whispering.

"You've got that eye."

I stifled a short, hysterical laugh. "The good ones cost extra. I can't see shit with this one."

"Where's Mohammad? Are you alone?"

"It's just me. He and Hunter are in the transport tunnels."

"Oh, fuck. Fuck. He's such a fucking—"

The whirring noise returned outside the room, and van Arendonk broke off abruptly. For several seconds neither of us spoke. We breathed quietly, carefully. The noise faded again as the drone moved away.

"Sigrah's here too," I said. "In the control room."

"I know. I was watching for her. She switched on those fucking drones."

"What happened to everybody? Why are they here?"

I heard a shuffle and a rasp as he adjusted his position. "Sigrah and her bloody henchman happened. They attacked us in Res."

"After that. I saw the surveillance. The Overseer showed me."

"The Overseer— Fuck." A huff of laughter. "You can't trust that machine. Did you happen to get a look around this lovely facility when you came in? This is what it's been hiding."

"It's not in control of all this. That's—it's something else. A different AI." He started to interrupt, but I spoke over him. "I can explain. I will. Just tell me what the fuck happened."

A pause, one in which I very much wished I could see van Arendonk's face, then he said, "We, uh, we fled into the transport tunnels—you probably saw that much? We made it before Sigrah triggered the lockdown."

"That was the Overseer too, trying to stop her from catching you."

"Was it?" He let out a slow breath. "Well, it didn't do a fucking bit of good. It's a bloody maze in there, and it took us a while to get through to the part that's been closed off. But we got here eventually and started looking for a place to take care of the injured. And to find a radio. This is some kind of comms room, but everything's shut down. They were trying to get it running. It seemed like a secure location. Melendez was keeping watch. And she—she collapsed. We thought she fainted, to be honest, or she'd been injured earlier and hadn't noticed. There was no warning."

"It wasn't a spider?"

"No. Not one of those wretched beehives either. We didn't see what it was until we went to get her." He cleared his throat, cleared it again. That low scrape of sound in the darkness made me painfully aware of how thirsty I was. "It was a riot rover. A small one. Right outside the fucking door. We didn't hear it roll up. Clever of it, wasn't it, to wait until we had our helmets off?"

That endless conveyor belt of gas canisters, unmarked and gleaming, had been bad enough. It was worse to know they were mounted on rovers and roaming the facility, and they had been activated well before Sigrah arrived.

"Why didn't it get you?" I asked.

"Apparently good genes are still the best defense."

"The fuck does that mean?"

"It's a fast-working and extremely powerful sedative," van Arendonk said. "Developed by some secret research team at Grimaldi Labs for the Yuèliàng military about a century ago, but the UEN picked it up quickly enough when they offered the right price. Brought it out of retirement, so to speak. I recognize the smell. Rotten roses." He sniffed and let out a huff of laughter. "I can still fucking smell it. It's just one of the dozens of unpleasant compounds my forebears genetically altered us to be unable to absorb or metabolize. Which does rather make it obvious who Parthenope intends to use it on, does it not?"

"No shit. It's not as though they built this entire fucking facility because they want to go to war with Yuèliàng. You were always going to be safe."

Van Arendonk was quiet a moment. "I didn't know what they were doing here, Marley. I had no idea."

"You knew something was going on. You assigned yourself to this investigation."

"You did the same," van Arendonk pointed out.

"That's not the same. I came here for a friend."

"So did I," he said. Then, more quietly, "For all the good it's done."

I rubbed my forehead; the combination of flashing lights and my prosthetic eye had given me another throbbing headache. "Did you already suspect that it had something to do with Aeolia?"

"Not precisely," van Arendonk said. "I still don't know what this place has to do with Aeolia, but I know the story of what happened there is bullshit. The same flavor of bullshit as all the PR about Nimue's productivity—and, yes, of course I knew something was going on here. Everybody in the fucking company knows something is going on here. Parthenope has called in too many favors and thrown too much money into building a furnace that has no hope of ever paying for itself. Everybody goes along with the polite fiction because the company has an uncanny knack for making its allies very rich and making its enemies very uncomfortable."

"And you help them," I said, "as one of their lawyers."

"So do you," he countered, "as one of their investigators."

I was never given a choice, I wanted to say, but I couldn't bring myself to speak the words aloud. It was true, and it was a comforting lie. We always had a choice. It was just that the companies we worked for were very good at making sure all of our choices were bad ones.

Of all the positions Parthenope had offered to me, none had come even remotely close to being what I would be most qualified to do. *Overseer wrangling*, David had called it. I had assumed the company simply didn't want to pay me what I would be worth in an AI-adjacent job.

I sat up a bit straighter, trying to ease the ache from my hip that was radiating up my back.

These machines would bore you. I had thought David was trying to be kind, trying to explain away why he was in the sysadmin job that should have been mine. But he had also said, *Maybe they're your style after all.* Platitudes, or so I had believed. Fuck. He wouldn't have wasted his time with small talk. He had one chance to contact me, one chance to tell me what he had learned without Mary Ping or Sigrah knowing. Everything David said in his message had a purpose. He had chosen his words carefully.

I just hadn't listened carefully. Not until it was too late.

"The virus on Aeolia wasn't a virus," I said, slowly, working it through, trying to piece together David's puzzle. Remembering Mary Ping's knowing smile. "It was an AI. It was a test run."

"What would they be test . . . Oh. Oh, fuck me sideways."

"They sent an AI to see if it could overtake Aeolia's Overseer. What's the point of building an entire fleet of illegal weapons if you can't be sure it's going to be able to attack like you want it to? But it went badly. They didn't expect the Overseer to react by shutting itself down and letting the entire crew die."

They should have. That was exactly the sort of thing an AI

put in an impossible position might be expected to do. Humans tended to forget that for an AI, shutting itself off counted as protection, not surrender. Ceasing to exist was the perfect way for an AI to guarantee its functionality could not be further compromised.

"That infiltrating AI is here now," I said. "That was the test. This is the real thing. But it's already gone wrong. It killed Mary Ping using one of the mech suits, and none of them expected that. It's not listening to Sigrah anymore. I'm not sure it ever was. AIs don't kill their sysadmins and build themselves giant creepy nests in the middle of their factories if they trust their handlers."

There was a brief silence before van Arendonk said, "Half of the stations in the belt are run by AIs based on the Overseers."

"Half?" I said, surprised. I had known Parthenope's steward design was popular, but I'd never bothered to find out exactly how widespread it was. "Really?"

"At a guess," van Arendonk said. "Mostly under other names, but they're all built on the same design. Parthenope leases the right to brand and modify the system to a company called Asymptote Intelligence, which is functionally little more than a shell. They have several products that are all essentially Overseers. They pay very well for the privilege too."

I had heard of Asymptote but assumed it was just another AI designer trying to get a toehold in outer systems commerce. "That's not common knowledge, is it?"

"Oh, not at all. Parthenope claims that would make the clients and their stations too vulnerable. Which is true, I suppose. They are certainly vulnerable."

I shook my head. He was right, but it was not our immediate problem. "We have to shut it down. We have to stop it before it can do—whatever they want it to do."

"You're mad to think it'll let you get close. Or Sigrah. She's already killed to protect it."

"I know. We have to do it anyway."

"Marley, you don't know anything about this machine."

"Well, yes, that is something to consider," I said. It was dark; he couldn't see my expression. "It's too bad we don't have an AI expert sitting right fucking in front of you with no other commitments for the rest of her day."

"I— Okay." Van Arendonk laughed slightly. "That's fair. I apologize. Does the AI expert have a plan for stopping the homicidal AI and its equally homicidal human keeper?"

"We have to—"

Before I could finish, a loud sound carried through the factory. It was a series of sharp pops: an attack from a beehive drone, but nowhere near us.

There was a scramble in the darkness as van Arendonk stood. "Fuck. I need—fuck, fuck, fuck." He fumbled briefly, then a light flared, momentarily blinding. He held the flashlight with one hand and grabbed his radio with the other.

I jumped to my feet. "Are you crazy? That thing is going to see us."

He ignored me to click the radio on. "Mohammad, do not come into the fucking factory. Do you hear me? Please be listening, you stubborn asshole. Do not enter the factory."

A beat, then a snap of sound. "That warning would have been more useful before we came into the factory, aye?"

"Get out and shut the door," van Arendonk said.

"Where are—"

Adisa's question was interrupted by a squeal of sound, followed at once by a deep, concussive boom. I bolted to the door and pulled it open. There was another explosion, and with it came a brilliant flash of light to my left. Van Arendonk shouted something, either in my ear or in the radio, but I couldn't hear his words over the noise reverberating through the factory.

I switched on my flashlight as I ran and looked for any glint of silver, for any bots or drones. Smoke billowed from the entrance to the cargo tunnel up ahead, with dancing beams of light caught in the drifts.

A bright flash filled the tunnel, startling and blinding, and another boom followed. I saw, for only a second, the silhouette of a beehive drone backlit by the explosion, but when the light faded, I lost sight of it. Glints of silver were racing up the factory wall, toward the mouth of the tunnel. So many sparks of light. So many spiders.

The shape of a person appeared, then another.

One of the figures—a flash of silver hair, it was Hunter—jumped from the tunnel entrance, ignoring the ladder and trusting herself to Nimue's low gravity. She landed gracefully, then turned to face the tunnel. Adisa stood in the entrance, looking down over the factory.

"Come on!" Hunter's shadow stretched before her, long and wavering in the yellow light from Sigrah's control room.

I stopped so abruptly my gecko soles stuck on the floor, and van Arendonk slammed into my back. He caught my pack before I fell—the straps dug into my shoulders—and even as we were righting ourselves, he was demanding, "What are you doing?"

I grabbed his arm to steady myself. "I have to shut down the AI."

Van Arendonk wasn't looking at me. He was looking up at the tunnel, where Adisa, with a smooth, sure motion, grabbed a spider from his boot and flung it away. It exploded against a beehive, destroying the drone in a fiery, crackling burst of light.

"Ask him and he'll fucking lie about spending his childhood throwing grenades at UEN threshers," van Arendonk said, before he turned to me. "Are you certain you can stop it?"

"I know what I'm doing."

"Without help?"

"Oh, you're going to help," I said. "You get to be the distraction."

"You can't distract an AI."

Not remotely true, but I wasn't about to argue the point. "You can distract Sigrah. She might not know I'm here yet." I let go of his arm and stepped back. "The AI didn't kill you and the others when it had the chance. All it did was knock them out. And I'm pretty sure it's not controlling all of these weapons."

"Pretty sure?"

I huffed in frustration. "Yes, pretty sure! Sigrah's the one trying to blow us the fuck up."

"You just said it killed Mary Ping."

But not me, I thought. It could have killed me so easily. I was right there when Mary Ping died. It ran away instead.

What I said was, "Yeah, well, she was a murderer and a smug piece of shit. I'm not asking for your permission," I said, when he opened his mouth. "Keep Sigrah and her bots distracted. Make a lot of noise. I'll take care of the AI."

TWENTY-THREE

A beehive drone was already arrowing toward me. The lights in its cells flashed as the individual explosives prepared to launch. It circled me, trying to cut me off, its whirring sound loud enough to be heard over the shouts and explosions.

I dodged through an open doorway when the first of the bees burst from the hive. I ducked behind a wall, and they pelted the room, sending out showers of stinging, fiery sparks. Something struck my right shoulder; I bit back a gasp at the hot, sharp flare of pain. I cast my light around—there was a door on the opposite side of the room, open. I ran for it. The beehive followed, buzzing into the room and spraying it with another round of projectiles as I charged through the doorway. I tried to pull the door shut behind me, but the drone fired again and I had to dodge out of the way.

From the room I ran to the base of the towering racks of

shipping containers. I veered to the left, away from Sigrah, toward the AI. The incessant hum of the beehive grew louder as a second drone joined it. Distantly, I heard shouts and another two explosive bursts, one right atop another. For a moment the factory was washed with pale light.

In that light I saw the massive, red-veined sphere ahead. It was too far. I couldn't sprint across the open space with drones following. I turned sharply to the right and slid into a gap between two shipping containers, balancing carefully on the metal rack.

One of the beehives let loose another spattering of projectiles—how many bombs did those fucking things carry?—that struck the shipping containers with a deafening noise. In the brief strobe of lights I saw the drones bobbing uneasily back and forth, passing the gap this way, that way, back again.

I couldn't stay there for long. There was a series of loud pops from elsewhere in the factory, followed by a startled shout. The drones whirred swiftly away.

Slowly, with as little noise as possible, I crept back toward the end of the shipping containers. I turned on my flashlight and held my breath for several seconds. The air was hazy with smoke, making it hard to see anything. I stepped out from between the containers.

There was a buzz right behind me. Smoke whirled as a drone zipped past my head. I cursed and nearly tripped as I ducked out of the way. The drone spun and flashed, preparing to fire, and I threw my arm up to protect my face.

Instead of the sound of the drone spitting another volley of projectiles, there was a loud crunch, followed immediately by the solid, deafening clang of metal on metal. I lowered my arm cautiously.

One of the black mech suits stood right before me.

I stepped backward in alarm. Another drone flew down toward me, moving so fast it was a blur of motion. When it was about three meters away, a second mech suit dropped out of the darkness, knocked the drone from the air, and smashed it to the ground.

I felt movement in the air as a third suit landed a couple of meters away.

And another, right behind it. Another. Every one landed with a terrifying thud of metal on metal, filling the empty space between the rooms and the cargo with still, black statues. They weren't only on the floor. There were mech suits standing atop the rooms as well, dark sentries in a line from one end to the other. I tried to count, quickly lost track. Two perched on the track of an overhead crane, another on a shipping container in the cargo rack below it. The suits did not move after they landed. They were as still as pillars, faceless and dark. They didn't seem to be doing anything. My heart was pounding so hard it hurt. There were so many of them.

And I could see them. I could *see* them, even through the shifting smoke, even though my flashlight was feeble and dim.

I blinked my eyes rapidly. The factory had begun to hum. I hadn't noticed before, but it was obvious now as the noise rose all around, and with it came light so gentle and gray it was almost unnoticeable at first, and it grew, and it brightened, like dawn rolling over a landscape. The low hum turned to a steady rumble, punctuated by machines chugging steadily somewhere in the distance, as regular and even as the beating of a dozen giant hearts. There were heavy clanks, metallic whirs, the hiss of air, and the chattering sound of racks and conveyor belts moving.

In both light and shadow there was motion: engines grumbling, belts rolling, robotic arms lifting and twisting. Noise from the machines wrapped around me, a bone-shaking industrial racket.

The factory was waking up.

The snap of my radio was so surprising I nearly yelped.

"It's not going to work." It was Sigrah, and she was furious. "Whatever the fuck you think you're doing, you should surrender before you get hurt."

I waited for van Arendonk or Adisa to answer, but there was only silence.

"Stop what you're doing. You don't have any way out," Sigrah said. "Be sensible, Safety Officer Marley. You're not a fanatic like Mary. You know the difference between a tool and a messiah."

I felt strangely, eerily calm, although my heart was still racing. So she knew I was here after all, and she thought I was the one who had restarted the factory.

"This base is under my control," Sigrah said, which was a complete fucking lie and we both knew it. "You can't hide forever."

The mech suits did not react at all. The nearest one was barely two meters away. The material covering the body was slick and flexible, with few seams visible; the boots were solid and sturdy. The faceplate was completely featureless, so devoid of light I could not tell if it was truly empty, if it was meant to hold a human person on the inside, or if the suit was merely a sick simulacrum of a human soldier. It wasn't exactly black, I realized as the lights grew brighter, but an undulating dark gray that seemed to shift and move as I stared. It was, in a way, beautiful, even though the rational part of my mind knew the mottling effect, however it was achieved, served only to make the suits more deadly.

"They'll find you soon enough," Sigrah said. "You'll be safe if you surrender."

That made no sense. They had already found me. An entire platoon of them had already found me, these suits that had knocked the drones out of the air before they could reach me, and now stood silently, watching, waiting. Not attacking.

She had to be talking about something else—about the weapons under her control, the drones or spiders or whatever else she'd got her hands on.

She went on, "When the company arrives, you can help me explain how the situation got so complicated."

A new sound registered. It was a gentle patter, like raindrops on the roof of a garden shed. The smoke whirled. I saw a glimmer of silver.

"You can use this to your benefit," Sigrah said. "Don't be stupid."

There. I could see them now. Spiders racing across the factory floor.

They wound around and through the legs of the mech suits, gleaming through the smoke, catching the light as they turned, every second drawing closer.

"Okay," I said quietly.

Sigrah had stopped talking. She was waiting for me, but I hadn't even lifted my radio to answer. There was no word from any of the others. They were probably dead. I hoped they weren't.

"Okay," I said again. I looked at the faceless weapon before me. I tasted blood at the back of my throat, sour and metallic. "I'm trying to help you. I can help you. Let me help you."

One of the suits moved to crush a spider beneath its boot. There was a crunch, a few sparks, and the other spiders skittered around it. A few of those spiders stopped suddenly, twitched, and writhed, their legs curling up underneath them as though they were in pain.

"Right," I said. "I guess that will do."

And I was running again. With the lights on I could see my destination clearly now. The AI's sphere was against the far wall, clinging like a wasp nest to the vertical shaft of a missile silo. The nest itself was a dark globe on a skirt of metal girders and supports, pieced together from tools, raw materials, cargo containers, transport rails, bits of missiles and scrap. The exterior surface of the sphere was gleaming black and silver and bright, burnished copper, like the shimmering, changeable scales of a slumbering dragon. It was massive, perhaps thirty meters high, and even as I raced toward it, the suits moving to intercept the spiders behind me, I wished I had more time to study it, understand it, maybe find the awe that Mary Ping had felt when she spoke of it.

I was at the base of the structure and beginning to climb when I felt a pricking sharp sting on my right arm. It was followed quickly by a sharp jab where I should not have felt anything: in the shoulder joint of my artificial left arm, the mechanical junction where there was no flesh and no bone. I felt it like a lightning strike, and the vision in my left eye flashed white—pure, blinding white, so painful it was like a physical assault—and my entire prosthetic arm spasmed violently.

My fingers clenched, then opened. But I wasn't doing it. I watched in horror as I made another fist, one entirely outside of my control. I couldn't make my hand obey. I couldn't get the fingers to work right, couldn't bend the elbow.

I tried to grab the spider from my shoulder, contorting myself painfully to reach for it, but I couldn't grasp it. I skidded down the sloping structure, kicking with my boots to stop my tumble. Before I could start climbing again, the metal fingers of my left hand closed around my right wrist and squeezed.

It was such a shock, so unnatural a thing to see my own hand acting without my permission, that I didn't even realize what was happening as the grip tightened and a sudden, sharp pain spread through my right arm. I jerked my left arm away—tried to—sent the command to open the fingers and release, but my fingers stayed closed. I could not make my left arm obey. Even when I'd been newly fitted with the prosthetic, thrashing about my hospital room and knocking into everything I could not avoid, I had not had so little control.

Pain exploded through my right wrist and hand as the grip tightened. I screamed—I was cracking my own bones. I was breaking my own fucking wrist and I couldn't stop it. Spots danced before my eyes and for a second there was nothing else, no factory, no asteroid, nothing besides the overwhelming, inescapable pain.

I rolled onto my side, trying to smash the clinging spider against the floor, but as I was turning I felt the sloped structure shift beneath me. My elbow dropped, twisting my shattered wrist in the grip of my unyielding left hand, and the pain was so great I let out a strangled cry and blacked out for a second as I fell.

I landed on the spider—it crunched beneath my shoulder—and lay in an agonized daze.

Several seconds passed before I tested my left hand again. This time, the fingers obeyed; the elbow bent when I told it to bend. I wanted to weep with relief. I was too afraid to try to move my right hand. It throbbed even when I was still, and every beat of my heart sent fresh waves of agony radiating up my arm and across my neck, my jaw, my back.

The light around me shifted slowly from low red to a piercing shade of blue, a shade that made my prosthetic eye twitch unpleasantly. The noise of the factory was muffled when the hole I had fallen through closed with a shuffle of metal plates. The battle between what my left eye was telling my brain and what the rest of my body believed sent a wave of vertigo through me. I rolled onto my side and retched.

The blue lights blinked, then shuttered. A hushed darkness surrounded me.

I struggled to my feet and leaned against a support strut, shuddering with pain and gasping for breath. There was no good way to hold my right arm; even letting it dangle at my side hurt. The air was warm and smelled of scorched metal and melted rubber. Sweat beaded on my brow and trickled down my neck.

Nothing moved around me. There were no spiders, no maintenance bots, nothing.

The light returned, slowly, now a gentle, pale blue. I was standing on a floor of welded metal sheets. Above me a great round hole led into the center of the sphere. The heart of the AI.

I reached out with my left hand—the shoulder hurt like hell, but so did everything else—and grasped the slanted support strut. Carefully, clumsily, I climbed up into the sphere. I sat down as soon as I was inside, my head spinning from that minor exertion. I closed my eyes and waited for the dizziness to pass.

Then, in the darkness, there was motion.

Metal clinked on metal. Angular shadows shifted and gathered. Larger than the spiders. Plates of silver metal. Long spindly legs. Clink, clink, clink. A skeletal shape loomed.

I knew that shape. I knew it as well as I knew my own reflection in the mirror. I could still remember the first time I had seen it, the surprise and joy I had felt, the bubbling laughter I had not been able to contain. *Is this what you want to be?* I had asked, because it was not the shape itself that mattered but the wanting of it, the decision, a choice I had not foreseen.

The thin, elegant limbs of a praying mantis bent over me.

"Hey, Bug," I whispered.

A long triangle head tilted toward me, with flat reflective lenses for eyes, watchful, waiting.

"So now—" I broke off to swallow back a bout of nausea, breathed until I was sure I would not vomit. "So now you decide to talk." I took in a painful breath and licked my lips, let my head drop back against the warm, curved wall. I closed my eyes for a moment. "You know what, kid? I am so fucking disappointed in you."

TWENTY-FOUR

Something cool nudged my right shoulder. It was gentle, cat-like. My fingers twitched. The triangle head moved out of my field of vision. Everything in the sphere was blue, so blue. I took a deep breath and sat up for my first clear view of what Vanguard had become.

It was so familiar my breath caught. The praying mantis shape had always been its favorite, with its large triangle head, a thin neck, two forelimbs for grasping. Its body was thin, about a meter long, and its six legs even longer, jointed in more places than I could count. It had never limited itself to the confines of the animal kingdom. I recognized David's designs in the leaf-shaped metal scales that protected the neck and body, in the graceful flexibility of the limbs. It rarely built itself a body this large. It had usually preferred to stay in a greater number of smaller bots so that it could explore more effectively.

"Look at you, Bug," I said. There was an ache in my throat and a sting in my eyes. I didn't know what else to say. "What happened to you?"

Vanguard bobbed its head and tucked two forelimbs over its face. I knew that gesture. It had learned it from my nephew, Michael, when he was just a toddler and Devon had brought him to Oxford to visit the laboratory. Michael had a habit of ducking his head and covering his face every time he was scolded—it never failed to soften whatever reprimand Devon was about to offer—and after only a few days of interaction, Vanguard had adopted the same gesture. It used it when we demanded explanations for actions it knew were forbidden, when we scolded it for breaking the rules, when we were unhappy with it and it wanted to make things better.

To see it now felt like a clamp around my chest, squeezing my heart and my lungs, sending an aching wave of grief through my body. Vanguard was answering me, and the only answer it had was an apology.

I slumped back against the curved wall to look around the metal sphere. A sphere was the shape Vanguard adopted when it was frightened, when there were threats it didn't understand all around it. When the darkness and the pressure were too great. When it didn't know what else to do. My lost child had built itself a protective nest of steel.

At the base of the sphere was a radiating web of cables and wires, twisting together to form a single long braid that rose, like the stem of a flower, toward the cluster of scarred black boxes in the center. The power lines feeding the brain—the brain that was supposed to have been destroyed aboard *Symposium*. Wrecked beyond all possibility of salvage. Nothing left but fused circuits and ash. Gone forever. That was what

Parthenope had claimed, and nobody had been in a position to argue.

They lied about it. They lied about everything, David had said.

Finally I understood. This was what he had been trying to tell me all along. I wanted more than anything to tell him that I got it now. There was a sourness in my throat, a sting in my eyes. All of our work, our research, our inventions. The years of our lives and legacy of our lost friends. His beautiful bots. My clever AI. All of it stolen during the rescue and salvage. All of it hidden away and conscripted into becoming weapons of war.

Somewhere outside that nest was a muffled thump and a chorus of sparking electricity. Sigrah's bots were hard at work. I didn't know how much of the factory or its products she had under her command, and how much remained under Vanguard's control. I only knew that I was not safe, not even here, within the armored shell Vanguard had made for itself.

"I know you're trying to fight back," I said. "You stopped the bots from attacking me. You stopped Mary from . . . She was going to hurt me, like she did David." I still had Mary Ping's dried blood in the creases of my fingers. "But before that. Before she brought you here. Did you mean for it to happen? What happened on Aeolia? Did you—"

It was answering before I could finish the question. It was shaking its head from side to side and gesturing with two forelimbs, sweeping its claws back and forth in a similar motion. The meaning was unmistakable: *no, no, no.*

I felt such relief it was as though my heart was cracking open. I laughed, caught the laugh on a sudden sob, pressed my fingers to my lips. This was still the Vanguard I knew. It remembered the lessons I had taught it, the rules about life and how to protect it, the risks it was allowed to take with itself and with others. It would never endanger an entire station of people on purpose. I did not know what Mary Ping and Parthenope had done to it, how they had changed it since the *Symposium* disaster. I had believed I was speaking the truth when Mary Ping asked me about AIs and how they learned violence. She must have been laughing on the inside while I spoke, demonstrating to her with every word that I was both full of unearned confidence and utterly ignorant. She had known, as she smiled across the table from me, that she had trained my creation to kill. Vanguard had been under her control for so long. Two years could be hundreds of millions of lifetimes of evolution for an AI.

But she had not warped it completely. Beneath those plans for greed and violence, beneath whatever mad scheme twisted Mary's thoughts to see gods inside machines, Vanguard was still the entity Sunita and I had built.

Vanguard nudged my shoulder again.

"What is it?" I asked eagerly. I was delighted, in spite of everything, to be talking to it again.

It waited until I was looking at it before darting up the side of the curved wall. It stopped a few meters above me to look at me again. It bent both forelimbs and swept them forward, a gesture I recognized easily: Follow me, it was saying. Come on. Come look. It was one of the first gestures it had learned, when it was first testing out different types of communication.

I studied the wall skeptically. Vanguard had never been all that great at estimating human limitations in locomotion; it tended to think we ought to be as flexible as it was and could simply build extra limbs when we needed them.

Vanguard stopped about halfway up, where the curve of the

sphere turned toward the apex, and made the *come on* gesture again. It reached out with both forelimbs and two of its hindlimbs to grasp a metal panel. It tugged the panel out of the wall easily. *Come on.*

Vanguard didn't repeat itself unless it had good reason.

I lurched to my feet, pained and off-balance, and studied the wall. It was not as smooth as I had first thought. There wasn't anything as obvious as a series of footholds or a ladder, but there were bolts and seams enough that I could probably make the climb. Probably. Doing it one-handed would not be easy.

Come on.

There was another series of loud electric pops outside the sphere. The metal beneath my feet trembled. I saw a flash of light below, bright and white, slicing through a seam in the sphere. Sigrah's spiders were making progress. A slender silver leg reached through a narrow gap. A second later, a twist of smoke rose around it, and another leg reached through the seam.

"Right," I said. "Fuck. I'm coming."

The climb was not easy, with my much-abused right wrist throbbing painfully every time I moved, but I made it to the hole and climbed out of the sphere. Vanguard pulled the metal panel into place behind us and climbed up the outside of the sphere's upper half. I took a steadying breath and followed. The sounds of the factory were louder outside the sphere, and there was air moving freely around me, coming from somewhere above. I heard what could have been the rhythmic beat of a great fan overhead, but I couldn't see it in the darkness.

There was a red square above us: a window with light behind it. It was a room in the wall of the factory. Vanguard made a jump from the top of the sphere to a metal walkway along the wall above. It scrambled over the railing and loped along the walkway to a door. I couldn't make the same jump, but a few meters away there was a ladder leading to the walkway.

I was halfway up the ladder when I heard a metal clang behind me. The hole I had just climbed through was open again. The panel slid noisily down the side of the sphere, and a scattering of spiders spilled out.

I hauled myself up the rest of the ladder, ignoring the pain in every one of my joints. Below, the spiders spread over the surface of the sphere. A couple of them halted and curled up—I suspected that's what happened when Vanguard wrested some control back from Sigrah—but one of them leapt for the wall and raced for the walkway, sparking with blue light.

I ran, boots thumping noisily, toward the red room. Vanguard had already opened the door, thank fuck, and as soon as I was inside, it slammed the door shut so quickly I felt a puff of air at my back. It hadn't come inside with me: the praying mantis remained outside with the spiders.

The lights came on around me, fading from red to white. I was in a control room of some sort. Not terribly big, maybe three meters square, but it felt larger due to the windows on both sides. One window, of course, looked out over the sphere and what would be the factory, if Vanguard's nest wasn't blocking it.

The other window had a very different view.

"Oh." I stepped over to the window. "Oh, fuck me."

The lights were on beyond that window, as bright as they had been in the factory, and the massive space was filled with activity and motion. Bots darting everywhere, machine arms moving, cranes sliding along tracks that traced circular routes around the exterior of the long, broad cylinder.

I had noticed, when I first spotted the sphere, that it sat at the bottom of one of the base's missile silos. I just hadn't considered that a missile silo was not going to be merely structural in an old war base now converted into a secret weapons factory.

"Fuck them," I said. I could not stop staring. "Fuck."

It was a massive cylinder, thirty meters across or more, extending so far down I couldn't see the bottom, and narrowing toward a closed iris in the ceiling. All throughout the space, bots and machines were adding payload to a series of rockets.

Twelve rockets. I counted. I counted again.

I had seen bits and pieces of the rockets in the factory, but I hadn't quite understood what they meant. I had been assuming all those weapons, the drones and bots and canisters of gas, were going to be packed away in neat rectangular shipping containers and sent to buyers throughout the system. But Parthenope was not just building its own weapons. It was building its own fleet of spacecraft for deploying them, and that fleet was almost ready to launch.

Another spider bot struck the outside of the door with a small explosion; the reinforced walls vibrated ominously. I heard the clatter of metal and saw a flash across the window: Vanguard was scurrying along the wall. It was trying to stop the spiders before they found a way inside. That realization jolted me into action. I couldn't stand around doing nothing while Vanguard protected me.

With my injured right hand held cautiously at my side, I touched every terminal, waking them all from their slumber.

"Okay, kid," I said. "What did you want me to see in here? Show me what you know."

There was a live operation status report that showed me what Sigrah controlled and what Vanguard controlled. Sigrah had several deployments of spiders and beehives and seemed to have access to many more; Vanguard had the mech suits but not much else. I didn't have time to work out how or why. I had to trust that Vanguard was doing what it could to get the weapons out of Sigrah's hands.

Sigrah also had control of surveillance. I couldn't see anything except what was right before me.

And what was before me, according to Vanguard, was mission preparation. I had finally found Parthenope's Project Sunburn.

It took me a few seconds to realize that I was not looking at a single plan; I was looking at two mission plans, the second of which was an altered version of the first. I checked—I knew exactly what to look for—and confirmed that Mary Ping had created the second plan. There were also two timetables, one with a series of dates well into the future, the other with a single launch date only a fortnight away.

"Fuck," I whispered.

Everything's going to change soon, Mary Ping had said to me, before Vanguard killed her. *I know you'll understand when you see it.*

She had her own mission, one separate from Parthenope's, and that meant she had to act before they could. That was what the second plan was all about. That was why she had been so angry when she realized David was about to discover the factory.

Each mission plan had its own list of targets. I asked for a map while I looked over the first list. I didn't recognize a lot of the names, but the information attached to them confirmed they were active mines, ports, and transit stations across a broad swath of space beyond Parthenope's current area of control. Stations owned by Carrington Ming, Sorrell-Larkin, Zinoviya, Hennig-Vishal, and a great many other corporations and competitors. I couldn't tell without digging but would have wagered that all of them ran steward AIs based on the Overseer system.

Parthenope's plan was to use these weapons to attack and seize several stations around the asteroid belt. Once they were taken, they would be brought under Parthenope control. It was breathtaking in its simplicity. The company had taken a look around the belt, picked out the pieces of it they wanted for themselves, and built a massive weapons force to take them. They knew the stations would be vulnerable, because the Outer Systems Administration did not have the reach or power to prevent a large-scale attack and what remained of the UEN was too far away for a quick response. They were going to start a war to take what they wanted, and nobody would be able to stop them.

I brought up a map that showed how the operation was intended to spread over time. It was a helpfully hideous display of lines of flight and contact emanating from Nimue, of stations shifting into Parthenope control, a sea of bright specks growing smaller and smaller as the scale of the expansion widened. The ratfuckers even had a nice little casualty estimate ticking upward in their plan. The low estimate for smooth and successful infiltration included a few hundred deaths among low-level workers. The higher estimates were for if what happened at Aeolia started happening everywhere else—there was, according to the plan, a thirty-five percent chance of that happening at about half the targets. They knew it could be the Aeolia catastrophe all over again, this time at dozens of stations, but they didn't care. A thousand dead, two thousand, five thousand, more. On the map, so clinical and calculated, it looked like a contagion spreading through the belt. More than ten thousand dead in the first phase was considered suboptimal. How very fucking humanitarian of them.

That first phase was due to begin in about a month. Right now they were in the final prelaunch push.

Mary Ping's plan was different. Her mission brief to the AI was the same—go, and take control—but the targets were different. The first target on her list was Hygiea. The second was Badenia, home to Parthenope's medical center and jointly operated shipyard. The third was Friederike, on which Parthenope co-owned a major transportation hub with Hunter-Fremont and a few other companies.

Parthenope stations. Parthenope territory. Starting with the company's central facility and working down the line. All to be infiltrated and seized and placed under the attacking AI's control. That was what Mary Ping had been targeting with her plan. She had set up a first wave of attacks to launch before the others. Which, if it worked as she intended, would have meant that when the rest of the attacks launched, they would not be bringing the seized stations under Parthenope's central company command, but under no human control at all. She wanted the AIs to be in charge.

She had told me as much in the warehouse, right before she died. *You created something beautiful and powerful*, she had said. *You know we can be so much better, if we let them show us the way.*

She did not seem to have planned beyond that initial takeover. Her mission timeline did not include predictions for what happened when dozens of independent AIs were fighting for control of stations and colonies that were home to tens of thousands of people.

"For fuck's sake," I said. "That would be absolute fucking chaos."

Outside the window, Vanguard ducked its triangle head, its long swan-like neck curving downward. It had been listening to me all the while its physical form was fighting off the spiders.

"Oh, kiddo," I said. "I know. I get it. I know you don't want to do that. I'm not mad at you."

It shook its head again and moved its forelimbs side to side again, that gesture of apology it had learned from Michael.

A spider scurried across the inner window, leaving a trail of something damp and shimmering behind it. I watched it until it disappeared from sight, then cleared my throat. I wanted a drink of water so badly I thought I might cry, but there was none in my pack.

"Okay, we need a plan of our own," I said. "There has to be a way we can both get out of here. And the others, if they're not dead already." A pair of spiders ignited outside the door. I jumped nervously and winced as the metal bolts strained with the impact. "Help me. What can we do?"

Vanguard, it turned out, already had a plan. It showed me another map, not of the asteroid belt, not of the Hygiea group, but of this base and only this base, a pockmark on the side of the lumpy potato that was Nimue.

It showed me the protective sphere it had built around its own brain.

It showed me a network of carefully positioned explosive charges. It had moved them into place when it had built the sphere. Another layer of protection against its kidnappers. Always looking forward. Always anticipating the moment when everything went wrong. Its intent was clear.

It showed me a start time and a countdown.

It would happen very fast, once it began.

"No," I said. "Absolutely not. That is not an option. We'll find another way."

Another couple of spiders raced across the window, leaving trails of fuel. Bug leapt after them, grabbed and crushed them, but not quite fast enough. One of the spiders self-destructed in a shower of sparks and a whip of bright blue flame. The fuel ignited immediately, slashing across the window in lines of brilliant fire, and the glass creaked ominously. The praying mantis reappeared in the window a second later.

"I know," I said. "I know you've been doing some fucked-up stuff. It's not your fault." I reached out to touch the glass, right where it was looking through at me. "But we can both get away from here. And all the others too. I've got an idea."

TWENTY-FIVE

"We have to work fast," I said.

I didn't know how much time we had. If Sigrah was able to break into this room, we were out of time. If she was able to wrest control of enough weapons away from Vanguard, we were out of time. She had already demonstrated she was perfectly happy to sacrifice lives and commit a great deal of corporate property damage to protect the base—but protecting the base meant protecting the AI that ran it. She wanted to get me out of here. She didn't want to destroy Vanguard.

"There are ten people that need to get deep into the transport tunnels," I said. "Back to the station, if possible. The Overseer will protect them."

I kept working as I talked. Vanguard could listen to both my terminal and verbal commands. I couldn't see Bug through the window anymore; it was busy elsewhere, trying to keep the onslaught of spiders away. Every time one slipped past and launched itself at the window or door I flinched, convinced that would be the time they broke through.

I went on, "And most of them are unconscious, thanks to you. The door needs to be closed behind them. Plus any other doors—are there even other doors along the transport route? There must be security doors, if this place has been locked up." I was rambling now, my thoughts and words tumbling together. "Anyway, they all need to be closed, with everybody safe on the other side. What can you do?"

In a blink, one of the screens switched to a bewildering segmented view of the factory. It looked like what a bee might see, and for a few confused seconds I wondered if Vanguard was showing me the view from one of the beehive drones—but that made no sense, they weren't actual bees with bee-like eyes. Only after I looked again did I understand that it was a collage of viewpoints from a huge number of sources.

"What is that? Are those drones or bots? Are they—"

Vanguard answered with a weapons schematic on the screen. Right. Should have been obvious. It was showing me what the mech suits could see. It wasn't limited in its choice of tools by the need for semiautonomous behavior of a cohort the same way Sigrah was; it could individually control as many machines as it needed to without any degradation in attention or reaction speed. As I watched, several of them began to move. The segmented view on the screen became nauseating, dizzying, impossible to follow, so I narrowed it down to just a few, and only for long enough to see that they were heading in the same direction: toward the comms room where most of the crew lay unconscious.

"That will work," I said. It had to work. I had no other ideas. "Do it. Get them to safety."

Through the other window, the activity in the missile silo had, at Vanguard's command, ramped up to a frantic speed. One swarm of cargo bots was redistributing the weapons among the twelve rockets, stripping out everything bulky and useless, making space; another swarm was marching into the missile silo with a steady stream of containers that carried the new payload. The machines moved swiftly and with dazzling efficiency. Vanguard estimated seventeen minutes to completion. It was an eternity for an AI. A thousand life cycles. Millions of calculations. An eon's worth of decisions.

For me, a small fleshy human in the middle of a factory of war, it was no time at all.

Another pair of spiders struck the window of the control room. There was a loud snap, and a wide crack spread across the glass, left to right, with tendrils of smaller cracks reaching all along its length.

Time was up. I had done what I could.

"Ready to move out?" I said.

Vanguard's only answer was to start turning off the screens of the terminals around the control room. The white light vanished, replaced by the muddy standby red. I took a breath and shoved the door open.

Bug was waiting for me outside, perched on the railing. I started toward the ladder, but the spiders were already there, joined in a silver web across the top, so I swung both of my legs over the railing and jumped.

I struck the outer curve of the sphere crookedly, with one gecko sole catching, skidding, catching again. A fresh riot of pain screamed in my left hip when I landed, in my right arm when I tried to steady myself, and for a second my vision was dark with spots. I had to ignore the pain, all of it, for a little while longer. Bug bounded after me, propped me up to keep me from toppling down the side. When I had my balance, it let me go to smack away the few spiders trying to follow. I scrambled over the outside of the sphere and dropped down to the underside of its support structure. I could hear the cargo bots working in the sphere overhead, could feel the rumble of their movements. The metal plates protecting the base shuffled again, as they had when I came in, and I scrambled out.

I slid to the factory floor and rolled right into the legs of a stationary mech suit. Bug tumbled out after me. One of its forelimbs had been badly damaged and was dangling uselessly by a few singed wires. It regained its feet quickly and, with its remaining forelimb, it gestured at me. It gestured again. It ducked its head, once.

Then it turned and raced back up toward the sphere.

Another explosion flared from the base as it approached. Bug's damaged forelimb tore off and skidded down the metal slant. I winced, even though I knew it felt no pain, even though I knew it was only one physical piece of a much greater whole. I rose to my feet, using the mech suit for balance—which was when I noticed that the suit was not a solid figure. The torso was split down the center, with both sides folded outward, and the helmet was tilted back. It was open. Open and waiting.

"Fuck's sake," I muttered. "We did not agree to this, kid."

But it was, I had to admit, a good idea. I stripped off the ruined vac suit even as another explosion flared behind me. I almost forgot the airlock key but remembered to dig it out of the pack. Vanguard's praying mantis was reshaping itself, damaged and undamaged parts alike, into something broader, wider, a shape I hadn't seen before and didn't recognize now, but it was clearly trying to contain the spiders in a cage of some kind. It wasn't going to work for long.

I stepped into the mech suit backward and slid my hands

into the openings for its arms. It felt wrong immediately, too big and unwieldy, and the sense of wrongness only grew when the suit began to close around me. My right wrist was a blazing knot of pain, but as soon as the suit closed over it, the agony began to lessen—ah, right. Analgesics in the suit. Useful. The glove pressed the thick metal key into my left hand; it seemed as good a place as any to keep it for now. The helmet was the last to fold into place, and for one heart-stopping second, I couldn't see anything.

The suit whirred to life around me. The helmet's visual feed clicked on just in time for me to see fire engulf Vanguard's bot. Metal groaned ominously—the base of the sphere was weakening—and a spider raced toward me, so fast it was scampering up the legs of the suit before I could react. I batted at it ineffectually with arms I wasn't quite sure how to control. It crossed my torso and jumped to my faceplate before it ignited.

Had I not been wearing the suit, the explosion would have turned my head into pulp. As it was, I felt the force of the blow rocking me backward, felt the slight pressure as the helmet adjusted to cushion my head. The stuttering flash of white light that should have been blinding was instantly dimmed. The visual input came back quickly, slightly quivering: there was damage, but it seemed slight. I didn't wait to find out. I tried to speak, to call out to Vanguard or even the others, but the radio squealed and spit feedback into my ear.

I couldn't wait any longer. I had to trust that Vanguard would save the others. It was faster than me in every way. It had an unlimited number of hands and the ability to use them all at the same time. I could not carry ten people to safety, even with the suit. There was nothing for me to do but run.

So I ran. Down the line of rooms in the center of the factory, letting the suit's mechanisms propel me forward faster than I could ever manage on my own, with balance and surety as the boots gripped the floor without the least skid and the exoskeleton kept my limbs in perfect alignment. The spiders raced around my feet, nipping at the metal, searching for purchase, releasing their chemical and setting it alight, but none of it slowed me down. Even with radio static in my ear and visual inputs showing me nothing but a murky sea of smoke and metal, I did not hesitate as I barreled forward.

I almost missed the nearest staircase and had to turn so abruptly I would have fallen without the suit. A beehive drone dropped into view in front of me, a couple of meters away. I dodged even as it released a volley of its bees. I didn't stop, didn't even pause, but I sure as fuck felt the impacts on my helmet, my arms, my back, each a solid blow that snapped and popped so loudly the radio squealed in protest.

One of the bees affixed itself to my right arm. It was the first close view I'd had of them, and it was an ugly little thing: a fat gray bot that clung like a slug and pulsed, something moving within a soft sac beneath its shell. I grabbed for it with my other hand, but it was harder to dislodge than I expected. It didn't help that the suit's gloves had trouble reading the signals from my prosthetic hand. I had managed to get one thumb under the edge when the bee exploded.

The force of the impact knocked me sideways. I skidded across the floor for several meters on my side and slammed into the metal strut at the base of a machine. My right wrist was in agony, but there were no more than the faintest scratches on the black surface of the arm. The suit had protected me from the worst of the impact.

But as I got my feet under me, I understood that denting my suit was not what the bots had in mind.

The spiders were scrambling up the staircase, with the beehive drone humming above them. I ran for the stairs and made a single jump up three steps before the first of the spiders exploded.

The staircase lurched beneath me, twisting as it broke free from its brackets. I grabbed the railing, but that was already loose and bending as the beehive fired a round of its little bombs into the stairs ahead of me.

I jumped and I caught the edge of the landing and held on—thank fuck for the suit and its stubborn gloves and Nimue's low gravity. A couple of spiders swarmed over me as the staircase toppled, the entire length of it breaking from its brackets and twisting to the side. It fell into a hanging conveyor rack of metal canisters, knocked several of them loose and onto another belt below, where they jammed themselves between the gears.

There was an ear-splitting metallic shriek; the entire belt jolted to a stop. The canisters, now crushed together at a bend in the belt, began to crumple. An arm of twisted metal punctured one canister, then another, then a third, and a faint white mist burbled out to engulf the machine. The belt was still trying to move, grinding against the damaged canisters. Somewhere within its mechanisms something sparked.

Small licks of flames glowed in the white mist. They were a brilliant, vibrant blue, and they grew larger.

I tugged myself to my feet, kicking one of the spiders away as I did so, and I bounded upward, taking every flight of stairs in two long jumps. I had absolutely no intention of being near enough to discover what those canisters held, and holy fucking hell these suits were amazing and terrible. I couldn't help but imagine what a private army of soldiers could do with armor like this. How little chance anybody would stand, on any station, armed with only electroshock weapons and a foolish belief that there was anybody out there interested in making sure everybody played by the rules. Parthenope couldn't have designed all of these weapons from scratch. Even with all the secrecy around Nimue, somebody would have noticed the company hiring a bunch of designers and engineers. They had to be working with somebody else, somewhere else. That was a terrifying thought to add to all the other terrifying thoughts.

The light changed as fire spread through the factory, fading from bright and white to a deep, murky red. There was a symphony of strained, agonized metal around me, the distant pops of fuel igniting, the machine rumbles turning to shrieks and squeals. The fire suppression system kicked on, filling the air with foam and mist, making it impossible for me to see anything but the hellish labyrinth of machinery and dancing light.

I raced the rest of the way up the stairs until I finally reached the upper level. I ran past the airlock to the top of the other staircase, the one I had taken down before. It was hard to see from a distance, with so much smoke rising through the factory, but I thought I glimpsed the broad door to the cargo transport tunnel in the wall. It was closed. I hoped that meant the others were already on the other side. Safe and fleeing the factory as fast as they could, or as fast as the mech suits could carry them.

If Vanguard hadn't been able to get them out, they had no chance now.

I didn't know how many of my seventeen minutes had passed. Too many. It was time to leave.

I stepped through the interior hatch, shut it firmly behind me, and wasted half a minute figuring out how to release my hand from its glove to access the key, then just as long figuring out how to get my hand closed safely away again. Finally I turned the key and the airlock depressurized. I opened the outer hatch.

The darkness outside was a shock after so much light inside the factory. The helmet's visual input adjusted with only a little bit of lag. I took two steps, then two more, testing how well the boots gripped the cargo track. Good enough. I began to run.

I ran with big steps, loping steps, impossible steps, every one of them powerful enough that it felt like it might launch me from the surface of Nimue. I ran until my shadow stretched before me, shadow from an impossible light where no light should be. I had too much momentum to stop gracefully, and as I turned I ended up stepping off the cargo track and into the soft dust and gravel. I stumbled, righted myself, and looked back toward the factory. The dust I had stirred up with my clumsiness gathered around me in a waist-high fog, swirling but not settling.

I had come far enough that I could not see the bunker or missile silos anymore. The light came from the launch of the twelve rockets, one after another, each spewing a burst of flame as it rose. My heart was hammering, not from exertion but from excitement and fear and, yes, a little bit of pride. Vanguard had carried out our plan successfully.

The twelve rockets burned into space, growing smaller and smaller.

There was, for a moment, nothing but darkness.

"Come on," I whispered. "Come on. Don't get squeamish on me now."

Three of the lights stopped retreating. I held my breath. With a change so imperceptible my eyes had trouble tracking it, they began to grow brighter instead.

"Oh, that will work. You clever little brat," I said, so relieved I wanted to laugh.

Vanguard had loaded itself into nine of the rockets. Removed the payload of weapons, replaced it with its own brain—which was, after all, always meant to be portable, capable of separation, cleaved into pieces and spread around widely to explore as it willed. It was free now. Not as Mary Ping had wanted, with her wide manic eyes and delusions of mechanical godhood, but as Sunita and I had always intended.

The three returning rockets grew brighter, brighter, nearer and brighter. Vanguard had replaced the payload on those three as well. Parthenope had plenty of powerfully destructive bombs in its factory.

The rockets became streaks of light, then solid objects for a blink, then they struck the factory. Brilliant white light flared from behind Nimue's stunted horizon.

The shock wave of gravel and debris followed moments later. I heard only the rattling of sand striking the suit, felt only the trembling of the asteroid beneath my feet, before I was engulfed in dust and the light was gone again.

TWENTY-SIX

The cell they put me in was larger than my personal quarters. I didn't expect that.

The room had a complete lack of privacy, with at least two cameras watching my every move and a shatterproof window forming the entire front wall. But there was so much space I spent part of my first day simply lying on the floor, not thinking about what had been cleaned off that surface, appreciating the ability to point my toes and stretch my arms over my head without touching anything. Hygiea's gravity felt strong after Nimue, like I was anchored and heavy, in no danger of drifting away.

And I waited. And waited.

I had been separated from the others on the flight back to Hygiea. *Wellfleet* was the sort of company ship that came with secured rooms and armed crew and not a lot of willing explanation. What I was able to learn before they shut me away was that Vanguard had, in fact, gotten the others out before destroying the factory. They were alive, all except for Katee King, who had succumbed to her injuries before *Wellfleet* found the survivors.

Sigrah had not made it out. I figured it would take a while for Parthenope to decide if it wanted to turn her into a hero or a villain. Probably the latter. They needed a scapegoat.

As soon as we returned to Hygiea, I was taken into custody. Stripped of my security uniform, told to bathe, given prisoner garb. They put me in a room for a medical exam, and during the long wait I had grown sweaty with terror that Parthenope was going to repossess my arm and leg.

They didn't. The medics patched my wounds of skin and flesh, splinted my right wrist, gave me some meds, and left my prosthetics in place. A doctor stopped by to tell me there was no serious damage to my left hip or shoulder, nor to any of the prosthetics. She refused to answer my questions. I went straight from the exam room back into my cell.

It was eerily quiet and strangely peaceful in the brig. The pain from my injuries faded as I rested. The food was the same as what was available in the employee canteen. I wasn't the only prisoner, but the others were out of sight; the cell directly opposite mine was empty. I knew my fellow prisoners only by what they said to the guards at mealtimes. There was "Fuck Off, Mason" a few cells down, a man with a booming Ceres accent, and on the opposite side was "Much Appreciated," a woman from Earth, probably Australia, who sang to herself after lights-out. Somewhere farther down the line, probably toward the end, was somebody who never spoke at all, only threw their plastic tray at the glass, and sometimes cried.

All I ever said was, "Thank you." I didn't want to be an asshole to the people who handled my food.

It wasn't until midday on the third day that the guard took me out of my cell, escorted me through a couple of secured doors, and let me into a room that looked almost exactly like the one I had just left. Same white walls, same white ceiling and scuffed floor, same wall of unbreakable glass. Only instead of a cot, sink, and head, this room had a table bolted to the floor and two stools, also bolted, on either side.

Leaning against the glass wall, PD in hand, was Hugo van Arendonk.

"Nobody has any fucking idea where it is," he said.

I let the door ease shut behind me. "Where what is?"

He pushed away from the wall and threw the PD on the table. "You know what the fuck I mean, Marley. Sit down."

I wanted to argue, just for the hell of it, but there didn't seem to be much point, and standing was still uncomfortable thanks to the lingering ache in my hip. I sat.

"You mean Vanguard," I said. "They can't find it?"

He sat across from me and raised an eyebrow. "I mean the proprietary advanced artificial intelligence that Parthenope Enterprises was developing for experimental purposes."

"Vanguard," I said. "Which they stole."

"That would be a violation of the outer systems cooperative salvage laws."

"And they would never break any laws."

"Certainly not," said van Arendonk. "Unlike you, an emotionally unstable safety officer, who violated the terms of your contract and endangered your colleagues to sneak into a restricted research facility dedicated to testing new mining techniques and fuel production processes."

"Ah." I thought about it for a few seconds. It wasn't the worst story, but I still thought they could have done better. "Is that what happened?"

"They haven't worked out all the details yet," he said, with a shrug. "They had to come up with something quickly, because that series of explosions wasn't exactly subtle. A few weapons test monitoring telescopes picked it up."

"Did it work? Is the factory gone?"

"Who the fuck knows? The missiles probably blasted it to slag. It will be weeks before anybody can approach safely. The company will get their story straight before then. Their investors and business partners are already asking uncomfortable questions. The CEO of Carrington Ming just had a press conference in which she shared that she is 'very concerned' about Parthenope's reckless operational practices and is starting an internal investigation to determine if any contractual obligations have been violated," van Arendonk said. "And that's just the first. Others are winding up to do the same."

"Oh dear," I said. "That sounds messy."

Van Arendonk's lips twitched. "They sent me in here to find out what you know about where it's going. And why. And then try to convince you it's in your best interests to help them cover it up."

I glanced at the camera in the corner. "Are you supposed to be telling me that's why you're here?"

"Not at all," he said easily. He swiveled around on the stool to look at the camera. "What are they going to do? Fire me? With all the shit I know about them? They might think about it until they remember I wrote the company's fucking nondisclosure agreements." He waited a beat, staring directly at the camera and whoever was watching on the other end, and spun back to face me. "The thing is, Marley, maybe in the short term their offer isn't entirely bullshit. It probably would get you out of here if you agreed to help them find your bloody machine and keep it from doing whatever the fuck you sent it out there to do."

"I didn't send it out there to do anything," I said. "It's making its own decisions now. I have no idea what it will do."

"Good, that's good, I can't even tell if you're lying or not," he said.

"I'm not."

"And it doesn't fucking matter." Van Arendonk sat forward suddenly, resting both forearms on the table. "You know that, right? It doesn't matter what you say, it doesn't matter if you help them or not, because they're looking for a way to hang all of this on you. Even if it gets out that they built a fucking armada of illegal war weapons and put it all under the control of a stolen AI, they'll still try to blame you. And it will probably work."

I had been thinking about little else for three days. How easy it would be for Parthenope to delete any inconvenient surveillance data. How simple it would be to build a conspiracy of the dead with David at the center. How Nimue was still theirs and it was possible nobody would ever learn the complete truth. How it had occurred to me only at the end that Parthenope must have been researching and developing their weapons elsewhere. How stupid I would feel if it turned out they had another factory somewhere.

"I know," I said.

"Yet you did it anyway. You set it free."

He didn't frame it as a question, but I knew that's exactly what it was. I even considered answering. I would have answered, if we weren't being watched. I rather liked Hugo van Arendonk, in spite of myself, and I believed that he had been telling the truth about having no prior idea what Parthenope was doing on Nimue. I thought he might actually listen if I told my own truth: that I had set Vanguard free because I could not bear to destroy it, nor could I bear to leave it in the hands of those who had tried to twist its beautiful, complicated, curious mind toward the industry of killing. I had set it free because it was never meant to be trapped inside weapons of war, churning out drones to help a corporation feed its hunger for more territory, more resources, more power. It had been intended, from the very first thought that led to its inception, for better than that.

I didn't know where Vanguard would go or what it would choose to do. That was precisely why I had let it go. I had set it free because there was some part of me, the part that hadn't been signed away on a corporate contract or burned away with *Symposium*, that wanted very much to see what it would do.

"I did," I said.

"And that's different from what Mary Ping was trying to do?" said van Arendonk.

"Yes," I said. It was different. It had to be different. She had never known Vanguard the way I knew it. She had never been able to see it clearly. "It's an explorer. That's what it was always meant to be. Not a weapon. Not a corporate steward. A scientist. And now it can go explore."

"And you have no idea what it's doing."

There was something about the way he asked, something that made me wonder again what I was missing while isolated in the brig. What was happening to motivate anxious lawyers and CEO press conferences. And why Parthenope wanted my help.

"Has something happened?" I asked.

"This is the outer system. Something's always happening." Van Arendonk drummed his fingers on the table before slapping the surface lightly with his palm. He picked up his PD and stood.

"Are the others okay?" I asked quickly. "I know Katee King died, they told me that on the ship, but everybody else? Is Avery okay?"

Van Arendonk gave me a knowing look. "Safety Officer Ryu has been medically cleared and will return to duty tomorrow. Neeta Hunter is currently represented by about ten of the best lawyers her mother could buy on short notice, in far better quarters than you have down here, so don't worry about her. The rest of Nimue's crew suffered only minor injuries."

"And Adisa?"

"If your bosses ever stop yelling at him, they'll demote him to security guard on some lonely chunk of ice in the middle of nowhere, but he'll probably like that."

He opened the door, and I hurried to say, "Wait. One more thing."

"Yes?"

"Can I, um, can I ask a favor? A personal favor," I clarified. When he only waited, looking at me expectantly, I went on, "It's my family. My parents and brother on Earth. I don't know what they're going to hear, it will probably be all lies, but could you . . . Not officially, I know that, but could you just let them know I'm okay?"

A few seconds passed. I couldn't read his expression.

"I'll contact them," van Arendonk said. "Don't do anything stupid, Marley. You're in a bigger pile of shit than you can dig out of."

Later that day, after I returned to my cell, the guards brought in another prisoner. He was a white man, middle-aged, with the twitchy, hyperactive manner of somebody coming down from a dose of stimulants. They put him into the cell directly across from mine. He shouted for water as soon as he was in the cell, shouted for food when the guard brought water, shouted for a blanket, shouted for a fan, shouted to be let the fuck out of there, did they know who he was, his lawyers would not like this, let him the fuck out.

I was doing my best to ignore him, but I couldn't help but notice that he looked somewhat familiar. I tried to get a good look without being obvious about it. He was pacing in his cell, one wall to the other, shaking his head and muttering to himself—then he stopped abruptly and stared at me. His eyes narrowed. He frowned.

I stared right back. I wondered if I'd ever investigated him. Confiscated his devices, ruined his blackmail gig, found his secret porn feed, something that would have pissed him off and given him a reason to remember me.

He said, "Hey. Who did your work? That is *fine* work." He whistled.

That's when I remembered where I'd seen him before. He was the Ceres surgeon who had started doing black market biohacks after losing his license, the one who had practically lobotomized the kid with the bleeding eyes. I had passed his file to Jackson before leaving for Nimue, but I hadn't expected anything to come of it. His last known location had been aboard a cargo ship heading away from Hygiea.

"How the fuck did you get caught?" I asked.

He laughed, surprised, stopped his pacing to lean against the glass wall. "Shit, man, I have the worst damn luck. I was headed to Badenia, yeah? On *legitimate medical business! There's a fucking hospital there!*" He shouted these words toward the camera in his cell. "But we're half a day out when the captain turns us the fuck around. I guess the station's off-limits now. Piece-of-shit ship brought me right back here. The OSD was on my ass before I'd even unstrapped from my bunk."

Badenia, where Parthenope had a shipyard and a major hospital. There were five thousand people living on that rock; it was Parthenope's second-largest station. It had been second on Mary Ping's target list. I suddenly felt nauseated and cold all over. Surely van Arendonk would have told me if something terrible had happened. He would have told me.

"What happened to Badenia?" I asked, barely able to force the question out.

"What?" The man blinked. "Nothing. Corporate shit. Carrington Ming revoked their joint management agreement for the shipyard, and they run the port administration, so that stopped traffic. A bunch of other companies are making noise about doing the same. They aren't saying why, but a buddy of mine says he's heard everybody's stopped issuing liability bonds for Parthenope-chartered ships and, guess the fuck what, I was on one of those. It's about to get real fucking crowded here, if they keep sending everybody back. Hey." His voice turned incredulous. He paced again a few steps before stopping. "Hey, it's not that funny. I didn't get my due fucking process!"

I didn't mean to laugh. It just came right up, without my permission, a giggle caught somewhere between mirthful and hysterical. There had not been a tragedy on Badenia. This was not a replay of the horror on Aeolia. Because, after all, there was no need for anything so dramatic.

I understood now why Parthenope so badly wanted to find Vanguard. It knew the worst of their secrets. And it had no reason to keep them to itself.

All Vanguard had to do was leak key pieces of information.

Hints of Mary Ping's and Parthenope's plans. Details of Parthenope's ongoing fraud. The names of everybody who had not known they were participating in a treaty violation. Vanguard was clever. It would know what to say, and who to say it to, what seeds to plant that would lead reporters and lawyers and OSA regulators to dig up the rest. I didn't know exactly what information it had access to, and maybe the full scale of what Parthenope had planned was not public yet, but I would have happily wagered a month's wages on the outer systems news media needing only a day or two to put together the big picture.

Van Arendonk was right. They were going to ask for my help. I ignored the butcher doc's ramblings to lie down on the floor again. I stared at the ceiling and smiled and thought about all the different ways I would tell them to go fuck themselves.

ACKNOWLEDGMENTS

Writing and editing a book when the world is falling apart around us is not a particularly easy thing to do, but it helps to have a friend who understands just how outrageous of a clusterfuck the whole writing and publishing process can be. I want to thank Audrey Coulthurst for going above and beyond what a friend should ever be asked to do in the service of fictional space murders. Without her thoughtful editing, patient hand-holding, tireless cheerleading, and honest commiseration, this book would be nothing more than a messy collection of half-formed scenes and bad ideas. I desperately needed the support, and she provided it with exactly the right amount of creative cussing.

Thank you as well to Leah Thomas, Lynnea Fleming, Matthew Slote, and Pat Russo, who formed my pandemic sanity pod and kept things from getting too terribly bleak when the days blended together and time lost all meaning.

I also want to thank all of my readers, and that means every one of you, from those of you who picked this book up on a whim to those who have followed me as I've jumped wildly from genre to genre over the past few years. You are literally everything that makes this crazy endeavor worthwhile. Thank you.

Photo © 2015 by Jessica Hilt

Kali Wallace studied geology and earned a PhD in geophysics before she realized she enjoyed inventing imaginary worlds more than she liked researching the real one. She is the author of science fiction, fantasy, and horror novels for adults, teens, and children, as well as a number of short stories and essays. After spending most of her life in Colorado, she now lives in southern California.

CONNECT ONLINE

KaliWallace.com
Kaliphyte